DEVIL PREACHER

by

Christopher DeWitt

For

Mom, for your creativity
Dad, for your love of history

Prologue

BLYTHESBURG, GEORGIA
August 12, 1877

Transcription of the account of Mr. Stephen
Hue, approximate age of 70 years

Taken by R.E. McElhany, Esq., on behalf of
the offices of The Forepaugh New and Colossal
All-Feature Show, A. Forepaugh proprietor.

* * *

THEY CALLED him The Great Western Land Pirate.

Well, some did, anyway. He probably hated that more than any of the other things they said about him. I suppose mostly it was because it conjured up images of fellas with feathers poking from their hats and black flags and oceans and the like, and what we did couldn't get any further from that than a bobcat to a fast-running crick. Worse, it was dreamed up by a politician who wrote it in a book for the sole purpose of getting elected in some Podunk county somewhere. "Sensationalized," I think they call it these days. Like one of those silly dime novels. Naturally, it was full of all sorts of prevarications, none of which John or anyone else could put up a defense to at the time.

Devil Preacher. Now, that's the name he preferred over anything else. Mainly because it described him more to a tee. In his mind — and everyone else's — it was a hell of a lot more sinister and carried real heft to it, especially in those days, when it came to scaring folks. Made them jumpy, you see, and more apt to have their wits leave them and make our jobs as villains and robbers that much easier.

The organization itself was called the Murrell Gang, mostly. That one was also used more to scare people, kids more than others, to keep them in line and such. There was also the Murrell Clan and then a more colorful and romantic Clan Mystic, which John took a warming to, for he did have something of a romantic flair to him, and not in a way with the ladies, necessarily, but how he saw the world, and how he wished it to be.

Like most men, John Murrell was many things, and sometimes different things to different people, according to the occasion.

He was my friend, though, and a good one, through it all.

I suppose I should cut to it. I know you have important folks waiting for you, and you've been after it for a long time now, this "artefact" you've been looking for. Don't ask me why I would hold on to such a grisly thing all these years. Part of me just couldn't let go, I guess.

Honestly, I am a touch mystified why anyone would still be interested in the thing. It has been many years since the Mystic

Clan haunted the Trace, after all. I'd expect the legend has faded, much like the folks who originated those events.

You first must hear some things about John Murrell, before I hand it over. I believe you should know some of the truth about the man and his days. Don't be caught up in some of the fanciful tales that have been woven about him, if you're going to take this thing away and treat it like some curiosity. Prop it up in some museum or drawing room of some wealthy collector, to be admired over whiskey and cigars.

This is going to take a spell, young man. You'll want another of my dear wife's lemonades to help cool you. Make yourself comfortable. I know it's hot as Hell's hinges, especially for one of you Yanks. I trust you brought along a good clutch, more pencils, and another scratch pad or two. You're going to need 'em.

Now, as I said, John Murrell was a lot of things. He was an artist, of a sort, a rapscallion, a freebooter, a damn good sharpshooter, a burglar, a libertine, a low character, a poet, a visionary, and what my dear mother would call a "constant vanity"...

1

Buzzard's Roost is where John and I first laid eyes on each other, and it was not under the most pleasant of circumstances, to be sure. It was a home for wayward boys, which was something apparently new to those parts. I was sent there because I was a thief. You could say I was an amateur criminal at that point and be dead on accurate. Don't ask me why I embarked on a life of crime, petty as it was at the time. I suppose I would lay it to me just being a farm boy looking to light a bit of a spark in myself, dig into something new and actually exciting. I needed something to take me away from the drab existence of digging furrows in the ground and herding pigs and sheep, and there were not a lot of things to choose from for a Tennessee farm boy.

"There's a certain dignity to it," Father said to me one day, hunkered down in one of our fields, digging into the earth with his big hands. I always envied those hands of his, strong and manly and callused with work. I looked at my own, and having to adjust for my young age, had to wonder if they would ever attain such a stature. He stood, towering over me and looking down with a satisfied smile. I didn't know what to say to him, for I just could not see it at the time. We turned together and started making our way through the field and to the house, in time for supper.

Indeed, it had been a fine day, and I remember it well. I'll allow that working by Father's side all day did exhaust me some, but there was a satisfaction to it, a sort of peace that set in at the end of the day.

Still, something I hadn't quite put a finger on was wrestling around inside me, even as we trudged up the fine stone walk that Mother had just freshly swept. She stood there on the porch, broom in hand, watching us, a faint smile on her mildly pretty face.

I felt a pang of something right then, in my chest. It was sort of an ache, like something telling me to catch that moment, with the sun settling down to pass things over into night, the smell of something delicious and rib-sticking wafting from the kitchen, and Father and Mother looking at each other, tired but so happy. Something was telling me to catch that moment and keep it forever.

"Don't you two look like you've done a week's work in a day," Mother said.

Father's smile broadened. "That was, in fact, our aim."

He walked past Mother, and she gave a little theatrical sniff. "Smells it, too."

We bathed and then sat to dinner. Chicken and dumplings it was – Father's favorite – and I will tell you it never tasted better.

"We'll all be chickens ourselves before long," Tiffany, my sister, groused.

"That was impolite, daughter," Father sternly chided her. "Apologize to your mother."

I glared at Tiffany. She had just about shattered my

contented experience by introducing a minor spat into our circle. And at dinner time, no less!

"Oh, no call for that," Mother said, reaching out to pat Tiffany's hand. "I'll make your favorite come this Sunday. How would that be?"

Tiffany's face transfigured at once to an expression of self-satisfied smugness, her eyes darting to take in my disgusted reaction and to bask in it.

My thoughts instantly went to what Mother's pronouncement meant for me, and that was to assist Father in slaughtering a lamb, for lamb chops, in a few days' time. I had the notion to propose that Tiffany herself should take part in the operation in my stead, since that was supposedly her favorite meal. But I did not want to add to the moment's impoliteness and choked it off, aiming to preserve a near-perfect day.

Tiffany tied it off then, by relaxing her squinched-up face long enough to stick her tongue out at me when Father and Mother happened to not be looking.

I again offered no response, trying very hard to keep my face made of stone, and was pretty proud of myself for it.

At eleven, Tiffany was two years younger than me. It was high time that I elevated my comportment around her, mostly since Father had, of late every once in a while, taken to addressing me as a "fine young man" and "stout youngster" as we went about our chores together.

Even so, I felt that pull again, some kind of inner tug of war. This life was a good one, one I should be content with. But even the word "content" rubbed at me like coarse sandpaper, and I couldn't lay a hand on why, exactly. It was a calm life, yet too calm, at least for me. It was rewarding in its way, just not rewarding enough. I felt like hell about it, hated myself for thinking it, but I just could not see myself doing it for the rest of my life, day in and day out, slopping hogs, rounding up geese, slaughtering lambs. There was not the least bit of buzz to it, no excitement.

* * *

Having said all that, I have to say it was sad and strange to find myself, sometime later, in the self-important and ornately appointed office of one Magistrate McAllen.

"Sir, you are to be brought to heel," McAllen pronounced, his voice booming in the stuffy room.

I flinched despite myself, and to this day I do not know if it was the sound itself or the words it carried that made me do it. Whatever the phrase meant, it sure had a heavy feel to it, having been applied to me under the magistrate's stern gaze. I could not entirely meet that gaze, I admit. His words also bore an extra dose of doom.

I stole a glance at Mother to my left. Her features betrayed both anger and shame, and also a hint that she was likewise uncertain where the magistrate was taking us with this phrase. She sat up straight, her hands resting ladylike in her lap, her tiny fingers tangling themselves with quick, nervous twists.

Father was at her side, but I could not look at him directly, not just yet. Maybe never again, I thought grimly.

I felt like a wretch about to be sent to the gallows. Part of me wished, in fact, that I had been.

"To effect this change in you, Master Hue, I regret that we must send you off," said McAllen. His eyes slid off me for a moment to Mother and Father, as if to somehow back up his first pronouncement, and to punctuate – weirdly, in my opinion – that it was the correct remedy.

There was a high, squeaking sound, almost like the chirp of a bird to my dazed mind.

Mother had let out a quick, startled cry but had just as

quickly stifled it. From a soft rustling, I knew Father had rested a reassuring arm on her shoulder.

"But he is just... Just a boy," She gasped softly, a hair short of a sob.

"Just a boy, Mrs. Hue?" McAllen's chair groaned across the floor as he stood, to give his utterance more weight, I imagine.

"This is true, madam, but he is a boy that has been brought before me this third time. Third! In two months' time. For thievery!"

His slate-gray eyes gave me the up and down as if taking in a creature worthy only of the harshest condemnation.

"I will say it does not speak well to his future, as you might well realize. A bible. The lad even stole the Good Book, of all the insults. And to add to it, tried to defend that outrage by saying he only took it because he saw Mr. Willis put a few bills in it for safekeeping. The sheer audacity of it!"

His chair groaned again as he sat back down, letting out a gruff, heavy breath like he had just pushed a wagon up a hill.

"I do not order this with any joy in my heart, trust this," McAllen intoned, looking out the window adjacent to his desk. The lonely echo of a horse clopping by made its way into the room.

Mother and Father were what some would call the salt of the earth, bless their souls for it. They were given to trust the instincts of someone like McAllen, who had managed to set himself up as the authority of the land. As far as I knew, his pronouncements were never questioned by anyone and were always final.

Myself, I could not see it. How could this person, one who had no real intimate knowledge of me, my family, or our life, decide to root me up from all of it like a turnip from the ground and send me off to be looked after by strangers? And they were to just carve out any wrongdoing I might have done like a gizzard from a roast turkey?

I sat there, tears of rage welling up inside me like a teakettle on the boil.

A husk! A mere husk is what they would send back to my folks, I was sure of it. There would be nothing but an empty vessel, and everything that was Stephen Hue would simply have been tortured out of me.

I finally made myself look at Mother, and the tears let loose. I tried to angrily blink them away, to no avail, and they streamed down my flushed face like a spring river, and I didn't care one whit that they did, either.

Father's eyes finally found mine, and I saw something there far, far worse than I had yet experienced.

Disappointment.

It struck me to the bone, it did, sucking all the marrow from them in one brief, breathless instant.

As I looked at my parents, and they, back at me, cold reality set in. I was to be sent away, and maybe would never see them again. Even at that young age, I knew most people in those days faced the reality of a randomly harsh world. Floods, tornadoes, earthquakes, bad men, and fire were events that did transpire from time to time in the weird and eccentric ways only this world could cruelly devise.

* * *

I stood at the end of the stone path that led from our home. I dared not look back at it.

Mother and Father stood behind me in stoic silence. Tiffany had already been sent off to school, but not before we had said our awkward goodbyes. She had tried to be stoic herself, in her own innocent little girl way, but her eyes had shone with threatening tears of her own. Behind them, I could tell, was also a kind of terror. I knew it because I, too, had felt so when I first looked at my parents after Magistrate McAllen's pronouncement of doom. She had torn herself away from my room's door with a violent dash. I heard a tiny sob as she ran down the hallway.

The coach pulled up, heavy wheels grinding against the hard-packed road, the driver uttering a muted "whoa" to the horses. My heart clutched to my throat as I stared at the dark cavern of the coach's interior. My stomach became a heavy, ponderous thing.

Mother knelt to my side, wrapped an arm around me. The smell of lilac soap came to me, offering me a brief comfort and the promise of memories.

"It's for the best, Stephen," she said, so very softly. Before my next breath could come, she crushed me to her. My tears flowed freely once more, and again I didn't care.

"Ma'am," I had heard, in a low, careful voice. The driver, gently reminding Mother that he had a schedule to keep.

"Yes," said Mother. "Yes, of course." She straightened, tried to put on a brave smile.

I looked up at the driver and was relieved that he appeared to have a kind, open face. He greeted me with a brief nod, his mouth turning up slightly.

"Master Hue," he said.

Something grasped my shoulder just then. I winced a little, as it was fierce, almost painful, but not quite. I knew at once this was the hand of my father, and I did not want to look at him. I did not want to see that expression again, the one I had seen on him in Magistrate McAllen's office.

His grip on my shoulder lessened a bit, and I thought that he, too, might kneel at my side as Mother had.

Instead, he gave my shoulder a little squeeze, gentle but

firm. It told me, all at once, that he was there, and though he did not approve of the present proceedings, that his affection was there. Always would be. His hand went up to my cheek, and gave it a little pat. In doing so, he wiped away a tear.

My legs felt like they would not – could not – move of their own accord. The driver stepped forward and grabbed my small duffel from the ground beside me. With his other hand he reached out to me, urging me to the coach.

The springs of the coach creaked only slightly as I climbed in. The faint, dusty smell of stale cigars and the worn horsehide of the seat covers assaulted my nose. Dark, unlit interior lamps gazed back at me, sullenly observing the lone occupant of their domain.

The driver drew back the curtains, allowing the sudden light of the burgeoning Tennessee morning. One of the horses snorted impatiently.

Sitting back on the coarse, stiffly upholstered seat, I could see only the bright spring sky and part of Father's perfectly-farrowed fields.

The springs of the coach groaned again and the coach tilted a little as the coach driver took his seat. I heard a "ha" from him and a slight slapping of reins. The coach started ponderously off. The clop of the horse's hooves on the dirt sounded heavily alien and distant. They might as well have come from the moon.

After a moment, I sat up quickly, with the thought of looking back out the window, for a last look at Mother and Father and the home they had built for us.

But I sat back again, for, just as quickly, my young mind told me that to do that would make things even worse.

I sat there, now numbed by the reality of it all closing in around me, my body swaying back and forth and side to side with the coach's motion. I no longer cried, because there were no more tears to give.

Up to the point where I had been sent off to Buzzard's Roost, I had never been farther than twenty miles outside of the county back in Tennessee, so my imagination had to do the work of constructing this place they had seen fit to send me. It was no pleasant place, not by half. In fact, it was a boy's vision of Hell, complete with dark, jagged ground covered in the blackest of ash, and an entire absence of God or anything pure or clean.

It was in the month of May, 1820, that I arrived at this place that should have been a boy's dream instead of a nightmare. It was a place "rightly sorted and groomed," as my Grandpap used to say. The grounds were well kept, with a lovely barn – freshly painted, it looked to be. An equally lovely house was there too, and gentle green hills that swooped gracefully away in all directions. Old oak and sycamore trees were in abundance, earnestly beckoning me to climb them as high as I was able.

It did not look – by any measure – like a place that would have a scraggly, forlorn name like "Buzzard's Roost." It was set not far off the Natchez Trace, or what many called the Chickasaw Trace. The Trace was a long road, that started out, it was told, as a series of hunting trails formed over many years by the Indian tribes that peopled the region, before America was even America. It went from Nashville all the way down to Natchez-Under-The-Hill, now known as just Natchez. There were places all along the Trace that appeared over time, called stands. These were mostly places where travelers would rest up, take on provisions and the like. Stretches of the Trace were none too friendly for average travelers, as you may imagine.

Bandits and what were later called road agents were known to prey on them.

It was not advisable to go it alone.

Anyway, Buzzard's Roost really was insidious, for it was a place that I should've hated, and from which I was already plotting my escape. But I didn't hate it at all, not right off. And the only reason I absolutely had to escape was to get back to my home in Carter County and back to Mother and Father and yes, even Tiffany, the sister who possessed boundless ways to annoy me.

I blinked happily against the brightness of it all, taking it in after being deposited on the side of the roadway leading into this sunny place, my one tote bag having been set next to me by the coach driver.

A large form brushed by, its shadow blotting out that joyful sun. A deep voice uttered something brief and guttural, like the sound of an exotic or fictional beast.

This form had been speaking to the coach driver, who now went on his way.

I turned to find an immense cask of a man looming over me, glowering down with gray, baleful eyes under the darkest, furriest brow I had ever encountered.

This being had a large lantern jaw, seemingly made exclusively for the beard that adorned it, framing a large, square head. I daresay now that the beard probably made his head appear squarer than the Creator originally meant it to be. An old-fashioned broad-brimmed hat somehow rode atop this head, providing vast amounts of additional shade. In one giant fist, he carried a riding crop that looked like it was used often and with purpose.

"Mr. Bucschalter, please introduce our newest student," an impossibly sweet, lyrical voice said, from somewhere.

This human eclipse named Bucschalter stepped to one

side, and there stood a small woman in a very modest, dark blue dress. Her pleasant face and kind eyes were a direct opposite of this intimidating creature.

"This would be young Master Hue, ma'am," said Bucschalter. His strong Teutonic accent bent those words in ways they were never designed to go. Still, everyone present understood them anyway, for this lady stepped toward me and bowed her head politely and folded her tiny, white-gloved hands primly in front of her.

"Master Hue, it is a pleasure to make your acquaintance. I am Mrs. Coffee. But you may call me Auntie Charlotte, or even Auntie. I permit that."

I could hear Bucschalter grumble something, but Auntie cast him a gentle but warning glance.

For some reason, I was profoundly relieved that she did not introduce herself as "Mrs. Bucschalter."

I repeated her move back to her, tilting my head in what I thought was a perfect imitation of her polite nod, but not sure I succeeded. My head felt like just a loose ball on top of a skinny stick. I folded my hands before me as she had.

Just then, I heard a collection of giggles. I looked over to see that a herd of about eleven boys of various ages had somehow gathered up silently nearby.

"Now, you boys," Auntie Charlotte carefully admonished them, and they promptly corked off their laughing.

"Please, let's welcome Master Hue politely, as you have been instructed," she said.

The herd of boys awkwardly and reluctantly migrated my way. One even ventured to shake my hand. I looked up at him, for he was a bit taller. He had humor in his eyes, and gave me a quick, somewhat lopsided smile, and perfect teeth for which I should have hated him.

"I'm John Murrell," he said. His grip was firm (something Father taught me was always a desirable trait in another man).

I liked him right off.

Bucschalter broke up the herd with some further guttural orders.

"Oh, Mr. Bucschalter," said Auntie Charlotte, she appeared disappointed in him for ending the greeting ceremony so abruptly, but allowed it nonetheless.

She turned her attention back to me, for which I was greatly relieved.

"Mr. Bucschalter will show you to your quarters, Master Hue. You are well aware of our standards and rules here, I trust, and what is expected of you."

I nodded vigorously.

She was quiet all of a sudden, and looked steadily at me as if expecting something. After a few moments, this did unnerve me to some degree.

"Are you a catbird, boy?" rumbled Bucschalter, "bobbing your head so?"

Auntie Charlotte's gaze had not wavered.

"Yes, ma'am," I finally blurted.

"Good!" was her only reply. She turned and made for the lovely little house.

Bucschalter looked at me, and I was struck by the fact that his expression had altered a little from glowering – what I thought up to that point was its natural state – to one of stern appraisal.

And then he said something, strangely not directed right at me, for his eyes stared just off of mine, sort of like something had just come to mind. But there was more of the quality of an oath or even a prayer.

"Tod soll sich nicht trennen," is what it sounded like, if I'm remembering it rightly.

Thinking on it later, it about gave me the shivers, as it seemed he sort of placed himself in a trance, or had transferred his mind somewhere else somehow, from that brief, vacant look to those gray eyes.

It spooked me something fierce.

That night, after I had settled in, I was given a letter by Bucschalter, back to glowering then. Judging by the handwriting, it was from Father to be dispensed to me on my arrival.

My Dear Stephen,

If you are reading this, then you have arrived at the place we have chosen for you to right your ship and see out the remainder of your schooling.

Please know that your mother and I came to this solution mostly owing to your age, and a desire to firmly extinguish undesirable predilections in you before they rooted into your soul and thereby set you on a path that will lead only to your destruction. This was our only impulse.

I hope and pray that you will improve every moment of time to the utmost advantage and that I shall have the satisfaction of seeing that my expectations are not disappointed.

Remember, my Dear Son, that the present is the moment to lay the foundation for your future greatness and security in life, that much money must be expended before your education is satisfactorily concluded, and that time lost can never be recalled.

I hope to God I shall be spared until I see you arrive at an age to give protection to your dear mother and little sister. Remember that they will look to you for protection should it happen that my life should be shortened. Keep in mind, this may happen.

Your Loving Father

· · ·

This last line shook me to my core, as it left me wondering if Father had kept hidden from the family some grave and uncertain illness that he may have learned of, or a reckless endeavor for which he was bound.

Further shaking me was the fact that this did not sound like Father at all, but a complete stranger. I had to settle on the fact that he was a farmer, and accidents and injuries befell farmers quite a bit more than other occupations.

Maybe that was his only thought.

I turned over in my tiny bed and looked at the window across from me without really seeing it. Tears I thought I had no more of welled just a little in my eyes. The window became a blur of a soft, deep blue of the night growing just beyond it, paled a bit by the lonely moon of this strange new land.

2

"You undt... You."

Bucschalter was standing there in all of his stern vastness, looming over a collection of us boys. We had no idea why he called us out of the barn which we had been mucking out, but we welcomed the brief interlude, nonetheless.

I had been at Buzzard's Roost for about three weeks, all settled in for the most part. At least, as settled in as I wanted to be, for I was working on ways to make good an escape. I had never been confronted with this sort of problem before, but I found it intriguing and exciting, having only read of similar situations in books and stories. Even the thought of pounding feverishly through the forest with the bloodhound Bucschalter fast on my heels was exhilarating!

I would reflect later that Bucschalter's choices that day on what boys to take to town were greatly fortuitous. He had selected me and John Murrell.

John looked over at me with that handsome grin, eagerly wiping his hands on his pants.

Bucschalter motioned off to the Roost's lone, ancient work

wagon, and we both happily jumped into the back of it. We knew, of course, that it meant more work for us at some point, loading and unloading the thing with various supplies, but we couldn't have cared less. We were going into town, and that in itself was its own reward.

The other boys watched us gloomily, like we were being freed from the clutches of Buzzard's Roost forever. I couldn't blame them, for I had already felt that myself, more than once.

As I settled in for the ride into town, I felt a happy glow warm my insides. Somehow the air smelled clearer and the sun shone brighter.

The wagon rumbled off, creaking and rattling. It seemed too frail to even be pulled by two horses, much less loaded with anything. Bucschalter dug into one of his impossibly deep coat pockets and drew out a pipe with an old-fashioned, over-long stem and sparked it off. The smoke from it drifted lazily back, and I welcomed it. The smell instantly reminded me of my old Grandpap, sucking blissfully on a similar pipe whilst by the fireplace.

Pontus, Bucschalter's sturdy pony, trailed faithfully behind us, not even needing to be tethered to the wagon.

John looked over. His arms were resting on his bent knees, his hands dangling loosely before him.

"Looks like you're settling in alright, Master Hue," he said, a mischievous sparkle in his eyes.

I shrugged. "Doing the best I can is all," I said. I had wanted to come off as worldly but wasn't sure I had accomplished it.

John just grinned back at me, and I squirmed a little because it felt like he was looking right through me, knew somehow what I was trying for. I had noted already that John did carry himself that way – a young man worldly beyond his years, and somehow knowing something about somebody before they did themselves.

He pointed at me with one of those dangling hands. "You'll get there." Instead of coming off ridiculous and cocky, his tone gave me a satisfied comfort, just like he knew what he was talking about, as if he himself had lived my experience. Could be that he had.

We rolled into the town of Burkesville, and John and I silently took in the sights and smells, almost like rubes. It seemed forever that I had been in any kind of civilized place, where people went about their business seemingly without a care in the world. The clanging of a blacksmith's hammer reached from a distance, and it was like music to me.

We jumped out of the bed of the wagon, each of us rubbing our haunches after the long ride on the hard boards.

Bucschalter climbed down and skewered us with a fierce look, silently ordering us to cease our rubbing and behave like civilized creatures, if we could manage it.

"Wait," he said with a deliberate nod at us. Naturally, to our ears his curt order sounded like "vait." He then stalked heavily into the mercantile store in front of which he had parked the wagon.

John watched him for a moment, then half-turned to me.

"Damned old Hessian, anyway," he said under his breath, with a crooked grin. Now, John said it this way: "Hess," with an "ian" on the end of it, like the name Ian.

"Huh," was my articulate and well-thought-out response.

"What is it?" John asked, leaning back on the wagon's side.

"You say that word like my old Grandpap does."

John looked at me blankly.

"Most folks I've heard say it 'Hesh-in.' You say "Hess-ian."

John stared at me a moment, clearly bemused. "That word come up a lot with your folks?"

"My Grandpap does, sometimes," I said with a shrug. "He was in the Revolution and fought 'em."

John stared at me again. "That a fact?"

"It is."

Now it was John's turn to shrug. "I guess a lot of people did."

I stared into the darkness just beyond the door of the mercantile, vaguely wondering how much stuff Bucschalter was arranging for us to load. Some boys were playing at the far end of the street. They were too far away for the sound of their voices to reach us.

"Anyway, that damned old Hess-ian should speak proper English and not taint it with that damned *Austrian* of his."

"Austrian ain't a language, though."

John looked at me. "What?"

"It's German. That's the language. Austria is a country. And they speak German there."

"Aren't you just a smart one?" John said, and for the first time, I saw something of a sneer and an ugly glint in his eyes, rather than his seemingly ever-present grin. He straightened up, and appeared to be squaring off on me. I took a step back, preparing to be pounded, but also fully ready to deliver a few licks of my own.

He took a step toward me, and I saw out of the corner of my eye that one of his hands had been balled into a fist. He had a strange, flinty look in his eyes now, as if I had challenged some authority he thought he had over me. My mind raced, trying to grapple with the fact that this older boy, this John Murrell, had so far treated me decently. At least, a little bit more decently than the other boys at Buzzard's Roost had. It seemed like the boy before me was an entirely different person. It had happened so suddenly, too, as swift as a summer storm.

I couldn't square any of it, and even though I tried not to

give any ground, I took another step back. I really did not want to fight. Not due to any cowardice, though. I didn't like to think so, anyway.

Some kind of ancient, primal instinct in the town boys at the end of the street must have tickled at their brains, alerting them to our alien presence. They stopped whatever nonsense they were engaged in and, one by one, their heads and faces turned to us. I could make out one boy pointing in our direction.

They started toward us in a herd.

John must have taken stock too, for he cocked his head at me. There was still that curious, flinty look in his eyes, but there didn't seem to be nearly as much resentfulness.

A smattering of voices now came to us: a variety of those kids' excited chatter. I thought, just briefly, that this may be a friendly bunch, after all. One boy appeared to be in the lead of the herd. He wore a tattered straw planter's hat, maybe a tad too big for him. His thumbs were hooked into frayed suspenders. As they neared, this boy's gait became more pronounced with intent, looking less and less friendly as they closed the distance. At least I imagine so. My mind was still swimming with what had just happened as I tried to fight down my welling anger.

John leaned in, grasping my arm. "We'll settle this in our own time, Hue," he said to me in a low, husky whisper. He looked down for a quick moment, his shoes scraping on the dirt. I looked down, too, and he was positioning his feet for a certain stance and clearing away any loose dirt. I was not some veteran of brawling, not at that stage of my young life, anyway. But I had witnessed at least a couple of kid fights, so I knew when someone who knew what he was about was squaring for one.

The group of town boys finally stopped, and the boy with the straw hat tipped it up to get a better look at us. He looked us up and down, his mouth turning up into a nasty smirk. His eyes were set too wide for his face, and a pug nose to beat all pug noses that I had ever seen. It is not very Christian to say, as Mother would've put it, but this boy was downright ugly.

"You them boys from the Roost, aintcha?" he said. He twisted the "Roost" part with a nasty, sarcastic turn.

"Maybe," John responded, after a moment. He flattened out the "A" and to me it sounded like "mebbe," and was purely from the deep South.

Straw Hat turned his head back to his troops with a derisive chuckle.

"'Mebbe,' he says."

The troops laughed dutifully.

John didn't move. Straw Hat didn't move, either. They stood there, sizing each other up. From what I could tell from my angle, John's expression hadn't altered the slightest, but Straw Hat's went through an evolution of changes within the space of thirty seconds: from haughtiness to a mean indifference and then to a tiny hint of uncertainty. I attached all this to John's stoic quiet, his unchanging stance. Straw Hat clearly had no idea what to make of it all.

"Well," Straw Hat said, finally. "We don't truck with you *Roosters* around here."

Though intended as a manly and tough challenge, it landed with all the force of a baby duck struggling to make its way out of its egg. One of Straw Hat's troops let out a small, involuntary giggle. Straw Hat's too-wide set eyes squinched up at the sound.

"That a fact," said John, and it struck me that it was the same thing he said to me when I was talking about my Grandpap, but this time it had more of blunt feel to it. Not a question, but a gauntlet thrown down.

I heard a dull clacking sound. One of the troops had pulled

a small cloth bag out of his pocket and was tossing it up and down in his hand idly.

"Come on, Louis," this boy said to Straw Hat, possibly trying to sound bored. It came out sort of whiney and pleading instead.

The marbles in the bag clacked again and again. "I wanna get that taw back," said the boy. He did not appear to be at all comfortable with how public this face-off was, regardless of the fact that they outnumbered us, three to one. I am not too proud to admit that I silently thanked this lad for being a voice of reason.

"You'll never get that shooter back, Sammy," someone else said.

"Shut up," Louis said, flat and low and menacing in the way a cornered cat's growl is.

We all stood there, forming a tableau that has been observed countless times in the annals of boyhood. A gang of bullies versus the innocent few, or one.

"Verdammt boys!" a voice roared from somewhere, and I swear to you that all of us troops, Louis and even John, jumped right out of our knickers at the suddenness of it, much less the sheer volume.

Here came Bucschalter from the mercantile, and I could have kissed him. He barged between us and the troops like a furious bull buffalo. His riding crop was out, lashing about without any discrimination to speak. A glancing blow off John led to a square-on shot to the boy Sammy with the marbles. His bag flew off, some of the tiny balls sailing into the dark under the wooden steps of the mercantile, sending up small dust fountains like miniature cannonballs.

Bucschalter was yelling, a great deal of which I believe was authentic German swearing and cursing. The troops scattered wildly. Louis lost the straw hat, and Bucschalter took a brief respite from his tirade, picked it up, and threw it after the ugly lad. It didn't travel far, naturally. Louis looked back, running, his unfortunately-spaced eyes somehow looking even wider apart than before.

Even though John and I were also a subject of Bucshalter's wrath, it all was just so glorious.

The enemy having been suitably set to fleeing the battle-field, Bucschalter turned to us. He was breathing heavily and his face was as near to beet red as I have seen a person's. He tugged at his coat to bring it back into form and stared at us. He then straightened his hat with a quick hand. With the other, he tapped the riding crop on the side of his leg with angry, impatient twitches, as he stalked forward.

To my great relief, he walked right past us to the wagon's driver seat.

Between ragged breaths, I heard him say, "Fighting. Alvays verdammt *fighting*." Bucschalter gestured with his large head toward the mercantile, picking up a box he must have dropped.

"Go see Mr. Patton about ze goods to be loaded here," he deposited it in the wagon's bed, his voice back to its usual grunt.

We walked into the dark coolness of the mercantile. Mr. Patton stood there waiting, hands on his hips. He was probably the thinnest stork of a man I had ever beheld. He had thin, reddish hair and a short, neatly trimmed beard. He surveyed us with beady eyes that looked like they didn't miss much.

"Boys," he greeted in a high, reedy voice. He nodded to a stack of goods that had been set aside for us to load into the wagon.

Mr. Patton turned to a lady who was clearly waiting for his attention at the pickled goods. He started chattering away to her, his voice already scratching at my eardrums like a rat.

John and I bustled out of each other's way as best as we

could in silent, busy tension, still taking pains not to look at each other.

We came in for one last trip, to make sure we had gotten it all. Apparently, we had, because Mr. Patton whisked us off with an impatient gesture, screeching, "Good! Good!" He turned back to the lady again, leaving me wondering about the need for such a lengthy discussion regarding pickled eggs and hog snouts.

We went out, back to the wagon. Bucschalter reached for the reins and fiddled with them a bit. He fished around again in one of the enormous pockets of his coat. This time it took longer for him to locate his pipe. He pulled it out and stuck it in his mouth. He searched again, found the matches, and started sparking the pipe. A cloud of smoke at last emanated from his mouth.

"Vell?" he asked, head cocked to the side, not really looking at us, and we climbed in.

* * *

The ride back to Buzzard's Roost was quiet. A bit too quiet for my taste, especially given the fact that our beautiful day of brief, relative freedom had been shattered by the threat of a street brawl and Bucschalter's awesome Teutonic fury endangering life and limb.

The wagon rumbled heavily along with its new burden of cargo, smoothing the ride to some degree. Our bodies swayed with the motion, and under happier circumstances, it might have put me to sleep.

I stared off into the forest. The uneasy thoughts of what recent events meant for my future at Buzzard's Roost flitted around my head like annoying gnats. The boy across from me, who still would not look fully in my direction, had started as a potential ally and then turned a mortal enemy.

The turn had happened so suddenly that there was no question to what had so offended him. And now, after that terse face-off together with the lads, I faced a right puzzle as to where the lines were drawn. It simply made no sense.

Just then, something flashed between the trees and brush at a stone's throw from the wagon. The quickness of it stood out well unnatural. Though I was no Daniel Boone, I knew enough to know that someone was following us.

John was looking at me now, but without challenge in his eyes this time. It was more of a questioning expression. Without realizing it, I had drawn in a quick breath, and he must've heard.

He looked over my shoulder, then sat up straight and leaned forward some, just like a hound dog picking up a scent.

I looked over at Bucschalter. He showed no sign of having picked up on anything.

My blood ran cold, my imagination conjuring up images of bloodthirsty bandits or other savages coveting the goods in our wagon, and our scalps as a bonus.

A flash of dingy red, betwixt the bushes, and I sat up straight. John continued to scan the forest behind me.

Now I heard something positively eerie and sinister: A shrill, ghostly giggling echoed in the forest's shadows.

My skin crawled. The forest seemed to grow suddenly darker. What was the time? Where had the day gone? How far were we from Buzzard's Roost? It now seemed to me like the safest, most beautiful haven.

John's eyes appeared to stab into the woods with all his focus. I glanced at Bucschalter again, and he still had not moved, staring dully ahead to the road, the reins loose in his hands as though he had no care in the world.

Just then, the wagon descended into a pronounced dip in the road, our bodies leaning forward with its motion, and we had to grasp the side boards to steady ourselves. We must have approached Litch's Creek. From there, I could roughly calculate the remaining distance to our salvation. My mind at once gibbered back that it still was not close enough by half, given our current predicament.

The wagon creaked louder than normal, and I felt it lurch forward and down alarmingly. There came what sounded like the sharp crack of a rifle. I'm not certain it was reality or again my imagination running wild, but the sound echoed spookily in the darkening woods.

Bucschalter let loose a string of words that left no doubt that it was, in fact, a foreign form of cursing and that his supply of them had not been exhausted. He dropped the reins, jumped down, and went around to the side of the wagon, now dipping unnaturally low at the front.

"Dschunke vagon!" he muttered. He bent down a moment, continuing to mutter, then popped back up, looking supremely annoyed.

"Verdammt axle broke," he announced. He stormed around to the back of the wagon and stood there a moment more, hands on hips, plainly trying to decide what to do.

"Told Mrs. Coffee this would happen one day," he huffed, sweeping off his giant hat and running a sleeve across his brow. He stared our way concentratedly, but I got the sense he wasn't really seeing us at all.

Bucschalter crammed his hat back onto his head, decision made.

"You boys stay here," he said. "I go back into town. Mr. Denny will give us assist."

I didn't know who Mr. Denny was, or anyone in town, for that matter. Mr. Denny was probably a blacksmith or wainwright. It really didn't matter, I thought miserably, as I considered myself a dead boy walking, stuck out here in what was the wildest of woods, full of beings who intended me great bodily harm, including a boy who now hated me. What was that he had said to me last? *We'll settle this in our own time, Hue.*

John jumped down from the wagon. He put his hands on his hips, copying Bucschalter and assuming the stance of confidence and authority.

"Yes, sir," he said, with a slight, courteous nod.

Bucschalter appraised him with what looked to be a somewhat satisfied eye. "Don't leave the vagon, hear?"

John nodded again.

"Gut," said Bucschalter with finality. He stalked over to Pontus and mounted the faithful pony, riding off without further ceremony.

John glanced at me, a purposeful look in his eye. He then resumed his beacon-like scanning of the forest. My heart gladdened a bit at the prospect that his previous iciness was at last melting away and we would again become at least friendlier. At least it looked like he had no longer intended to beat on me, like he had threatened to.

John jumped into the bed of the wagon to improve his view, and my mind instantly returned to the matter at hand: survival.

It was incredible that Bucschalter had taken no notice of the movement around us – or had appeared not to, in any case. Certainly, it was no imagination, for John had seen it too! What did Bucschalter think we would do if we were accosted by villains? We were weaponless. Panic started creeping up from my slightly aching belly. I swallowed it down as best as I could.

I watched Bucschalter's form until it was swallowed by the distant woods. The quiet of the forest descended on us again. The horses stood placidly on the other side of the creek, heads low to the ground. I suddenly felt bad for them, still harnessed and all, with no idea how long Bucschalter and Mr. Denny would be. I walked over to the creek and navigated carefully across it on some dry stones. It was not all that deep here, hence the road crossing it at this point. I looked over at the wheel that was sunk in a trough in the creek bed and had to shake my head. That was astonishingly poor luck, the wagon finding that one hole that would break the axle. Perhaps it might have something to do with Bucschalter's lackadaisical driving. Had he been asleep?

A quick fluttering movement broke my ruminations. John was urgently flapping his hand at me to get my attention. Once he had it, he motioned into the distance somewhere behind me. When I looked, my eyes must have grown three times wider in a heartbeat, for there, peeking over the edge of a bush, was the very top of a familiar straw planter's hat.

We exchanged surprised and excited expressions, all anger forgotten, for the moment.

He quietly left the wagon and moved silently into the shadows of the woods. Not wanting to be alone, I followed as quickly and quietly as I could, imagining myself as a savage born to the stealthy hunt, like I had read about in books. My heart started pumping faster. I could feel its beat in my eardrums, like the war drums of the Mohawks.

Hushed and hurried voices came to us now, before one rose above the rest. The unmistakable commanding voice of Louis, the leader of this pack of town boys.

"I told you to watch, Jemmy, you idjit!" he said. "Now where'd they get off to?! Anybody see?"

There was a rustling of leaves and branches and then a sudden thump. From the sound of it, I could only conclude that idjit Jemmy had been felled somehow.

"Hey!" came another voice, and I believe this was Jemmy. "I'll –" Jemmy bit off his retort for some reason.

"You'll *what?!*" came Louis' challenge. "I swear, Jemmy, if they find it, I'll crown you plenty. Your head'll swell like a summer melon! You won't be able to wear a hat the rest of your life!"

A morose silence fell over the shrubs. I could see a bit more color now, through the woods, and more of Louis' straw hat, which showed a bit more wear and tear up close owing to the row back in town. They were picking their way through the woods, and we followed them, still in cover, as they approached a small clearing. There were only about half of their number from before: four boys. Sammy was missing. Perhaps he was still under the mercantile gathering his marbles.

The group stopped and stood there, looking at Louis. One boy's face was clouded with a tight, angry expression, glaring into the woods. That had to be Jemmy.

"Nobody will ever find it, Louis," said Jemmy defiantly. "It's hid real good."

"*We* found it, didn't we?" Louis finally shot back. The boys just stood there in sullen silence.

Something rustled the brush near me. John was standing from his previously crouched position. He approached the boys in the clearing. Not knowing quite what to do, I followed him.

"That's right," John said in a clear voice that echoed across the clearing and into the surrounding trees. "We found it, already. It's ours now, so you all can clear off."

I had no idea what he was talking about, naturally. I also did not know why I was fully prepared to back his play, but I was.

Clearly, Louis and his gang had no idea what was going on themselves. John had taken them so by surprise by his sudden appearance and brazen announcement that they stood there, mouths gaping open stupidly like hungry pigeon hatchlings.

Louis' ugly maw finally snapped shut after a moment. His oddly-spaced eyes focused on John with amused contempt.

"We knew that was you all in the woods," I blurted. I don't know why I even said it. It lay there flatly in the clearing as everyone tried to absorb its meaning. "Following our wagon," I added helpfully. A crow cawed in the distance, as if mocking me.

The boys looked challengingly back at me.

"You didn't scare us any," I said, feeling more confident. I heard a scuff and knew John was shifting his feet as he had done before. This must be his way of backing my play.

"Now, git," John said. His voice was low, firm, and direct.

Louis just stared back, his mouth curved into a crooked smirk, somehow making him twice as ugly.

One of Louis' gang put his fists on his hips, sizing us up. They still outnumbered us, but John was bigger than them all by a bit. That might have been an equalizing factor.

Jemmy looked the least certain in the enemy ranks. His feet stirred the leaves nervously on the soft floor of the forest.

"Make us," Louis said, and there the gauntlet was thrown again. He stepped forward, reinforcing his position and intent. "You don't got any giant square-head to help you, neither. Not this time."

John spat on the ground right in front of him, his eyes never leaving Louis' hideous gaze.

"Hell, I don't need any damned old Hess-ian to do my fighting, I'll tell you that."

Louis let out a nasty, moist scoff.

John charged.

Louis' eyes went wide with this unexpected turn of events, as John sprang from the ground, flying through the air and hitting Louis squarely, knocking him backwards so hard that his feet left the ground. His straw hat flew off, and his head almost hit the thick trunk of a sycamore tree as he landed hard.

John's fists commenced to fly in a wild blur. Louis had no chance. He got his arms up to attempt to ward off what blows he could, which was not many.

The other boys watched, frozen in horrified fascination. One of them kind of hopped around on his feet, like he wanted to join in, but was unsure as to when or how.

Now, I had tensed up, as you might imagine, but something was flowing through me like some kind of feral energy. My heart was pounding like a steam engine. When I thought about it after it was all over, that energy was the only thing I could think that made me do it. I ran at the boy hopping around on his feet, just as he was about to go to Louis' aid. I tried to copy John's last-second leap but botched it and hit Hopping Boy sort of sideways. It was enough to knock him down, though; leaves and twigs and dirt flew in all directions.

He tried to scramble away from me, partially getting to his feet. I was a mite quicker and tripped him up. He fell again, on his hands and knees now, and I jumped on his back. He collapsed with a loud 'oof' as his head hit the ground.

I started raining clumsy blows to the back of his head, rapping my knuckles painfully on his skull. A voice in my head was telling me this was not exactly the proper way to go about this, being not very sporting and all. I stopped hitting him and stood back, panting, giving him one last push on his back for leverage. To my surprise, the boy scrambled quickly away on all fours, like a wounded raccoon, a comical sight, really. He gradually gained his legs under him and ran off, not looking back even once.

I was still gulping deep breaths, feral energy still coursing through my veins. I was surprised I had all that in me. This was my first ever brawl, and it was exhilarating.

Surrounding noises finally broke through my recently-discovered fog of war, yelling, cursing, and grunting, and I remembered John was still engaged in the main event. I turned and saw only one other of Louis' troops remained. The other had headed home; apparently, he thought my victim's skedaddling was the more prudent recourse when facing a determined foe. It was Jemmy, and as if unsure what to do, he was kind of leaning in and out over John and Louis, who were still engaged in mortal combat.

Jemmy finally looked over at me and jumped, like he had forgotten I was there in all the excitement. His eyes took on sudden wariness and he backed off from me. I imagined my eyes bore a wild look, fresh from battle and raring for still more, like a miniature berserker.

A weird sound broke through the cacophony of war. Louis was crying.

He was begging, really, and gradually John eased up on his blows and stood up. Louis lay there, squirming as if still fending off the attack. John gulped air, eyes shining with victory. The knuckles of his hands were a dull, raw red that would soon darken into purple bruises.

Louis was still sobbing as he scootched back on his hind end, heels digging into the soil, trying to push away from John. His red face was wet with tears and blood from where John's fists had landed true. His bloody mouth worked like it wanted to throw further insults, but it wouldn't work right, only producing an incoherent mix of guttural gibberish and heavy gusts of breath.

John casually bent down and picked up Louis' hat, now crushed beyond usefulness by the stampede of combat. He threw it down with a careless, sideways motion. Louis flinched, adding to his humiliation. The hat struck his face with a soft brushing sound and tumbled onto his lap.

"We don't truck with no townies," sneered John.

Louis got to unsteady feet with one final dig of his heels and was off running clumsily into the woods.

Amazingly, Jemmy stood there still, watching Louis disappear into the distance. It was like he was nailed to the ground by the shock of indecision.

Then he glanced at us, his eyes revealing that he had come out of his stupid daze. Surely, he thought his life hung in peril.

He turned to run, and without thinking about it, I dashed forward and was able to slide to the ground at the last second, extending a leg to trip him up. Jemmy went flying much like Louis had done, only he went forward instead of backward. He hit the ground hard with a loud grunt and John was on him. He straddled Jemmy and turned him around. The boy's face was white with terror.

All the air had been knocked out of Jemmy. His eyes were bugging out, and his mouth was working like a landed carp. He raised his arms to protect his face, but John quickly grabbed them and pinned them to the ground.

"I ain't gonna hurt you," said John, and Jemmy's eyes registered startled surprise, then relief. "But you're gonna show us where *it* is."

Jemmy looked at him, his chest heaving as he gradually regained his air. His brow furrowed like he didn't quite grasp what John was saying.

"It's hid real good, you said," John said, low and pointed. "Right, Jemmy?"

Realization lit Jemmy's eyes, followed by a tired resignation.

"I will," he breathed. "Yes, I will."

* * *

We stood at the bottom of a ravine where once a decent creek had run, and was likely a place that flooded after a hard rain.

There was a jumble of boulders at the narrow end, almost like they were heaped there with purpose by a giant being.

Jemmy just pointed at it, looking like he would at last be free of us, and he could run home like his friends.

"Show us," John said, in that weighty and serious tone.

Jemmy reluctantly stepped forward and started climbing over the nearest boulders. We followed, and a small cave shortly came into view via a small maze created by the boulders and some fallen branches from dead trees that past floods had gathered there. We had to crouch on our hands and knees to get through the cave's mouth, but once inside, we were able to stand, though a full-grown man would not nearly be able to.

The air was musty and dank and darkly mysterious, as is proper for a cave.

John looked steadily at Jemmy.

"This? This is it?" He didn't say it in a disappointed way, for most boys will approve of a good cave, hideout, or fort.

Jemmy shrugged slightly, then shook his head timidly.

"Well?" John prompted, putting his fists on his hips.

There was just enough light seeping in that we could make out a little shelf of rock near the back of the cave. Jemmy turned to it, fiddled with something for a moment. There was a scratching sound, a flash of light, then the unmistakable smell of sulfur, and just like that, the boy had lit a small lantern.

The soft glow grew more to life. We beheld a right cozy shelter as our eyes adjusted quickly.

Jemmy smiled a little then, seeing our looks of satisfaction. He squatted down just under the lamp. We heard a slight grinding sound as he moved a flat slab of rock to reveal a hole in the cave floor. I could see something in the hole, wrapped in rough cloth. Jemmy stood back. "Here."

John and I exchanged intrigued looks.

John bent down and retrieved the bundle from the hole. It contained something fairly long and angular, and I started tingling with excitement. John laid it on the ground, carefully peeling back the layers of cloth.

I stopped breathing for a moment, and I like to think John did too.

It was a big, rugged flintlock pistol. I knew this from illustrations in books.

The barrel seemed enormous, at least more so than the few pistols I had actually seen. It was rusted from end to end, too, and appeared quite old, but I could see there was the promise of a deadly grey gleam underneath, and loud smoky violence along with it. The butt of the weapon was long and rounded, to fit in the palm of a man's hand, and even after its single shot would still be useful as a blunt instrument to brain one's foe. There was metal plating all along the sides, graced with engraved floral designs that instantly brought to mind a Spanish galleon, all sails filled as it prowled the high seas. It had obviously missed many years of the loving touch of a caring master.

It was damned beautiful.

John reached to pick it up, his hand hesitating, as if with a sort of reverence.

When he picked it up, it seemed impossibly large in his hands. He looked over at me, an awed smile forming on his face, then at Jemmy, who was smiling brightly, though his eyes still hinted at fear.

John reached up with his thumb and drew back the hammer. There was a soft, metallic grating at first, then a fine, satisfying click as it locked home. It snicked loudly in the little cave, Jemmy started a little, one hand almost going up to his mouth in an old lady's "Oh my!" gesture. His body quivered slightly sideways, like maybe he wanted to run.

Looking a little more confident with the weapon in hand, John aimed it at the mouth of the cave. His hand wavered slightly with the weight of holding it with one extended arm.

He pulled the trigger, and the hammer came down on the frizzen. No sparks were generated there; the flint for the weapon long since gone, but it scraped down and slammed onto the flash pan. It sounded like thunder compared to the cocking of it.

Jemmy let out a little yelp of surprise.

"This," John said, rather dreamily. "This is something."

He turned and held it out to me. The worn butt of the gun was smooth, despite its aged wood. It felt solid and purposeful in my hands. I had held Father's rifle before, of course, when he taught me to shoot, but that was long and cumbersome. Father had told me that the rifle, for a farmer, was more of a tool than anything else, to deal with varmints or predators fixing to get your livestock.

This thing, though, was something personal. A weapon not just to tuck into your belt and draw when faced with bandits, but to duel with when your honor has been challenged.

My hands were too small to aim it with one hand, but I could see how the gently sloping, rounded butt would fit easily, even comfortably, in a grown man's.

Its awesome weight surprised me some, but at the same time it did not. I cocked it just as John had done, only I needed two thumbs. For all its obvious age, it felt still solid and lethal. The hammer hung above the frizzen and flash pan like a snake poised to strike. I could not hold it steady as I too aimed at the cave's mouth. I had to use my other hand to steady it. I put my finger delicately on the ancient trigger. Remembering what

Father taught me, I didn't pull it and instead squeezed it, letting out a breath slowly as I did.

The hammer came down, and I felt it slam like a tiny blacksmith's hammer. I imagined a brief flash, followed by billowing smoke that partially obscured my intended target, leaving me wondering if my shot had hit its mark.

I was not all that well-versed in firearms, being just a lad and all, but some instinct told me that the craftsman of this marvel had surely known his business.

It seemed magical.

My trance was broken by John taking back the pistol and wrapping it back into the cloth. He was looking at the mouth of the cave. "We are losing the light," he said.

He returned the bundle to the hole, covered it again with the flat stone, and turned to Jemmy. "We'll be back for it, and make no mistake, Jemmy."

Jemmy looked at us with nervous uncertainty.

"If Louis comes for it and moves it, we will find you."

Jemmy took an involuntary step back, then finally nodded.

We crawled from the cave and headed back to the wagon. Coming back to reality, I began worrying that Bucschalter had already returned to the wagon with Mr. Denny. Our goose might be as good as cooked.

* * *

We made it back to the wagon with not much time to spare. I breathed a relieved sigh as it came into view, the poor horses still standing there patiently, half in, half out of the creek.

We heard manly voices in the distance and took up positions on the wagon that hopefully looked like we had been overtaken with an inhumane dose of boredom.

Mr. Denny set to work immediately, and we were soon on our way back to Buzzard's Roost. The sun was meeting the horizon and the gloom of dusk slowly enveloped us. The horses trotted along, eager to get to their feed and stable.

I looked over at John. He smiled a knowing, satisfied smile, and I smiled back, a lively day of adventure, a found treasure, and a shared secret between us.

He opened his mouth to speak, then shut it again. He glanced over at Bucschalter, back to contentedly puffing on his pipe like a steam train.

John dropped his arms to his sides, using his hands to scootch a little toward me. He leaned towards me and said, softly, "I regret what happened back there."

I looked at him quizzically. So much had happened, I wasn't quite sure if I knew it exact.

"In town," he hushed his voice, and I had to lean in too, to better hear him. "About..." He gestured toward Bucschalter with a thumb. "The German language and all."

He genuinely looked shamefaced, and it came back to me.

"That?" I whispered back, surprised. That is indeed what it had been: I had corrected him about the language used in Austria.

"I'm just... Not used to it."

I nodded slowly, smiling a little.

"Being wrong and all," he continued. "It's kinda embarrassing."

I shrugged back. "No need, John. No need. I meant no harm by it."

He stuck his hand out to me, and I took it.

"Friends," he said, and it was not by any means a question or a plea.

"Friends," I said firmly.

We shook hands vigorously, smiling broader smiles now. I saw Bucschalter cocking his head slightly, followed by a low grumble, like he was clearing his throat a little.

I still think to this day he heard the whole exchange, and wonder if that grunt was one of approval.

INTERLUDE

1877

Mr. Erastus Vinning
Secretary to Mr. A. Forepaugh
The Offices of The Forepaugh New and Colossal
All-Feature Show
Trust Company Building
Philadelphia, Pennsylvania

August 13, 1877

Sir,

This is to inform you that I have concluded my travels in my quest to locate Mr. Stephen Hue, having arrived at the town of Blythesburg, Georgia, this past 11th of August. I have the happy duty of informing you that I have begun an investigation and interview of this man — as the instructions of your last correspondence detailed — to determine the veracity of Mr. Hue's claims as to the authenticity of the object you seek, and his possession of such. Owing to the potential sensitivity to this matter, I have determined that the best course of action is to allow Mr. Hue to expound on his exploits with the original "owner of the object," shall we say.

I would like to add that the hospitality afforded me by Mr. Hue and his wife exceeds all expectations, and further supports the reputation held in the South. So much so, however, that the speed of this investigation may be at times hampered by the languid approach to almost everything in life here.

I will, of course, elucidate to you as to further developments in my mission as they arise.

Your Obedient Servant

R.E. McElhany, Esq.

3

"I HAVE no choice but to dole out punishment to the lot of you since no one among you will confess." This was from Auntie, who had devised that a boy had absconded with an extra dollop or two of cream, somehow. This cream was kept in the cellar of the main house. Only Auntie had a key, as far as we knew, which meant that someone was industrious enough to cop it, help themselves to the cream – and who knew what else – and return it to her person undetected.

She had detected it somehow anyway. No doubt with Buchalter's assistance.

Presently, he was scowling at us, one fist clenched at his side, and I had no doubt he would have loved nothing more than to club us with it. He always seemed to have a barely contained fury, just a hair trigger away from being unleashed on us. His other hand gripped a riding crop, and I could just see it twitching, just itching to get at one of our hides. He only managed to use it on us when Auntie wasn't looking, resulting in us boys rather liking her around. It was at that moment that I realized that this dread form towering over us was some kind of darkly opposing force put there to specifically offset the lovely surroundings. To a boy, it was almost to the level of a cruel joke played by an angry, ancient god.

I was happy enough with the mutton or slab of pork that we received on a usual evening, and being a small-time thief myself, felt little need to indulge in such criminal activity. There was also the matter that once I was "brought to heel" enough, at least in Auntie's eyes, I might be brought back to hearth and home.

"I've got the prize," John Murrell confided to me, as we mucked the stalls of her meager stable, which housed only two horses and one skinny ox to work the place, plus Pontus. Auntie was good to her word, seeing us all punished for one boy's crime.

"The prize?" I asked.

"I am apprised of the villain's identity," John replied.

I must have looked a stump. I was no sophisticate who casually used four-dollar words.

John glared me up and down, and thumped my head with a filthy knuckle.

"I know who did it, you lunk."

I stared wordlessly. John took this for further density. "Why did you not tell Auntie?" This seemed like a reasonable question.

But John just scoffed. "Because I am not a fool."

Did John Murrell fear the thief? I was learning more about my friend.

"Clearly I misjudged you. I should not have told you. Forget it."

Taken aback that I was being judged by Murrell, I returned to my muted state.

We completed the mucking in silence and trudged to the trough to sluice off the horse stink as best we could. Overall, I got the impression that he regretted bringing me into his confidence. He cast sidelong views my way whilst he shook his hands dry.

"I intend to use this intelligence to gain advantage. While I am here, leastwise," John said sullenly at last. I marveled at this young man's ability to craft sentences. Up to this point, I only knew of fictional beings in books able to express themselves in such a fashion.

"I'm with you," I said. With luck, it sounded more earnest than I felt at that moment. I had found thus far that, given enough time, my brain would catch up to events as they unfolded. Not to say I viewed myself as a dullard or halfwit, but this wouldn't be the first time that it seemed apparent I lagged a step or two behind John. This was a constant frustration for me, I'll admit.

I hazarded a question to John. "Uh, who is it?"

John leaned my way conspiratorially. "Hermie," he said. My face betrayed clear shock at this revelation. John read it in an instant, and I burst out laughing.

"It just can't be!" I managed to blurt out, shaking my head.

John was gathering himself up to defend his claim. He paused for breath, then let go a bray of laughter himself.

"I almost didn't believe it myself once I learned it," he said. "But it's true." You see, Hermie was the least likely candidate for any kind of illicit activity to begin with, and the aspect of his crime was just too much to contemplate.

After several minutes of unbridled guffaws betwixt us, John stopped abruptly and cast a stern eye on me again, which cut off my own laughter like someone stuck a gourd down my throat.

"We cannot tip our hand," John said. "When we see Hermie at dinner and lessons, we can't even look his way.

Better to be safe than risk looking at him and us give in to such fits."

Right away, I knew I was in trouble. Why, the thought of Hermie's face even now, coupled with my knowledge of what he had reportedly done, was enough to give me at least the giggles. Hermie always seemed to wear a face like a mouse's looking up at a hungry cat. We all wondered how he ended up at a place like Auntie's to begin with.

When we sat down to dinner, I found every reason not to look Hermie's way. I had no trust in my ability to control myself.

John, however, committed himself to engaging with Hermie at every opportunity. He would offer up an extra helping of dumplings from his plate, and Hermie accepted in his faltering, scared-mouse way. He smiled at John, but you could see in his eyes that he couldn't figure why this older boy would treat him so nicely, and he looked around like he really did expect a joke was being played on him.

At lessons, John assisted Hermie in memorizing his assigned Bible verses. I was astonished at this exercise, as John quoted them with near pinpoint accuracy while only infrequently consulting the Good Book.

Auntie was greatly impressed, and John became the favored student right off. He used this to his advantage, of course. Boys being boys, it fostered some ill will with the others, but John exhibited no concern over this. As for Bucschalter, he too seemed to pay extra attention to John, but not in a good way at all. Rather, he watched him closely, ever with a suspicious eye.

Over the next few weeks, I became more accustomed to being around Hermie without losing myself in laughter or betraying our knowledge of his recent thieving ways. As we were paired off together for certain chores, I even came to find him pleasant enough company, if not frightfully quiet and shy.

After some time, I learned that his folks had perished. He did not elaborate on the circumstances, but it explained why he looked and behaved like a scared rabbit. The poor kid was orphaned! And then thrown into a whole alien world, like nobody wanted him. I guess he had no other kin to take him in. There was a whole melancholy aspect that draped over him now, and having benefitted from the gift of both parents my whole life, my heart did go out to Hermie.

Consequently, I took to treating him more as a friend and less of a mechanism to the larger worldly aim of making my life easier at Auntie's. John kept at it though, keeping Hermie practically scared of his own shadow, and everybody else's in the bargain.

I was not privy to all John's designs – he tended to keep his plans close until he was ready to spring them, or he needed something from you.

Life at Auntie's did become at least routinely tolerable over a time, regardless of Bucschalter's disciplinary efforts, which he doled out at will, without rhyme or reason, it seemed to us. John said it was just to keep us boys as a group off balance and in a constant state of fearfulness. The trick, he said, was "all in the head," and to not let Bucschalter "affect your mind." He could make your body sore and scraped up some, but can never touch the mind, he said. Easier said than done for a kid, but I kept that to myself.

Anyway, Bucschalter chucked out daily thumpings with that damnable riding crop of his – out of Auntie's view – and would occasionally growl at us through his thick German accent that he was, in fact, the true master of Buzzard's Roost.

We managed scraps of solace with a quick chat betwixt ourselves when we happened to be out of his line of sight, with the added benefit that we were getting away with something. This only came about by way of Bucschalter's faulty hearing, a result of his reported participation in Tecumseh's Rebellion and all of the noisy ruckus that goes along with rebellions.

At least, that was the story that went the rounds amongst the boys. This claim had met some dispute, but of course, could never be proven or disproven. Nobody had the nerve to ask Bucschalter about it. It was known he would merely growl something at you or clop you on the head with that cussed riding crop of his if you got the least bit familiar with him. I always thought the tale was just a boy's imagination working extra hard, just laying a more mysterious and even tragic layer over an already near-legendary figure.

Besides, fearsome and mighty though he appeared to us, Bucschalter never struck me much as the type to have engaged in any soldierly life, despite his occasional martial airs.

4

I SLEPT the sleep of the dead.

That was normally the case during my time at Buzzard's Roost. Most of us were so dog-tired at the end of each day, between studies and chores, chores and then to studying again, it was nothing to fall into a dead sleep right through until morning. I would climb into my little rickety bed, lie on my side, and stare at the window across from me, which I had started to think of as a portal into another world. I looked through it, framed with plain white curtains with no frill to them, and imagine my mind's eye transferred to a great bird – perhaps a mighty bald eagle or a condor with wings spanning six feet – to soar all those miles to home, where I could watch my family and farm from the heavens. That was my escape for the time being, and one peaceful enough to lull me into a deeper sleep than I had ever known.

A hand clasped my mouth, another forceful hand gripped my shoulder.

Violent, bloody images skittered through my suddenly

waking brain, my eyes clinching tight with fear. I struggled mightily, but that hand held me firm.

This was it, I thought. The Roost was being overrun with angry, savage warriors, and I was their first victim. I could already feel a tomahawk's blade opening my throat.

My chest heaved with exertion, and the hand over my mouth surged me to greater panic. My heart pounded like a piston, pushing blood through my ears in a torrent.

My mind, at last catching up with things, commanded me to open my eyes.

John loomed over me, decidedly not a savage. Nevertheless, he might have been one, with my brain still trying to make sense of things in the darkness. My panic gave way very quickly to anger. I was never one to find being scared a funny thing like some folks seemed to. My eyes must have told John that, so he held up his other hand, as if saying, "Hold on. I come in peace."

I breathed a bit easier then, blinking a few times, still irritated, but signaling that I understood at last what was happening. John released me.

I sat up, the bed creaking a little, and scowled at him. He held my shoes out to me, and I scowled at him some more, but with a questioning tilt of my head.

"Let's go." He made for the window. I scrambled to follow him quietly, after hastily putting on my drawers. Thankfully, the other boys were still fast asleep. The soft snores of a few helped mask the sound of our movement.

John motioned me to follow, right out through a window which was already open. It was a late summer night, and we were permitted to keep the windows open to allow a breeze, what little there was of one.

We picked our way very carefully through the grounds. I followed John's lead at every turn. When he stopped, I stopped. When he paused and struck a pose as if to listen, I did the same. We must have made a comical sight, now that I think back on it.

I was ever alert for Bucschalter's presence, of course. He was known to lurk about the place at all hours of the night like a wraith from Hades itself, muttering that strange, Teutonic oath of his. He had no detectable pattern of sleep or waking hours, right unsettlingly. It also added another layer to the man's primordial, monstrous lore amongst us lads. In fact, nobody was quite sure that he was even a human being at all, but a sort of golem that Auntie had created from her celebrated knick-knacks that she had collected from all over the country.

Somehow, we evaded Bucschalter's detection. My relief was indescribable, as we had all heard the screams and groans of those miserable boys that he caught from time to time, being out of their barracks without permission or otherwise up to no good.

However, we would have to endure the same procedure to remain undetected upon our return.... If we returned at all, for at this point, who knew if permanent escape was John's intent?

We made our way through the dark woods, me trying not to think too hard on the dangers lying in wait for us there: Indian braves, for instance, cougars, even werewolves.

Just then, a thought came to me. I reached out and tugged on John's sleeve.

"Isn't it thataway?" I motioned off in another direction.

He looked at me quizzically. "What is it, *thataway?*"

I was further confused. "Why, the pistol, of course."

John looked blankly at me a moment, then waved his hand. "Oh no," he said. "We can get that old *pistole* any time. This is better than that, Master Hue." His face took on a devilish grin, leaving me still puzzled but plenty intrigued.

We continued through the dark woods, and I must say I

was impressed with how John seemed very familiar with them, like he was a born tracker.

Eventually, far off, I could hear the friendly, tinkling sound of what seemed to be a piano. This struck me as a very unlikely sound in these parts. I hadn't heard one since my family had visited the La Barges' home back in Elizabethton. They had money and a piano, and little Lucinda La Barge gave us a recital. I even managed to stay awake through it, too, controlling my squirming and fiddling, which made Mother happy.

There was a bit of light coming from some building in the distance, and John barred my way with an arm. We stopped and peered through the underbrush and brambles at a house.

It was a two-story affair, but rough. In the middle of the woods, there was enough of a house here to sport a porch, even.

There were men on this porch, smoking and talking. One of them was drunk. Well, they were all in various stages of drunkenness, but there was one drunker than most. I knew this from observing my Uncle Olson at a county cookout and it stuck with me ever since, so much more because it had infuriated my mother that my sister and I had witnessed it. When a child of about eight first sees a family member acting out in a way completely unlike the person they always were... Well, that sort of thing tends to stick with you. How do I mean? Uncle Olson broke into song very randomly, made a hash of every lyric, and commenced to climb a tree overhanging a creek, before falling into said creek and had to be rescued by Father, who then tried to explain hastily that he was just revisiting a childhood event and got a bit carried away... You see?

I don't think I had ever seen Mother so angry. Poor Father took on the full might of her fury that day, and only because Uncle Olson had already passed out, so the fury had to go somewhere.

We studied these men on the porch from the relative security of the bushes and brambles for several minutes. I began to wonder why, in fact, we were watching them so. I started to whisper this when John held up a hand. I followed his gaze, which had not left the porch for one instant, and spotted the very drunk man making his unsteady way toward us.

He tripped and fell more than once, causing his fellows on the porch to burst out laughing.

The drunk muttered angrily, then lurched himself back to his feet. He managed to keep slowly navigating toward us. I sucked in a quick breath as he shambled closer.

He suddenly stopped short as if he had heard it. He stood still – as still as a drunken man can stand – and appeared to listen carefully, his head wobbling around like a top about to lose all of its remaining spin.

"Uh oh," said one of the men. "He seed another Mohawk!" This unleashed another gale of laughter from the porch crowd.

The drunk turned his head back to them and sputtered what sounded like a curse. He was much drunker than Uncle Olson ever was at that cookout. He turned his attention back to the dark woods for a moment, before shrugging, and tilted his head to one side, mumbling what for all the world sounded like, "Mmmph show trtit dirty injuns, Mohawks... Ffft I, I took three them prrt Mohawks m'self. Shhht." He belched, sounding perilously close to vomiting, then recovered. "Injun. Uggg. Fighter... Way back, I did, and y'all kin..."

All this time, he was fumbling with his trousers. We suddenly heard the loud spattering of his urination in the bushes directly out front of us. John and I scrambled back as best and quietly as we could. We tried to stifle our laughter. Grinning like an idiot, eyes wide with shock, I clapped my hand to my mouth. It felt like I really couldn't stop my giggles unless I stuffed my whole hand in there.

The drunk's stream of piss seemed to have no end, which

tickled us further, naturally. It was all over when he finally let loose a roar of flatulence which seemed to quake the timbers all around us. I still wonder as to how his trousers survived that blast. He then proceeded to pass out in a heap of filthy disgrace.

Our laughter was masked by that of the men on the porch. And then the door of the house banged open, spilling a few more men. The sound of the piano likewise was unleashed upon the surrounding woods.

A woman emerged next, dressed in a very florid, flowing gown, low cut at the neck to expose as much of her breasts as might be allowed without being completely exposed. I had never seen anything like it and was firmly rooted to the ground, my eyes fixated on that vision.

This woman and her gifts immediately grasped the attention of the men on the porch. They hollered and hooted like I imagine the Mohawks must have when the drunk had battled them back in his days of glory.

Us boys, too, were fixed on this vision of female wonder. My mouth must have been gaping, as I do believe I swallowed a bug or two while taking this whole spectacle in. I jumped a little at a hand on my shoulder. When I glanced over, John's mouth hung open like a landed trout's. He had probably grasped me only to ensure that I too was benefiting from the view.

Now, if we had been paying closer attention to anything north of the woman's chest, we would have seen that she was a significantly older lady, probably in her mid or late thirties. By any fourteen- or fifteen- year-old's estimation, that would be considered positively ancient; well, under more normal circumstances. And if her breasts weren't just about hanging out.

Of course, we could not have cared one whit. We stared and stared until our eyes were likely to dry out like sunbaked raisins, and we would have stared more if The Vision had loitered out on that porch much longer. She eventually reached out and tugged a man's sleeve.

He looked at her appreciably, but shyly too, and the other men had another guffaw. They laughed and chided him, and it was pretty clear this was a kind of initiating event of some sort. One gently pushed him toward The Vision, prodding him on.

She looked at him sweetly, brushing her hair with her hand. I expect this was supposed to make her look more dainty and somehow more alluring. Then she said something to him in that weird sing-songy way I had heard girls use around boys, for some reason or another. She pursed her lips and planted a kiss on his whiskered cheek, and you would think that alone was the funniest thing the porch loiterers had ever seen. The young man hung his head bashfully and entered the house with The Vision on his arm. She waved a hand at the men on the porch as if to say, "I never!" and hush them up.

John and I retreated into the gloom of the night-shaded woods.

"What is this place?" I asked. My face must have still reflected some pleasurable glow, because he looked at me and chuckled.

"It's what my daddy called a den of iniquity."

I looked at him, puzzled beyond measure.

"A pleasure house."

My vexation wasn't alleviated.

"A house of ill repute. Of ill fame."

Ill repute? Ill fame? To John, I'm sure I looked the very picture of a dolt.

"My Lord, man, what did you do back there in that backwater town of yours? You've not seen anything of the world, have you?" said John. He sat back, waiting for something to sink in.

Finally, he blurted out, "It's a *whorehouse!*"

This term I *was* familiar with, thanks to Johnny Portnoy back in Elizabethton. We had managed to escape church that day and, following the theme of the day, which was to do things contrary to things decent and wholesome to our spirit, by discussing what we knew of the world.

Unfortunately, this outburst also gained the attention of the porch dwellers.

"What?! Damned rascals!" I heard from one of them. "Likely those Bender boys again. I'll hide 'em good, since their pap won't!" and also an absurd "Devil's in the bramble!" There was even some laughter in there, too, as a brief chase erupted through the woods, apparently becoming sport to some of our pursuers.

With John's silent, panicky direction, we managed to evade them a short distance, finally stumbling into an old, dark gully. We followed its path, thinking we'd lost them for good, since their yelping and drunken guffawing dwindled a bit with some distance.

"There you be, you young villains!" a rough voice stopped us short. There, blocking our way after a turn in the gulley, was one of the porch lurkers. He had outfoxed us, I daresay owing to the fact that he wasn't quite as fumed as the others. Not to mention more familiar with these woods, if that was indeed a woodsman's hatchet that dangled menacingly from his belt.

Hence, we were unceremoniously dragged back to the establishment, literally by the ears.

We found ourselves in the midst of what had just been a place of deep and yet strangely satisfying mystery. The wonder of it collapsed around us, revealing itself as a simple, rough clapboard house, fairly dingy in its surroundings, with not much to offer in the way of décor. There was a wide plank set down on a couple of crates in one corner, forming the bar of the main room. Two shelves containing bottles of various shapes and sizes were on the wall behind this bar, and more than a few jugs. A weapon hung there too, looking very much like an antique. I believed it was a blunderbuss, of all things. A tall man stood there, older than the others, with a bit of a paunch on him. He was wide in the shoulders though, and had a look that didn't suffer trifles from anyone. As he wiped his huge hands on a grimy towel, he stared at us from under a bushy, furrowed brow, plainly displeased.

The piano had stopped abruptly. The pianist spun around on a creaky seat and looked at us with some fair amusement.

Most of the surrounding men glared at us, though, like the bartender.

"Huh. Just lads," one of them said, and spat into the fire in the fireplace. The spittle sputtered on a hot, blackened log.

"What do we do with 'em?" asked one of them. He was probably the youngest of them and also the dumbest, by the looks of him. The rest ignored him.

Another sitting near the fire, took a deep swig from a brown jug and cast a mean, bleary eye at us. The thing that caught me about him was that his eyes, sort of amber tinged. It looked downright unnatural for a human. The glow of the fire added to the effect. From a scabbard on his belt, he drew a knife, which looked as mean and as dangerous as he did. Blade and handle alike bore a series of nasty notches and jags. The edge itself told a long, colorful tale of violence and blood.

"I say we split them like eels," he said.

My throat clicked dry as it tried to swallow my tongue.

"There will be no splitting, damn your hides," rang a female voice. All eyes shifted.

The Vision descended the stairs with the man she had earlier kissed in her trail. He looked sweaty, tired, and satisfied all at once, which struck me queer.

"What in hell's name is wrong with you brutes?" said The

Vision, and I could have kissed her. "They are but kids, can't you see?"

"Oh, we was just funnin'," said the dumb one.

"Shut up, Mills," said the bartender. Mills glared challengingly back, but the bartender's stare made him wilt.

Amber Eyes just laughed, sounding like a mix of hissing air and some dead, heavy thing being dragged across rough ground. He reluctantly scabbarded that ugly blade, thank the Lord.

The Vision walked over to him and kicked his foot off the stool where his foot rested, pulled the jug away from him, and sat down. She wiped off the mouth of the bottle with part of her gown and took a deep pull on it herself. She then wiped her brow with a frilly hanky produced from somewhere and gave a wink to the man she had kissed, who was still on the stairs. It seemed like he really didn't know what to do with himself. In the end, he completed his descent down the stairs and left through the front door, closing it quietly behind him.

There was a silent pause long enough for a breath, and then the men burst into laughter. Once it subsided, all attention turned back to John and myself.

I was paralyzed. Even if I had been capable of anything, no doubt it'd have been easily snuffed out by the roughs surrounding me. I spared a quick glance at John, and to my shock, he did not look the least bit concerned. In fact, in some strange way, he looked like he belonged. Almost as if he were among friends, even.

The Vision was appraising John.

"Well, you are a handsome lad, aren't you?" she said. "Look at that curly brown hair. Lustrous, it is. My girls might give you a toss for free one day soon, eh?"

John simply smiled. This strange reaction seemed to unbalance even some of the men.

"Come on, Ma," said one, finally. Even as a dumb kid, I could tell that The Vision was not this man's mother. "What say we dispose of them?"

The room fell silent all of a sudden, with the audible pall of death itself. Now I was unnerved anew. The man at the piano started playing, God bless him.

"Now, why would we do that? Seems wasteful. And foolhardy," The Vision replied. "Sides, they haven't hurt nobody, have they? Might be useful."

Someone huffed and went out the back. Amber Eyes just rattled off another low laugh.

The Vision, still looking us over, snapped her fingers, and the bartender seemed to magically produce a pipe. He came over to hand it to her, a clomping sound coming along with him. Only then did I see that he had a well-worn peg for a leg.

The Vision deftly packed her pipe with the contents of a small pouch that hung from her waist. The bartender had already produced a smoldering twig from the fire that she used to light it. She puffed it to life, her eyes never leaving us throughout. I know I looked startled at the presentation, as I had never seen a woman smoke before. The Vision smiled.

"Helps me think," she said, as though knowing my thoughts. She winked at me. No girl or woman had ever thrown a wink my way before. Right then, I tried to swallow my tongue.

"Lads, this place is known as Ma Surgick's," she said. "I'm Ma."

The scene then suddenly and with perfect grace took on a whole different aspect altogether. Another person appeared from the staircase, on dainty and silent feet.

If the woman who sat before us was The Vision, owing almost entirely to the scandalous display of a vast portion of her bosom to young boys previously deprived of such scenery, then the heavenly creature that stepped – no, floated – into our lives from above could only be described as The Dream.

Indeed, as I pondered the moment in the following days and weeks, I was sure that I had in reality been dreaming this part. I know that all seems awfully melodramatic, but I'm trying to frame it as it was in our minds all of those years ago. To us mere lads, no such being could have existed on a mortal plain. It was just that simple.

She positively glowed up there on those stairs. And it wasn't just us that she affected so, oh no. All activity in that rough room simply stopped: the piano, the drinking, the card-playing (some had resumed their previous activity during our interview with The Vision).

Her hair floated about her elegant face, much like the haloed archangels depicted in the colored glass windows of some tall churches.

She even wore a white gown that seemed to flow off her like a mountain waterfall of the purest water. It cascaded onto the stairs at her feet.

"Ma?" said The Dream, and it was music.

"Yes, dear?" answered The Vision sweetly, not looking at The Dream. Her eyes were still fixed in our direction, but I noticed with some alarm that they now had a flat glaze.

"Why are you down here, my dear?" The Vision asked, her voice now equally flat and distinctly razor-edged.

More music, as The Dream prettily stated, with a pout, "He pissed himself again."

The Vision's face turned from flat, menacing annoyance to one of pure disgust, mixed with a touch of rage for good measure.

"That sot has sullied my girl's crib for the last time! Hieronymus!"

An enormous black man entered from a room behind the

bar. He looked up at The Dream, then around at the assembly, clearly looking for the man who had harmed her in some fashion. He ascended the stairs with a slight limp, carefully making his way past her.

Hieronymus disappeared into the rooms above, and there was heard a bumpy commotion. He reemerged onto the stairway where he maneuvered a clump of soiled clothing and man down and out of the building.

"And you will not be welcome back here, sir!" Ma called after the clump. She waved a hand dismissively to The Dream, who floated back upstairs like a delicate cloud to the heavens.

"A damned shame," Ma continued. "The judge's purse will be missed around here, sure." One of the men let out a quick chortle.

"As to you, then," Ma purred, her attention back to us, "You didn't say from what quarter you sprung."

Neither of us took her meaning. Amber Eyes stuck the toe of his boot into my side.

"What hole did you two rats crawl from, anyhow?" he asked. "Where be your home?"

"Auntie Charlotte's!" I blurted. John gave me a fierce, warning glance, but of course, it was too late. I reflected later and defended myself to John by saying that it was a natural reflex, what I had hoped at the time was one of self-preservation.

"Ah, I see," said Ma with a chuckle. "That old biddy a-spying on me, is she? I might have known. They'll be shore missing you come the dawn, though, won't they?" This didn't seem so much a question as it was her running things through her mind aloud.

"Want I should take 'em back?" one of the men said. Ma shook her head.

"I know well the place." She grasped the jug away from

someone. She absently wiped the mouth of it again with her dress and drank generously. "Auntie Charlotte's a congregant of Pastor Purdy's, is she not?"

"She is, I can attest," said a lanky fellow with a hank of hair jutting from the front of his scalp and not much else behind it. The bartender snorted at the man, then spat a wad into a deplorable-looking bucket festooned with patterns of rust. It made a sick, wet sound when it landed.

"My wife attends there," the man said, shrugging meekly.

"And you lads attend as well," Ma reasoned.

She puffed on her pipe, eyeing us in an intense, considering way that made me more uncomfortable than I already was.

Hieronymus stood in the doorway behind the bar. He was looking at us in such a way that made me think he was sympathetic to us, which alleviated my nerves some.

"I do believe these boys will provide us some use," Ma said with some finality. It seemed we were to survive the night after all. "Indeed, they will."

And she proceeded to tell us just how.

5

"Now, GIT," sneered Amber Eyes as he put a boot to John's hindquarters and shoved. John nearly toppled to the ground, face first.

Hieronymus was at his side. Apparently, the largest man ever in existence was needed in case two boys roughly one-third his size put together got out of control. In fact, this being just about made Bucschalter look like just another average-sized human.

They escorted us within sight of the place. We could see dark forms of its buildings just through the woods, murkier now in the pre-dawn light than when we had departed hours before. It seemed ages since we had left, and now the place seemed from another life entirely, as welcome as the bosom of my own family farm.

My head was pretty well fogged up, grappling with the mission that Ma had commissioned us. Hear this madness: We were to steal into a church office, of all places, and pilfer a book. Now, you might think I would already have considerable experience there, since my very presence at the Roost was partly owing to the fact that I had stolen a Bible, if only for the money nestled within its well-read pages. But that particular Bible was just sitting out on a bench by itself, not locked up in a desk within a pastor's office. I just couldn't figure how to go about it.

When I looked over at John, I was mightily annoyed to make out a blissful smile.

"What's all that about, John? Are you a fool? We'll be cooked, for sure," I huffed.

"Hmph," John said. "This is nothing. Why, I lifted a wallet the size of a dictionary from a police captain's coat once. And he wasn't even drunk!"

I grunted unhappily and stared at the dark path ahead of us.

"Don't be such a worrywart, Master Stephen." John tapped his head with a smirk. "I have it all worked out. And you even have a starring role."

I stopped in my tracks right there, while John sauntered along, hands in his pockets, like he didn't have a care in the world.

I started, realizing I was being left in the woods with the werewolves. I hurried after him while trying to look like I wasn't hurrying at all.

* * *

Reentering the fold of our billet was comically easy. To the point where, once I was back in bed with the covers comfortingly drawn about me, I half expected Bucschalter to tower above me from the surrounding gloom, tear me from my warm, comforting nest, and nail me to the wall with his hell-spawned glare.

I crawled into bed, my head a flurry of the night's events, and tried not to worry about our mission. My frenzied thoughts soon calmed to the serene image of The Dream. I felt a warmth in my belly at the memory of her floating into my world, and eventually drifted off to sleep with the notion of sometime maybe even talking to her.

It felt like mere moments later that I was roused by the usual bell ringing us to the chores that had been set for us before breakfast.

John fell in step beside me as I made for the stables. We were to tend to the mule and horse and, of course, muck out the place again.

He jostled me with a sharp elbow, not the most pleasant sensation when first waking. I looked over to see a grin to beat all had lit up his handsome face.

"That was a right good time, eh?"

I looked at him as if his forehead had sprouted an extra Satanic eye of a goat. He laughed, then ducked his head a bit and looked slyly around to ensure Bucschalter was not within hearing distance. The man viewed any boy engaging in any form of merriment as a sure sign that they were up to no good. It therefore must be immediately investigated, then horse-whipped into extinction.

"I was scared witless, John." I instantly regretted that; it sounded babyish. John just chuckled.

"Those, to me, are the best times."

At my puzzlement, he just smiled crookedly.

"The times when I was most afraid, when I know I am surely about to meet my maker, why, those pack the most thrills," he said, then paused. "Though I suppose you don't realize that until you have made it through. I guess it isn't fun at the time, now that I think on it." He barked another laugh, then quickly checked again for our friend Bucschalter.

He ambled on ahead, happier than I had ever seen him.

And now that we had been hitched, together like horse and

buggy, I had to consider just what breed of horse I had been hitched to.

It wasn't but three days later that a group of us gathered for a special task. We knew not where we were bound, but Bucschalter had conveyed in his clipped Hessian fashion that we had been hand-picked to attend to a neighbor's needs.

John looked at me with that ever-present smile and winked. I knew by now not to ask how he came by certain intelligence, but I could tell he knew our destination, for he looked fairly excited at the prospect.

We struck out on foot, trailing behind Bucschalter on faithful, sturdy Pontus.

John again sidled up.

"This is our chance," he spoke in a stage whisper. "Ain't it excitin'?"

John had earlier apprised me of my part, which was to create a distraction. Beyond that, he didn't say much, as always.

My skin went a-tingle of a sudden, because I happened to be staring straight ahead at the back of Bucschalter's planet-sized head. When John said that, that head twitched a touch to the side like he had heard something.

I managed to keep from letting out a squeaking noise. The whole situation made me more nervous than rhubarb in a pie shop. I didn't find it any fun at all.

John had observed all of this and laughed quietly, damn him. He really was enjoying himself, and my nervousness must have add to his entertainment, which made my forehead and ears hot to the touch.

"You're going to do me little good in such a state, son," he said.

John lately had taken to calling me "son," and I couldn't figure it. It added to my irritations, as he was only a few years older, after all. I chalked it up to something he picked up at some point in his travels and tried to leave it at that.

I now recognized the road we were heading down. We were bound for what we called Pallwick's, short for Pallwick's Primitive Baptist, the church that Auntie dragged us to on Sundays and sometimes Mondays and Wednesdays too, if we were deserving of it for acting extra uppity that week. Now I knew of John's earlier excitement.

I didn't really want to believe Auntie was the mercenary type that paved her way heavenward, but I just couldn't shake the notion that we were being marched down to Pallwick's as forced labor just to grease those skids for her. That wasn't something Bucschalter would do of his own accord. Matter of fact, he no doubt saw it as a means to head us off from the path of mischief that boys naturally spin off to. On that score, he would get no argument from me. The workers were few on Pastor Purdy's grounds, so to speak, and off we dutifully trudged.

We set about doing the chores under the forced labor contract which the Lord demanded. I was scraping the side of the church building itself, making way for a new coat, something I admit I did not know was necessary before repainting. I always assumed you would just slather on new paint to hide the shortcomings of the old one. So, I at least learned something.

We scraped and dug and moved and piled and had no fair opportunity for much else but continuous work. It was a while before we were finally able to set for a while and had a bit of cold chicken and an apple a-piece to fortify our energies for the next round.

All it took was but a few minutes for a spot of trouble to

find us, thereby bolstering Bucschalter's views of the natural villainous impulses of boys gathered in herds.

It was discovered that there was a crick nearby. And really, that is enough to lay the idea that calls for some kind of adventure, for cricks (or "creeks" as you might call them) attract boys with the same efficiency as bloated cow carcasses attract blue bottle flies.

This crick lazed along just past a small bluff that attempted, rather half-arsedly, to hide the aquatic treasure lying just beyond, for you could see a sliver of water and reeds and cattails that were typical of cricks, and they called to us like the Sirens of the ancients.

Bucschalter, we understood at this point, could not be everywhere at once, supernatural gifts or not, and we took full advantage. We boys knew when to make hay while the glorious sun shone, and had the philosophy that even when caught manufacturing said hay, sometimes it was worth any punishment.

Thus, most of us gravitated to that crick almost at once.

It was in these quick moments that John gave me the look. We can likely chalk this up to another auxiliary level of boy instinct, but I read it as "This is it. You know what to do." I didn't, really, but I had to think fast.

I followed the herd to the crick.

The water had the most inviting aspect to it. Its surface positively glistened with the promise of escape from the heat of the day, our cruel masters, and dismal toils.

Some boys took to skimming rocks, another instinctive impulse of a young, healthy lad. If not skimming, it's throwing anything else that might be at hand into the water. They do it without thinking anything at all about it. Where there is water and there are rocks, there is skimming to be had. It happens as sure as the Earth turns.

Elsewhere, where the crick ran shallow, boys went to hunt down the wily and elusive crawdad, something else that kicks into gear without a thought.

I rounded the bluff and spotted something of a small lagoon that had formed below it. I nearly waded into the water, stopped myself, and retreated up the shore a ways to remove my shoes. I stepped back in carefully, feeling the silty crick mud squeeze between my toes with a satisfaction beyond description. The water felt blessedly cool, and even its clean smell was like a balm.

I waded a bit further, now just about up to my knees. Minnows were darting about now, deeper water ahead beckoning me. In I went, and I had no idea just how deep it was there until too late. I felt a foot slip down a slippery crick shelf and in I went, suddenly past the top of my head. My hands darted out all around me, desperately grasping for some of the growth of water plants near the edge of the crick - reeds, roots, anything. Truthfully, I could swim a bit, so they say the best acting needed a drop of actual emotion – panic, in this case.

Finally, my hand grasped a bit of cloth, and I felt something moving around behind it, felt other hands trying to grasp back at me.

I had already swallowed a lot of crick and continued to thrash and grasp about, like some kind of drowning ape. Boys were now all about me, trying to help, it seemed. Well, I like to believe some were trying to, but for all I knew, some were assisting in drowning me.

I windmilled my arms with renewed energy, needing to prolong this drama as much as possible, in the name of the mission. This created quite the maelstrom. I even managed to lay in some blows on those who were "rescuing" me while I was at it.

Little did my saviors know that I had discovered a fairly

firm footing on the crick bed by now, and was merely enjoying the pure spectacle in belting a few boys and getting away with it because I was "drowning."

Of course, there was a lot of shouting and screaming that went along with all of this. Some of it reached a note that I believed only females were capable of. Were there some girls about that we were not previously aware of? Must have come from some of the younger lads.

Back then, it was actually fairly rare to find someone who knew how to swim, so it stands to reason there would be a reasonable fear of one of us drowning.

I was suddenly grasped by frightfully strong hands on my shoulders, and these iron vices hauled me out of the crick as unceremoniously as a river trout on a hook.

There I dangled, in the grasp of a very irate Bucschalter. He glowered at me with the fearsome gaze of an angry god - Zeus or Odin came to mind. He was breathing quite heavily, and it did not seem to be from any particular exertion, but more from fear, which I detected – for an instant – a glint of it in his grey eyes. Some of his heavy breath reached my face and nostrils, and the muscles there right away clenched defensively. It was laced with whatever spice from Hades, or dead things that had garnished his last nine meals. He gusted more of it out, smothered me, robbed all air of anything my lungs could find of use, and rendered me even more inert.

At last, he laid me on the shore with surprising gentleness.

The boys had all silenced their hysterical caterwauling upon Bucschalter's arrival. My eyes were still half-closed, and I tossed my head from side to side, sputtering as if my mouth and throat still contained further gallons of crick. Throughout those thrashings, I tried to squint through to detect if John was in the vicinity so I could conclude my theatrics.

He was not.

I continued the scene.

Bucschalter had cleared the area around us with his massive arms. The boys stood with decent respect away, no doubt at least half of them were expecting me to give up my own ghost right then and there. Probably a third of them hoped for it, as it would make a right dandy tale in later days.

Bucschalter loomed over me. He grasped my face with his over-large, meaty hands and inspected my face, as if searching for signs of life or the spirit to fight for it. He clearly did not know what to do with this newly beached trout-boy. He started to sort of slap my cheeks, no doubt thinking these were gentle in nature. To me, it felt like I was on the losing end of a prize fight.

"–on his side!" Some boy squeaked.

I could barely squint the confusion on Bucschalter's slab face. Then he nodded and turned me on my side with his enormous paws as easily as a normal human would turn the page in a book.

On cue, I dutifully managed to spurt a quantity of crick from my mouth. It really was just some spittle I managed to produce on the spot, as I was out of crick. I gave a little cough for additional effect. It appeared to produce the desired reaction, as the lads yielded a gasp, and some of them moved in a little. I heaved some more, just to put a loving, dramatic touch on the scene. *Might as well heap some ham on the thing, I* thought, *as I may not get another chance at this level of fame any time soon.* I blinked around at the circle of boys and saw expressions that ranged from relief – a little one was still crying – to profound disappointment.

"Huh," one of them grunted. He crossed his arms and walked away, shaking his head just as his own disenchanted parents must have done.

I looked up at them and uttered, in as weak and pathetic a voice as I could muster:

"Shoes...?"

One of the more sympathetic observers disappeared from my view for a moment and then carefully placed my shoes before me. As far as I could squint, Bucschalter moved them closer in. Apparently, this kinder version of Bucschalter – kinder than any of us had ever seen – wanted to be sure I knew they were there. I was truly touched, given all I had ever seen this man display was a distinctly stern, Germanic disciplinary air at all times.

He gazed at me for the first time without a scowl or cold condemning stare.

"Tod soll sich nicht trennen," he muttered.

The group of us then trudged up the bank of the crick, toward the church proper and whatever chores still awaited us.

Pastor Purdy was there too, having been drawn by the hubbub. He cast a stern eye, but at the same time gave me a quick up and down to ensure my true welfare. His face had a peculiar pallor to it, as if he also was affrighted at the aspect of an awful death befalling one of his flock.

This was an altogether fresh experience. True, I was still but a boy, but I had never before seen any concern for my safety displayed by anyone other than my family. A comforting feeling, of course, but after my theatrics, it made me shift and squirm in my wet clothes.

Thus, I was grateful for John's return to my side. In all the commotion, nobody had noted his absence. I did get satisfaction from that, at least. He looked at my soggy clothes with some amusement.

"Well done, son," he said in a low voice, when everyone was again out of earshot. Bucschalter was already off rousting some boys to another chore. "That was just enough. I feared

Purdy might never hear that commotion and leave his office. That man must be half-deef."

His pronunciation of the word gave me pause, but then I took his meaning.

"You mean deaf," I said, remembering too late how John took no delight in being corrected.

To my relief, he just shrugged. "It worked for us," he said with a sly look. "I've got it." He patted the waist of his trousers, where I saw the faint outline of a square, flat object.

He winked and threw me that crooked smile.

6

Hieronymus peered at us with dark, fierce eyes.

"You best not have come with empty hands," he rumbled like thunder. I was taken a little aback at the sound, for I could not recall having heard him even speak before, certainly not to us. His voice had a kind of musical lilt; clearly, he was not from around these parts at all. "Ma will have your hides, elsewise, and have me to do it, too."

"Yessir," John mumbled. Any sign of cockiness or self-assuredness seemed to melt away in the very presence of the huge man.

Hieronymus stared at us a moment or two, I suppose to assure us that he was not a man to tolerate any foolishness. There was no doubt whatsoever that if we were not producing the demanded item, he would be the one to harvest, cure, and tan our skins.

He led us into the house's rear quarters, past a small room containing only a cot and a small table on which a lantern burned low. Hieronymus' quarters, perhaps? He led us to another small room with a couple of rough chairs, a small round table with some playing cards around it, and a musket leaning in one corner. A small lantern hung there, burning low.

"Sit," commanded Hieronymus, and we did. He left.

Piano music drifted in from the room next door, with men's and women's laughter mixed in it, and a bit of singing here and there, too. Peculiar thumping and jostling noises could be heard from above as well. I looked at John, but he looked completely unfazed.

"You're sure it's the right one?" I asked John. Now that we were here, the prospect of escape, if needed, appeared to be dim.

"Course I am," he responded, but I detected a flicker of doubt in his eyes. Something cold stabbed right through the length of my body right then. "Couldn't be many others like it, could there?"

"You look inside it?"

"Course I did!" he snapped. His face betrayed another hint of doubt. "Only a little."

The music from next door seemed to reach a loud, unhar-monious crescendo; the piano player banged out the last notes with a fury, as if hoping to finish off the mangling of a song to end its misery. There was a loud overhead slam of a door, and suddenly there was a confused muddling of voices, some forced female laughter, and a drunken guffaw.

A man appeared in the doorway of the room we had been deposited in. It was the man who had escorted us back to Auntie's alongside Hieronymus. He peered at us with those ugly, unsettling amber eyes and spat on the floor, as if to be rid of a rancid taste.

"You lot, again."

My belly shriveled at the sight of him, and, as impossible as I thought it might be, shriveled even further as I watched his filthy hand crawling over and fingering the hilt of the enormous knife hanging off his belt. He leaned against the doorjamb, clearly enjoying watching our wits leave us.

Hieronymus reappeared in the hallway, saving us from a sure, torturous death. For a big man, he moved ever so quietly, even with that little limp of his. Even Amber Eyes seemed surprised. Hieronymus gave him a look, and he slunk away reluctantly, yet with a malicious smirk.

"Ma will see you, now," said Hieronymus, with the gravity of a butler in some English lord's manse.

He led us into the main room in which she had interviewed us several nights before.

There was Ma Surgick, in all her glory, a generous glimpse of her treasures to be had, as always. I believed at the time that it was an attempt to further dazzle us boys and keep us off balance with our minds and thoughts distracted with the suggestion of earthly pleasures.

Of course, this worked to great effect. At least, on me it did, I'll admit. I was always a touch nervy around women anyway, and still am, truth be told, even at my now advanced age. John never was. It was one of those things I admired about him despite myself.

"Well?" Ma Surgick smiled at us expectantly, but her eyes were flinty, challenging. "Let's have it, then."

John reached into his shirt, pulled something from the inside waist of his trousers. It was a simple, cloth-bound book with an intricate, fancy design on its cover. He laid it carefully on the table, and I could see a lacy frame surrounding the image of a bird. A grouse? A partridge?

Ma didn't move at once, her eyes going from the book back up to John and me more than once. I couldn't shake the feeling she was trying to build suspense for some reason. As if things were not suspenseful enough.

"Looks right," she said, finally. A very slight nod from her had Hieronymus picking up the book, flipping through a few pages, before nodding curtly back. Ma held a hand out, and he passed it over. She then held it up to us.

"Did you look at the contents yourselves?"

"No, ma'am," John answered. "Well, I had to, a bit, to make sure it was the right one."

Ma laughed lightly, the fingers of one hand fluttering over the intricate bird design.

She looked right at me. My eyes could not hold her gaze. I looked away and muttered, "No, ma'am. I didn't neither."

"It was about three months back," Ma said. Her eyes darted to Hieronymus, who nodded solemnly. "Old Pastor Purdy got some of his flock all riled up in one *hell* of a righteous fervor."

She reached into her ever-present pouch and produced her pipe. She daintily packed it with tobacco.

"Oh yes, much to my regret, it was a slow night and they fairly stormed in here, stomping about the place. Even threatened to burn it to the ground. Held poor Hieronymus here at gunpoint, too. What customers I did have rightly skedaddled rather than face the good Pastor's wrath."

She scratched a match to light and put it to the pipe, watching us.

"Now that I think on it, it was probably to my fortune that there weren't many menfolk here that night. Elsewise, they wouldn't be coming back for a while. Bad for business."

She sighed out a cloud of blue-black smoke.

"Sure enough, there were a few men outside with torches waiting for us when they marched me and Hieronymus out. Then that old Pastor, why, he came out with that there book in his hands, and I will tell you he grasped that thing tighter and more passionately than he ever did the Good Book."

She chuckled then, without an ounce of mirth. Her teeth made a soft clacking sound as they clamped the pipe.

"Purdy looked at me with no small measure of triumph in those beady eyes of his, I'll tell you. He didn't say a word to me, but he tossed his head up to his flock and they mounted up and lit off, the job done."

She exhaled another gust of smoke.

"The fool," Her voice was low, almost to herself. "Thinking it was over somehow. They would have to burn *me* down for it to be over."

She picked up the book.

"Lists, boys, are useful things, even to people like us, you'll find. We know who are frequent guests, who are beholden to us, who owes us."

She opened it, turned a few pages. "And who will not be welcomed back."

A look passed between her and Hieronymus then, and he smirked slightly. She closed the book and held it up to us again. I was already tired of looking at that damned bird.

"This, boys, was the real reason for Pastor Purdy's raid," Ma said. "It contains all of those things, including the esteemed Purdy's itself. He wouldn't want it passing into the wrong hands, you see. He would have burned it, sure, but I guess he figured it was a useful thing for him, too. See how it is?"

She sat up straight with this last, and we nodded that we did, in fact, see her meaning.

"You've done me good, boys. Just as I thought you might." She pointed at John. "You... You have a certain look about you..." She waited for his name.

"John, ma'am," he said.

She did not ask my name. I sat there feeling dumb and, for some reason, slightly offended.

"You both come around here of an evening, when you can get away from that place. We'll find you some fun and excitement, which I am sure you need. Isn't that right?"

We both nodded dumbly and dutifully said our "yes ma'ams," and Hieronymus escorted us from the room to the yard behind the house. Off in the distance, and most definitely upwind of us, could be heard the grunting of pigs and hogs.

"She likes you," Hieronymus told us. At least I thought it was meant for both of us. I looked up at him, and he was glowering down like an unnecessarily large, vengeful golem. I wasn't sure if Hieronymus cared very much at all for Ma taking a liking to us. Perhaps he was a jealous golem, too, not just vengeful.

"Best not squander it," he said in a deep rumble that even Hercules himself would not likely argue with, if he knew what was good for him.

7

Thus began our careers working for Ma Surgick.

John devised something of a system of getting around Bucschalter's erratic and oddly timed ground wanderings. We were never together during these escapes. That way was sure death. We tried to always be apart from each other once we got through the window, as opposite as we could possibly get and as quick, too. We had perfected the art of imitating the noises and calls of the region's fauna, until we believed we were fit for the mightiest war band of Comanches. With this marvelous mimicry – and Bucschalter's poor hearing – we stayed miraculously undetected.

Anyways, when we could get out to Ma's, we would typically be engaged in generally menial tasks, cleaning up here and there, which usually involved puke or piss. Only once was there shit involved. Yes, a grown man had actually shit himself, and I didn't know what was worse, cleaning it up from the floor where he had fallen in disgrace, or seeing the poor sod muscled out with Ma berating him for the new level of shame he had managed to discover amongst men. He was drunk, naturally, and my young conscience grew increasingly shocked at realizing the number of grown men who could not hold their liquor. For the record, this time the wretch who had shit himself was a different man than before, on that night we had first seen The Dream, who reported that a man had soiled himself. Hieronymus remarked sourly that he had detected something of a recent theme about the place, and he was decidedly not in favor of it.

Whereas we kept well apart while sneaking away from Buzzard's Roost, we were careful to stay as close together as possible at Ma Surgick's, at least to within a holler's reach. I can't really explain it, but John right off took to the place like he had grown up there himself. By that, I mean he seemed to know how things worked in a world that would be downright jarring to a boy hailing from a normal, civilized upbringing. That might sound cruel to most, and indeed it is a cruel world. But John seemed to have adapted to it readily.

This served me well, as he kept me out of trouble in a place bursting with it. I rarely left his side, though after a while I did gain more confidence and could move about the place somewhat independently, without anybody paying me much attention.

All about us were grown men and we were the only boys. Now you might wonder that a couple of kids hanging about a whorehouse would draw all kinds of attention. The sad fact is that in those days it was not all that uncommon, for often as not you'd find that girls – women – who worked these places would have kids of their own. Many of the kids were bastards, or their fathers had long ago lit out for sundry reasons, none of them good.

It helped, naturally, that the men who gravitated to Ma's were mostly intent on more carnal pursuits, and not much interested at all in some kid. That said now, many of these men, like Amber Eyes, looked to be, in large part, of a villainous persuasion. They tended to cast a suspicious eye upon us, particularly because, besides being new appearances, we were known to be inhabitants of Auntie Charlotte's. So, some suspicion was at least understandable on that score. I got the impression more than once that these men were dead sure we would call them out to the law. John was sorely amused at that notion. The only law we knew, in our limited existence, was the one back home that had sent us here, and Bucschalter, the law of Auntie Charlotte's.

Of course, we often saw menfolk from nearby villages and towns, too. Sometimes farmers that we knew from our occasional excursions with Bucschalter for picking up goods and various supplies. You could tell them easy, too, for they carried themselves with a certain awkwardness until they got some liquor in them. You might not believe it, but much of the time those men would attend Ma's place just to have a drink and enjoy the companionship of the other menfolk, maybe a song or two. Very often, a spirited political debate would break out and reduce itself to a brawl. Some of the regulars never went upstairs with a girl at all, even. Either they couldn't work up the nerve, or that kind of sport didn't appeal to them, there was no telling.

It wasn't for lack of the girls' trying either. They sidled up constantly, displaying their wares to the men, many of whom would shyly buy them drinks. If the girls got annoyed with their bashfulness, they would move on to the next mark. It was part of the job, part of the game.

Us boys had in our young brains some vague notions of what they did with those men who did succumb to their feminine wiles, in the rooms above us. We were not allowed to go upstairs, you see. Even Ma had her limits as to what mere lads should be exposed to, I guess.

She did make sure to take care of us for our efforts, though. A coin or two stood us just fine, and since we really didn't have anywhere to spend it, it built up and we saved a decent purse of money between ourselves. Enough so, John said, that it went from merely "walking around money" to "escape plan money."

Eventually, Hieronymus too seemed to welcome our presence, as it freed him to better attend to the girls. Ma employed four or five at a time. He might be a Negro, and therefore an inferior in the eyes of many who frequented the place, but they clearly feared him, mightily so. None would admit it, sure, but even Amber Eyes steered him a wide berth.

Now, up to then, I had already believed Hieronymus was a free man instead of Ma's property or anyone else's. I had not had a lot of experience with black folks or slaves, mind you. Whenever I had seen the rare slave in my early days, say, one who had been sent to town on an errand, they, like as not, avoided looking most people in the eyes.

There was a certain way this giant carried himself, though. He was always quiet and respectful to folks around him, be they white or black or other, but he was in no ways at all ever cowed or beggarly in his manner. Hieronymus looked at everyone straightforward, non-flinching, when speaking to them.

This was first made evident when a customer blew into Ma's with his slave in tow. It looked like this man was treated fairly well, in somewhat clean clothes and appearing to be in decent health, with no sign of recent beatings or abuse. Hieronymus did look directly at this man, and not without pity. I found it to be the most interesting exchange between two people without any words being employed that I ever did see. The slave met Hieronymus' gaze with a kind of understanding in his own right, like he knew something instantly about him without being told outright. And this was reciprocated by Hieronymus. It was most peculiar and fascinating.

When Hieronymus sized up this man's master, the coldness behind his eyes stopped short of malice. Whether the customer even picked up on this is in much doubt. In fact, I don't believe he was aware of Hieronymus' existence at all, being so preoccupied with addressing his carnal needs, on top of being already half-drunk.

Hieronymus was even more so respectful and gentle with the girls. Part of his carriage, too, not just his size, had people generally avoiding any confrontation with him. And when it came to Ma, his attitude was of a respectful vein that seemed reserved for a boss, more than anything. At the same time, I got the sense she stood for more to him than a boss, or the person who simply paid his wage. He was steadfastly loyal to Ma, though for what reason we never really learned.

As mentioned previously, fights did break out, at least one every night. Over girls, cards or just plain drunken stupidity. I saw one fight start just because one drunk bumped into another and his foot jostled a spittoon. And the spittoon didn't even fall over or splash its innards or anything, either. There was the jostle, a tinkle of metal and then it was on, bloody as anything.

We witnessed more than one "knock-down-drag-out," as Hieronymus termed them, and we were nothing short of astonished that anyone ever survived these at all.

Yes, some were quite bloody, those involving the odd knives and various edged weapons. It was generally fists, clubs, rocks, and dirt when things spewed outside – anything and everything at hand. I one time saw a man bludgeon another with a saddle. Hieronymus usually ended things before they got too out of hand, just by his imposing presence, backed by the authority that even these hard hands acknowledged.

We would typically get the summons from Hieronymus or

Weatherby (the bartender with one stump for a leg) for our clean-up duties in what the men jokingly yet loftily called the "Main Hall." They never hollered our names either, just "Buckets!" and we came a-running.

All the while during our janitorial apprenticeship, we kept an eye out for any little excuse whatsoever to catch at least a glimpse of The Dream (we still somehow had not learned her name). Lord above, she was lovely, whenever we did catch that glimpse. The tiniest fraction of the sight of her was worth toting out twenty piss pots to be emptied, rinsing them out at the crick, and returning to scrub off ten crusty layers of a drunk's manure.

Such was the extent of the "fun and excitement" that Ma had promised us.

It was about here that John and I had our first real disagreement, which rapidly blew up into what my father called a "donnybrook." If "donnybrook" means a fairly mutual pummeling to both parties, I'd say it describes it to a tee.

Besides that matter with the townies, we both had been involved in an occasional bout at Auntie's, as boys tend to do. Boys will fight for what might be the obvious reasons, but what also might not seem obvious is that boys just plain *like* to fight. It's a mite different with menfolk, for all but the drunkest fool knew a fight could mean permanent harm, if things went enough sideways. Such stakes were never there for us lads, and so we could take those risks, be a little freer with our tongues and fists.

More times than not, Bucschalter would break it up – right quick, too, I'll tell you that. That man's strength was bested only by that of Hieronymus (although just barely, I wager). It took him nothing to yank kids apart, regardless of how badly they wanted to murder each other. Which is why the boys took to settling their differences when out a-field, when they were supposed to be working or gathering or some such. In those cases, one or both parties would usually display some evidence of a row, a cut lip, torn clothes, or the occasional black eye. This would be rewarded at the appropriate time with a beating doled out by Bucschalter, sometimes before dinner. Believe me, the ironic aspects of that were not lost on us.

You likely would not be surprised to know that our brawl was over a girl. There could really be only one woman within our sphere of existence that could inspire two fast friends to go at it so hotly, and that was The Dream herself.

We were returning from a task Weatherby had assigned. For once, it was not taking what kitchen slop there was to the hogs.

No, we had to retrieve a nag that had strayed into the woods, having gotten loose from one of the customers who was – as you might guess – drunk. Often as not, such an occurrence would go generally unaddressed until the man shook off enough of his drink to locate his mount himself. However, Weatherby insisted that this one was an exception, and we must offer additional services to them who frequented the establishment far more than the typical. It didn't hurt any that this man was a politician of some local note, and Weatherby allowed later that the purpose was partly to "keep the paths smoothed," as he put it.

So, we found the critter and were returning it through the woods when John suddenly put forth, "I'm a-going to marry her."

This statement just popped out like it plum dropped from the heavens itself, unconnected to any former topic of discussion we had that night. Or any night, for that matter.

Well, it stunned me proper. I stopped dead, dropping the traces of the horse onto the trail.

"You never," was all my stunned trap could manage. My brain was telling me to say something, and no kind of congratulatory statement was in the mix. My still-numbed mouth could not produce even the slightest noise to fill the silence. So, John did it for me.

"Yup," he said proudly, a smug look glowing on his moonlit face. "She already agreed. Said yes on my first go at it, too. Why, her eyes shone like stars when I told her what fine things I'd provide her: Dresses all the way from Paris, necklaces from Persia, all the sparkly gewgaws girls take to."

I stood there in disbelief for a moment more, and that smugness on his face appeared in my eyes right then as the ugliest of smirks.

Next thing I knew, my head went down and I barreled toward him. My arms were swinging already, like sideways-angled pistons, and I had no idea if any of them would really land anyplace on him. I didn't care.

All thinking and reason had fled my skull. The shock of this full bull rush gave me a momentary advantage over my bigger friend, now mortal enemy. As far as I was concerned, this was to the death. My arms pistoned back and forth, now hitting mostly brush and bush branches. He took a tumble after tripping over those bushes momentarily and sort of scrambled on his hands and knees for a second. He then was able to regain his feet, for I got tripped up too in those damnable brambles.

I could swear John was laughing, which clouded my brain with a redder fury than ever, rendering my vision ever more blurred. It was my second taste of the Fog of War, and boy, was it a bigger flood than the first.

John backpedaled, back up onto the trail. Beyond him, the horse had preceded leisurely, meandering back to Ma's like it knew where it was going, doubtless from dozens of repeated procedures.

I continued pursuing John, up to the top of the trail, which emerged into a clearing that led up to what was Ma's back yard, where there was a well and a chicken coop. John had stopped laughing now, because he could see that I was not funning about. In fact, soon enough I managed to tackle him and sit astride his chest.

Yes, he was a bit bigger than I, but my instant insanity gave me a berserker-like speed, and I had taken him all by surprise, so he was considerably off balance. Plus, I don't think he thought I had it in me to start with. I was normally the docile, polite type, you see.

Why, I surprised even myself as my fists started to make meaningful contact with his face and skull. A glance at his expression, through my blur of blows, told me that he was experiencing a real, honest-to-God bewilderment about it all, more than anything.

I really wasn't even making any sound either, save for the grunting and gasping of breath which typically accompany such exertions. John told me later this had spooked him more than a little.

He was about to holler out, I could tell, and he wasn't hitting back at this point, just trying to ward off my blows in pure defense. I was luckier for it, too, come to think of it

His shout was cut off quick by a high, lilting voice from across the yard. It wasn't any grown up hollering at us to knock it off, either. In fact, it sounded like singing.

On a night with horses lost in dark woods, a boy declaring he was to be wed to a girl he had never so much as spoken to, and me astride my friend beating all hell out of him, came a song from another world. And it was sung by the loveliest voice you would ever hear, too.

Something like that will sometimes break up even the worst

of fights right quick. Probably more so than a gunshot or whipcrack.

I don't recall the song. The only thing that mattered was who was singing, and it was none other than The Dream.

She was perched on the low wall of the well, beside a bucket of fresh water. She was dipping in her dainty little hands and running her wet fingers through her hair in the prettiest fashion.

We were as dumbstruck as could be, and every other concern, large or small, was blasted from our conscience like it was never even there to begin with.

She sat there in her gossamer gown, washing her golden hair and singing like a siren from one of those old Greek stories.

I sat with a sudden slump onto my behind, and John rolled over and righted his head as best he could for a better view. We were almost afraid to move right then, like two hunters afraid to startle a deer we had come upon in a broad meadow.

What sound during the fight went unnoticed somehow by her; she must have been so engrossed in her own hair. And I can't rightly fault her for that. But then the very cessation of the fighting seemed to snare her attention.

"Lord, boys do like to fight, don't they?" she said. "I just don't understand it."

Then she laughed, looking at us with those wonderful blue eyes. We remained transfixed, but I thought right then it was impossible for this creature to have been sullied by the insensitive, pawing hunger of brutish men in any way. Also in that moment, my foolish mind told me I would never do it to her myself, and I would not permit others to engage in it, from then on.

I resolutely stood from my sitting posture and found myself taking a step toward her. To this day, I do not know where I found the courage.

"Ma'am, I do apologize," I said. I know it sounds dumb, and I don't really know why I apologized, but I said it. After all, she did seem entertained by our set-to, despite her musings. And I do know that from time-to-time, women appreciate when men fight over them, despite what they might say out loud. Sammy Hodges, back at Elizabethton, had told me so, with great authority, so it had to be true.

She let out a delicate titter at that, turning her full attention to us, with two hands ahold of a healthy strand of her long hair, now a darker version of lustrous gold, from the water she was presently ringing out of it.

"Oh, there is no need to stop on account of me, boys," she said, with a wry look. The lantern she had brought out with her bathed her in the mellowest of saintly glows.

I must have appeared a ridiculous stump to her. I had been mesmerized watching her wring that flaxen hair.

She looked directly into my eyes, "Even I know it ain't polite to stare, boy." She didn't say it mean, though. In fact, she still had that amused light in her eyes, and a very slight smile remained on her lips. Caught, I looked away quick, face burning red. John chuckled, but I could tell it was also because he had been likewise caught out committing the same transgression. It simply could not be helped.

She casually flipped that tress over her shoulder, stood, and walked toward us. What does one do? Running away would be unseemly, not to mention unmanly. I would never recover from that in a thousand lifetimes.

"You know, I have seen you boys around here. Though you have not seen me, I reckon. Seen you through that window, right there." She pointed to a window on the second floor. Even we dumb kids knew enough not to admit that we already knew which window was hers, from constant reconnaissance and careful observation, although we had never seen her looking out from there, which was a puzzlement. It just added to her already profound and delightful mysteries.

"I see you two running about and tending to some chores, mostly. I have wondered what kids are here this time of night, and where they might come from, too."

This last had the saddest tone to it, and she got a kind of faraway look in her eyes, like she was trying to recall something. In that moment, she looked as much a child as we were. It made my heart ache, more than a little.

We didn't rightly know what to say to that, so we kept our traps shut.

"Minerva!" Came a call from the innards of the house. It stood out easily from the usual racket and piano tinklings, for we could tell it was Ma Surgick right off. She seldom raised her voice, but when she did, it stuck out like anything.

"That's me," said The Dream, smiling sadly. She looked at us, kind of apologetic. Like she wanted to stay a while.

The call came again, with obvious impatience.

She quickly extended her hand out and hung it, limp-wristed in the fashion of those high-toned types. I had no idea what to do. John did, though, thank the Lord, and saved me from looking the complete rube that I really was.

He reached out gentlemanly and took that pretty hand, and, later recalling it, I seethed with jealousy, though I got my turn too. He was first and it ate at me. Dumb, I know, but it did.

"Minerva," that lyrical voice said. "Minerva Underwood."

"Pleasure," said John, just like he knew what he was doing, sort of bending a little at the waist and dipping his head a bit. For one terrifying moment, I thought he was going to kiss her hand. In my fevered mind, I saw two things at once: A renewal of our previous exertions, wherein I removed his skull from his miserable shoulders with my bare hands. I then ran away and lived like a hermit for the next fifty years, ending it all like Judas, hanging from a lonely tree in the wilderness.

She then turned to me, as Ma hollered again. I barely heard anything save for the rush of blood through my melon. I mimicked John's actions as best I could.

She politely backed away after delivering the prettiest of curtsies.

By now, Weatherby was standing at the back door, wiping his hands with his ever-present bar rag. "Now, Min," he said with an admonishing smile, "She's in a fair mood tonight. Don't chuck it."

"I was only washing my hair, God's sake," she said.

Weatherby chuckled, letting her pass. "I know, darlin'."

Minerva Underwood. The Dream had a name. A full one, even. A first and a last.

With that, we returned to Buzzard's Roost and slept the remainder of the night with pleasant dreams of golden hair, soft hands, and a pretty song in the night.

8

After one particularly lively and entertaining bout in Ma's house, an especially splattery affair too, we heard "Buckets!" and retrieved those things. We made it to the hall with such speed and efficiency that a St. Louis fireman would blush. Amber Eyes was in attendance, as always, and looked us up and down with that ever-amused but threatening stare of his.

"And here's the brigade," he said. "Heh." That crusty hand of his was always fingering the handle of his huge, ugly knife. I truly believed – no, I *knew* – that notched blade itched for our scalps.

We got to it with the rags and water, only a little bit of suds in it from some weak tallow soap they kept around the place, for some reason. It was not much used, after all.

I stopped my scrubbing a moment, and peered at the floor in the erratic lantern light.

There were bits of something scattered about the red bubbles on the rough wood surface. I carefully picked up a piece. It was too slippery, and I dropped it back into the muck. There was plenty to be had, though, and I nipped another shard, holding it up so John could examine it too. He squinted at it for a moment and then just shrugged.

"Yep, it's a tooth!" he announced.

Being a boy and given to collecting odds and ends and various grotesqueries whenever encountered, I wiped it on the front of my shirt and stuck it in my pocket.

One of our first tasks when we were able to get out to Ma Surgick's was tending to the hogs. Feeding them, more precisely. Now, I was not especially keen on this chore, being about done with that type of thing back in Elizabethton. But with John new to the task, there was a bit of an entertaining aspect for me. He was a mite skittish around the animals at first, and teaching him the ins and outs of the caring of hogs put this errand in a fresh, surprisingly happy light. We had yet to see Ma's place by the light of day, but it was at first strange to us to think of it as an everyday working farm – or at least a hog farm that nobody would look at twice if they could see it from the nearest road.

Rather, one could find the hog pens downwind of the house, over a hilly path curling around a couple of knolls crowned with low scrub and a few trees.

We trudged out there, our pails filled with table scraps and other whatnot to toss to those hogs, usually without so much as a lantern most nights to navigate our way to it, for we've reached that point after so many repetitions. The smell often helped guide us as well, when the wind was right, or wrong. And naturally, the sound of them, too.

I suppose I ought to mention Old Bit, the big boar hog that ran the place.

He was a mean one who had made a good account of his name. Put it like this: Hieronymus himself had a small chunk of his leg removed by Old Bit (which accounted for his limp), and it would have been a whole lot more if he hadn't been as quick getting out of the pen. Hieronymus hated the old boar with all his being, enough to fill his guts, he said. Small wonder he passed on the tending to these animals to us, but with repeated warnings never to turn our backs on Old Bit. Never.

One night, John and I commenced to deliver the evening's repast to Old Bit and his harem of sows and their piglets. This night we did bring a lantern along, as it was a nasty one, storming and raining. It was fearful dark besides, when the lightning didn't glow up the woods for us. It really was not a night to be about at all, but to us it added yet another layer of high adventure.

We made it to the pen and tossed in the morsels, but even Old Bit had the sense to remain under what shelter was available to him, this rough lean-to in a corner next to a stable stall. He was clearly content to await a more temperate climate in which to enjoy his feast.

As we turned to make our way back to Ma's, a dark figure awaited us on the path, blocking our way.

John held the lantern out, but its weak light was futile against the murkiness of the night storm. He tried to squint in the rain that lashed his face.

"Hello?" he called. No response. "Uh, mister?"

John looked at me. I just shook my head.

"Mr. Hieronymus?" John called to the figure in a hopeful voice. It was useless, though, because this man was not near Hieronymus' bulk.

The figure stepped closer to us. The faint glow of distant lightning told us that it was our old friend, Amber Eyes. I'd swear those eyes were a starker flavor of amber now, more than ever. My spine tingled so and the nerves of my neck and scalp were set instantly to an electric jolt. And it wasn't any lightning that did it, either.

"You boys," he took another step toward us. His boot

splashed in the mud, and my nerves jangled to the bottom of my feet.

"You've got something belongs to me," he said. His voice was that of what I imagined a strangled man's dead voice might produce, if some sinister force somehow allowed him to speak.

My now nerveless body took on a life of its own, and I felt my feet backpedaling on the soggy turf, felt them slip. If I took a tumble, old Amber Eyes would be on me like a starving tick on a hound.

John was stepping back, too, and he did fall once, losing the lantern in the scramble. He recovered right away, while all Amber Eyes did was chuckle that strangled man's laugh, turning what blood that still managed to run steady in my veins to a slow, icy river.

Amber Eyes continued to leisurely advance on us. I had little doubt he could catch us if he really had a mind to. We could not beat his stride in a long haul, or that damned knife of his thrown that distance. He was tormenting us solely for his sick brand of fun.

Oh, hell, this is how I go out, I had thought.

And doesn't that beat all, with only thirteen and a half years of walking the Earth left on the table, with nothing to show for it but a soggy corpse all carved up like a sorry field-dressed rabbit.

Amber Eyes finally grabbed at John, who was closer and had tripped up some more. I thought, being the coward that he was, Amber Eyes would rather have seized on me, since I was smaller. But then he would have to contend with the somewhat larger of us maybe sticking a pitchfork or some other sharp farm tool into his back.

A scream burbled up in the back of my throat, and another hysterical thought rose up – I was thankful it was a wet night, because I was sure I had pissed myself.

It occurred to me also, in my last minutes, to wonder what it was we had of Amber Eyes. What was he after? The only thing my panicked brain could conclude was that it was that old tooth I had picked up off the bloody floor of the bar that night. But that made little sense, as Amber Eyes was not involved in that particular event. He'd only been a spectator of that affair, as far as I could recall.

Now, Amber Eyes had yanked up John from the mud and was shaking him about by his coat. A button flew off, winking in the glow of distant lightning.

"Give it to me!" he shrieked, "You know it's mine, you filthy thief!" He cuffed John with a backhand swipe. "I'll show you what happens, hornin' in on things!"

I didn't know what to do. I scrambled away, looking toward the hog pens for a moment, hoping, I suppose, for that imagined pitchfork or some other farm instrument to plunge into Amber Eyes.

He'd gone plum mad. He always appeared to be a half-collared lunatic, always staring at us with those predator eyes and making threats to our being. John once made a joke of it, shrugging and saying, "Oh, the old bastard just doesn't like kids. One day, when we are growed men, we'll get drunk and piss on his tomb, don't doubt it!"

This was an Amber Eyes we'd not seen before. Like as not, it was only because he hadn't had the opportunity yet to get at us when we were apart from Ma Surgick's. Now he was filled with unreasoning rage, hell-bent on tearing us down to nothing.

He cuffed John again, knocking him to the ground with a savage blow, and loomed over him, striking a wide stance, looking every bit an insane demon bent on nothing but blood and revenge.

Then he reached for that damnable notched blade.

With a cackle that would take the starch out of Satan

himself, he raised it dramatically as he pulled John up by his coat collar with his other hand. True, he was still but a lad, but Amber Eyes' mad strength was something to behold as he now lifted and shook him like a little girl's rag doll.

The storm's light gleamed off that nasty blade, and I thought he was going to drag the edge fast across John's gullet, but instead, he slowly brought it up to John's throat. No, he wanted to enjoy the slaughter, which surprised me none at all.

Me, why I was utterly useless. My bladder was further emptying but there could not be much left to piss out. I was froze to the ground, for I had never witnessed anything like this in my short life. Here I was in that boys' home for a trivial crime, what I considered fun in my small town, and now I was about to watch my friend be slaughtered like the hogs we tended to, my own end was not to be long after.

John was petrified in place, too, for no more sound came from him through the remainder of this torture, and his eyes were as big as mail-order China plates.

Right then, I felt a quick regretful sadness for having gone after John the way I did over Minerva, and a smidge of shame, too. How tiny a matter, how stupidly tiny that was...

"I'm a-going to enjoy this," Amber Eyes dug the knife edge into John's neck, and here came some blood.

Of a sudden, he reared back, his feet backpedaling and splashing in the mud but hardly connecting with it, looking truly possessed of the Devil now. That cursed knife went flying out of his hand and landed near me.

My frozen brain thawed just enough to urge me to grab the thing, but I didn't. When I looked up again, I saw Hieronymus, now with Amber Eyes firmly in his grasp.

One giant fist reared up and came down like thunder, square into Amber Eyes' ugly hatchet of a face, making a tremendous cleaver-into-meat sound if there ever was one. I admit great satisfaction in seeing the look of the hunted in those formerly predator eyes.

"Hier–!" was all Amber Eyes was able to choke out, his maw already a bloody mush. Hieronymus punched it again, before following up with a blow to the belly that lifted Amber Eyes up off the ground at least two, three feet.

Well, that blasted out all of what remaining air was in him, and Amber Eyes crumpled to the mud with a breath-starved groan.

John scrambled further back, for he had been flung into the mud when Hieronymus had grabbed his attacker.

I managed to uproot from my position and likewise scurried away from the combatants, the knife still somehow gleaming through the mud.

Old Amber Eyes was enough recovered from Hieronymus' mighty blow to his midsection to begin getting up from his crumpled position. Still crouching, he looked up at the big man with hatred the likes I have yet to see in any creature's eyes, even over what he had previously directed at John and myself.

"Figured you to come protect these sewer rats," he growled, spitting blood and broken teeth every couple words. "You ever was the worthless cur yourself, you damned black bastard."

Hieronymus looked at Amber Eyes with a kind of pity. His enormous fists clasped and unclasped with menacing intent, and I swear I heard knuckles popping from between those iron sinews.

"I'm inviting you," Hieronymus said, "to depart this place." His voice rumbled like a river in a deep cavern. It gave his appeal the overall feel of something very different than an invitation to anything other than a proper beating.

"You'll hang for this," Amber Eyes said, with a weird finality, as if he had the upper hand. He croaked out something that barely passed for a laugh. He looked over at us with pure loathing. "You'd stretch for the likes of these? Right stupid, it is."

"They are only kids, you dog," replied Hieronymus. Amber Eyes was starting to circle slowly around, stumbling at first, but becoming more sure-footed with each step. Hieronymus's eyes followed him warily, his stance moving only slightly. He reminded me of a giant cat readying itself to spring.

I scooted further away from that knife.

Amber Eyes continued his move toward his favored weapon. Hieronymus' eyes took on a curious light, and in that moment, I could see he wanted Amber Eyes to go for it.

I believed he would, too. A man that consumed with evil and hatred would not suffer for very long the humiliation of being exiled by a black man. Not in those days, and not in those parts. His threats of hanging were rather hollow, I suppose, given that Amber Eyes was on the wrong side of the law himself, not likely to seek justice at the hands of any real authority. Who knows what crimes he had done.

So Amber Eyes dove for that oversized belly sticker like he was leaping for life itself, and in a way he was, I suppose. It really was his only card left; he had to know that. There was no way on God's earth that he could fight Hieronymus hand to hand, even to a draw. He could have either lit out right then or be properly dispatched by Hieronymus. So, nobody could blame him for making a dive for that knife of his.

Just as his hand wrapped about the haft, clumsily, owing to the slick mud, Hieronymus stomped on that extended arm. Through a sickening crunch, Amber Eyes howled to the rain-filled sky. He tried to twist himself out of reach of Hieronymus' fearsome power, so desperately it seemed like he was trying to pull his own arm out of its socket, like an animal gnawing its own paw off to escape a trap.

He reached with his other hand for the knife, twisting his

body around awkwardly. Hieronymus hammered him again, this time square in the jaw, and stepped off the crunched arm just in time to allow Amber Eyes to fly back with the blow.

A beating like that is indeed a thing to behold. Everyone should witness one at least once in their lifetime, if anything, just to know what to avoid in life.

I admit feeling a real, almost electric titillation to the spectacle. It was about how I imagined it was for the old Romans, watching gladiators beating the hell out of each other in their day.

Miraculously, it seemed old Amber Eyes had successfully held on to his beloved knife, despite the monstrous blow.

Hieronymus stood there now, feet spread and a mite crouched in a waiting stance, as Amber Eyes steeled himself to charge.

Charge he did, his stomped-on arm flailing around on its own. It would have looked comical if it weren't such a deadly situation; he went at Hieronymus with all his remaining steam, screaming like a gut-shot Comanche. A weird, unnerving sound that defies any description. From another world, really.

It really was a lesson for us in how losing your top in a fight is the final undoing of a man if he permits it to happen. Amber Eyes, coward and despicable creature though he was, was an expert knife fighter, at least listening to the talk around Ma's place. He had plumb let his mind get away from him – probably because it was a black man who had undone him to this point.

He held the knife above his head in a basic sort of way, without any touch of finesse, and Hieronymus just did a little sidestep – nimble on his feet for a big man, even with that slight limp – grabbing Amber Eye's knife arm. Quick as you please, he folded it in as Amber Eyes closed on him.

Like that, the knife found the wielder's mid-section, just

under the rib cage, I'd gamble. It was deep, too, which we could see even from where we were in the dark.

Amber Eyes' scream quickly twisted into a surprised, disappointed mewling. It was not a sound I care to hear again from any human being, mortal enemy be damned.

Hieronymus let him crumple to the ground, staring at him a long moment. His sides heaved with exertion, though it looked to us like he hardly expended very much at all.

When he turned to us, he still held this flinty look that told me he was still caught up in the excitement. I found that I could not breathe. In this insane, waking nightmare of sudden violence, the only thing that I could picture happening then is Hieronymus dispatching us, the only witnesses. None of us in that murky tableau had any other illusion that Hieronymus would indeed hang.

His eyes transformed to a sort of lost one as that seemed to sink in, back to the world and its harsh reality. Somehow, I knew then that he meant us no harm.

"He aimed to kill me," he said.

I simply nodded shakily. John uttered a quiet, "Yes."

Then, with quick resolve, Hieronymus dragged Amber Eyes' corpse over to the hog pen. He picked it up without ceremony and heaved it into the pen. Old Bit rustled in his sheltered wallow a bit, as if to better view the morsel that had been added to the mix.

All at once, I felt my gorge rise up. My limbs had gone from quivering to being just numb, but they still managed to move me away from the hog pen, step by faltering step, to empty my stomach in the most violent upchuck I had ever experienced. My belly pulled and pushed and heaved onto itself like it was a bagpipe. My eyes watered considerably, and it felt like the convulsions would never end.

Amidst this, I managed to pick up the vague sights and

sounds of John going through the same right at my side. I chalked all of this up to the full realization of what we had just witnessed: the brutal end of a man's life, right before our eyes.

With nothing left in our bellies, the heaves eventually wore down. I wiped my mouth as best as I could with my wet shirt's sleeve and looked around to see Hieronymus leaning on the pen's rail, his eyes looking off to the gloomy horizon. The storm had moved on by then, the lightning looking like firefly light in a fog.

I went to the railing myself and averted my eyes from the corpse just inside the pen. My body was still limp and weak, and tried as I might, I could not keep my bottom lip from trembling. I tried swallowing, but my throat was as dry as dust and still tasted of bile.

"You boys," Hieronymus said, finally, "been stealing, I know."

Now, this was a revelation. Surely all that was just a man gone buckwild crazy, like a coyote stalking us after getting drunk on human blood. But John shuffled his feet uncomfortably, telling me there was something to Hieronymus' words.

"Yep," was all he said. After a moment, he pulled a small leather pouch from his pocket and threw it on the muddy ground, where it came open, spilling some gold coins glistening in the thin water. He spat on them, grimacing with disgust.

"It was just money I took."

Hieronymus huffed out a deep sigh.

"Burdett here," he nodded toward the sad corpse in the hog pen, and I was jolted at a name applied to him; now that he was dead, it seemed starkly appropriate. "He was the sneak thief. Those boys to the house, they pass out after laying with the girls. This one would take from them what he could. Sometimes, split it with the girl." He looked up at the horizon again.

"But I cannot abide a grown man beating on a child. That been done to me and I won't have it."

John hung his head between his arms, now resting on the pen railing like Hieronymus. Not in shame, but to spit again.

"You were interfering in his action," Hieronymus stated.

"Yep," John said again, and I never knew him to be so limited in his expression until then. He almost always had a gab or a line to offer some shine to something, no matter the situation.

There was a long pause, and here came, finally, that gab. Although I wasn't sure that was the intent, for it wasn't just polish but rang true. There was almost a shame in there.

"Learned it from my Ma. Pop was a preacher. Road preacher, you see. When he was on the trail, he'd be gone a lot. Long stretches. Months. Said otherwise, if he stayed too long about the place, he would be after Ma like a boar during the rut. So, we had to fend by taking in travelers now and again. When he was home, he tried to break her of what he called "her sultry ways..."

A share of resentment and disgust was in John's voice now. The hogs began to emerge from their various shelters as the rain abated. Old Bit watched their activity from his sovereign wallow, with his mean beast eyes.

"Pa said he had a time trying to break her from her swinging hips and 'undulating breasts.' Sickened me. All of it did."

John spat again, head still down, as if trying to rid his mouth of the taste. "Here that son of a bitch would come, beating her down, sometimes with that damnable wolf-head cane of his. Pulling her about by the hair, even. Who knows what would've happened to her if I hadn't..."

"So them travelers stopped at our place and were spent by their activities with my Ma, and she taught me how to sneak thief the especially drunk ones. Over time, I got good enough for even the not-so-drunk. Ma used to say they was so weary from the sport she gave them that they'd have slept through a typhoon. The sound of it, all that grunting and pawing at her, just filled my head and my guts with poison. You don't know – I wished all the time I could puke it all out. Left with nothing, though, a body's got to eat. We did – she did – what she had to do."

He looked up for the first time, and his face wore a tired smile, like that of an old man who had seen many things that had aggrieved him.

"I swore I would give her things – fine things – to make up for all of it, once I got to be one of those big city bugs, with a grand house and servants and a fat purse."

Old Bit finally emerged. At his commanding, imperial approach to the corpse of Burdett, his passel of hogs parted for him without argument.

"Anyhow," John said at last, "I'm sorry for any trouble I caused. I just wanted to build a means by which Stephen and I could eventually skip here and find our fortunes abroad."

The hogs were really starting to root now.

We watched as they began devouring the corpse, a most ghastly sight, the most terrible my young eyes had yet beheld, which was saying much after tonight. I just could not tear my eyes away.

"I'm a man freed," said Hieronymus suddenly, with some tone of declaration. "Did it myself, I did. Earned and bought it."

He bowed his head, and I swear I heard something of a chuckle. "But I did it!"

Hieronymus stared at the hog's feast, almost without seeing it.

"I came here as a slave. I was a little boy, but a slave. A little boy whose father was a slave. Whose mother was a slave." His words were really flowing now, perhaps not even to us, who knew. But flow they did.

"We were the property of Monsieur Alarie, along with his other properties he held in Saint-Domingue. This is Haiti now, but to us, it was home, but also Hell. A French colony it was, and M. Alarie's family held great parts of it and a great many people, too. Mainly, it was sugar made there on his lands, but also coffee and cotton, like here. Lord, they worked us hard, but pretended that we were happy, and that it was how everything had always been and how it was supposed to be.

"Then that night, there was a terrible storm. A storm within a storm, as it turned out. The lightning lit the sky, and the thunder rolled and rolled on. We didn't think it would ever stop.

"A man we knew from two plantations over came to us. His eyes were wild; I had never seen that on a white man before. Hell had arrived, finally, he said.

"M. Alarie ordered us to load furniture and goods from the house into a few wagons, and his family too. We did, of course, and before we knew it, we were bound for who knows where. Just away, it seemed. Just away."

He chuckled mildly.

"But it's an island, you see. Where you going to go?

"Along the way, I caught young Master Bastien, M. Alarie's boy – about my age – looking at me. Just looking at me like he never saw me before, and his eyes wide as little moons. They were glassy, too, filled with fear. This filled *me* with fear. Just two boys, two scared little ones, just looking at each other, sharing our fear. That's all we were, just then.

"We had made it to a shoreline, and there was a boat waiting. We quick loaded that boat with what we could, which was not much, since there had to be people in there too.

"M. Alarie looked at us for a long time, there on that beach. His eyes kind of had that same glassy look, too. A most odd look on his face, since none of us had ever seen him like that. It made no sense to me.

"Papa told me later – much later – that M. Alarie was deciding should he kill us.

"Of course, he did not. He ordered us into the boat instead.

"M. Alarie was many things, but he was no murderer. Yes, we were his slaves, and he would do whatever he liked to us. I did not know it at the time, but his world was being destroyed all around him in that moment, and we standing there, to him, might have been what he saw as the instrument of it."

Hieronymus' massive shoulders rolled in a shrug.

"In his mind, later, he might have decided he should have killed us, but I do not think he had that inside him. Punishments on the plantations were always done by others. Men who he paid for that. Maybe that made him a worse kind of man. I don't know.

"The boat took us out to a schooner, one that had put out from St. Marc, somehow.

"I say somehow because it was only then, once on that schooner, we learned what it was all about, what was happening all over Saint-Domingue.

"The slaves had revolted, and the slaughter was terrible. Many whites – grande blancs, even – were killed. Their children, too. Old people. Many, many of them. Then the whites retreated to some areas, and a struggle went on for some time after."

"But we... We had come to Louisiana. And I remained a slave, still. My papa a slave. My mama a slave." Hieronymus' face looked like something chiseled from grim stone, almost frightening in its stoic bitterness.

"Oh, M. Alarie came out just fine. Yes, he did. He acquired

land and even bought more slaves in time. Old French money he had. Rich family.

"But then something happened.

"He came to us, one day, my family. And he said we could buy our freedom back from him. It was just us, and no other of his property, could do this, you see. We, the slaves that stood with him on that beach, and he held our lives in his hands. And even knowing what was happening, and that his world was killing itself, and if we learned what was really happening ourselves, it might have come out different for him and his family.

"I think that weighed on him. I do. That in some way we were the ones who saved him or had some fateful hand in it in some way. This was his way of paying us back for that."

He let out a deep sigh, and everything was quiet for a while. This somber story had lit this man in a whole new light. The fearsome being watching over Ma's place was replaced with a man with a heart and a soul and a true purpose. And who is to know if it was partly to bring him here to save our skinny white hides? That seemed a tall and self-centered order to me after all he had been through, I'll own that, but well, if that was the case, we had best make it all worth it.

It was quiet then, save for the remnants of rainwater pattering through leaves and the nearby creek whispering through the woods. A hint of sunrise glowed soft on the horizon, threatening to steal some of the distant storm's glory.

"I suppose I should dispose of this," Hieronymus said. He was still holding Amber Eyes/Burdett's blade carelessly over the hog pen.

"We need to get back, John," I said quietly. The sky was telling us that sunrise was not far off. We started to turn away.

"You boys don't need to be worrying about this," Hieronymus rumbled, his eyes fixed on the hogs stripping the grisly remains. "This has been coming a long while now. This man, he was no-good, nothing but a hound, and there is many a man in this county that marked him for needing to be put down." He shook his head, "Hell, he sometimes acted like he *wanted* putting down. Talk was he's wanted for murder in Kentucky, and various crimes in other parts too. Like as not, this skunk's stink won't be missed. Not at all."

John looked bleakly at the big man, the closest to tears that I would ever see him. "I'm sorry, Hieronymus."

I could tell he meant it.

"You kids get, now," Hieronymus said. "And don't come 'round here, least for a while."

"Yessir," we said in tandem.

We arrived back at Buzzard's Roost just in time to beat the sun's rise.

INTERLUDE

1877

Mr. Erastus Vinning
    Secretary to Mr. A. Forepaugh
    The Offices of The Forepaugh New and
Colossal All-Feature Show
    Trust Company Building
    Philadelphia, Pennsylvania

    August 16th, 1877

    Sir,

I have received your latest communication
via telegraph. As the town in which Mr. Hue
resides does not, as yet, have telegraph
services nearby (as ludicrous as that may
seem in this day and age), I have secured the
services of a young lad to act as a courier
in order to retrieve your communications in
as expeditious a fashion as is practicable. I
have also arranged to have my communications
to you via Mr. Forepaugh's various connections from here to Philadelphia to deliver
these letters to you and keep you informed as
to my mission's progress.

I again assure you that I am conducting
the interview and evaluation of Mr. Hue's
reliability as best as I am able. Those
efforts, however, are sometimes frustrated by
Mr. Hue's insistence on relaying adventures
of Hue the Younger, which, although colorful
in their roughhewn, back-woods way, are fore-
stalling the real meat of the quest, if you
would pardon the expression.

That said, I personally am hard put to

reconcile the tales of the infamous Devil Preacher with such vivid illustrations of vulnerability during his youth. One could never have imagined.

The delays are also owing to Mr. Hue's predilection for treating me to endless pauses and "rests" involving sojourns to the nearest taverns and other eateries, and his insistence on introducing me to anyone he may know in the town, which appears to be everyone, including mules, dogs, and even someone's pet ferret.

I have taken it upon myself to serve as something of a secretary, jotting down Mr. Hue's ramblings for, if anything, posterity's sake, thereby allowing you to review the written record of his testimony in your own good time. This will also serve to attest to Mr. Forepaugh himself, should he be so disposed.

Your Faithful Servant,
    R.E. McElhany, Esq.

9

We stayed away from Ma Surgick's for a fair length of time, several weeks, I would guess, and settled into the routine of Auntie's without too much resistance. I'd wager a piece of that had to do with us being very much rattled by our recent experience. I'd say it was a jarring introduction into the low, more grisly sorts of life that society had to offer.

Despite the fact that Amber Eyes was our mortal enemy, there was a certain guilt nestled inside the horror of his death that laid an overall sobering aspect to our lives. Seeing your first human death, and that death dealt by the hand of someone you know, will shake you down to your roots, believe me.

So, with a will, we fell to most activities around the boys' home, our routine schooling, and studies. Even memorizing bible verses and such. John knew most of them anyway, even becoming a good tutor for many of the other boys. He helped us get through the Sunday school portions of our lessons without too much chastisement from Bucschalter or Auntie. Throughout, I could not shake the feeling that Bucschalter knew we had been up to something. There were the longer looks and colder stares than before. He was an adult, after all, and travelled in circles where adults talked about adult things. News, gossip, and rumors would always find a way to circulate among them.

After a while, though, I admit things got dull as dishwater. You would think our brush with death would have been enough to ward us off from being within the orbit of that world for the rest of our days. It was not to be, though. Without much discussion, we knew we needed to add some pepper back into our lives. It even took longer than I ever thought John would go before he reached a restlessness that finally drove him to my bedside one night. It picked up the way it all started, with his hand clapped over my mouth, waking me in an instant with my heart pounding out of my chest. His eyes peered into mine with that unmistakable and excitable meaning in them. He didn't even have to whisper anything or make any added gestures. I knew what we were about to get up to again.

A real thrill spiked through me as we checked those familiar corners of the various buildings of Buzzard's Roost. They were all coated in that lovely moon shadow, and breathing the brittle night air was a tonic. It all came back to me at once as we stole away that night. I was truly happy again, rather than just living day by day, breathing the normal air of daylight and doing whatever the world expected of me.

Then, of course, there was the possibility of getting a look at The Dream – ah, Minerva Underwood – that added another dose of thrill to it all. I had dreamed and daydreamed of the time that I might even get a chance to speak to her again, if I could ever manage to screw up enough courage to do it. She really didn't seem to be that much older than we were, after all. I tended to nudge that notion aside when it came to the reality of why she was even at a place like Ma's to begin with. It was all just too sordid to contemplate, so I endeavored to keep it in my mind's deepest recesses.

I experienced another startling pang of jealousy when I once happened to spy John from a distance, speaking to her. It was a brief exchange in reality, but to my mind at the time, it was an eternity. She had dropped something – a hairbrush perhaps – while ascending the stairs from the bottom-most step. Somehow, John was there to pick it up and hand it to her, and for all it was worth to me, it may as well have been the trail of her gown or a hanky she had purposely dropped so he could display what a chivalrous hero he was. She smiled at him, damned his soul, and in that instant, my heart shriveled to a fragile husk, filled with little but a sudden sadness. Some of that old anger flamed back up, I won't deny, but soon that took me back to when Amber Eyes was about to end us, realizing that my feelings about Minerva shrank to nothingness next to my friend's life being in jeopardy.

Any time I was not directly at John's side after that, I found myself wondering if he was secretly meeting with her, wooing her with that handsome smile and fiendish charm. But curiously, even under that ache in my heart, I found myself looking at my friend differently. What he had said about the fine things he wanted to give to his mother, the poor woman. To set things aright, in the long run. Make her life a joyous existence and not a tawdry one. It could be he saw something of his mother's plight in Minerva, too, and wanted to take her away from it. Part of me, at least, wanted to wish John luck pursuing this dream, truly, but there was too much turmoil in me to think too much on it, so I tried to shake it off. It hurt like the devil.

Anyhow, we settled into the routine of Ma Surgick's place without having missed the slightest step. It was as if nothing had happened at all, and I guess in that world it hadn't. Hieronymus himself had taken off to who knows where for how long, but no one lifted a brow, it seemed. There was nothing at all unusual about people being there one day and gone the next, apparently. For the folks populating what would later be called the underworld always have a wide variety of reasons to make themselves instantly scarce, otherwise they would be scarce made *of*, if you take my meaning.

These people asked no questions neither. Like as not, it would invite unwanted attention. Always best to keep one's head comfortably down in your cups, dice, or the shadows.

That said, it made me melancholy that nobody thought to ask about Hieronymus, for he certainly was a loyal fellow, in Ma's service for quite a time and always doing right by her, and she him, no matter what.

After a while, I imagined that the silence was something of its own due respect, not to mention the notion that if one didn't talk about him or ruminate too much on his absence, maybe he would return to the fold.

Somebody we knew who would never come back, of course, was Amber Eyes. When it came time to resume our chores in the hog pen, I must tell you we did have to steel our nerves for what we might find there.

To our immense relief, we found nothing but those old hogs themselves, with Old Bit presiding over them like King George himself. We peered into every nook, cranny, and corner of the place for any remnant of our old nemesis, just to rest our nerves that he was truly gone, and that no artifact could identify him or expose some clue about his demise. This was more to protect our unexpected protector, Hieronymus, than anything else, for we were just kids. Who would hold us to account for any dark events here?

No law ever came around to look into what happened to anybody. The only law we ever saw was when the region's sheriff came by for his monthly servicing. Funny thing was, as far as the law was concerned, Ma's place didn't even take up any space on a map, just the way they liked it – both the law and Ma. It was a matter of convenience on many fronts to keep it that way rather than unraveling a fine mess of trouble for a whole lot of people, while at the same time depriving them of a valued, irreplaceable release the menfolk required.

Even if anyone came sniffing, Old Bit and his crew had thankfully dispatched of the remains quite thoroughly. Amber Eyes' husk had become a part of the muddy, putrid landscape that was Old Bit's empire, which was fine by us.

Now, there would never be a replacing of Hieronymus, but Weatherby, the bartender, took it on himself to resume looking after us. At first, it was with a grudging, frowning eye, but seeing no need to make a new enemy, we kept our noses clean, didn't intrude where we could, and made ourselves otherwise invisible. He really did seem to take a shine to us after a time, which surprised us some.

One night, when we were coming back from Old Bit's stately manse, we came across Weatherby out to the side of the house, taking some fresh air and fouling it at the same time with one of his cigars. He was resting on his stump leg and puffing out that smoke like steam from a locomotive at speed.

"Things well in hand at the pen, are they?" he said, as we neared his station.

Any communication from Weatherby up to then had been an abbreviated statement here, a bark there, so we had grown used to the gruff presentation of them all. He had never engaged us conversationally, so we found ourselves taken aback.

"Yessir," we muttered together. This had become something of our style lately, to some grown-ups' amusement.

An all-enveloping cloud of thick smoke answered us.

"You boys hail from Auntie's, I understand," he said. We were a mite surprised at that, too, for we thought our origin was well-known some time ago.

"Yessir."

"Ol' Bucschalter still runs the roost, that so?"

John and I exchanged looks. This night was full of surprises. This man seemed to not only know of Bucschalter's existence, but seemed to know him personally, too, from his demeanor.

Weatherby laughed knowingly, suggesting he knew our puzzlement.

"He's a hard hand, that one. I knowed him from his scalawag days."

Well, we were right intrigued, just then. I had never actually known anyone who was referred to by that term.

"Oh, yes," Weatherby leaned over to the side a bit and spat an impressive gob onto the ground. "He made his mark with the Lafitte crowd, believe it. He was a smuggler, and a fair hand at it, too."

He caught me looking at his stump of a leg, ending in a battle-scarred peg.

"Psshaw," he dismissed. "This warn't from any seafaring adventuring, boy. Damned wagon wheel crushed it right off me. Fool of a mule skinner let his team get away from him, down to Natchitoches."

John set his bucket down, flipping it over and making a seat of it, as did I. Bucschalter had become instantly more of a fascination.

"Yep, how he fell in with Charlotte Coffee of all people and that school of hers is one of those eternal mysteries with no answers any folks around here could sniff out, considering his background and all. But it's not all bad. Can't be, really. Every man gets at least one opportunity in his life to make things right, and I guess that was his, and he latched onto it like a horsefly to a nag's ear. And good for him, says I.

"When I says it's not all bad, well, by that I mean Bucky –

that's what some call him, but don't let him hear you say it or he might just throwback to his buccaneer days and take a pike to you. Mebbe a cutlass if there be one near to hand."

My head snapped around to John at Weatherby's utterance of that nickname. John's face wore a matching expression, mouth agape in a half-smile, wide eyes alit with silent amusement.

Bucky. If that doesn't beat all, and the name bent entirely the other way as to how we viewed the stern, intimidating Bucschalter. It just didn't square, but at the same time it did, casting the man in a whole new light for us, and not an entirely bad one, either.

Weatherby was deeper into his cigar now. Heavy blue smoke curled about him, and I just about saw the ghost of a true pirate in the light of his eyes.

"Anyway, Bucky's done some good with that outfit in between all that smuggling and stealing. Why, did you know that he had a hand in a colony, even? Yep, he and Lafitte's boys staked out a post they call Shacklefoot now – odd name, that's a fact – up Bayou Patroon on the Texas side of the Sabine River. True, it did start out as a base for Lafitte. Some say the name's taken from the shackles put on prisoners they took, but I take that as a stretch.

"Now, some say calling it a colony is alone a stretch, too. Some folks did take it on themselves to settle there, and it's still running, far as I know, as a ferry, across that Sabine."

Weatherby drew in his cigar again, his eyes searching ours in a serious, curious way, like something had just occurred to him.

"I take it you all have seen Bucky sometimes whispering to himself, something in his native tongue? Sort of like an oath?"

I nodded. "Right off. When I got to Auntie's. Kinda eerie."

Weatherby stabbed the stem of his pipe at me. "Right there. That one."

I found myself leaning forward on my bucket till it near tipped over.

"Story goes that when he got the calling, seed the nature of his sinning, whatever you want to call it, why, he took an oath to himself and to all of mankind, were it within his power, to make sure no other lad's lives were steered afoul like his did. So he repeats the oath, like a prayer, to keep his course true."

Weatherby looked up for a moment, like he was searching his memory.

"Something like Dee Toogend... Der Todd Nicked Trennen. I'm massacring it, and Bucky would likely take that pike to me."

"All I hear mostly is that "trennen" part," I said.

Weatherby stared through the smoke, past us, again speaking haltingly from memory.

"Means... 'Who virtue unites, death shall not separate,' or near to it, as I recall."

Everything was quiet for a time.

"Anyway, it's a worthy thought." Weatherby finally shifted again on his stump.

"Don't measure the man too harshly, lads. He's a tough lot, but trust that he means well by you."

He mashed out his cigar, nodded a good night to us, and stumped off back to his bar.

John and I sat there in silence for a while, looking off into the dark woods, not quite sure what to make of all we had just heard. It was just a lot of new information to apply to a being who had been mostly a subject of speculation and boyish myth-making. And next to Weatherby's musings back in his memory, all that was positively mild by comparison.

Finally, we upped and made our way back to the Roost, still

in awed silence. I climbed into bed, clutching my blankets up around me. Unknown to my conscience, my hand searched out under my thin and flattened pillow, where I kept my Dear Father's letter. Just touching it there gave me a tiny bit of a sad peace, and I fell asleep pondering Minerva Underwood, Hieronymus, Weatherby and his leg, even Bucschalter and his oath, and last of all, my friend John Murrell and his mother. All these folk make up such strangeness sometimes found out there, and the secret lives of some people that the world may never know.

10

It was about this time that John Murrell began crafting an escape from Buzzard's Roost. We had not seen much more of Minerva Underwood, and the routine around Ma's began to have more of a dull, repetitive aspect to it anyway. We had fallen into being laborers, and its thrill dwindled considerably. There were even nights when John came to me and I confessed I would rather just sleep.

John felt we had earned enough "escape money" anyhow, and the thought of returning to my family started to appeal to me more and more. I was, in fact, homesick. It was not something I got into with John, as he had no family to go back to.

John had been careful over these many weeks to keep our old friend Hermie in suspense and made sure the constant specter of his spilling the beans about the stolen cream still hovered over poor Hermie. Here, he used the boy's near-permanent state of nervousness to full advantage. Now, you would think the stolen cream escapade would have been long forgotten by the adults, and for all we knew, it had been. But John kept Hermie believing that our guardians were still on the prowl for the culprits and had him jumping every time Bucschalter barked about the slightest instance of rule-breaking.

We were, from time to time, allowed some leisure hours around Auntie's. I believe this was all her doing, and none of Bucschalter's. They seemed aware that each was the other's counterpart, and you could not have too much of any one thing or would have the reverse effect in the long run. Boys constantly under the lash will eventually just rebel and run away. Or maybe just haul off and kill you in the dead of night, then go on to lead a worse life of crime and disaster. We did not know this at the time, but upon reflection, as the years went on, and observing life as a whole, life makes one come to these conclusions on their own. Wisdom of the ages, I suppose.

During some of those days and hours, John and myself taught Hermie and the other boys how to fish. It brought back memories of my father, who was a devout fisherman and taught me when I was just barely able to walk. So, I found it nothing short of astounding that there were boys who did not know how to fish. It was downright scandalous. Their fathers and uncles mustn't have loved them one whit, to leave them so criminally ill-prepared for all things in life. These men should be punished mercilessly.

So down we went to the banks of Big Creek, where I personally introduced Hermie to the craft. He was a quiet but very attentive student as I went through the finer points, and surprisingly didn't wince or show any remorse whatsoever when we caught one and bashed it on the head with a rock to end its misery. In fact, seeing the pleasure on his face with his first catch kind of made me glow inside.

"It is time, Hermie," John said almost distractedly, just as Hermie clumsily threw out a cast. He faltered at John's utterance, making his cast clumsier.

"Time?" Hermie squeaked. He was notoriously ill-equipped for pretending ignorance, or playing coy, not two ounces of guile in him. Kid had a rough road ahead of him in life.

"It is time for you to provide for us a service. In exchange for your identity as the cream and sugar thief being kept to only ourselves." John said this in as deep and cryptic a manner as he was able. With Hermie, even the most theatrical of a performance would be taken as if from Beelzebub himself, with the same desired effect.

Hermie's throat clicked as he gulped air. He fiddled with his line.

"I remind you, son, that we are the only ones in possession of this knowledge," John intoned. "To keep it that way, you must do as we tell you."

"Yes," Hermie croaked, as a man marching onto the gallows. His eyes had taken on a vacant quality, as if he were staring off to somewhere very distant, perhaps the farthest reaches of the Orient or Darkest Africa. Then to my surprise, he quickly snapped out of it, and threw a defiant eye at John. I feared that he was going to say he would accept punishment rather than do John's bidding.

"Bucschalter," John said simply, cutting Hermie off before he even got started.

The mere name seemed to remind Hermie of just how terrified he was of the old Hessian. He wilted and lifted his head again to stare off to the Antarctic.

"If Bucschalter were to come by this intelligence, it would surely be the end of you," John said. This was the type of rhetoric that probably kept poor Hermie on the edge of suicide for a month or so now. I found it quite unnecessary to see John verbally beat him down, but truthfully, I found it equally fascinating.

To take a happy occasion, though, when a boy is unlocking the pure joy of fishing for the first time and turn it about into an instrument of horror and punishment was a spectacle. And I must admit a distasteful one at that.

John took a step towards Hermie, striking a commanding stance with hands on his hips.

"There is a thing you will do for me. Once it is done, the information will reach the ears of no one," he said, rather loftily.

This was a voice and an attitude that I had not witnessed from John Murrell up to that point. It was almost a theatrical performance, yet there was something irresistible in it.

* * *

It was at Sunday worship that John chose to exploit his hold on Hermie. Every Sunday, we boys walked the distance of about two country miles each way to church in dutiful, if not faithful, style.

Bucschalter would rise before everyone (if he had slept at all, that is) and see Auntie's modest carriage hitched and ready for the journey. He would ride in the lead on Pontus as a vanguard, and we boys marched behind or beside the carriage.

We were all wearing an assortment of rough-hewn jackets and cheaply stitched coats, owing to an odd chill in the air these several days. Nothing too mean, but enough for Auntie to decree them "precautionary," no doubt lest she be saddled with a host of boys come down with a case of sore heads and runny noses.

Still, it was a beautiful spring morning, and I was already bucking, in my mind, the notion of sitting on a hard church pew for the next several hours, fending off the dozes. Bucschalter's glare was not even enough to keep those dozes at bay, I feared.

John was trudging next to Hermie just ahead of me, head down and murmuring into his ear. I assumed he was reinforcing his hold, keeping the boy's terror up, but I confess a fear that John would push it too far and Hermie would simply tear off into the nearby woods, driven completely insane by the continuous prospect of being exposed as The Thief, and enduring the tortures of Hell itself at the hands of the Hessian.

I was not privy to the entire plan, merely a sketch of it, which was John's normal modus operandi. Apparently it was all I needed to know.

I was soon to learn in the coming whirlwind of events.

Pastor Purdy droned on in his sermon, something about a gentleman by the exotic name of Naaman. This unfortunate soul had been stricken with a ghastly ailment of noses, fingers, and assorted other appendages simply dropping off his body.

Naturally, this was horrifying enough to arrest my doldrums considerably, leastwise for the moment. Stories of body parts dropping off people will do that to a boy. Despite this, I did notice when John, seated two rows to my front, threw over his shoulder a conspiratorial wink.

Pastor Purdy was winding up his story of the stricken Naaman, who had obtained a cure by simply... bathing. To my young, sleepy mind, I figured the good pastor was just using the story to get us boys to be mindful of the benefits of regular baths. A clue was wretched Naaman subjecting himself to the act no less than seven times, which seemed excessive.

It was then that Hermie fairly collapsed into the aisle between the rows of pews.

"Mercy!" he cried.

He scrambled on hands and knees to the front of the church, looking up at Pastor Purdy as if he were Jehovah Himself.

"Mercy on my soul, O Lord! I have sinned! I beg forgiveness!"

The entire congregation was properly dumbstruck, even Bucschalter. Auntie was staring in awe at the lad, but there was a slight, glad smile turning up on either side of her mouth.

John whipped a quick view at me as if to keep me in place for now.

Hermie carried on with his histrionics, producing a suitable flow of tears. The effect on the congregation was devastating. A few ladies began quietly weeping, but with that same weird, sympathetic smile such as Auntie's. Clearly, they were caught up in an outpouring of Christian love and a friendly connection with his condition, but I found it all kinds of unsettling.

It was likely not difficult for Hermie to produce this crop of wailing and emotion. The way I saw it, he was drawing from the fact that he was The Thief and every ounce of it was being squeezed out of him all at once, in real terror of the Hessian mixed in with a generous amount of real regret. All this had been corked up in his fevered brain all this time, and now the cork had been fully loosed.

Bucschalter, recovering somewhat from his astonishment, took a few faltering steps toward Hermie, leaving his riding crop behind against a wall. This act alone spoke of his utter shock of what was taking place. Auntie likewise stood and moved up the aisle toward Hermie, cheeks wet with happy tears.

The boys and most of the congregation rose as one to view the drama better, and just then John retrieved me roughly by the collar. I was also too busy gawking at Hermie's sudden desire for divine mercy to notice his maneuvering my way.

John whisked me out of a side door, dragging me to where the congregants had parked their various horses and carriages. He dashed up to Pontus and fumbled with the reins a bit. The animal was hitched to a single post, along with a couple of others.

We could hear singing now from the church. Absurdly, even in my rushed state, I made it out to be O, *Worship the King*.

Finally, John had freed the beast, clambered atop him, and reached an arm down to me.

"Hurry, you oaf!" he exclaimed. Up I went without much thought to what was happening, and to this day I cannot fully recollect all the details of those hectic minutes.

Pontus pelted down the dusty road like a fellow conspirator to our escape. I do not know how I held on, other than my newfound, intense desire to survive the day. One could say I was literally holding on for dear life.

I was never a great horseman, but John appeared to be a stout rider, which fair surprised me. For this fact alone, I was eternally grateful. Without some skill, and the way we were tearing away, I feel I might have been flung into a tree and impaled on a dead branch or something. It was hold on or crack my head open like a hen's egg on the hard trail.

Now, Pontus was a real fine example of a strong Western Opelousa Relatively small compared to other breeds, with a head like an anvil. Tough as hell and built for travel. He could have run all day, and likely would have, too, if we hadn't eventually pulled up and walked him into the woods.

"We must get off the trail," John steered Pontus up a hill fairly tangled with brush and pine. He appeared to not give much care to any sign that we might be leaving, but I dared not mention it. John seemed to know what he was doing, while I was a mere amateur in the fugitive business.

We rode slowly, very slowly, through the pine-crowded forest. Up and down hills, through ravines and various crevices, until darkness fell.

"Here we make camp," John finally declared. He had given no sign that he had been even looking for a suitable place, but I was all for it.

It was a somewhat open area, which, from what I had observed in this part of the wilderness, was a scarce thing, which would account for John's selection. It was more or less a flat rock jutting out over a very small stream. It looked like it was put there just for us.

Pontus lapped water from the cool stream while we gathered firewood. We would need all the warmth we could get tonight. As I drew my coat tighter about me, John produced a few rough matches from his pocket.

"Managed to get these from Bucschalter," he explained, chuckling at my look of mild surprise. "Stole 'em,"

"Part of your planning," I said.

"Of course," he replied. "I always have a plan."

He lit the kindling, and once it took, he pointed the smoldering match at me, gesturing in time with each of his next words. "Always. Have. A. Plan."

These seemed wise enough words, and I made a note to remember them henceforth. Just then, John Murrell brought out something else from an inner pocket of his coat.

In the flickering firelight, out came the large, rounded butt of the Spanish flintlock we had obtained from the townies' cave, followed by its long, menacing barrel. John smiled at my astonishment.

"I about killed myself running back to that cave and back the other night." He shrugged. "Sorry. I just thought I could travel faster on my own. No offense."

"None taken," I said dazedly.

"Let's hear that old pistol sing!" John tapped his side with his free hand excitedly.

Holding the pistol carefully, barrel up, he walked to the

end of the slab of rock. He started to extend his arm into the woods, then stopped.

"You want to go first?"

"You first," I said, maybe a mite too eagerly. It had felt like ages since we found it.

He shrugged again, raising his arm. It wobbled a bit with the pistol's weight, as it had back in the cave.

He used his left hand to bring back the hammer. It clicked into place.

John took a breath, held steady again, and fired. The hammer came down, scraped along the frizzen, and slammed onto the pan with a mighty metallic bang. It boomed much louder here than in the cave, echoing closely about us. The woods were deathly silent in its wake. Pontus was still as a stone. The Opelousa must have brushed near firearms before, to be so cool. As for us, we looked at the weapon with a fresh awe, recalling.

"I did endeavor to find some flint and musket balls back at Ma's," John confessed apologetically, "You know that old musket hanging on the wall? I knew they must be about somewhere. But Weatherby was too cunning, too watchful. He hid them well."

There was a wistful pause before John shrugged and handed me the pistol. "Now you!"

I lifted the pistol with one hand. Much to my dismay, I still had to bring up the other to assist. I aimed into the woods, but I could see only my foe, clambering over the gunwale of my imagined ship, cutlass in hand, murder in his eye. I needed to clear the enemy boarder, and quickly!

I squeezed the trigger and the hammer banged home again, my hands shuddering with the impact. The smoke cleared, and the boarder had vanished. I had sent the villain to rest forever in Davy Jones' Locker. I grinned happily as I passed the pistol back to John. This time, he went through the motions of actually loading the thing, which was a nice touch.

We carried on like that for a while, but eventually tired of it. John put the flintlock safely back in his coat.

"Even with it empty, we could maybe use it to scare off bad folks, push comes to shove," he mused. "Or make a trade for something we're in sore need of. I reckon an antique like this could fetch more than a fine penny on the market. Anything could be put to use, so long as there's a plan, eh?"

"Always have a plan," I mumbled, almost sluggishly.

"That's right, son. Always have a plan."

The small fire cast our tiny camp in a soft glow. A light scent of early spring violets wafted to us in the delicate breeze whispering through the pine and oak trees.

Being a young man now on the lam, worn down by all the excitement, I fell asleep, dog tired.

11

I AWAKENED amongst the leaves and cool loess soil very much alone. You can imagine this was not a comfortable sensation, particularly when I realized that Pontus, too, had apparently abandoned me. I rose and climbed atop the highest point of a nearby hill and peered about for Pontus or John. This did little good, as one could not see more than maybe twenty feet before sight was obstructed by the thick vegetation of the woods. The silence that greeted my ears may as well have been the very Clap of Doom.

"John!" I hollered, already feeling like it was nothing but futility. The reality of the situation seemed to scramble up my spine and seep into my brain from the bottom up. It was a curious, almost physical feeling, enough for me to near soil my drawers. I'll admit that fully. These were the beginning stages of panic.

After a few minutes, I realized that I was shouting John's name to the empty woods pretty much mindlessly, like the natural reflex of a baby bird gawping its mouth open for a scrap of sustenance. I finally shut my mouth with a loud click. Tears were welling in my eyes now, and I fought them back, anger beginning to fill my gut. My erstwhile friend had left me to the wolves and savages inhabiting this region.

"JOHN!" I bellowed, this time with pure rage. A squirrel peered around the trunk of a tree to get a look at the noisome critter that had so rudely upset her quiet woods. The wind softly shushed through the trees, the most deafeningly mournful sound I had ever heard.

"You will right raise the dead with such caterwauling," a voice said nearby. It came, of course, from behind me, and I just about jumped out of my own skin.

I whipped around and there before me was a grimy fellow with flint in his eyes and something resembling half a grin and half a contemptuous sneer on his lips. The teeth that still managed to reside in that sneer displayed a minimal amount of ivory.

"Blood and tobacco," this man muttered in a gravelly voice, shifting a musket he was cradling against his forearm. It sounded like both an oath and a curse.

"I thought I mightn't bag at least a hare or a skunk, even, save for that exclamation of yorn. Now we'll like to all starve," he said.

He walked over to the stream, squatted, and scooped up a mouthful of water.

I confess at this point I was downright embarrassed, though I can't say why – I did not know this man from Adam. I hung my head low in this stranger's face. That said, I was eternally grateful at the same time, as I would rather be in the hands of this obvious frontier man instead of a wild Comanche or even a Chickasaw. Up to only a moment before, I had envisioned myself very much expired, my scalp being tanned by a Choctaw maid in a nearby barbarian camp.

"You two fairly burned a trail through these here woods,

you know. A blind pilgrim could track you, easy. Never seed nothin' like it a'fore this day."

My eyes must have lit up at the mention of my former friend, then burned with fury. "John," I grumbled.

The man waved impatiently down the hill. "Oh, he's trompin' over this a-way, don't despair. He did locate a bundle of acorns for your breakfast, if'n you still have an appa-teet."

This gentleman peered about the woods, sentinel-like, as John slowly approached.

As if reading my thoughts, the man pierced me with that flinty gaze, still sneering. "You all mightn't have had different visitors soon what with all this hollerin'."

Visions of my scalp decorating that Choctaw hut again gave me a case of goosebumps.

John walked up to us, finally, Pontus in trace. He looked at me with some bemusement. "Now, would I have dragged your corpse with me to this point just to leave you for the savages?"

I fixed him with a death stare.

"Pshht," our new friend opined in amusement. "Taint the Choctaws to be fretting by."

He started moving down the hill, gesturing for us to follow.

"The Creek – now, they'll square off among theyselves over your young pelts, true. You'd make one a rich savage at the slave markets, mark it!" And he guffawed with that. I did not find it the least bit amusing.

Nevertheless, having a keen interest in maintaining our pelts, we followed him.

* * *

We trudged after him for probably two miles or so with Pontus in trail. It seemed impolite to ride when our guide walked. Though now that I think on it, I doubt he would have minded.

Whenever we attempted to engage our savior in conversation to pass the time, or even to learn a little about him, he would abruptly bring a hand up in a sudden jerk. The message could not be clearer: Hush the hell up or be left behind for the Creeks.

As we walked on, I observed that he was much attuned to the wilderness about us. I felt supremely secure, no longer as much concerned with an encounter with a savage or beast. He had an air about him that he belonged more here than in any city.

We finally reached his cabin, and it was what I might have expected. It was a rough one, clearly designed for only one man, maybe two. After that, any semblance of comfort would be unhappily abandoned. It did have mortared logs in place, and even a door with leather hinges. A dying fire smoldered in a stone hearth. The interior was appointed with several furs of assorted animals. An elk skull leered down at us with black-holed eyes as we ducked in.

"Beevy," our rescuer announced, after propping his musket against the side of the hearth.

"Hosiah Beevy," he completed. He held his hand out to us. Apparently, now a formal greeting could be conducted within the boundaries of relative civilization. We likewise introduced ourselves.

"How came ye to be in these parts, lads?" he then asked.

John and I looked at each other, a bit hesitantly.

"Look to be in a hurry, you, what with no packs nor provisions to speak."

Mr. Beevy peered at us with those eyes of flint and amusement from beneath a bushy, permanently scowling brow. A deep scar was apparent on his forehead, which would account for this ever-present frowning aspect. I caught him more than once peering at me most intently, searching almost. One time, his scowling aspect even gave way briefly to a slightly sorrowful one, and he quickly looked away when our eyes met.

"Pa is a scoundrel to beat all," John exclaimed. "We had to get away, sir. We feared so for our very lives."

"Brothers," Mr. Beevy said, not a question, but a statement, almost to himself.

I elected to keep quiet and let John handle things from here on. He had already set the table, and I would let him serve up the meal.

"He's a ring-tailed terror when he's on the jug. I could no longer abide," John said with a conviction so firm that even I believed him, just for a moment.

Mr. Beevy grunted, rubbed his neck and then his scalp. I got the sense that he, in some way, related to our plight.

"Welcome to stay here the night," he said. "But I want no trouble if'n your Pa lights after you."

We both nodded, perhaps too enthusiastically.

The remainder of the day was spent exploring the surrounding area, when we weren't set on some frontier task by Mr. Beevy. He kept close to his cabin, brewing some kind of stew and working busily on some sort of hide garment. He generally behaved like a man happiest when alone.

At the same time, this man we had known for but half a day now seemed to fret over us like a mother hen, advising us more than once not to stray too far from the cabin, which he called "Rye-stead," for some reason.

Late in the afternoon, John and I were walking back to Rye-stead with another seemingly endless gathering of firewood.

"What's the plan, John?"

John looked surprised at this sudden query.

"I am working it out," he answered, a touch of defensiveness in his tone.

"I believe Mr. Beevy means well, but I don't wish to remain

here a slave," I said. I had had enough of the chores. We went from Auntie's, where it seemed endless work and toil was our lot, to God knows where in the middle of the wilds just to end up with more toil. I decided I did not want to be a man on the frontier after all if it meant all this work. The books and stories that hawked the adventures of frontiersmen like Daniel Boone and Davy Crockett had somehow left that part out.

"We are just earning our keep for the night, is all," John said.

"I see him, however, eyeing Pontus frequently. A suspicious eye," I remarked.

"I can't imagine the purpose," John replied, blowing out a gust of air as we climbed a rise. He dropped his parcel of firewood.

"I don't believe he means to take him. I don't sense ill intent. He means well and appears a good man. I think he's enjoying our company, for now."

"And his chores getting done with it, too."

John smiled wryly at that and picked up his load of wood again to deposit it on the now impressive heap near the cabin.

"And he looks at me, too, like he knows me. Makes me squirm."

"I wouldn't fret so about that. He's just a lonely old man," said John. Then his face brightened. "Maybe he thinks you're the long-lost fruit of his loins!"

I stood there for a moment, trying to cipher just what he was getting at. I felt my face flush when I took on that he was mocking me. Then I just glared at him.

That evening, we were seated by the fire outside of the cabin, where Mr. Beevy had been tending to his pot of stew. He served us each a bowl of it and sat down with his own. My belly rumbled with the scent of it; only then did I realize how hungry I had gotten.

"I do appreciate your efforts, boys," he said, and I felt a pang of guilt at my complaining earlier.

Mr. Beevy blew on the contents of his crude wooden spoon. He squinted over the dripping utensil at us with an anticipatory eye.

"Ain't you at all hungry? You been workin' a spell, figgered you could eat your own hoss!" he said.

With that, we quickly blew on the hot morsels on our own spoons and deposited them in our mouths.

After a moment of chewing on the plump meat within the concoction, John sat back with a surprised look. For my part, the taste of the meat reminded me of something, but I could not accurately place it. It was rather gamey, but not overly so, and had a certain sweetness to it, rather like pork.

Mr. Beevy looked pleased, nodding enthusiastically. "Better. Better," he muttered in between smacking his lips in satisfaction. "Not so much fat this time."

We went to work cleaning every bit of that stew from our bowls. John even went for seconds, after gaining permission from Mr. Beevy. This pleased the frontiersman even more.

Whilst we supped, we conversed on general topics. Mr. Beevy appeared no longer interested in our domestic situation, skirting the topic of our fictional father. Just fine by us.

Mr. Beevy tended, to our surprise, to elaborate on his own relatively recent history, which turned out about a thousand times more interesting than our own, anyway.

"... First seed these parts in '14, I did, in the company of Gen'ral Andy Jackson. We took the Trace mostly, south'rd, to wrassle with Ol' John Bull some. Liked it so much I come back after the war and settled in."

"You were with General Jackson?" I asked. My father had elucidated me to the so-called War of 1812. Being as they were somewhat recent events, and though I was but a baby at the time, most folks knew about it or had some familial connection with the war, and we grew up hearing tales about it many a time over.

"Pshht. You might say I was. I was Andy's Aide-dee-camp, true."

"That so?" John said excitedly, sitting up with revised interest.

"It is."

"You were there, then."

I had a vague notion of what "there" meant, but kept shut for fear of shining a light on my own possible ignorance.

"I was. I was with Andy throughout, for the whole haul. Yessir, I was at Old Hickory's side most times at Chalmette. Endeavored in that direction, anyhow." Mr. Beevy chuckled softly, "Hell, he couldn't shake off me, a-tall. But I took it on myself to look after him. I think he appreciated that, mostly."

Things got quiet for a long time then. I knew from some descriptions I had heard of the place called Chalmette. Most people knew the events that took place there as the Battle of New Orleans.

Mr. Beevy stared at the stew pot still dangling over the fire, then briefly over to me. Our eyes connected, and once again that sad look came to his.

"Son," he said, his gravelly voice low and heavy. "You look just like him."

I looked at John with newfound understanding, and he looked back, lips pursed and eyes cautious. Somehow, I had the mad theatrical urge to bring out the flintlock and show it off, given the subject of war. Maybe it would enhance my new image of being a soldier's lookalike. But something about the atmosphere held me back.

"Young Master Sam, poor lad," said Mr. Beevy, his voice trailing to but a whisper. His eyes took on a distant look.

I swallowed hard, not really knowing what to expect. We had only known this rough man for a day, but seeing him so affected by this memory was sobering. When he next spoke, it was in a voice from a faraway place.

"We seed a rocket go up early that morning, and we knew that it was their signal. It squirreled up and around in the air a bit, then dipped into the river.

"It was cold that morning, believe it, and there was a fog on the ground too. Some in the air. And I will tell you it gave some of us the haunts. Some of us the thrills, I suppose.

"The Brits were a bit late in coming, and that surprised us some. That rocket had gone up, and there was this long quiet spot; that gave us the haunts even more, I'll tell you. Eerie as sin. We looked at each other, not knowing if any of it was real, or if we was all in a bad dream together. Sounds touched now, but it's a fact.

"Oh, there had been other actions leading up to this, a'fore Christmas, matter of fact, over on our right. By the river, over to the Villere place. It was a lively action, too."

Mr. Beevy paused again. The fire crackled.

"Then their guns opened up. We could see them cannonballs, really see and watch them, floating through the fog. Looked like birds soaring about, in a way.

"Then we watched the columns approach, coming out of that fog. Some of them grenadiers, why they carried ladders and bundles of sticks – fascines, they call 'em, queer name it be – to lay across the ditches we'd dug in front of our breastworks.

"Then our artillery started on them, grapeshot and canister. The destruction was frightful. So very frightful. They was the enemy, true, but to watch it made your guts churn, and your soul shrivel a little.

"The sun had proceeded on its way, and our fire was getting heavier, deadlier, and fearsome bloody.

"It was all confusion, thunder, blood, and smoke. Some of them ran, which any man with sense would do, honest. But most of them just kept a-coming, and I have to tell you it was a sight to see. Such bravery is a severe uncommon thing. Marching right into the teeth of your own brutal death, knowing you are afeared but putting it away, and going forward.

"Fine, fine British soldiers – many of them of the elite class, the King's Own, fusiliers, and such. Fought Napoleon, by gum. Now they's fighting us."

Mr. Beevy shook his head slowly in wonderment.

"And they did come through the hell and the fire like the devil's own, they did.

"They came with their drummers and pennants, too, and it was a sight and a sound I wished lads like you could behold your own selves. Without the bloodshed, mind.

"We had our own drums too, though, and bands. They played various tunes to answer the Limeys'. I don't recall all of them, but I do know Yankee Doodle when I hear'd it. But thing is, I don't rightly know which side was a-playin' it!

"And by the eternal if both sides didn't cheer and rouse.

"They got into rifle and musket range, in time, and we gave them the buck and ball then.

"I hope to never see slaughter like it again, I can tell you that. Some did make it to our embrasures and even scaled up those redoubts, but our rifles made quick work of them at such close range, rest assured.

Mr. Beevy sort of shut down then, getting very quiet. He looked down at the ground for a moment, and when he looked up, his eyes held a shine from the seed of a tear.

"It was Master Samuel," he said, almost choking with a soft sob. "Saw him laying there aside us. Musket ball took him, most of his slim chest gone. His eyes were open and he still had a cask of powder in his hands. Was running powder to us on the line, he was."

Mr. Beevy shook his head fiercely, as if trying to throw off the memory and the emotion with it. He nodded at me.

"He gave it to the last, young Sam. His service. Yes, he did."

His eyes drifted back to that far-off place and time. He shifted on his seat and cleared his throat, getting back to the business at Chalmette, but his voice seemed slightly drained.

"Their advance, of course, slowed, then stopped in all of that fury. We found out later from prisoners we'd took that part of their slowing up was their Gen'ral Pakenham had been mortal wounded.

"In that situation, you almost feel sorry for your enemy, believe it. Old Hickory made sure their wounded were proper tended to. He had no love for Brits, mind you, since the time he was a lad 'bout your ages, and had a saber scar to tell of it, too, from the Revolution days.

"He had respect for them as soldiers, though, and these men showed a fierce lot of courage that day.

"But that line – our line – held firm, just as Andy said it would. Less than a mile of lumber, mud, and will held off the grand and proud British army."

Mr. Beevy looked at us then with a slight, sad smile.

"We held the line, January 8, 1815, we did, and mark it well, boys. Mark it well."

The camp fell to a melancholy silence. Mr. Beevy seemed to have lost his remaining appetite and scraped what was still left in his bowl out to the side.

His gaze then strayed over to Pontus, who was quietly grazing on the bushes just beyond the oak tree that loomed partly over the cabin.

"That is an admirable animal you have there," he said, seeming to come back to his previous demeanor. "Fine pony."

John glanced at me, and I smiled a bit into my bowl. Mr. Beevy pretended not to notice.

"He's for sale, if you are in the market!" said John, a bit too jovially for my taste, for I must have started some. Mr. Beevy barked out a surprised "Ha!" and one bushy brow shot up. This seemed to me to be out of his character, even for the short time we had known him. He did not strike me as someone who would be surprised at anything in life, let alone show it.

"I'm sure your Pa might have a say in that transaction," he said.

"He doesn't. Not anymore," John said flatly, a cold gaze overtaking him now as he looked briefly out into the woods. Something told me he did not have our fictional father in mind.

Mr. Beevy released a bottled-up breath. "Blood and tobacco," he grumbled.

12

Come morning, John and I, after looking about briefly while shaking the sleep from our eyes, determined that Mr. Beevy had departed his camp. At first, we thought he was off for his morning hunt or some other chore, but then we saw that Pontus was absent as well. We walked all about Rye-stead, looking for that pony, as if Pontus might appear in the brush, or had wandered around the cabin all on his own, as ponies will sometimes do.

"Don't say it," John said to me firmly, gesturing at me. He then expelled a long rope of swearing and cursing the likes I had never heard, particularly from him. It would have been enough to melt Auntie's eardrums, even at this present distance from her. And probably Pastor Purdy's too, in the bargain.

I have to say, as remarkable as it may seem, I never witnessed John curse again like that in the entire time I knew him.

Then, with that out and over with, John went about carefully calculating something; one could tell by the rapid, concentrated shifting of his eyes. This was a desperate situation, to be sure, and our next move was paramount. Not that we had that many at our disposal.

"How long, would you say, it has been since Mr. Beevy left us?" he asked me. Whether John truthfully expected an answer or was just pondering out loud, I hadn't the slightest.

"It could have been at any point after we had fallen asleep," I offered a small shrug.

John quickly turned toward me, and I half-expected a slap for stating something so obvious and dumb. But all he did was stare at me a moment, then let fly with another rope of blue words. If Mr. Beevy's cabin had had any wallpaper, it would have fallen off the walls and rolled up on itself at the very sound.

"By God, if I am not the most ignorant being to ever walk the Earth!" he said at last, when he came up for breath from all that cursing. "Let this be a lesson to you, Stephen. Let it be a lesson, at my expense, son. I let myself get prideful, I did. Downright cocky." He clawed a hand through his lustrous hair and squinched up his face in frustration. It reminded me of Father when I witnessed the few times I saw his anger get the better of him over something. It appeared a very grown-up gesture that struck me as odd in someone so young, but also kind of funny. I turned away from him, lest it make me cough out a laugh. John was in no way in a state for that.

It also dawned on me that I was feeling a certain satisfaction. One, that my suspicions of Beevy putting his squinty eyeballs on Pontus were right all along. But more that John, who had become something of a mentor to me, was human after all, apt to make mistakes when he got too full of himself.

"Why, that dumb old dead elk head has more mush in its skull than I could ever hope to!"

I turned back to him then, bearing a smile that I had no

hope of shucking. The dumb old dead elk head loomed just above him, and that was enough to set me off. My laughter spilled forth in a torrent, like dammed-up water set free. John grabbed my shirt in his fists. I didn't brace for the pummeling I was about to receive, because I really didn't care. The moment was just too delicious, like the aroma of a warm cherry pie freshly stolen from an old maid's window sill.

To my great surprise, John's face screwed up, going from anger into more of a quizzical expression, but then it washed away, replaced by one of sheer panic.

"We must flee," he whispered, as if it were his last breath in this world.

My laughter died a quick death at the urgency in his expression and voice.

Since we were all about the obvious things confronting us, I couldn't have agreed more. John set about grabbing up what few things we had, and then took to searching the cabin and area for useful things we might bring with us. Having arrived at Pastor Purdy's church the day before only to worship and perhaps catch a much-needed nap, we had no knapsack or other baggage in which to collect things, save our coats. We thus proceeded to stuff our shirts with whatever might be of some use, which, in our rushed minds, apparently was pretty much anything.

Not to say that Mr. Beevy had all that much to pilfer. There was an old powder horn with a sizable crack, a smoking pipe, some kind of animal pelt that looked like he cleaned other creature's pelts and bones with, and a spoon.

We departed in haste.

About three miles from the Beevy estate, or Rye-stead, we crested a gentle knoll to come face-to-face with the fron-tiersman himself.

He was not alone, for his entourage now included none other than Bucschalter.

* * *

Bucschalter had now been restored to the ever-trusty Opelousa, Pontus. He skewered us with a furious and fearsome eye from atop his steed, as he reached down to pat Pontus' neck, as if John and I had wronged the hoss somehow, other than the thieving of him.

Another man was there, too. He was short and stocky, with very close-cropped hair that was evident as he dismounted his dappled gray horse and took off his hat. He wiped his brow with it as he approached us. His face wore a grim expression, and he stated, very importantly, "I'm marshal in these parts, boys."

Mr. Beevy found it necessary to make introductions.

"Sorry, lads," he said, "but I had to. This here is Marshal Honey. He'll have to custodize you. I am sorry."

I have to say, Mr. Beevy did, in fact, look upon us with some regret. For a fleeting moment when our eyes met, I saw the ghost of the sadness I had seen yesterday.

The marshal looked at Mr. Beevy with some annoyance. It did not appear that he approved of the frontiersman performing a formal arrest or telling him his business. It could just have been that he didn't appreciate anyone taking away his thunder.

Bucschalter remained mute, but glared down at us plenty, as only he could. He finally turned Pontus around into the general direction of Buzzard's Roost. Our hands were trussed up,and we were installed atop a spare pony brought along for our transport.

Honey searched our coats with a brisk hand, raising his

eyebrows as he drew out the old flintlock. Bucschalter looked astonished, then scowled thunderously at us. His gray eyes cut to Mr. Beevy.

"I knowed they had it," Beevy shrugged. "No harm could be had to it. Anyhow, I fought alongside boys their age, and they had far better'n that."

Now, we had never really had a brush with the law in this territory, shut away at Auntie's place like we were supposed to be, not even when John and I had struck out on one of our escapades. So being ushered into the building wherein the judge of our crimes was seated, we were thoroughly daunted.

It lay about half a day's ride from Buzzard's Roost itself, so by the time we arrived, it was a particularly looming façade in the thin light of dusk. It was an impressive structure, sort of a proper plantation manse.

They led us to a shack somewhere well behind this manse, and down a slight hill, fair middling into the very swamp. We could see lanterns and small fires here and there, and the shadowy forms of other shacks scattered about. I had never seen any in real life, but I assumed they were slave quarters, for a soft murmur of voices drifted our way now and again, and a distant, lonely singing joined in as well.

Bucschalter cast one last baleful eye on us as the wooden door closed with an ominous creak, followed by the equally ominous clanking and clattering of a metal hasp and lock being thrown on it. He had not spoken one word during the entire journey, which in itself was plain spooky enough without all of this prisoner and confinement business. It had the feel of things changing for us in that we had moved up into another level of criminal activity, and this punishment loomed over us like death's own specter. For the first time in my life, I felt as though I were a true villain.

In that tiny, dank space, John looked me square in the eye.

"This will be but a brief interlude," he said resolutely. "Trust me in this."

I truly wished John was correct.

Some time later, we were brought some food. I had not realized how hungry I had become. It was a bit of pork and a portion of dumplings. John was likewise famished, and we set to the rations with a will.

The man who had brought us the vittles hunkered down and watched us closely. Too closely, for my taste.

He was a slave. Not the first nor the last I would see in my lifetime, but this one, unlike any of the others, acted a bit touched. His stare was unnerving. I had never – never, I say – seen a black man look so direct at a white person in such a way before, and that even included Hieronymus. Those eyes of his were as wide as saucers, which did little to reduce the spooky effect of this encounter. The white overseer who had accompanied him – escorted him, really – rested a few feet away. He wiped his brow of sweat and sat on a cask, puffing on his pipe.

The slave moved his head only slightly to his rearward, to indicate that the overseer would not take kindly to his engaging with us, but he proceeded anyway, in a rough whisper.

"You will be judged," he said.

I have to say it struck me fearsome ominous in a day already filled to the brim with the like, but I strived to outwardly shrug it off with the weakest of jokes.

"As will we all, in time, my good man," I said. I had borrowed the "good man" part from my Uncle Olson. My try at a cavalier response came out flat, even to my own ears.

The overseer looked over but appeared reluctant to give up his seat and pipe for the moment.

The slave did not move his body even once, but his eyes slid to me, and I braced for yet more eeriness to be piled on top of what we were already grappling with. Instead, I saw a particle of humor there.

"This is truth," he said.

"I have already been judged," John said quietly, "and have been found wanting. I do not fear man's judgment." There was a hardness to him that belied his years.

The black man shifted his weight on his haunches.

"This judgement you will fear, I trust, old soul," he warned.

John looked at him for the first time, defiantly.

"That'll do, Kitch," the overseer declared. He walked over to the doorway with a slight limp, spat an impressive gob, and shook his pipe out. "Gather them plates, now."

Kitch took the plates from us. That is when I noticed three fingers were missing from his left hand. I looked at him and his eyes told me that this, too, was part of his warning.

"Be stout, young sirs," was the last he whispered to us.

Next morning, I felt anything but stout. I had not slept but a wink here and there during the night. It is fair to say that that was owing in great part to the uncertainty of our present state, never mind the slabs of hard, rough wood that made up our beds. Many times I lay there, trying to ward off thoughts of home, for melancholy tears would do me no good. My hand even crept on its own to where there should be a pillow, searching for Father's letter.

The slave Kitch and the overseer retrieved us from our wooden cell, clattering the padlock as loudly as they could, purposely, no doubt, to irritate our senses and beset us with further foreboding.

The sun was still only peeking over the horizon as we stepped out. The cleaner air would have been refreshing had it not been for our unease, the overseer's wry, humorless smile, and Kitch's still unblinking stare.

They gave us biscuits and bacon, which at least spared me hope to the effect that they would not hang us on that day.

"You boys had a fit night, I see," the overseer said gruffly, then guffawed and spat. "Better'n horse thieves deserve, I wager."

A cold chill raced down into my innards at that term. I could swear my windpipe had frozen over.

The overseer, observing my discomfort, smiled again, with bitter humor in his eyes.

Off in the distance, the slaves were already working the fields. Their work song floated over to us, imparting an oddly peaceful moment. I found I could breathe again. I suppose you could say their singing eased my anxiety a bit, despite me being resigned to some grisly fate.

We were escorted to the back portico of the manse, where a desk and a chair had been set up, complete with an ink stand and a pen. And a gavel too.

Another man escorted us alongside the overseer, grabbing me roughly by the back of my neck to guide me. He seemed to be enjoying it too much. I could just about feel his cruel smile behind me, just about as present as his hot, rancid breath.

We stood before this desk for a time. Perhaps the intent was to make a show of us waiting to add to our torment. If so, it achieved the desired effect.

A well-appointed house slave eventually emerged from the house proper, clutching a sheaf of papers. He threw us a disap-proving look, and I reflected that here was a slave eyeing us as though we were something just scraped from the bottom of his boot.

He laid the papers on the desk and carefully placed a weight on them. This weight was in the shape of a curious-looking animal. It had a rather elongated face and a hunched back, something like a gargoyle, it appeared. Strange that something like that would have stood out for me, after all of these years.

Another man started to come out of the large portico doors, but stopped abruptly, his face turned from us as he was addressing someone still within the house.

"By the Lord Harry, I will have the last word on that score, mind you!" he exclaimed. "That parcel is to be tended as I instructed, or I will have his hide for a satchel! And you tell him I said it!"

He emerged fully from within the dimmer confines of the manse. He was thin and wiry, with a patch of thinning red hair and a scrubby tuft of beard that sprouted from either cheek, framing his narrow face.

He smiled at us, not very kindly at all, more the way of a bank or train station clerk who feels overworked and can't be bothered with the likes of you but has to anyway. I would take what I could get at that low point and was thankful that at least one grown person would show us a bit of kindness now, inauthentic or not.

"I do apologize for that outburst," he said. "'Tis fair indecorous to enter a place growling like a wounded peccary."

He then looked closer at us, and what smile on his face dropped off with eerie suddenness.

"These are the lads, eh?" he asked nobody in particular. The overseer shuffled his feet, as if not sure if he should answer. The man's gaze stayed on us as he sat at the desk. He reached for his pen and paper, set the weight aside and fastidiously adjusted it to what seemed a very particular position on the desk. I could see now that it was a baboon, made of some dull metal. I can't explain it, but my eyes were drawn to the damned beast like iron shavings to a magnet.

"Names!" he barked suddenly. It wasn't particularly loud, but it got everyone's attention all the same.

"J-john Murrell," spoke John meekly. The man did not look up as he started to scribble furiously, the scratching of it seeming to fill the portico.

"Your honor," the man said firmly.

John looked at me, puzzled. The scratching continued.

"At all times when addressing the court, you will address such as "your honor."

"Your honor," John said, darting terrified eyes my way.

This judgement you will fear, I trust, old soul, Kitch's words returned. I swallowed, both at the memory and at John, seeming indeed shaken.

The pen stopped its scratching. The man did not look up.

"John Murrell, your honor."

The pen resumed its torture of the paper. The man tilted his head just so slightly, as if straining for more.

I recited my name with a "your honor" tied dutifully on the end of it.

The scratching stopped again, and His Honor peered at us in silence for what seemed a lifetime. Behind him, the well-appointed house slave smiled a little smile. I decided at that moment that I did not like him very much, probably even hated him right then, just for making my existence that much more uncomfortable.

"It's a hanging offense, as I am sure you are aware," said His Honor. "This horse thievery."

I swallowed. The click in my throat sounded near as audible as the scratching of the pen. In fact, right then, I'd bet that it could have been heard on the moon.

"Of course, I can see you are but just lads," the man went on. "And the surest way to inhibit a life of crime is to end it entirely."

This time, I could hear the click in John's swallowing. Myself, I had no spit whatever left in my mouth, for it was all cotton and my brain a frozen mudball.

"It will save a countless amount of trouble to the public and end *your* suffering in particular. For there is nothing but grief and despair for you on the path on which you now find yourselves." He paused to stare at us some more, not without a certain pity in his eyes now. This was it for us.

"I have *seen* it!" he shouted suddenly, rising out of his chair about a quarter. Its legs scraped the deck of the portico with a loud, jarring squeak. This didn't help settle what nerves were left alive in my body.

He stood fully and held one hand out to his side, eyes never leaving us. The slave handed him a clean white handkerchief. The judge deliberately wiped his hands with it. I could not make out why; there did not appear to be any ink on his hands.

He reached down to the desk and rested the paper weight on the paper he had been torturing with the pen, placing it just so, in a ridiculously dainty fashion.

"I am inclined this day to be a mite more forgiving, however."

The way he was looking at us, I was convinced that he was thoroughly enjoying his power over our fate. "Therefore, I sentence you to corporal punishment. In the stead of a hanging."

I risked a questioning glance at John. Fear clutched at my throat like a demon's claws.

"Corp-oral? Your Honor?" I croaked. The baboon paperweight stared at me with malevolent, metallic eyes.

The judge's lips formed a tight smile. "Just so, lad."

He gestured to the black servant, who left the room and returned with a brazier hanging from a chain, held by his gloved hand. Coals smoldered in the pan and two metal rods with wooden handles protruded from the white-hot coals.

I knew then that this man had predetermined what our punishment was to be.

My resentment at that moment knew no bounds.

And I kicked. In my mind, I kicked and revolted, and I swear my short life again flashed before my eyes. I bolted then, or attempted to, but the overseer's man was quicker by far. He shoved me to the floor, where I looked up at John, who had not flinched once, not even a muscle.

"Jeffrey," the judge's eyes still had not left us, and I knew true hatred for the first time in my life. "A simple inscription, if you please." He gestured again, and Jeffrey approached respectfully. The judge whispered something to the slave.

Jeffrey then backed away, solemnly grasping one of the metal rods by the wooden handle.

The overseer had seized on John, forcing his left hand on the nearby porch rail. He whipped a leather strap around it, binding it tightly, no doubt painfully, to the rail. Jeffrey approached with the steel rod, its end glowing a most villainous red. My entire body quivered with each slam of my heartbeat, the bones in my legs no longer of any use.

John stared at me as Jeffrey applied the length of steel to his hand, silent tears of pain and rage coursing down his face. I was astonished that he made no sound whatsoever. Bile rose to the back of my throat as I gagged against the acrid smell of searing human skin.

It seemed to go on forever.

Jeffrey methodically kept at the task, returning to the brazier a number of times.

The stench of burning flesh seemed to render the portico into a smaller, closer space.

Jeffrey, his gruesome work finally concluded, turned his gaze upon me, and my blood ran as cold as a deep river.

The judge held one hand aloft, looking from me to John, who glared at a distant place and at no one, an empty hatred in his eyes. He shivered with a fury and pain that it was clear only he understood. His branded hand was still strapped mercilessly to the portico rail.

I confess that at no time during this procedure did my mind go to the question of how men could do such a thing to a mere boy, a child. Surely some of these men had children of their own? My mature mind in later years ascribed it to simply being a factor that a future people, perhaps considering themselves more advanced and civilized, would recoil from.

The judge turned back to me, and I saw a type of pity in his eyes. Somehow, from Jeffrey, I detected a resigned disappointment, almost as if he could read the judge's thoughts. Perhaps he could. After all, who knew how long he had been assisting in meting out such "justice?"

The now cooling steel rod drooped, its tip not venturing back to the brazier.

"Your friend made a good account of himself," the judge announced, as if I should be congratulating John on surviving unspeakable horror at this maniac's hand. "An impressive display of courage. Dare I say, manliness."

Jeffrey now rested the tip of the branding iron on the white-painted porch, his other hand resting jauntily on his hip. This must have been great sport for him.

The overseer dug his pipe from a breast pocket with one hand, tugged at the leather strap holding John to the rail with the other.

"As to you, boy," the judge addressed me, "The stink of your friend's punishment may be retribution enough for you, wouldn't you say?"

I cannot say today if the hateful glare I threw this man at that moment has yet been surpassed in my lifetime. Somehow, I knew he had seen that look before from souls such as mine, although perhaps not many from a child.

I did know that it would be worse for me than any branding on my own hide would have done.

Jeffrey sighed.

The overseer struck a match.

13

THE STONE PATH UP to the house had been swept clean. Mother always managed to keep it that way, so I knew it was not just for my sake, but it felt that way to me, in the moment.

The coach dropped me there, and the driver did not even get down from his perch to assist me like he had for the other passengers he had left off. Not that I expected it, you understand, since I was still just a kid and all. The coachman did at least tip his hat a little to me, which was the most acknowledgment he had afforded me the entire journey.

I stood there with my duffel in my hand, this time somewhat lighter to carry than it had been when I had departed from home before.

The clatter of the coach faded quickly into the distance, and the relative quiet of the farm descended on me. I was fairly surprised there had been nobody there to greet me, for most folks will notice right off when a coach or a wagon heads to their farmstead. For one thing, they will see the dust it kicks up a mile or two away, unless it's raining or snowing.

The quiet wrapped some wisp of sadness around me, what

with nobody to greet me. Did they think me already dead or elsewise occupied by other ill events? Surely, they had been informed of my return.

My eyes scanned about, taking in the barn and the fields, and my insides warmed to how they had not changed all that much in my absence. The comfort of being back home started to overtake my melancholy.

It was a farm, after all, chores had to be gotten to, and people could not just stand about waiting for a coach that they did not know for what hour it could be expected.

Suddenly, I spied Tiffany, standing on the porch, now somehow magically and silently appearing behind a post, staring at me with one eye.

I stared back, trying not to take on too much of the aspect of an apparition. To be honest, I was kind of stuck in place, not quite knowing what I should be doing, and my brain was catching up to how different she looked and yet the same too.

I looked around again, this time down the road the coach had just traversed, and where our fields lay, and then I heard a sudden clattering and before I knew it, Tiffany was upon me, grasping me in a hurried hug that about toppled me over. The duffel dropped from my hand and hit the ground with a muffled thud, and I hugged Tiffany back with a grateful little chuckle. She was saying something, but I couldn't quite make it out since her face was pressed up to my chest and her voice was choked with crying.

Then she looked up at me, her face squinched up, and smeared with tears. Right then, I recollected that her and I had never even hugged before.

Tiffany stood back a bit, wiping away her happy tears and looking up at me with a kind of smile I had never seen her use before. I heard a delicate, airy gasp and looked up to see that Mother now stood on the porch, one hand up covering her mouth, the other grasping the front of her apron in a tight ball.

She took a couple of faltering steps down the porch stairs. I met her halfway down the stone path. Her hand was still covering her mouth. She had tears in her eyes as her other hand let go of the apron and reached for me. She touched first my shoulder, as if she was checking to see if I was real, then her hand travelled shakily across my shoulder, softly to my cheek. It fluttered there for a moment, as if afraid to touch me. Then her other hand dropped from her mouth and went to my other shoulder. She pulled me to her as gentle as a newborn angel and held me for a moment. The delicate scent of lilac soap was to me like spring water to a man in the desert.

Mother then held me at arm's length, a hand on each shoulder, to look me over now that she had confirmed I really was standing before her on her stone walk.

"Goodness, how you've grown, Stephen," she said.

We smiled at each other, and Tiffany smiled too, looking back and forth between us.

Mother must have seen something in my eyes. She gestured off toward the large barn.

I stood there still, just looking at her. I guess I was still smiling dumbly, trying to work out to myself that I truly was home, or maybe to simply ensure that I would remember the moment forever, and never lose it. Mother gestured off again with a quick sweep of her arm, wiping away a tear with the other.

I turned and looked at the barn. I took a few steps and felt something in my hand. I looked down, seeing that it was Tiffany's warm hand. She looked happily up at me.

"Daughter," I heard Mother say in her soft but firm way that expected no argument. "I need you in here."

Tiffany dropped my hand with a disgruntled look. "Hmph." She stalked back to Mother.

When I looked back, Mother nodded in the direction of the barn.

"He'll be glad," she said softly, turning back to the house.

Father was at his workbench in the corner of the barn. The doors were open, and he was hunched over, working on something in the corner of light the open barn doors provided.

He was deep into whatever he was doing, so he didn't appear to hear my purposeful shuffle behind him. I knew enough not to startle a man with an awl or blade in his hand if I could help it, even my own father.

I gave out a polite little "ahem" to signal that I was there. His hands stopped. I could see a harness strap in them. He lowered the tool on the bench and looked at me for a moment.

"Stephen," I couldn't make out any kind of meaning in this. It seemed like just a word sort of plopped there, as if he was looking out at the farm, saw a starling and marked it by just saying "bird."

My body tensed up a bit, drawing in a breath, poised, I thought, for anything. The notion that Father may not be all that glad to see me squirreled across my brain. The Earth started sliding out from under me, like it was telling me to just turn and run back the way I came as fast as I could. Then I thought of the letter from him that I had kept inside my pillow back at the Roost, how it kept me connected to the farm and to Mother and even Tiffany. And to him. My despair then seemed like it could fill a universe.

Father inspected me up and down for a long time, his face so serious, and I swear it felt like Bucschalter all over again, searching for any little item for correction.

He finally stood up, wiped his hands on a cloth, and came over. He looked me dead in the eyes, as stern as Judgment Day.

Then the ghost of a smile came to his lips, and his eyes took on the very slightest shine. He put a hand on my upper arm and squeezed it firmly.

"There he is," he said. "There's my fine young man."

* * *

I was set to work right off, that very day, on the farm. I didn't mind at all, truthfully. I was glad to be introduced to a normal, day-to-day existence again.

We sat down to dinner and it was just about spectacular: fried chicken, corn bread, black-eyed peas, potatoes, and gravy. I had plum forgotten how good a home-cooked meal could be.

"What was that Rooster place really like?" Tiffany blurted out, not two minutes into the meal. She and I hadn't had any real time to talk, as I had spent most of the day tromping around the farm at Father's side.

"Now, daughter," Father said, his mouth set firm, shaking his head slightly.

Tiffany's mouth pulled to the side in an admonished grimace.

"In any case, not at the dinner table," Mother said, more gently.

Father cleared his throat, reaching for a chunk of bread. He showed his slight, soft smile.

"Now this sets me just right," he said, looking around the table, and everyone smiled back, even Tiffany.

Now, I may not be the keenest blade on the plow, but I did get the sense that Father and Mother simply wanted to put the whole episode of the Roost and our family's experience with it well behind us. It was over, and that was that.

* * *

Later that night, I lay on my bed in my room, tired and happy. Fine night air blew gently from our well-kept farm through the open window, stirring the curtains ever so slightly. I breathed it in gratefully.

At a stirring at my door, I looked over. There was Tiffany, peering in at me.

"Stephen?"

"Yes, Tiff?" I answered, my eyes going back to the window.

She came over to me, looking down at me for a moment. She then climbed into the bed and lay at my side. I wrapped my arm around her, and she released a contented sigh. Just as I could not recall us ever hugging before, my little sister had never shown this kind of affection for me, but this seemed like it was something we had always done, in some form or another, and it felt good and right. It made me feel whole, somehow.

I stared out the window at the dark Tennessee sky. Maybe, in some way beyond my youthful understanding, I was meant to go off to the Roost for a broader purpose than just to be "brought to heel" as Magistrate McAllen had put it. Looking into the night, though, I also saw past it to the wild lands about the Trace and the beckoning of the wide Mississippi River beyond it, and the look and smell and taste of adventure that those things offered, all that the farm never could.

I thought of John, and grew a little sad, wondering what chapters had been written in his story since the branding at the order of the porch judge and Jeffrey, that house-slave fiend. That judge had created someone – something – that probably even now was going on to a ruinous, lonesome fate through the world, fueled only by hatred and resentment. I drifted off in a supreme melancholy state of mind. John was out there somewhere without hearth and home, burning lightning-fast through a short fuse.

14

THE SHOP CLERK looked at me with an inspecting eye, to what purpose I could not decipher. Mother had dispatched me to town for some items, so I had trundled in on the farm's service wagon. I was very happy to do it, of course. Most times, any excuse to go into town would do.

Growing up, I had been to town only a handful of times before with Mother and had visited the same general store. But this clerk was new. I believe it was his father who had attended to us then. Mr. Tandy had been friendly, in a business-like way, paying almost no attention to me. But Young Tandy looked like he had no intention of letting me escape his eye, even as he finished up our transaction. The boy version of Bucschalter, this one.

My irritation continued towards its peak. About the time I had opened my mouth to voice it, a young lady slipped into the shop, and I guess the lad's attention found something far more pleasant to fix upon. He and the girl instantly launched into a lively discussion of some sort.

I drowned out the noise and snapped my trap shut, taking in the store again for old times' sake as I turned away.

The young gal and the suspicious clerk gabbled on, and I became embarrassed for the boy then, only because he sounded as much like a spring hen as she did, babbling away on day-to-day niceties with no meaning behind them other than to flatter and puff up each other. It was downright humiliating to behold.

She was there for gloves she had ordered, all the way from Boston, looked like. I had no idea Boston gloves were any better than gloves from St. Louis or Philadelphia or wherever, but I suppose that is the difference between me and some trussed-up, self-important girl who fancied herself a big-city socialite instead of just another town girl in Elizabethton, Tennessee.

I ambled around to the back of the store, soaking in happy memories of tagging along with Mother as she examined various bolts of cloth, sewing threads, and hankies, occasionally haggling with the shopkeeper. I was more interested in the paper-wrapped candies, if they had any, and always prowled for any of the latest toys.

Perhaps up ahead, they had some of that licorice I enjoyed so much as a younger lad. It would be a treat for Tiffany, whom I'd made my mind not to take for granted so much. As I mean-dered back to the storefront on this new hunt, the girl briefly glanced back at me, but after a moment, quite unexpectedly gave me the prettiest smile. I don't care who you are, but when a pretty girl smiles at you – whatever the reason – it'll make you feel ten feet tall, ready to tackle Genghis Khan himself, and all his hordes, too.

Her smile had the opposite effect on the clerk, who frowned down at the counter, swiping his hand across it, clearing it of some invisible dust. The girl pursed her mouth in polite disapproval at his angry gesture. This appeared to rattle him even further, as he then slapped the counter with a sharp rap. He tried to catch himself with a deep breath, straightening an apron that did not need to be straightened and offered the girl a strained smile. But he had already lost the day, his weak and phony smile squandered, for she was looking away, out the window.

All saggy and defeated, the clerk produced a small package from somewhere and deposited it on the counter. "Should I unwrap it for you, miss?" he said, in a small voice, depleted of any air or hope.

"Thank you," she replied, with just a hint of frost. "That won't be necessary." She reached out with a delicate white hand and picked up the package, and held it to her midsection. She must have waited quite some time for those gloves to be delivered all the way from Boston. She clung to that package like it was all she had left in the world. There is no figuring the female mind sometimes, I'll tell you that.

She seemed to look about the shop for me on her way out while trying to act like she wasn't.

For my part, it was a dual win. I had vanquished a perceived rival and possible enemy while attaining the attentions of a pretty girl. While she may be a townie, likely a rather uppity one in the bargain, I figured I could forgive her those things. I decided to try to carve her image into my memory for future consultation and was already plotting my next journey into town to seek her out.

The bells of the shop's door tinkled as she stepped outside. I would've followed, but, just then, Mr. Tandy appeared from the back. The boy-clerk, looking immensely relieved, stepped to the safer spaces of the back room, but not before stopping to whisper something to him. Mr. Tandy glanced my way for a moment, the clerk still running his mouth into his ear. From time to time, the boy threw me a hot, scathing glare. Mr. Tandy's expression turned from businesslike and uncaring to a slightly surprised look, flowing right into one of suspicion rivaling that of the clerk's. I happily deflected it with my new-found shield of victory like Perseus against the glare of the Gorgon.

At any rate, I hadn't a need to dawdle there much longer. I hadn't found any licorice, but Mother's goods were bagged and paid for, my nostalgia was satisfied, and I even drew me a comely girl's eye. John Murrell would be proud.

I tramped on out.

* * *

To my disappointment, I never did spy the girl again as I guided the wagon through the woods that edged the Stover place, just off Stony Creek. It was a sprawling farm, probably the largest in Carter County. It was a pleasant enough interlude of late-afternoon shade before the road straightened out and was bracketed by dull, flat farmland.

I let the reins dangle freely in my hands, the horses knowing the route home better than I.

A stand of trees lay ahead, the road bending around it into something of a blind turn.

The horses stopped dead in their tracks mid-turn. There in the road stood another horse, a lovely blue roan. It didn't even turn its head as we approached, just staring off into the woods like it was a statue. I sat there, looking at it, half-waiting for it to just move on its own.

It did not.

It was saddled. Might be the rider had to tend to some business or another in the privacy of the trees. There was a rifle still in its scabbard on the saddle, so it was not likely the rider was hunting.

There was no room to go around this pony, so I got down

from the wagon and went over to it, patted it on its nose, and murmured a few kind words to let it know I was a friend.

I stood there for several minutes, just listening and looking about for this animal's owner. I heard nothing but a soft wind soughing through the trees and some tinkling, pleasing bird-song. Finally, I took the traces of the horse and gently led it to the side of the road as much as possible and it obliged me, even giving out a friendly little whicker for the trouble.

I climbed back aboard the service wagon, clicked my tongue, gave the reins a little slap, and we were back on our way.

After a while, I fell into daydreaming, mostly about the pretty girl back at the dry goods shop, the haughty boy-clerk who had acted like he had something over on me somehow, and how I had felt like I really had won the day. I may not have won Minerva Underwood over, and mind you, she still was The Dream to me even now – after all, they say you never forget your first love – but this was its own gift.

I sat there, my head lolling with the motion of the wagon, self-congratulation warming me, when I was rudely snapped out of that state by the sensation that I was being watched.

I looked around, seeing nothing but flat, uninteresting fields lying fallow, with nobody working them and nobody about at all.

Then I turned around. It was that cussed horse. The foolish thing had been following the wagon. By that time, I reckoned it had been about two miles.

Now, horses will just simply follow other horses from time to time. But I felt this was a tad unusual only because it was saddled, and there was somebody's gear on it. A well-trained horse will stay put forever, awaiting its owner and rider, and they generally will stay there until kingdom come.

I am not a cruel person, especially to animals, but I couldn't help but think what a dumb beast this thing was. Why the hell follow me? It wasn't like I gave it a lump of sugar or an apple.

"Shoo, now!" I told it, not expecting it to shoo at all, at least not at first. It was a good twenty yards behind us. I felt ashamed for not having heard any clopping of hooves or snorting or breathing it might have done. I told myself it had been covered up by the wagon creaks and rumbling of the wheels, not because of my foolish daydreaming. No, sir, not that. I did fancy myself to be a better woodsman than that, after my turn at Buzzard's Roost and the things I had learned of actual worldly value.

I stopped the wagon again and went to the animal.

"You get, you hear?" I said to the horse, motioning with my hands to whisk it away like some ridiculous wizard. "Somebody's looking for you, you idiot!" For some reason, I thought insulting the brute might do the trick.

"Get lost, will you? I don't want you!" I continued as it stared at me with big brown eyes. Meanness can never be discounted as an effective tactic, either, I assumed. Animals are dumb, but they do have feelings. At least some of them possibly do.

I huffed a bit in frustration, hands on my hips. I thought for a moment about turning that wagon around and leading the lost horse back to the woods, but it was getting late and there was still a ways to go. I didn't want the folks to get to worrying about me.

I got back into the wagon and started off again. I looked back for a minute, and the horse hadn't moved. I hoped against hope that things would stay just like that, or better yet, the dullard would turn that long head back to those woods and rightful owner.

Lo and behold, there it came again, slowly clopping after us. Now I started feeling sorry for the thing. Did it somehow know that it had truly been abandoned? Or worse yet, had its owner befallen some dastardly accident and it had stood obstinately in the road to communicate it in its own horsely way?

These thoughts ricocheted through my brain all the way back to the farm and only Father's appearance on the road, aside one of our fields, snapped me out of my vexed reverie. He cast a questioning eye at the extra beast. I shrugged.

"Followed me all the way from Stover's Woods."

"Hmph," Father grunted, his brow furrowed, apparently as vexed as I was. He walked over to the horse, his eyes appraising it. "Fine-looking animal. This saddle doesn't look at all familiar to me, though." He patted it on the head, murmuring softly. "Well, I expect somebody will come looking for him shortly." He led it off to the barn. "Meantime, let's get you comfortable, shall we?"

* * *

"Father says to come quick!"

I did not like Tiffany's saucer-eyed look when she breathlessly blurted it out. I was out in the east field, harrowing out a stubborn weed patch. I hastily propped the scythe on the fence and trotted after Tiffany.

Three men were sitting on their horses in the yard before the barn. Father had brought out the blue roan, a simple rope halter on it.

I stooped near Father, panting, Tiffany at my side. The three men's gaze went to the two of us. I had never seen them before. They stared at my sister and I, their faces grave and unchanging. Their focus shifted to me alone. A heaviness started to grow in my belly, and a heat went to the back of my neck.

"Daughter," Father tilted his head to the house. She

scowled, but trudged dutifully off. Mother was on the porch, staring our way, her hands wrapped in her apron.

"Stephen Hue," said one of the men, his slate-gray eyes piercing right through me. He wore a black coat and a wide-brimmed hat to match. He seemed all business to me, an unsettling sight. This was clearly no social visit.

"Y-yes," I answered. "Yessir."

"What do you know about this here nag?"

I looked over at Father. He nodded. "This is Sheriff Hernon, Stephen."

"Well, sir, I...I came up to it over to Stover Woods."

There was a creak to a saddle as another of the men leaned over and spat a juicy gob onto the ground.

"Came up to it,' he says," he scoffed, a smirk twisting his mouth.

"That's what the boy said," Father's voice was firm and deep, with a menacing ring I don't recall having ever heard before. He and this man locked eyes. After a moment, the spitter looked away, muttering something inaudible to himself.

"Mr. Tandy and his boy put you in town just before this hoss went missing," said Hernon.

I looked at Father, but he was staring at the men.

"It was just standing there in the road," I continued, fortified a little by Father's steadfastness.

The spitter guffawed anyway and spit again. I had never seen anyone so filled with spit.

"We put it up, figuring the owner would be by soon enough," said Father. He let go of the lead rope and put his hand on the roan's neck.

"And here I am for my property, said the third man, turning to me again more pointedly.

"And here it is. Your property." There was that sound again in Father's voice. I was starting to like it. This side of him was a revelation I confess I sorely needed right then. "You'll see that this is your saddle too, sir."

"I marked it," the man said with a curt nod. He had a narrow face and coal-black eyes like a crow. He wore a dirty vest, and his pants and shoes were overly worn. "Thing is, I don't see my Hawkins."

"I took it to the house for safekeeping," replied Father. "Seemed the wisest course."

The man leaned against the pommel of his saddle. "I'm sure it did," he said in the oiliest of ways.

"Son, fetch that rifle from the house." Father's gaze was locked on Crow-Eyes.

"You stay put there, boy," interjected Hernon. His tone was firm, like a man used to wielding authority. But it was not unkind, either. "Mr. Coggins," he said to Crow-Eyes, "Retrieve your horse. That's what we're here for. I'll collect your Hawkins."

Coggins got off his horse and walked over to the roan, his beady eyes watching Father warily. "A man can't just park his horse to answer the call without some damned horse thief making off with his goods– "

"What did you say?" Father growled, pivoting to Coggins as he picked up the roan's lead.

"You heard it," Coggins pointed at me. "This'n here is a tried and true horse thief, and everyone here knows it. Everyone in the cussed *county* knows it–"

Father hit him.

It was a powerful blow, lifting Coggins clean off his feet. He hit the ground backwards with a heavy grain-sack thud, miniature cyclones of dust flying around him. I recoiled from the shock and suddenness of it.

"Now wait a damned minute!" Hernon shouted when

Father stepped over Coggins and grabbed his filthy vest, pulling him up for another punch. It was a sight to see.

The spitter guffawed loudly again. Hernon cut it short with a sharp look.

Father stayed his hand, balled fist hovering over Coggin's ugly bird face. Father let him go with a push and stepped away, breathing heavily. I got the sense it was not from exertion.

"We'll have to take him in, Mr. Hue," said Hernon. "Just 'til things get sorted out."

"Not without a warrant, you won't."

Hernon looked at Father evenly for a moment. Finally, he said, "Yes. Of course."

Coggins had collected himself off the ground, casting me a withering glare. He exchanged it for a fearful one as he had led the roan past Father. "Ought to put a hot iron on his skinny ass too, just like that other brat–"

"That's enough!" barked Hernon.

The spitter chortled and did what he apparently did best, and spat. "Hot iron." Hernon shot him a look, and the spitter averted his eyes, wiping his ugly mouth with the sleeve of his coat.

Coggins threw the saddle on the roan and hurriedly cinched it down enough to hold it in place with no rider. He led the horse over to his other one and mounted.

"You stay put, young Hue." Hernon looked squarely at Father. "I'll be back for that Hawkins as well, Thomas." He nodded toward the house, a hint of regret in his eyes. Father nodded curtly. Out the corner of my eye, I saw his hand tighten into a fist again.

The men turned their horses. We stood and watched them for a moment.

I heard Father's voice, from a million miles away.

"We'd best wash up for supper."

* * *

Three days had passed since that matter. I stared through the window of my room, as I always did, waiting for sleep to overtake my senses. This night, though, I knew it would never come. I turned and lay back down. Not after the dreams-turned-nightmares. The brawl with the townies, my frenzied blows raining down on the one in the woods, my blood up, pleasure churning through my veins. Then I was blasting through the forest on Pontus, wind in my face, heart drumming away in my chest nearly as loud as his hooves on the trail.

Then abruptly, all that vanished. Scorching heat swam up my nose, so furious my brows are surely singed clean off. Worse still, there was the ugly stink of roasting flesh. It thickened and thickened till it was downright choking.

About this time, I would wake, gasping in clean air.

I lay there thinking of all that had transpired since arriving back home. The comfort of being at last back in the bosom of my family, a new appreciation for them having been attained thanks to my time away at the Roost. Not that it was all bad there, I reflected. My memories flitted by like moths. First of meeting John, quarreling with him, then making steadfast friends, discovering first the flintlock and then Ma's, pulling off our first heist, squabbling again over Minerva, surviving that vicious man, Amber Eyes, learning of Hieronymus' and John's sordid tales, and running away. What a short but good time.

I tried to banish the grim, horrid end to all those rapscallion adventures. Still, it had dogged me those past nights.

Time and again, that burning stench doused my nose, until I imagined myself in hell. Will it plague me even miles away?

Next, I thought about Tiffany and her new-found affection for me, and mine for her. I thought of Mother and Father's welcoming me back, absent of any chastisement, all transgressions forgiven, much less mentioned. Knowing John and poor Hermie had none of these, I should have been ever so grateful and not throw it away.

I looked out that window, hating myself. For having put my family through all of that, for having brought more of it back to them, even though it was not my fault Coggin's cursed old roan followed me home. I hated Coggins for owning the stupid animal to begin with, and saw in my mind Father driving more blows to his grotesque, crow-eyed face.

Tears welled in my eyes as I cursed myself for the worst sin of all, in my head: I *wanted* to go through that window. I wanted it more than anything. Riding in a hell for leather escape on a fast pony, trading blows with my fists in the dirt...

Damned me, I desired the life of adventure and danger more than I wanted farm life, the church life, civilized life. There was that pretty girl at the store, wasn't there? If I was smart, I should have gone after her, wooed her proper, then married her and settled down, and generally come to my senses.

But Hernon and Coggin and Tandy were all in town too; doubtless they'd turned the town on me and mine. Our family name was stained, surely. Hell, I *wanted* the excuse of not putting Father and Mother and Tiffany through any of that again. Why not go through that window, open the glass panels, part the calico-patterned curtains, and go back to the Trace and the River and the free life, forever. Then the gossip and whispers would follow me away from my home, wouldn't they?

Tears charted a path down the side of my face. The perfect square of the window and the night beyond beckoned. I knew that it very well could be the portal to my hell, and possibly a worse fate, in the end, than Sheriff Hernon or the court or a jury of my peers might provide.

I pondered all of these visions and dreams, and sadly

wondered if they really meant something. Was I being cautioned away from a life of danger, long incarceration, or death? Something beyond my understanding, but steering me to a better path?

But in the end, it was no use. I... I made up my mind.

The world around me was a dark blur as I gathered a few things, looked around at what was one day going to be a distant memory.

And I went through the window.

It bit hard, and it was the hardest thing I had ever done; I did not look back as I took the road West.

15

Mose Bunton stared at me with his one good eye.

"Listen here, Hue," he said. "If you think it's you earning this, you're wrong. It's just that you're the only blamed one left to turn to."

I had learned to hold that one good eye's gaze, for a spell. Just long enough, mind you, not so long as to throw any kind of challenge to him.

I wasn't sure what he was getting at. Sometimes Mose just blurted things and you weren't able to decipher their true meaning until the next day or the next week, sometimes never. Well, we all on the crew of his keelboat, *Jasmine Moon*, knew that if we followed one of his pronouncements with a question, we might get a swipe from his ever-present cane sword. The first time was enough.

Tonight, the *Moon* was nudged up securely at New Madrid, on the Kentucky Bend, where the Mississippi River looped to make a horseshoe betwixt Missouri and Kentucky. A late summer evening breeze had the river lapping at her hull, the peaceful sound at times overtaken by the happy roar of revelers from a nearby saloon. Lunk Masters and Joe Harper, my two crewmates, had gone and left me here with our fearless skipper.

Mose shifted in his chair to get a better view of me. It was not entirely necessary; he had already watched the last year of river life make me heftier and broader of shoulder. We were perched atop the cabin of the boat, taking in the night air, which was his usual custom. Somedays, when we were moored up on a bank for a night or two, he liked us to keep a watch in shifts. Said it'd sharpen our ears and eyes some, like a knife on a whetstone.

He was a big man. Old, but one could still see he had been cut from stout timber, and that he had to have been a fearsome enemy and a powerful ally in his day. He had a beard, gray and long in the old style. His right eye had been taken from him years ago in a river quay knife fight. His face there showed a grotesque scar that he took no pains to hide. Word was that it was in that very squall where he got the cane sword from an Alabamian gambler, after the man accused him of cheating at cards. Mose joked from time to time that he exchanged the eye for that cane, which served him better than the eye had. Friends and foes alike said that Mose Bunton's carcass carried more scars than any being on the river or beyond it. And just about as many bullet holes, too, just to keep things even.

It often made me wonder how a man could carry such a reputation with pride, other than the effect of appearing tougher beyond human imagining, almost immortal-like. Mose did revel in it, though, before he got old.

"It reduces the tangles a mite," he said to me once, after he got used to me lasting longer than he expected, as a full-time crewman. I asked him what he meant.

"Ain't no bar or alley I can go into where folks will bother me no more," Mose said, casting that cyclopean eye on me with some humor. "Was a time I enjoyed it, too. I could hold my own, and I was far too good at it. Else-wise I wouldn't be here shooting the breeze with you."

Finally, Mose's gaze strayed back to the river. I thought I even heard him sigh. This would be an unusual event in itself, for men like Mose Bunton weren't given much to sighing or any other brand of emotional exhibits. The urgent trill of a whip-poorwill's call drifted to us. A raft came lazily around the bend in the distance, a man and a boy fishing from it.

He tore his one-eyed gaze from the moon-silvered river and onto me again. The expression there was not unkind this time, and it stayed on me a long moment. He seemed to be carefully weighing his next words.

"I'm a damned liar, I am," he said. Then slowly, his mouth hinted a crooked smile. That, too, was a rare thing, and I thought right then that I ought to well remember this moment, for something important seemed poised to occur.

"Hue, I never seen anyone to what the ways of this here river road comes so natural."

His chair complained with a few creaks as he sat back, watching me now with satisfaction, some unexpressed decision made.

It was true that Mose had taught me what seemed like everything there was for a keelboater to know, even though deep down I knew that could never be true. The river has a way of showing a man new things even after decades on it, as if one of its jobs was to keep him humble.

Mose taught me how to read the river, to take in and use the signs the surface will give you, almost as good as any traffic signs on a city road, if you look for them. Like a rippling fan of water telling you there is a reef there, a greasy spot that signals shoal water, the difference between a bluff reef and a wind reef, where to square up a turn and where to fall off, the tell-tale signs of a nasty sawyer – a dark slant in the water that meant a giant log of dead wood was looking to tear the guts out of your boat.

Even what taverns to frequent and which to give a wide berth, which saloons you could find a good fight at, which captains will back your play, the difference in attitudes of keel-boaters and flatboaters. Flatboats, Mose said, were nothing more than one-way floating kindling, little better than a raft, fit more for the furnace. Keelboats were the stauncher breed, any keelboat man will tell you, and takes more skill to pilot than any old raft. To skipper a keelboat held far more heft and pride. This debate alone had caused more fights on the river than anything else, even more than money, or women, or cheating at cards, believe it.

During all this river apprenticing, Mose battered me about the head only about a dozen times or so, but strangely never with his fancy cane sword or sword cane, like he did more often on Lunk and Joe. I almost hoped he would, from time to time, use those things on me rather than his open hand or fist, lest they resent me for not getting the same treatment. When it came to it, I guess you could say I endeavored to limit my mistakes and keep all his lessons from leaking out my brain. Fellows like Joe and Lunk seemed to keep it only as long as it took them to get to the next port, the next brown jug, the next whore.

"You are right river-rigged, Hue, and I am here to say I ain't seen nothing like it in all of my days."

"Thank you, sir," I uttered, not really knowing what to say.

"Don't let those wharf rats Joe and Lunk give any trouble about it, ya hear?"

"Trouble, sir?"

"You'll know what I'm breezing about soon enough, Hue. You'll know."

Of course, I had no idea what Mose was talking about. I tried not to puzzle too much about it as he trundled away to his cabin, leaving me to my watch. It did keep me from falling off to sleep, to be sure. Maybe that's what the old rooster wanted, damn his hide.

A pastoral gloom slowly draped itself over the river. Stars began to gradually dazzle the firmament, and, one by one, bull-frogs roused their throaty serenade. Joe and Lunk still had not returned from the saloons.

Later, sleep still having eluded me, I rose and went to check about the boat. The lines were secure, the roar from the taverns and saloons quieting some. The lantern was still lit in Mose's cabin. The door was slightly ajar, and I went to it, thinking to shut it securely. I peeked in, surprised that I did not hear a great snore venting from within. Mose Bunton was the undisputed World Champion of Snorers and would have served well as a warning in the fog.

Mose indeed was in his bunk, his mouth wide open, one arm splayed out to the side, clutching a wad of something in his hand. I gingerly approached, but not before scouting the little cabin to see where he had parked his sword cane, lest he use it on me for interrupting his rest. It was off in the corner, out of his reach. Relatively safe, I stepped quietly to his side.

Mose Bunton had passed away. Not a breath, not a heave of his chest. Just to be sure, I held a hand over his mouth. The air was still. I carefully folded his arms over his belly, and some paper he held dropped to the floor. I picked it up, unwadded it, and in the guttering lantern light read:

I, Moses Aristeus Bunton, being of mostly sound mind at the time of this writing, and not near of body, absent one right eye, two fingers

and a bit of scalp where a drunk Cherokee liked to prove his bravery against me and meeting a grisly end for his efforts, and knowing my time in this existence is well beyond its expiration, do hereby bequeath this here keelboat and all of its affects to one Stephen Hue, the only man known to be aforesaid Moses Aristeus Bunton's immediate orbit to possess any kind of mind for the furtherance of the Jasmine Moon's (the aforesaid boat) continued operation on this here river, or even the Big Muddy should that be expedient or necessary in any way. Any challenge to this here bequeathment by Joe Harper, Lunk Masters, or any other river rat or miscreant shall be met with Judgment from Beyond, and failing that, the courts of mortals and existing U.S. and territorial laws that may apply.
Signed this Day of September 13
The Year of Our Lord 1829

Well, if there was a feather nearby, it would have knocked me over, I'll tell you that.

I sat heavily down on the cabin deck and just stared at Mose, waiting for that old chest to rise, breathing, and that lone gray eye to scowl at me, him reaching for that cane sword or sword cane or whatever it is called to brain me with.

But he just laid there, and I didn't quite know what to make of it all. I folded Mose's will up and put it in my shirt pocket. Just to be extra sure, I grabbed an old shaving mirror Mose used to trim his beard when he felt like it (not often) and held it over his mouth. After a minute of seeing no fog, I grabbed up his blanket and gently covered him with it.

Now, men would come about their vessels in a variety of ways, usually involving violence of some kind, so a will was rarely ever heard of. Most times, a man would not even think of a will or even have time to write one before being nastily dispatched.

My old friend John Murrell lived by the philosophy, "Always have a plan." Indeed, a plan would've served me well here. But in the end, there was nothing to it but to present my crewmates with the will, along with some heartfelt words.

Certain men would've suspected foul play, maybe with poisoned food, which adds up; I often fetched Mose his supper. I braced for Joe or Lunk to make a fuss, but they didn't. I suppose they knew deep down that I was loyal to a fault, not the sort to do in the man who sheltered, protected, and taught me fiercely all that time, even for my own fortune. That, and no person or phenomenon could sever old Bunton's life before the Lord's appointed time.

Anyway, I was glad they didn't want to mutiny. I had fought by their side a time or two, so it would seem kind of unnatural to fall out. I guess that is one of my vices, though. Being loyal and whatnot. The riverside can be a flinty, dangerous place. Why that is, I don't know, other than to say I suppose it just folds into the whole aspect of the West in those days. Unforgiving and only for the stoutest souls.

Anyways, Lunk and Joe didn't even squawk when I renamed the boat after Minerva Underwood. Lunk even said, "Hell, Mose gave you the boat. It's yorn to do with what ya see fit." Not given to ambition, sure, or the sharpest blades aboard, or even close pals of mine, but they were alright, really, those two. We enjoyed many an adventure in that time, maybe enough to fill another book, if anyone has a mind to put it on paper one day.

* * *

Natchez-Under-The-Hill was, to many, a paradise of activity, much of it brazenly criminal and dangerous in nature.

One night, I found myself outside an establishment known as The Red Algerine. Besides being famous for their pork loin, which I was here for, this groggery had the enviable reputation as among the worst haunts of disreputables. That's to say the clientele was populated with what would politely be termed as border ruffians.

The amusements to be found were plenty. Cards, dice, and adventuresses abounded, accounting for The Algerine's popularity. Men with newfound coins clinking in their formerly empty pockets alighted here like crows to corn, which then drew other local mudsills, those who would relieve drunken rivermen of their gains, right expeditiously too. I myself had acquired a taste for the game of Faro in my time on the river. But I made it a habit to keep one hand on the purse in my pocket as much as I could, and always a weather eye out for sticky-fingered villains.

The Algerine at last hove into view as I tried to dodge mud puddles in the street. My mouth stung and watered at the smell of crisp pork, the welcoming ruckus of the lively saloon music to my ears.

Just then, the front door blew up into a thousand splinters, along with the cured gator skin that had always held it together while serving as splendid décor. Through the debris, into the street sailed two poor gentlemen, all tangled and cursing and bloody. Above them loomed Doaks, the enraged bartender of The Red Algerine. He was low-slung, shorter than most men in these parts, but made up for it in being built like a bull buffalo with the same disposition to match, not to mention having a nose for trouble like the best of watchdogs. I quickly stepped back, perilously near tripping over a pile of firewood.

"–and if you ever so much as darken yon Algerine's door again, you will be skinned, and I'll do the skinning!" The walls of the surrounding establishments quavered with this declaration.

It was then that Doaks realized he had destroyed his own door during this operation. He looked about at the crowd that had developed to observe this spectacle, sputtered for an awkward moment, then recovered enough to grab up the gator skin. He shook away the remaining splinters and stomped back into the Algerine, daring anyone to so much as eye him sideways.

One of the men had ended up face down in the muck, mere inches from a mound of soggy horse dump. His hat had skittered across the muddy street in this hubbub. I retrieved it and stood over him politely. "Your cap, sir, I believe?" I said.

He scrambled to his feet to regain some shred of dignity, which wasn't much. His companion, a rather gnomish, podgy sort, attempted to do likewise.

The first one who had gotten up reached out his hand in a somewhat absent fashion, not looking at me right away. He sported a roguish, chestnut brown mustache.

"I thank you, sir," he said, taking the spattered chapeau. "Very kind." He was preoccupied for the moment, glowering at his friend.

"I told you, Hercules," he went on. "I told you that you were pushing it. Did you not read my signal? Or have you forgotten that as well? Expand, I said. Expand, and not linger. We should have upped stakes for Vicksburg. I said it a month ago."

Hercules looked mighty peeved himself. "Vicksburg. Shhht. Nothing to it. It's a wasteland for this grift and you know it."

This man deposited his stained hat upon his head and finally faced me. My mouth plopped open in astonishment, but the rest of me froze on the spot. It was the smile that grabbed me first, for nobody could ever forget its wry crookedness. His blue eyes, even previously annoyed, held that familiar glint of mischievous humor as they looked me over. Now, I don't know how much I looked the same over the years, but those eyes did open a bit wider, and he belted out an astonished laugh.

"By thunder and Moses! It's you!" John Murrell declared.

Hercules gave me a sidelong look. "And this is?" he asked.

"Why, this is none other than my partner and criminal compatriot from my boy's school days. I told you about that old Buzzard Roost haunt, did I not?"

"You did, I wager a time or two, John," Mr. Plumb said. He extended a hand and we shook. "Plumb, Hercules Plumb. Pleasure, Mr...."

"Stephen Hue," I replied. Mr. Plumb nodded. "Indeed, a pleasure," he said without much trace of it evident in his voice.

John and I looked each other over again, assessing what the interval of years had done to the other. We, of course, had become young men, fuller and stronger in body. Once you looked past the mud and dirt, John had grown handsomer, damned his soul. The mustache fit him well. He had the devil's own smile to go along with it, too, with the most perfect set of choppers you might ever see. I realized at that instant that my resentment equaled my pleasure at encountering my old friend again. One's pride will do that, from time to time, raising its jealous head in just about anyone. That said, I felt myself immediately drawn to him inexplicably, as if our old friendship that had melded together all those years ago had never dimmed in any way. The only way I can really explain it is that the world seemed to have just become more comfortable, and I did not want to leave it.

This sense of unwavering confidence seemed to waft off him, even as he continued to straighten and set aright his various accoutrements.

"What brings you to these parts, dear boy?" he smoothed his splendid mustache.

"Been here a while, in truth. Riverman business," I said, not managing to reduce a sudden exaggerated, manly tone. Who knew why I even did it.

"Oh ho! We have us a Mike Fink roustabout, do we?" he answered, smiling at Mr. Plumb, who returned it noncommittally, looking down the street at some rag-peddling women.

I looked about self-consciously, but the crowd that had assembled for the earlier extravaganza had disbursed.

"I have no allusion to Fink, but I can hold my own in a squall, if that's what you mean."

"A simple jest. Of that I have no doubt. Mr. Plumb, on account of meeting my old friend, I'm afraid our present business must take a rest for the evening. I shall call on you tomorrow." Hercules seemed all too fine with this, and made off.

We ambled down the street.

"The life and work of a riverman can be useful, to be sure. Not just for the steady work, but also connections and opportunities all up and down the Mississippi," John pontificated, his thumbs riding in his vest pockets.

"There is no doubt of that," I replied. "There are always goods to transport and people to meet."

We wandered a sufficient distance from the Algerine to explore the comforts of an establishment where John was hopefully less known. This one was known unimaginatively as "Number 23."

We secured a table and began to drink and catch up, as they say. I knew I would be paying for it, somehow. And I really did not mind at all.

It turned out John and this Hercules Plumb were the agents of a confidence game that had since well fallen out of favor with the criminal class, as the general populace had become too familiar with its insidious machinations. Doaks had exposed them as charlatans, and of course, acted as Doaks would.

"Welcome to The Red Algerine," I said deadpan, and we had a good roar. Did that feel good, I swear.

"I didn't figure I'd ever run into even one of you rascals from the Roost." John wiped his mouth with a handkerchief.

"The world's a big place."

"And the river wide." He looked at me with a contented smile. "By jings, you ever wonder what happened to 'em? Bucschalter, blathering his damnable–"

"*German!*" we said together, laughing again.

"Lord, that old pirate," John sighed.

"We'd have never known if it weren't for that scalawag, Weatherby."

"True enough. And good old Hieronymus. By God, I think he actually enjoyed throwing so many white men out of Ma's!" We laughed once more, throwing back another swig to his health and Samson-like strength. My head was starting to swim like a cork in a storm-tossed sea, and it was glorious. Recalling Hieronymus brought me a warm feeling, like pride and respect, too.

Our eyes locked. I saw something unmistakable in his.

"Do you remember Minerva?" I said the name carefully.

"Do you wonder?"

"I do." I toyed with my mug a bit, lifted it to my lips, but didn't drink. Instead, I said, "Tell me you went back there and took her from that place and married that beauty."

John's smile faltered.

"Would that I could, brother. Would that I could." *Brother.* The name threw me a little, but filled me with warmth. Our friendship hadn't cooled all that much over all these years.

I finally took that sip, for something to do in the silence.

"In any case, this would be no life for her," he said. "Out of the pan and into the fire, eh?" His smile tightened, his eyes betraying a touch of sadness.

John suddenly hoisted his mug. "To Minerva Underwood, wherever she is!"

"To her health, fortune, and long life!"

"And to all our fellow Rats of the Roost! To Heaven or Hell and Perdition!"

Any sadness and regret vanished as we clicked our mugs and drank deep the rotgut rum.

John slammed down his mug, patting his coat pockets.

"Stephen, I'm ready to take some of that river air." Out came a long-stemmed pipe. I thought it amusing, as it reminded me of Bucschalter's.

We walked to the edge of town, taking a meandering path further into the woods. The air was cleaner, the noise and clatter of Natchez-Under-The-Hill becoming muted behind us. Moon-glow peeked between some gathering clouds, sifting through the trees, glistening off the rippling surface of a small stream.

"I smell rain," John said softly. The wind whistled some.

"Reminds me of Litch's Creek. Remember, where that old wagon broke? We got that Spanish flintlock from those townie boys' cave?"

"Yep. That was something else." John puffed away.

"S'pose that old son of a bitch Bucschalter sold it—" I

stopped, realizing I was getting to some darker territories of our recollections. Eight years we haven't seen one another, and here I go raising that horrendous memory like a damnable fool.

"Oh, forget that relic of a *pistole*," Thankfully, John's mind didn't seem to wander down that path. He was busy reaching deeper into his coat's breast pocket. "Look at this." Out came a pistol, not as long as that flintlock, but newer, somewhat block-ier, certainly deadlier.

"This here is a Collier five-shot." He leaned in. "Don't ask me how I got hold of it."

He handed it over, and I carefully examined it. It looked vastly different from the flintlocks I was used to, having a round cylinder under the pan and over the trigger. It looked somewhat odd, less elegant, and more business-like.

"Revolver," said John, with authority.

He took it back and raised it at a large oak tree across the stream. When he fired, flames roared from the muzzle, the report echoing loudly into the woods, setting my ears to ringing. A storm of blue-white smoke enveloped us, adding a sulfurous tang to the air. A sharp crack quickly followed, splinters show-ering as the ball tore apart a branch thick as a man's arm.

It was wonderful.

John grinned widely, pulling the hammer back again, using his other hand to pull the cylinder slightly back toward him, turning it. This aligned the next chamber with the barrel.

"This is where the 'revolving' comes in." He pulled the frizzen, which had a small box atop it (again, unlike a standard flintlock), down to rest against the pan.

"This here frizzen is filled with powder, you see, and each time you bring it down, it primes the pan all on its own. Clever, eh?"

"Indeed, John. Indeed." I was entranced by the mechanism.

"Now for you." He handed me the pistol.

I aimed. Once, I had to use both hands to lift the Spanish flintlock. This newer weapon felt good and solid in only the one. I squeezed the trigger, and it bucked mightily, smoke again wrapping us in an acrid shroud. John stared at the oak for a moment, then grinned impishly at me. "Well, it's your first try," he shrugged.

I laughed. This felt so strangely familiar, as if we had just done this very thing only days ago. John nodded, and I cocked the gun, carefully pulled back the cylinder, and rotated it.

"That's it," John approved. I locked the frizzen into place and took aim. Bark sheared off the side of the oak this time. "Huzzah!" John whooped.

We shot that clever device for a while, the wind blowing a bit more fervently as time passed. The smell of rain grew stronger.

"Come morn, this will need mighty good cleaning." John was sitting on a tree stump, tilting the copper powder flask delicately, loading the cylinder and the priming box. "But it's worth it. A fine weapon for old John Murrell, yes-sir, a fine weapon."

He laid the pistol across his lap and tipped his hat to me. "You're about a dead shot there, Stephen. That oak tree is wishing it had set its roots deeper into the woods, I'll say." I smiled and tried to wave it away modestly. This revolver was leagues from the Spanish antique we found so long ago. Fascinating technology.

After a minute, John looked up at the threatening sky. Thunder grumbled moodily in the distance. His expression turned stony. "Takes me back, this weather." Somehow, I knew right away what he meant.

"That wolf-eyed son of a bitch. That damned ugly knife."

"And us barely lads then. It just shouldn't happen. Not to kids."

Not to kids. Those precise words I once thought, but about something else. I couldn't say anything. What to say? My mind was racing through all those events, and all I could think of was that awful branding, the disgusting odor of melting flesh smothering my senses. Not to kids indeed...

John stood, putting the pistol safely away into his coat pocket, turning to face the twinkling lights of Natchez-Under-The-Hill.

"I confess giving this some fair thought over the years, old friend. In a world where men would slit up mere boys, and many innocent souls about like Minerva Underwood, folks in these parts need something like a protector. A clan with numbers enough to guard against the wolves."

I kept silent. John seemed to be mostly thinking out loud, talking to the air.

Then, ever so softly: "We were just kids..."

INTERLUDE

1877

Mr. Erastus Vinning
Secretary to Mr. A. Forepaugh
The Offices of The Forepaugh New and Colossal
All-Feature Show
Trust Company Building
Philadelphia, Pennsylvania

    August 20th, 1877

Dear Mr. Vinning,

    I have received your latest communique on
behalf of Mr. Forepaugh

    The interview of Mr. Hue continues apace.
It had eluded me how he still was in possession of the object after he and Murrell had
parted ways, but it came clear upon learning
of their reunion in their juvenile adulthood.
In rare form, Mr. Hue seemed to bask in a
fine appreciation of the object. And I quote:
"The finest weapon of John Murrell, young
sir, the finest weapon for the likes of him!
Such grand aim and focus, yes indeed."

    Notwithstanding, while I do appreciate Mr.
Forepaugh's eagerness to obtain the object,
you must understand that we are at the mercy
of Mr. Hue's stubborn demand that the whole
of his tale be told, object or no, and most
importantly, that of Mr. Murrell's is faithfully relayed. I daresay that Mr. Hue's realization that I am taking his dictation has
reinforced this notion, but I must insist

that this is a critical component in maintaining the integrity of my mission. Mr. Hue further insists that this all must be done to understand that John Murrell's entire existence must not be boiled down to just this one physical object alone. This idea seems to be unseemly in the extreme to him, and when I have brought the matter up, he becomes visibly agitated, even angry. This leads me to exercise extreme caution, as I do not want to throw the whole thing into jeopardy. I have thus approached with a great deal of patience and allowed him to expound further on the Clan Mystic's history, as it were.

I understand that Mr. Forepaugh's desire to secure this object is fueled by the possibility of his chief rival, P.T. Barnum, first getting hold of it, but I do not believe it will be in his show's interest to obtain it if it is proven to be a phony or a fraud. That development in itself could be contrived by Mr. Barnum as a matter of public ridicule and may be harmful to his reputation. I beg you to revisit the episode involving the proposal to find the horn of a pachyderm buried in the Netherlands, of all places. The one some Dutchman brought all the way from the Orient some century ago, if that even happened at all. Small wonder none of our agents agreed to take it on.

As a business matter, I believe Mr. Hue's object and story are something that should be considered on a serious basis.

Awaiting Your Speedy Reply,
R.E. McElhany, Esq.

16

Next morning, I met with John and Hercules Plumb at Connelly's, a tavern renowned locally for the blackest coffee and the heartiest grub. John had wanted to discuss prospects that might be ahead. I was open to it, just to jaw-jack with my old friend again, if anything.

It was during this unexpected reunion that John Murrell held forth on a grand design, a roadmap toward his future fortune – and mine, if I dared to ride along.

His scheme was still in its infancy, but to my shock, it involved about four large plantations along the Mississippi River. He had managed to become connected and friendly with various workers, and even Negroes, some of them slaves. Others were freed men who worked on and still populated these plantations.

As he began detailing this plan, I could see that Hercules Plumb had heard this plot before because he started to pay attention to the serving woman. She wasn't the type that would catch my eye, but Mr. Plumb did not strike me as a particularly choosy man in that regard.

"I've come upon a place called Rooks Hope. Perhaps you have heard of it?" John said.

I shrugged, as it did not ring a bell.

"It's a half mile or so inland from the riverbank, not too distant from Kaskaskia. Has its own wharf and dockside to accommodate their trade. Really an impressive plantation, as they go, in those parts."

Mr. Plumb had now wandered off to try his hand with the serving woman.

"There is a lieutenant to the overseer at Rooks Hope, a Loney Pilver by name. Mr. Pilver is a man not satisfactorily compensated for his talents, as he sees it. He told me of his frustrations while in his cups one evening. Seems he was passed over for the head overseer's position and is looking to account for that in some way."

John could see me waiting for the reason he might be narrating this.

"Your boat and skills might be useful in assisting Loney in his endeavor. If you could be so persuaded, that is."

Well, that sure did not take long, I reflected. Just reunited with the man and already roping me into his schemes. Sounded about right.

My expression must have told John that I was not so persuaded.

"I have to get upriver for another haul, John. No time for side jobs."

"Side job? Oh, no, sir. This could be *the* long haul, son."

I must have looked vexed beyond repair.

"But, for your purposes, a side job for now," John shrugged. "Potentially quite lucrative."

"John, I am happy with my lot. Business is fair."

"For now, maybe," said John. He sat back, looking more self-assured than ever, which rankled me some. I took another drink, sat back myself, and sighed, half annoyed and half amused. My best friend, even after all these years, and still, damn his cocksure insolence.

"I know you have seen those double-stackers on the river," John probed.

Of course, I had seen them, as had everyone else plying the river. They would indeed be very difficult to miss, these marvels of modern technology. There were at least two of what were called "steamboats" that I had seen several times on my regular route. Naturally, these double-stackers, these steamers, had been on the river for years, creating a large measure of competition for us smaller operators. In fact, many flatboaters and keelboaters would move their cargoes down-river and then sell the boats or break them up for firewood rather than work them back upriver for another run. They would go back upriver by ground, by the Trace, and start over again. This is where the steamers held a great advantage. A sight to admire for sure, but they also signaled the keel boat's eventual demise.

We still had an edge, though, in that we could reach tight, hard-to-get-to places along that river, much quieter. That could be a very useful thing, and I knew the type to put it to use.

"There are more and more of them, seeming to appear by the day. The competition on that river is getting fierce," continued John.

This had, in fact, crossed my mind, as well as many river-men's. I had developed something of a business savvy, even at my youthful age. One had to, in order to survive the river game. I resented John a bit for making that aspect even more lively in my mind.

"What I mean to say is you might as well find your grease now." John took a casual pull on his own tankard. He set it down.

"Of course, a man could find a passable slot working for the steamers, maybe even a snag boat come the tougher times."

Now, I was raised to appreciate honest, good work, believe it or not. And while the notion of working a snag boat – a vessel designed for the express purpose of clearing the river of navigation hazards – certainly fit that bill, it was not my ideal picture of where I wanted to be in life. We both knew John had set the hook.

"So, what does this Pilver need to move?"

Yes, Stephen Hue was a right snagged catfish just then. Once again, I felt like I wanted to meet John's approval. I couldn't account for it then, but even so, I cursed it, just for my personal lack of independence and mental fortification.

"Loney has set aside enough goods on his own to set things aright, for now," John said.

"For now," I said.

"Rooks Hope is a producer of many desirable goods. Chief among them is a somewhat refined tarantula juice."

I could not prevent a grimace. "There is no such concoction, John. 'Refined' and 'tarantula juice' do not go together. You might have better luck refining an actual tarantula."

Tarantula juice was really just a hell-spawned liquor – even the term "liquor" applied to it was overly generous – contrived typically of alcohol, tobacco plug, and scorched peaches. I wouldn't serve it to a pack of Comanches that just had their ways with my sainted mother.

John laughed. "The still masters at Rooks Hope have encountered a means to tame the untamable. There is a demand for it, believe it."

I shook my head, waving a hand for the servant woman's attention. The mere mention of tarantula juice made me dry for a more palatable spirit, just on principle.

"Well, chew on that a while, Stephen. That won't hurt.

Meantime, I have an entertaining diversion in the works. Only a spot of fun, you understand. You're welcome to string along if you've a mind to."

I raised my brows as the lady drew close, as though I wasn't committing to anything yet. And maybe so for the tarantula juice, but for this "entertaining diversion", I knew I was already caught and ready to be reeled in. A diversion was just what I needed.

17

That late afternoon, we continued north near the Trace until we came up on the town of Brashear's Post, meeting up with two men who had been dispatched there by Hercules Plumb. John addressed the senior of the two, who looked to be a veteran familiar to John and his operations. His name was Spurlock, and he was tall and stringy, but he looked to be well aware of his business, serious at all times. The other man, built similarly, was Spurlock's nephew, and he was quiet, awful quiet, as watchful a man as I ever did see. Likely nothing in his surroundings ever escaped him.

Both men gave me an unmasked, suspicious up-down look. With John's introduction, Spurlock seemed somewhat more comfortable with me, though not friendly at all. Then again, he didn't look the type to ever be friendly with anyone, even his own kids if he had any.

"You have it?" John asked Spurlock.

"Of course," he frowned, slightly offended. "It's why Herc sent me, isn't it?" He patted a case that had been strapped onto his hoss.

"And the others?"

"They are ready."

I suddenly started itching at all this. What had I gotten myself into? Adventure I wanted, yes, but I had made something of an effort during my journeys to steer clear of criminal activity, owing partly to being "brought to heel" as Magistrate McAllen demanded (Alright, it did influence me after all). Mostly, it has been a stout dedication to dear Mother, and despite not being around her, I hated thinking of her heart shattering. If she or Father were to be watching me from Heaven, the least I could do was give their spirits no need for unrest.

But this was just a one-off dallying, not a long-range turn for the worst...

We made camp on the outskirts of Brashear's Post.

* * *

Next day had me rising the earliest in the camp. Spurlock nodded a grudging good morning to me, and I wandered off to a nearby creek to refresh myself for the day.

When I returned to the camp, there before me was a John Murrell I had not yet seen. He was resplendent in what appeared to be a black frock coat, a clean white shirt with a smart black cravat, and a blocked gentleman's hat on his head, the kind preferred by the pastors of the day. And he was freshly shaved, too.

I have to say he looked altogether sharply presentable.

"Fit for a preacher, would you say?" he asked me with a grin.

"I'd say!" was my flabbergasted response.

"Ride with me, sir," he said.

We mounted our horses, which Spurlock and his nephew

had made ready for us. John winked at Spurlock, who unsmilingly tipped his hat to him as we departed.

Brashear's Post was a pleasant enough town, not too big and not too small, but a size somehow appearing to be just right for itself.

We wandered down the main street, found an out-of-the-way spot to park our horses, and began strolling happily along.

We came upon a merchant setting out some goods. John struck up a conversation with him in his easy-going way, probably made easier owing to his friendly attire.

"I've not seen you in town, before, Pastor..."

"Mylgrew, good sir," John replied. "Pastor Mylgrew, it is. And this is my long-time companion and manservant, Mr. Good."

The merchant smiled civilly and nodded toward me. I wasn't at all sure I liked being assigned the position of "manservant," if a pastor would even have one to begin with. It was as if John had elevated his position to pope in one breath.

"We are merely itinerant brothers in the Lord, sir. Bringing the Gospel to all and as far as we are humbly able. Walking, as it were, in the shoes of the Apostle Paul."

The merchant continued to smile real polite, wiping his hands on his apron, then attempting to mop off a bead of sweat on his brow.

"Well," he said, "that is as worthy an endeavor as any, to be sure. Brashear's Post always welcomes honest and worthy travelers."

"I'm sure you do," said John. "This is a pleasant, hospitable-looking little town." Then, to me, "Mr. Good, please be so kind as to pay this fine merchant for one of those apples, if you please. I dare say they have been tempting me all this time. And get one for yourself, too, while you are about it."

I tried not to bristle at this new pompous tone. He seemed

to be letting his playacting get the better of him, and he was abusing it. I went along just for the moment, knowing I was playacting for a blessedly abbreviated time. What else could I do?

We strolled on, leaving the merchant in our holy wake. John said, "We must find the tavern."

I must've looked startled at the prospect of entering a tavern right then, not only due to the hour of the day, but because John was currently in the accoutrements of a man of the cloth. This would gather certain undesired attention.

"Not to imbibe," John said, tugging primly at the lapels of his fine frock coat. Then he gave me a small, tight smile and settled back into his preacher ways.

We found the tavern: a modest building offset slightly from the main street. At a distance, it resembled part of another barn-like structure or stable. That is to say, it did not start out as a tavern, from the looks of it. As we neared, we spied a man emptying the contents of a bucket into an open ditch that ran around the back of the place.

The man nodded a greeting to us. The bucket clattered to the ground as he dropped it and wiped his hands on his filthy apron. For a horrifying moment, I thought he meant to shake our hands. Instead, he just squinted our way. His scraggly hair wisped around his face in the breeze.

"Place be open," he said. He leaned back on one foot and arched his back, stretching it. "Though it don't look it," he groaned.

"Thank you, but no, good man," John said. "I see how your customers enjoy your fare, sir."

Toward the end of that, his tone had taken on a lofty air, into a slight tenor of one who has taken offense at something.

I followed his suddenly baleful gaze, coming to rest on a

figure slumped near the end of the ditch. The one the tavern keep had just dumped the contents of the bucket into.

I instantly remembered the multiple rumpled heaps we had seen carried out of Ma Surgick's place when we were kids.

John went over and hunkered down near the man, his expression taking on severe disapproval, like one smelling something foul and disagreeable. Then he looked like a man placed in some trance, his eyes going distant. And he started to speak, as if to himself.

"Noah did the best thing and the worst for this world. He constructed an ark against the deluge of water but introduced a deluge against which the human race has ever since been trying to build an ark. The deluge of *drunkenness*!

"Ever since apples and grapes and wheat grew, the world has been tempted to unhealthful stimulations. The intoxicants of olden times were an innocent beverage, a harmless syrup, a peaceful soda water compared with the liquids of modern inebriation."

As John carried on, his voice rose ever higher. The tavern keep continued squinting through his wisps of hair. Now he rested a hand on his hip, settled back on one foot, and just listened respectfully.

"An archfiend arrived in our world, and he builds an invisible cauldron of temptation. He built that cauldron strong and stout for all ages and nations. First, he squeezed into the caldron the juices of the forbidden fruit of Paradise. Then he gathered for it a distillation from the harvest fields and orchards from the hemispheres. Then he poured into this cauldron capsicum and copperas and logwood and deadly nightshade and assault and battery and vitriol and opium and rum and murder and poverty and Death..."

I could see people from the main street taking notice of something interesting happening by the tavern. Most just paused in whatever they were about, trying to figure out what it was, it all being something out of the ordinary in their humble town. By and by, some trickled over to listen for a spell. One man rode in on an impossibly large dray horse. He stopped the horse mid-street, dismounted, and tied it to a post. He then walked over and sat on the ground to listen to John, well away and upwind of that ditch.

"...If I could gather all of the armies of the dead drunkards and have them come to resurrection, and then add to that host all of the armies of living drunkards, five and ten abreast, and then if I could have you mount a horse and ride along that line for review, you could ride that horse until he dropped from exhaustion, and you would mount another horse and ride until he fell from exhaustion, and you would take another and another. A great host, in regiments, in brigades. Great armies of them. And then if you had a voice stentorian enough to make them all hear, and you could give the command! Forward, march! Why, their first step would make the earth tremble...

"I tell you, folks gathered here, what many of you may never have thought of, that today the Church holds the balance of power in America. If Christian people, the men and women who profess love for the Lord Jesus Christ and to love purity and to be sworn enemies of uncleanness and debauchery and sin... If all such would march side by side and shoulder to shoulder, this evil would be overthrown. Think of three hundred thousand churches and Sunday schools in Christendom marching as one! How very short a time it would take them to put down this evil, if all the Churches of God were armed on this subject!"

The eyes of some gathered shone with a sort of martial fervor, like they would take up righteous arms in the struggle if they were just given the word.

"Young men of America, pass over into the army of teetotalism. Whiskey, excellent to preserve corpses, ought never to turn you into a corpse. Tens of thousands of young men have been dragged out of respectability, and out of purity, and out of good character, and into darkness by this infernal stuff called 'Strong Drink.' Do not touch it! Do *not* touch it!"

John's shoulders slumped. He took a deep breath, sighed it out, and his head dropped some, like he was spent.

The crowd was silent for a long moment, staring at John. I'm not at all sure if they expected more or were just letting the message of his sermon wash over them, a sort of verbal baptism.

The tavern keep was still watching too with that ever-present squint (I don't think his eyes knew how to do anything else). After a moment, he leaned over and spat into the ditch.

"That was a goodly speech, mister." He then picked up his bucket and stalked back into his establishment, banging the door behind him.

A trio of ladies from the crowd approached John, led by a stout, matronly woman all trussed up in a dark blue dress, her hair hidden by a slightly frilly but generally modest bonnet. John tipped his hat handsomely to them and one to the rear-ward of the group, a moonfaced young lady with pretty blue eyes, blushed like a raspberry down to her ruffled collar. John likely had that effect on the ladies through the years, without so much as a sweat, either.

The stout, matronly woman was untouched by his gallantry, but did give him a courteous smile, "Sir, might I say that was quite a powerful essay on one of the many blights on mankind we presently endure."

"Why, thank you, ma'am."

"You must have benefited from extensive and exhaustive instruction from the seminary, Mr..."

John introduced himself, basically with the speech he had dispensed to the merchant, a humble traveling Apostle Paul type, so on and so forth. And I was still his even more humble "manservant." He then began expounding on the Gospel itself and his undying love of it. Although his real passion was taking The Word to the known Dens of Decadence and Iniquity along the Trace, he yearned to also bring it and sing it to the various flocks throughout the townships. This was, apparently, to keep his preaching "brushed up" and "polished to a shine." This last comment seemed a touch immodest, and I thought the ladies might recoil from that. But they didn't, which might have to do with that little sparkle I swore I saw from that radiant smile of his that likely undid many a gal.

I'd begun to wonder about the entire purpose of all this playacting – amusing as it was – although I had surmised some of it by then. At that point, I was just there to watch it play out.

And here it came.

"Why, Mr. Hapscomb – my husband," said the stout matron, "is a deacon with the church here, and I just know he could influence Pastor Bartholomew to lend his pulpit to you to assist in furthering your worthy message."

And she really did bat her eyes at him, stunning me good. I never saw any real female do that before, only read about such things occurring, so up to then, I thought it might just be some writer's flight of fancy. The very notion seemed so silly. What were such a gesture's practical aspects?

John thanked them profusely, fawning more than I felt warranted or even believable. Then again, he was in his element and surely knew his business better than I did.

The appointed day arrived, and after ensuring John's "preacher rags" were properly immaculate, we rode back into Brashear's Post, direct to their somewhat plain but somehow still pretty clapboarded church, shining brightly in a new coat of paint – at least on one side of it. It seemed to be a work-in-progress, but that didn't keep these good town folk from its utilization. It possessed no bell tower, just a bell the size of a small cask hung on the corner of it, presently being rung with earnest zeal by a serious-looking lad who had to be told firmly more than once to quit it.

"He'd ring it all day, if I left him be," said Pastor Bartholomew, a round, kind-faced man. "He's not simple, but he acts it some, and only on Sundays. It's a mystery."

"One can't help but admire his enthusiasm," John smiled.

With the bell's tone still humming in our heads, we settled in. John was taking in the congregation's measure, and his gaze fell on the moon-faced gal with the pretty eyes, the one surveying his landscape days before. Somehow, he got away with a quick wink to her, and she about swallowed a gallon of air all at once and made a loud, unladylike gulping sound. The boy next to her in the pew – maybe her brother, for he possessed the exact moon face, only his eyes looked like beady raisins – snapped a look over like he was expecting to see the hornet or horse fly that had given her a good bite.

Pastor Bartholomew got up and said a few words introductory to the day's worship, and a few songs were sung, including an invitational I recalled from my kid days. I don't know the name, but I do remember Mother saying these were her favorite words from that song:

Here see the bread of life, see waters flowing
Forth from the Throne of God, pure from above
Come to the feast of love; Come ever knowing
Earth has no sorrow but heav'n can remove.

She could not thoroughly explain it, she said, but that passage always moved her.

I got pretty sad right then, hearing those words sung again by good people. It even choked me up some, too.

John looked at me kind of sideways, then carefully handed

me his pristine, blocked hat, silently reminding me that I was his "manservant," and to restrain myself.

When John took the pulpit, it was with full authority, just like this was his own flock for his entire pastoral career, and he had been leading them to the Promised Land all this time. He paused, surveying the flock with a kindly paternal eye. Then he began.

"There is nothing that keeps wicked men at any one moment out of Hell, but the mere pleasure of God. There is no want of power in God to cast even wicked men into Hell at any moment. Men's hands cannot be strong *when God rises up!*"

Why, John had them in his grips right then, and he kept on it, never letting up. The folks sitting in that humble little church sure were mesmerized for a good while.

Sometime amidst this, the flock was jarred from their reverie by shouting from outside, followed closely by the unmistakable clatter of hooves. John looked concernedly at the main doors when they burst wide open.

The boy who had been forever ringing the bell was there.

"The hosses!" he shouted. "They's after the hosses!"

A pistol shot rang out, and the men jumped to their feet and tried to exit the main doors all at once. The women screamed, as did the girls. One boy tried to make an exit, a shocked, but excited half-smile on his face. Probably thinking, "At last, some excitement around here." Alas, he was held fast by a woman who was white as a sheet. She wasn't screaming or shouting, but her lower lip was quivering like she was a landed trout.

It was pandemonium outside. Spurlock was there on his own horse, holding two other horses' traces. There were about five other men there, too, mounting the other congregants' horses and riding off on them.

Suddenly, I could not move. I was doing it. John's arm

carried the mark of a very serious crime in those days: horse thieving. And I was part of it. I gagged on just the memory of the smell from the branding. Coggin's ugly, crow-eyed face loomed from memory, cawing *horse thief horse thief horse thief.* Father's dark countenance at the slander. I cursed myself, my heart breaking, because despite everything, I wanted this. I didn't know it until this moment, but I craved the danger of it, the wrongness. There was no reasoning or logic, but I *had* to have it, this ruckus, this chaos.

Spurlock's silent friend was there too, a horse ready for John. He sprang up onto it like an ape and whipped out that cleverly invented revolver from inside his coat. He fired it, apparently deciding there was not enough of a cacophony engulfing the church. A sharp musical note rose and lingered, vibrating above the other noises, drawing my gaze to the bell, now marred by an impressive dent on its top. A mad laugh barked out of me at the sheer audaciousness. I loved it. Dear God, but I loved it.

There was some screaming, crying, and moaning from the women and children, as well as dust flinging about copiously. And cussing, too, from some men, which surprised me as they were just listening to John's sermon like polite angels just a minute before.

Pastor Bartholomew stumbled forth from the church doors, looked about, and spotted John.

"The devil's preacher!" he hollered, his voice choked with outrage. "That's what you are!" He stabbed an accusing finger at John. "Devil preacher! And may you be damned! Damned for all eternity!"

The ever-growing clouds of dust seemed to overcome him, and he leaned falteringly against the wall of his church. "Devil preacher!" he managed to croak again.

John held out a hand to me.

"Mr. Good. If you please!" he shouted over all of the caterwauling.

I felt a happy grin splitting my face all at once, and I hopped on the horse, almost as ape-like as John had. The battle in me was won.

The horse spun around in a cyclone of dust, then dramatically reared up before tearing off down the road, and to this day, I wonder if that was by John's design. No telling how many lads' and girls' young minds this had left an indelible impression of excitement and daring. It would have for me, I know that.

Bullets were whickering by us now, and I felt one tug ever so slightly on the shoulder of my coat like an impatient schoolmarm.

Here we were, a dozen bad men, thundering away into the woods in a fiery escape, and a real thrill raced through me like it had never done before.

We rode hard for quite a time.

I was the happiest I had been in a long, long time, maybe ever.

<h1 style="text-align:center">18</h1>

We eventually reduced our pelting to a healthier trot. Our mounts certainly needed it, and we had to catch our own breath.

"A fine job, boys," John called to the gang, his eyes bright and smile broad.

"As lively a dance as we've had in a while, John," said a man with a face as long as his pony's, flashing a near-toothless grin.

"That it was, Pearson, that it was!"

"I'm a bad man," said another, this one chomping a cigar to death, still holding a heavy slouch hat atop his head as if we were still storming along. "But I never thought I'd ride with the devil hisself!"

"That's devil *preacher*, Donagal! And don't forget it neither, you ignorant heathen." This from a lanky, red-haired man with a full, impressive beard halfway down his chest, though his body brimmed with energy like a squirrel's. He guffawed hoarsely. "By God, Johnny, that was a hell of a shot on that bell. Best I've seen. You left them something to remember you by, too! Every time they ring it!"

"Obliged, Brer Lucias. Much obliged." John laughed, loud and deep. "Poor old Pastor Bart. I thought his ticker would fail him, right there on that church porch."

"He gave you a gift, John," said another man, this one riding a handsome sorrel like he was born to it. He was large of stature, easily the biggest of the group, bald as an egg but with a shaggy mustache as black as midnight, and sharp, intelligent eyes. John looked at him, searching. "Notoriety," the man said. "It'll go a long way."

"Mark it well, Matthews," John nodded. "I intend to use it."

* * *

The sun was dipping below the horizon as we made camp in a small, low valley, scouted out competently by the still sullen Spurlock. The men were freely passing a jug of rum.

They had taken to teasing Matthews, who had a disarmingly sensitive side despite his physical appearance. One of the younger, less tactful others was plaguing the poor man with all kinds of inquisitive questions about his moniker Clubber, which he clearly didn't cotton to. Eventually, he was so wearied that he gave in and began telling the tale.

"–Well, this old skunk wouldn't just let it be. I tried to ignore him. He was yapping at me like a damned rich woman's dog, too big for his britches, trying to prove something, I suppose. And drunk on top of it. So, I whirled around and before I knew it, I had one fist over his head and brought it down like a sledge. I just wanted to quiet him down, is all–"

"Oh, he quieted down, alright," Brer Lucias smirked. "Through all eternity! Ha! Eyeball sprung from his skull like a cork on New Year's Eve, too! Made a sound just like it too, didn't it Clubber?" Brer Lucias combed his red beard with his hand, all too happy with himself. "That's where it came from, that name. Clubber!" He let out a raspy guffaw, and the men joined in as Clubber scowled.

According to Lucias, muleskinner Clubber Matthews was the only man left standing after a brawl with the gang (they, of course, were the troublemakers). The rest of John's men were too afraid to fight him. John finally talked him into joining by pointing out no one else would riddle his hide with blade or ball from then on, if he helped them with the odd heist and security now and then. Damnedest way to enlist people I had ever heard.

"This man knows his business," John nodded in Donagal's direction as he broke out his fiddle, beginning to tune it up.

"Devil preacher," He brought out his pipe, sparking it to life. "Stephen, I am warming to it, now that I think on it. And christened on holy grounds too, imagine!"

I laughed softly and sipped at my tin cup of rum, staring into the crackling fire. The aroma of something tantalizing was coming from the stew pot hanging over it. I only then realized how hungry I was. Donegal struck up a lively, vaguely familiar tune.

"Ah," John grinned. "Soldier's Joy." He leaned toward me. "A favorite of the boys."

I looked over at the horses, picketed nearby, calmly chewing the bushes. A certain curiosity had nibbled at me for hours underneath all the excitement.

"Why, John? Why this? You know, horse..." The next word died on my tongue; I couldn't bring myself to utter it. "After..."

John followed my gaze, his satisfied smile faltering just a hair. He glanced at me knowingly, as if he expected this question in due course. There was a soft click as he clamped his pipe in his mouth, looking into the fire. His free hand absently grasped his sleeve.

"You witnessed it, Stephen. You saw the world mark me."

His voice became strained, bitter. "With its wisdom. Its *justice*. H. T. Burned forever." From across the fire, Matthews studied us with a serious eye. "I resolved to show the world. Show it if that's the way they wanted it, I'd be the best God-damned horse thief they'd ever seen. They'd remember it. Eternally."

Donegal's tune had reached its end. There was a loud pop and crack from the fire. "Another, another!" cried Brer Lucias.

"At least give a man room to breathe and drink some rum, damn your ever-flapping mouth!"

"He never runs out of steam, does he, the silly boy," Another man cuffed Brer Lucias, half-exasperated, half-amused.

Pearson stirred the stew pot, chuckling.

"Yes, they shall remember it, I wager you." John stared into the fire, paying the hubbub no mind. His eyes were distant. "And there would be more besides, things beyond even this old world's imagining. I see an empire. An empire that will carry my name through the ages."

The wind soughed through the trees. Donegal began a slow, sorrowful tune.

I thought of Father in that moment. A man such as he would never know the law's scorn or the exiling from polite society. It was for the better, naturally. But it was not for me. I didn't know why, exactly, but I knew it certainly.

"You're fixed in your path, Stephen." John had resumed his formerly content and relaxed state. "Your *Minerva Underwood* – a deserved christening there." He barked a laugh, reaching for his tin of rum. "But let us enjoy this for now, shall we? Then you can be on your way. I'll load you up with gifts first thing tomorrow – come, I'll hear no argument now, I won't."

I looked around at this camp of happy thieves. "On my way...?"

John cocked his head. "You have your own business, Stephen, and I respect that. Far be it from me to direct a man's course for him all his life."

I started a little. I might have been moved by such talk the day before, but now I was not so certain. "I... well, I might just tag along, John. For this one river job, if you'll still have me, that is."

His eyes sparkled, but he dipped his head as earnestly as he could, and hoisted his tin. "Whatever you choose, Stephen. I'll be content to have you at my side."

Our tins clicked, and we downed the rum together.

* * *

Loney Pilver stood on the riverside wharf of plantation Rooks Hope, appearing to be a man of confidence and no nonsense whatever. He was a tall man with bushy grey lambchop whiskers framing his face. He fastened penetrating blue eyes on me as I stepped onto the wooden platform.

John read Pilver's posture. "Stephen's a man what deals square, Pilver, not to worry."

Pilver spat on the wharf, his eyes not leaving me. "See to it."

I simply nodded briefly by way of greeting as I completed tying off the *Minerva* to the wharf, which looked seldom-used until very recently. Some hasty repairs had been done to it of late, where very old wood had been replaced. Rooks Hope appeared to be one of the older plantations, based on this alone.

A collection of three slaves swiftly and efficiently began loading the contraband, contained in various-sized crates and barrels, with Pilver finding it necessary to bat one about the head only once with his walking stick to accelerate the operation. They seemed experienced with this, and I had no doubt that Pilver used only certain slaves to conduct the work when it came time. Still, how long could even slaves be trusted to hold such information in confidence?

I ended up convincing myself that it was not my concern. After all, I was only the transporter. Even if others at Rooks Hope got onto the operation, surely their attention would be on Pilver alone.

John had previously arranged a transaction with a fence some twenty-five miles upriver. A secure enough distance to prevent anyone from tracing the goods very well. John had assured me that Mr. Pilver was careful in removing all indications of the goods' origins.

* * *

We sat on the *Minerva* in an inlet not far from Mud Hollow and divided up the take. John took the larger percentage, on the grounds of being the founder. Mr. Plumb's take was second to John's, but not by much, as they were longtime partners. As transporter of a healthy – or unhealthy – burden of risk, the *Minerva* herself could be seized and perhaps even destroyed in an altercation with the law or any business rivals, so I was generally happy with my portion.

Mr. Plumb produced a jug and began pouring a dram or three of celebratory toasts of tarantula juice for each of us. Against my better judgment, I did partake. John politely refused his, however. "Never touch the stuff," he said, chuckling satisfactorily. He dealt out cards on a keg table, and I proceeded to find inventive ways of losing some of my profit.

It was at this point that my life's path took yet another turn. The relative ease of this line of work, coupled with the thrill of illicit activity and the prospect of apprehension, has reminded me of the life I knew deep down was truly my destiny. The absence of danger – really of any sort, except maybe drowning – made the life of a simple cargo riverman seem dull as concrete, one worthy of complete abandonment.

19

FORTUNATELY, my latest career decision folded in nicely with the rising popularity of this particular brand of tarantula juice, as John promised. Conversations with Mr. Pilver, as infrequent and blunt as they usually were, led me to believe that he had discovered a secret ingredient that made it so. This, he guarded jealously.

For many months, the business thrived. I discovered I really was in my element once settled in. We had even begun making enough money to invest in new boats and had modified them to improve operations on the river and the many areas along it where we conducted the meat of our business – the bayous. A bit shallower drafts, where it did not compromise the cargo capacity, were used where possible. We also found a necessity for armaments, due to extra run-ins with river pirates operating from various shady islands all along the Mississippi.

The *Minerva* now sported a swivel gun on her bow when we were on the river. This addition came highly recommended from a Louisiana trader, who assured me it was of the exact design of the swivel gun that Lewis and Clark had employed on their famous journey of exploration. If I recall in my boyhood reading, Lewis and Clark often used them to scare off hostile Indians and salute any fort that they might approach. These were rather like oversized shotguns that fired grapeshot – a collection of small, marble-sized balls, generally for repelling boarders. Some forts were known to even use them on their walls. They were loaded from the breech, rather than the muzzle, like the larger cannons, and could be moved around the boat if called for. I mounted mine in a way that would allow easy removal before entering a legitimate port. The less attention received from authorities, the better, you understand. Old Mose Bunton would have boldly boasted such a weapon on his boat, but he was a different breed than I.

Our latest mission saw us setting off again from Rooks Hope to points north, ducking into an estuary close to Port Hudson. It seemed like regular business. We groped our way close to shore most of the way, just beyond reach of the tangle of tree branches and various river growth. John commanded our second boat on this outing. *Minerva* took the lead.

We listened carefully for our connecting merchants, using prearranged call signs and signals. Rarely did our shore-bound counterparts spark a torch, in the event they might be spied by another pirate about, or an officer of the law. Which is why, as we rounded a small jutting portion of the shore, we were shocked by a veritable collection of torches waiting for us on a flat-bottomed bateau bristling with armed men.

"Heave to!" a commanding voice bellowed from the craft.

"What the hell is this?!" John growled from the bow of his boat.

"A trap!" Hercules Plumb exclaimed unnecessarily.

Almost without thinking, I had begun bringing my boat about. John mimicked my orders to his own crew. We had fortunately acted in time to get the jump on the other vessel.

They had apparently relied too much on the simple element of surprise to shock us into paralysis. Also, it was a much larger craft than our two keel boats, and to my eye, it appeared to take much more to get it moving.

A large gun cracked to life on the larger vessel, sounding much more formidable than our swivel gun.

The ball whistled overhead. One of my crewmen scrambled to the swivel gun and made ready to load it, as we had drilled during firing practice. But I stopped him short with a thump to his head, which hurt my hand a little. Not that I noticed it much, owing to the flurry of action. These other boats were not in range of the swivel gun and would have been a waste of time and energy.

"Heave to, or I will fire into you!" hollered the voice again, still wallowing around to come after us. Just then, I detected a touch of Irish brogue to that voice.

Our boats completed coming about and came very near to taking the river main, the crews furiously plying long poles to push off of the river bottom until they could pole no longer. They then took to oars, or even any item aboard that would suffice to propel the boats.

The Irishman continued his bellowing as they continued the chase.

Another boom from their cannon rumbled unnervingly close by, sounding like a heavy runaway wagon on a rough road. An enormous geyser of water shot up from the river where the ball had struck the surface. We plowed the boat through the waterfall that followed the geyser, and as we emerged under it, the rush of the water was replaced by a curious, loud buzzing by my ear, like an overlarge, prehistoric bumblebee. It was followed very shortly by another, this one even closer as the air rippled by my head. My brain gibbered maniacally that our pursuers had now taken to their rifles.

My skin crawled knowing my back was exposed to them, and I shrank as low as I was able, still manning the *Minerva's* tiller.

My scalp felt like it was on fire, and my eyes darted about, searching for a way, any way, out of this fix. *What's the plan, now, John Murrell?!* His cocksure phrase pecked at my brain like a mad raven: *AlwayshaveaplanAlwayshaveaplanAlwayshaveaplan...*

I wiped water from my face with my sleeve and peered forward. A quick count told me my crew was all still there, but one man – the one who started to load the swivel gun – was now struggling with his pole, his eyes bright with panic. He was grasping at the pole, trying to pull it to him. The pole refused to move. I realized it was fixed fast to something on the river bottom, in the mud, or snagged on a sodden log. The current suddenly grew swifter. He would be dragged overboard if he kept at it.

"Leave it!" I screamed. A nasty crackling sound shredded the air as another rifle shot splintered the boat's rail. The crewman released the pole and hunkered down, looking for another he could use, or anything else he could paddle with.

Another boom, but this one thankfully sounded a bit further from us. Blessedly, the rifle fire had stopped. The river's swift current and the inky darkness were aiding us. Eventually, we managed to make another deeper estuary further south. Hopefully, we could conceal ourselves long enough to emerge and return to base.

John jumped to the *Minerva* after covering his own boat with branches and foliage near the shore. "Let us confer," he said quickly.

We walked to the low-slung roof of the cabin on *Minerva*. I rested an elbow there while John produced a pipe and began packing it.

"That was a close-run thing," he said, in a rather matter-of-fact and calm fashion.

"That varmint was intent, I'll say that," I said.

Mr. Plumb then joined our committee.

"I would wager my share that scoundrel was none other than Mandley," he said.

John and I looked at him.

"Surely you have heard," Mr. Plumb said, somewhat defensively.

"Do tell," invited John with a puff on his pipe.

"Works for Tedder and Company, is the word."

We waited for more. Tedder was a steam company, still fairly new hereabouts.

"They've set river patrols. 'Mitigate black market and piracy,' I believe the bill said."

"Bill?" I asked.

Mr. Plumb waved over a crewman by the name of Withey. "This bill you seen, down to Port Gibson, recruiting river crews. What's it about?"

Withey wiped his brow. "Looking to crew up patrol boats. They's wanting to grasp control of this stretch, for now. 'Smooth the trade out,' the Tedder man said to me."

"Smooth the trade," John said. He clapped Withey on the back and sent him on his way. He then turned to Mr. Plumb, who shrugged lamely. "They fancy themselves as their own government, do they?"

"I thought you knew," he replied plaintively.

"No matter," John said. "We must adjust to this, that is plain."

He gave instructions to the crews. We split up and made our ways separately back to our headquarters.

By the time we had reached them, word had spread considerably. The name Mandley seemed on every tongue, and with it an air of mystique and danger. He had already become a thing of myth and imminent doom. Through much wrangling, negotiating, and greasing of skids, John reeled in some tangible information tying this Mandley to the real world.

"This man is a formidable force, it seems," he briefed us over drinks at our favorite doggery. "And he is no pretender. Served his royal majesty's Navy at none other than Trafalgar and on the West Africa Blockade. Ran down slavers."

"The man for the job, eh?" I said, and took a liberal puff on my cigar.

"Indeed."

I could see the wheels turning, John's mind burning the coal.

"Mr. Mandley's efforts to assemble these river patrols are in their infancy. Still, I do not believe direct confrontation is a solution, even at this juncture."

"Perhaps lay low for a time?" offered Hercules Plumb.

"We have customers," John replied. He puffed several times in quick succession on his pipe, always an indication his mind was churning.

I thought, with a wince, of my unused swivel gun and if I would ever get to hear it boom in anger. That opportunity may have already passed.

"Gentlemen," said John, "I intend to maintain our presence on this river, no question to that. Perhaps it is time to broaden our land-based operations."

Conversation then turned to connections that had been made on the Natchez Trace, at the various stands that strung along it. Thus far, our trade had made its way to the nearer stands almost exclusively. Establishments that catered to travelers going both north and southbound. There were still many travelers and traders who utilized it, depending on their given situation. From Nashville to Natchez and back. Some rivermen would take a shipment downriver, then sell or scrap the boat, and travel by land back up to Nashville or beyond rather than try to work back upriver against the predominant current.

We had fairly steady customers stretching even beyond Port Gibson, at Coon Box Stand and even as far as Haye's Stand, which lay just south of Jackson.

As we discussed the details of expanding our land-bound smuggling, I could see that the Mandley Problem, as it came to be known amongst the crews, still gnawed at John some.

It was not so much that he had been beaten – however temporarily. Indeed, he did not even see it that way. He characterized it as a mere setback, as anything a businessman might encounter in any other trade. A bad 'shine batch, say, or some crew members jailed somewhere inconvenient. I had seen John work around such things without agonizing too much, almost shrugging them off, with that wicked smile, "Just part of the trade, lads!"

In the case of Mandley, however, it seemed a challenge to something above John's ability to conduct business, instead closer to posing an obstacle to his overall burgeoning ambition for a higher criminal purpose, aimed well beyond mere smuggling of tarantula juice and other black-market products.

I had seen glimpses of this ambition from time to time, of course. Conversations around the drinking and card tables where he described a vast, far-reaching criminal organization at which only he was at the main control. It came up more often with him of an evening, in the taverns and at camp. He was always fishing around for a name to pin on it, too, to "give the organization more weight," as he put it.

In any case, John still plotted to stunt Mandley's effect on our river business, and I knew at some point that some kind of action would become necessary.

By this time, our crew had grown to enough numbers to

more or less expedite our expansion inland along the Trace. After all, many of them were from the area and knew the back trails and terrain better than anyone. They also knew the people who operated the various stands and establishments as well as they knew their own families. Their entire lives, in fact. So it did not take too long to establish a steady business, prodding John and myself to wonder why we had not already struck out on such a plan.

To aid our efforts, there was little to no presence of the law in most parts where we operated. Highwaymen and cutthroats could generally be counted on to appear anywhere at any time, but our crew was able to provide fairly reliable security.

It was like John said, after all: "Folks in these parts need something like a protector. A clan with numbers enough to guard against the wolves." Numbers indeed. Mandley or no, lawful fear or no, every week saw our ranks swell with men hungry for coin, and young fools thirsting for glory. And the Devil Preacher looked on this, and said it was good.

20

I MUST POINT out at this juncture that what our descendants will term the United States of America truly was the Wild West during my time. You might not think of the Mississippi River as such, but it was as wild as beyond, even to the Big Muddy. Any laws or regulations were more or less set up by various regions on either side of the river. Oh, there were marshals and sheriffs and even judges here and there, but they typically haunted the general areas of so-called civilization and not yet what was still the frontier terrain on the Natchez Trace. Any laws imposed were those of the stout men who formed the security arms of the merchants who hired them. Much in line, John said, with the practices of the ancient days of medieval Europe, when pack trains traveled here and about to sell their wares.

Though the river had absorbed the bulk of that traffic in recent years, there were still tradesmen and merchants who would brave the trail. Longer travel, but generally cheaper.

Which is where I came in. John had assigned me to supervise the bulk of the land operation, which I was happy to do, though most of my experience involved river traffic. Part of the reason is that I was still somewhat rattled at the memory of our first encounter with Mandley's boat, though I would never openly admit that to anyone, much less John.

I was also the supreme skipper over the *Minerva Underwood* and her crew, generally outside the oversight of John or Hercules Plumb, as we had agreed upon at the outset of the partnership. I had *Minerva* hidden in a secluded estuary, for all practical purposes, "laying low" until we had the Mandley Problem sorted out. I left one crewman with her to watch for pirates or assorted scalawags – or Mandley himself. He would instantly scuttle her if the need arose.

* * *

I was cooling my heels and relieving my thirst at Old Factor's Stand, where we had just secured a contract for our various goods. It had been a long trail, so the crew and I felt it was within our rights to rest and recreate. A lively dice game had attracted most of the boys, and I leaned against the wall to sip my ale in peace and observe.

"Well, I'll be hanged for a Philadelphia lawyer!" A man entered from one of the side halls of the establishment, beaming toothily. "Stephen, you seven-times-a-rascal! It seems a coon's age."

"It does." I smiled. Charles was always a friendly sort to me and the boys whenever we darkened his door, though this was the first time we were officially selling him our stock now that we were venturing landwards. He looked around, pleased with the turnout in the place.

"Business has never been better."

"I see it."

"You have a say in that, too." He threw me a wink.

I laughed, but it caught up short as I spied a pretty gal on the other side of the room. She was as petite as a ballerina, with lovely red curls.

"Pray, excuse me a moment," I straightened from my slouch against the wall and adjusted my accoutrements. I figured that I might go speak to the lonesome lady.

I took no more than a step when a young man approached her, a tiny baby in his arms. Defeated, I resumed my slouch against the wall. Charles chuckled good-naturedly, winking at me again. He had been watching slyly. "That there is Persephone. Ain't she about the loveliest thing?"

"Indeed," I muttered, playing along.

"My daughter, you lunk. And married just a year now."

"Charles, you have my sincere congratulations." I shook his hand.

"He treats her like a princess," he sighed, watching the happy couple with tender eyes.

As he bustled away, I thought of my own family just then. Father hunkered down, gathering chunks of earth from his plowed field in his big hand with a satisfied smile. Mother in her apron, sweeping her stone walk clean, as always. Tiffany scrunching up her face in a bratty smirk. I missed my parents more than I realized. They would be middle-aged by this time. How was Tiffany faring? She would no doubt be married herself by now, maybe raising a family of her own. Would I one day do the same? Meet a Persephone of my own, settle down, build a home together...?

But this business with John wasn't doing too shabby. Why, in a few months, we were hauling in what the average man might earn honestly in a year. I was pocketing five hundred a month when the everyday dock worker was earning eighty, tops.

Ruminations about domestication evaporated. I was having

a hell of a lot more fun adventuring, and my chest puffed with pride thinking about the gang and what it stood for: Independence, brotherhood, and true liberty. And I was with my old friend John.

In short, I was living the life.

In came three men with an immediate air of surliness about them. They looked around at the other customers, like they were all about swinging fists now, no questions later.

I observed them while trying earnestly to look like I wasn't.

They stalked up to the bar, where Charles had his back to them. When he turned about, he blanched immediately. A man never looked so guilty to me. There was no doubt he was a man who had been caught at something.

"Charles," the first man greeted. He had the clearest, most sonorous voice outside of Hieronymus'. It fairly pierced the hubbub of the bar and reached me as if he were standing right in front of me.

Charles was almost as white as the label on the bottle in his hand.

The man who had addressed Charles looked at him squarely, and apparently in a form of greeting, smacked his lips. A curious gesture, but Charles appeared to understand its meaning perfectly, for he quailed under this man's gaze even more.

"What's on the menu, Charles?" That bell-like voice pressed.

"Th-th-the usual fare," stuttered that shaken barman.

The man stared.

"Usual... Usual fare, I'm afraid," continued Charles.

The man looked slowly around the establishment. The gesture looked like it was strictly for the show of it, not to actually take in what his eyes beheld. For one heartbeat, his eyes rested on me, as if somehow I stood out to him. Then they moved on.

"I heard it warn't so usual, Charles. That you've come about some new stock."

"Well..." Charles said, trying to buy time. He grabbed up a filthy rag and started busily wiping the counter with it. His eyes involuntarily darted to me. In my mind, I heartily thanked him for that.

The man swiveled his eyes back my way and looked dead at me. He looked for all the world like a man who was used to his gaze alone wilting men on the spot.

Although I did not have a reputation as a scrapper – I preferred to employ what intellect and charm I possessed to propel me from tight squeezes – I could hold my own if hard pressed. I always carried a leather sap on my person in these places.

Several moments passed where this man let his steely, intimidating gaze do its work on me, even as he walked to where I sat. His two shadows advanced too, keeping a respectable distance behind him.

The clientele quieted a great degree, or at least reduced whatever activity they might be engaged into a crawl, so that they could take in whatever spectacle may have developed.

This was shaping up to be a standard bar brawl. Persephone and her husband gathered their child and made hastily for the door. Poor Charles was clearing what shelves he had of his best products, which took all of five seconds, belying his age. The rest, mostly in unlabeled jugs and other vessels of wildly varying shapes, sizes, and qualities, were left to suffer whatever damages were pending. I noticed in a fleeting moment that three jugs of newly-installed tarantula juice were among that number.

The man addressed me directly in that clarion voice.

"You're that lot from Natchez-Under."

It sounded all-in-one purpose, both statement and question. My thoughts ran by at an ever-quickening pace and observed that this was either a very efficient means of communication or a stupid waste of time and breath.

"Aren't we all."

Those same thoughts, now recorded for future consideration, confirmed that it was, in fact, an inane and useless response. Its design, of course, was to buy what little time was left.

My mind groped for a plan, considering our gang's numbers here in the stand. I had five men here, his three here before me, but how many were outside?

Fortunately, the man ignored my limp response.

"This stand, and all them stretching four up and four down the trail from here, is strictly Colbert-claimed."

"Colbert?"

Now I could see I had struck a flinty spot, for I saw a spark in his eye with that query.

His shadows advanced half a step more.

"I'm sorry. I am not familiar," I said calmly.

I was, of course, familiar. Everyone knew the Colbert name in these parts, owing to the efforts of Chief Levi Colbert's dealings with the U.S. government.

There were many Colberts about, though, and having never met Chief Levi, or the Itte-Wamba Mingo in the Chickasaw Nation, I could not confirm that this man bore any family resemblance.

The spark in his eyes betrayed some semblance of humor, for he knew well and good how far flung the Colbert name had reached.

"Just know that you've stepped into it, this time," he said. "*I'm* Colbert."

He assumed a stance that told me that, at this point, his shadows would begin the job of rousting me and my competing goods out of this establishment. My hand slowly reached for the sap.

At this moment, Providence took it upon herself to smile upon me.

Clubber entered the bar.

All activity ceased with a jolt of quiet. Colbert swiveled his gaze to the giant who had to literally duck his head to enter through the doorway built for average-sized mortals.

Colbert and his shadows did not betray the least amount of fear, if there was any to begin with. For that, I will have to give them unflinching credit.

Clubber moved through the room, making his way to the bar, wiping his hands on a white cloth naturally turning it dirty (it was his turn to tend the hosses). He looked over at me, and I tried looking serene – at least I hoped it was serene. He nodded to Colbert and his shadows by way of a friendly greeting, stepping between myself and Colbert.

"Now this here stuff," he said, picking up a crude clay bottle of our tarantula juice, "can make friends of anyone, Philistine and Israelite."

Clubber uncorked the bottle and poured three drams after Charles had proffered the glasses to him, quickly taking in Clubber's design.

Colbert looked at Clubber skeptically, then at me equally so. Finally, he performed a near imperceptible physical motion that could be a shrug and reached for one of the glasses. Clubber took one and handed the other to me.

I raised my glass to Colbert. "To the republic and all its people."

Colbert had raised his glass but paused at that. After taking in Clubber again, he shrugged more perceptibly.

Down the hatch that juice went, all five of us. Colbert's eyes now registered something of shock, but recovered quickly, almost before anyone could notice it. His shadows did likewise.

Clubber smiled at me and nodded.

Colbert also nodded, reluctant at first, then a mite more vigorously. He gestured for Charles to pour further drams of the stuff. In the old man's haste to please, a tiny splash of the juice ended up on the bar.

"Don't get that on your clothes," I warned Colbert.

And so we went on drinking, eventually working out a deal with the Colbert gang. They would get a percentage of the tarantula juice cut, which was fine by me. Sometimes it's just easier to work with an already established outfit rather than fight over turf. In the long run, it could even be more profitable for all.

Part of the compact also stipulated that we were prohibited from trading in any kind of grains or certain feed goods, which would impinge on the livelihood of the farmers of the area, a bulk of whom were Colbert's people. Fine and sensible by us also.

It was along these lines that our operation continued to grow and collect men and women of a wide variety of criminal stripes and talent.

With hundreds of folks at our disposal over a time, we eventually branched out into enterprises ranging from our simple black-market exchange, your standard horse-thievery, and some agents even specialized in slave-stealing.

In that racket, one of them would carefully cultivate a friendly relationship with a slave with a bit more leeway in going to towns or cities on certain errands, deliveries, or the picking up of goods, supplies, or equipment. After a time, our agent would convince said slave that he could assist in making good his or her bid for freedom. The fee for this service would be a portion of any amount collected from another sale, right after, in another part of the country. Our man would promise his assistance in a *second* escape. The end game – always promised to these poor souls – was eventual true freedom. At some point. Sometimes never determined. Some slaves did attain this gleaming prize, but very few, really.

One must try and understand, a reward was offered for every escaped slave. And where there's a bounty, the land sees no end of slave hunters, on foot and horseback, skilled at tracking and shooting. And with a major part of our outfit hailing from the white underworld, it wasn't too hard for an agent to get greedy, yes, even under John Murrell. Hard industry to break into, slave-stealing.

In some cases, our agents, who we took to calling "strikers," would hide the slave. After a time, according to the law in those days, the slave became property held in trust, and then they could be sold again.

Well, yes, *could* be sold. But we never exercised this. After a string of agents putting their purses before the operation, John began choosing strikers more carefully. See, what he really wanted were freed slaves who would work *with* him.

"What better way to form a loyal band?" he would ask. Not to paint it too cynically, for he saw them as souls that needed protecting, too, and we often talked about a debt we owed to Hieronymus for saving our worthless skins. It felt like the right thing to do for his people, whenever we could.

We finally assembled a handful of more trustworthy strikers who were becoming accomplished in this scheme, but one Billy Semple was becoming a damned fair hand at it. He seemed to know all of the angles and worked them near to perfection.

He worked the area south of the Tennessee line, and we happened to come up on him near a place called Pine Agency, while on what John called a "grand tour." He was a rangy-looking fellow with a sharp eye to him, and sometimes a sharp tongue too. Most of our other strikers didn't care to work with him, mostly for those reasons, so he developed into one of our "lone crow" type operators. John was not so much in favor of having their sort about, but whilst he was growing and arranging his outfit, he allowed it for the time being.

Semple welcomed us gleefully into his camp and set to plying us with rum and whiskey and even the ever-present tarantula juice. We right off noticed one of his stolen slaves hovering in the shadows, not even shackled or anything.

"Wouldn't do to bind them in any way," said Billy Semple. His voice was high-pitched, and he had a twang that beat all to hell anything I had ever heard. Most of us had southern drawls, but his made John and myself practically sound like the King of England and the Duke of Cornwall.

"They are not given to wandering off, not what with what is on the line for them. Hell, I don't even much use them as servants, or nothin', even if that is what they're used to."

I could see Semple still kept a wary eye on him. Most slaves, runaways or stolen or even former ones, were not so given to challenging white folks much anyhow. Most kept a careful distance, and only spoke when spoken to, with their eyes cast down. Just a habit, I suppose, one likely very hard to break given their situation. I had heard that the ones right off the boat, fresh from Africa, were a different matter altogether most times.

Those were raw to the whole idea of slavery, like as not, and like most men born free, were more disposed to keep that freedom rather than give it up easily, and even die for it if need be. Seemed to me a plantation owner might shy away from those types and just keep to the ones that were born into that sorry existence. The whole idea depressed me severely, if I'm at all honest about it.

And looking at this man, in the shadows of the firelight and looking at us, when he did at all, furtively and without any challenge to his eyes, my heart did go out to him, and I decided right then I didn't care at all for this slave-stealing business. It seemed to me most cruel to toy with just that idea of liberty and freedom, dangling it like bait to a poor soul that has had that taunting throughout his or her life. Most cruel, indeed. Say what you will about John Murrell, and there is much that could be said. But he was decades in advance of most people hereabouts on that score – believing black folks should be free.

"Not that you care any, but this one is named July," said Semple. "Funny how they name these blackbirds, ain't it? I mean, how you come by that? 'Name a month, any month! We'll tack it onto this blackbird over here!" He peeled off a loud laugh that sounded like a cracked, broken bell. It sure soured my face some. Despite him freeing some men in the process, I didn't much care for the way he spoke about these people, like they possessed no feelings whatsoever. They were people caught up in a miserable state.

John gave him a frozen smile. "Where does Mr. July hail from, exactly?"

"Oh, I acquired him up about Solyette, or thereabouts, I think. He and another were on this long, straight, dusty road, and had a cow with them. Why it takes two of them to find a lost cow escapes me, I swear. So, I stopped 'em and asked them about their home and all, like usual. Get a taste of if they might be up to skedaddling and all of that."

"There was another?" John asked. "What happened to him?"

"Oh, he didn't work out much."

We looked at each other. John struck a match for his pipe.

"How do you mean?"

"Well, when I was laying out my plan for them – for them to get free and all – this other one got mighty nervous. Fierce scared of their master, y'see, even more than their overseer, which is right unusual. This other one's eyes got so big it was comical. Thought they might pop right out of his head, I did. July did his best to get him calmed. July was for it, y'see. His friend there was right agitated. But I could see July knew this was his time, and it might not come 'round for a spell, if ever again. So, you could say he was worked up in the other direction.

"Finally, he did get this other one – his name was Sc... Scipio, if I remember correct. There is one of those funny names." Again, with Semple's grating laugh. "Don't know where they get these silly names."

"Roman general," John said quietly.

"How's that?" asked Semple.

"Never mind. Do continue, Billy."

"Anyhow, this Scipio was finally calmed a bit, but that night..."

"Yes?"

"Well, that night he got right *extry* scared and nervous and all, and was tearing at July's clothes, even, scared witless that some way that master would find them that night. Hollerin' and carrying on so that I thought I would have to cudgel him, or have July do it. I started to get afeared myself that someone may happen by, hear all that caterwauling and come looking into the camp and stirring up trouble for me."

John and I said nothing. Billy could see us waiting. He let out a sigh.

"I had to dispatch him, I did."

John puffed out a large cloud of smoke, squinted against it at Billy.

"Dispatch him, hmm?"

"I sent July off to look for firewood and took a knife to ole Scipio, sad to say. Had to gut him like a carp. Filled his carcass with rocks and sent him to the bottom of the river." He laughed that broken bell laugh again. I do not love violence the way some men do, but right then, I thought I just might use it on Billy Semple if I heard that bray again.

"At least I hope I sent him down and he stays down!"

Billy looked at us brightly, never doubting that we'd share in his grisly humor.

"July here came back to the camp, and I just told him Scipio just ran off, and there was nothing to be done about it. I think July stayed with me just because he was afeared to go back himself and get some awful punishment as a thank you."

John stood up and examined his pipe. Semple chuckled a little and tipped a jug to his mouth.

"I won't have it," John said quietly, almost to himself.

Billy looked up at him, wiping his mouth on a grimy sleeve.

I'd never seen John move so fast. He stalked around to Billy and grabbed his collar up in a heartbeat. He brought Billy's face close, his own dark with fury.

"I'll not have cold murderers in our ranks."

"Billy's eyes were wide with shock at first, then turned to a feverish, pleading look.

"What else was there to do, Mr. Murrell?"

John shook him furiously. Billy's tone took on a whining quality, but it didn't come off convincing. One of his hands crept and hovered about a knife at his belt.

"Mr. Murrell..." he sniveled, even while his eyes lied. "It won't happen again!"

"By God, it won't," John said, his voice even.

As if he had already sensed it, John grasped Billy's hand, the one reaching for that knife. He wrenched, and something snapped like a tree branch parting. Billy moaned in agony and crumpled to the ground. John threw the knife into the woods. His body was shaking with fury. "I won't have it," he breathed. He took his seat again.

Billy whimpered. He looked afraid to look John's way for a very long time. The sound of Semple's wrist giving kept echoing in my mind, taking me back to when Hieronymus sundered Amber Eye's arm. Bitter gorge rose in my throat.

Instead of sleeping that night, I took it on myself to watch Billy Semple, for I saw cold hatred in his eyes and knew he bore a close watch. I swore Hieronymus – his spirit, anyway – was there keeping watch with me. It felt like something of a tribute to the big man's memory.

Billy eventually did leave in the dead of night.

The slave July stayed in camp, though, with a look of uncertainty about him. Run or stay? What lay in wait for him in either case? When he did look at us, his eyes were wary.

Come morning, we settled down for our breakfast, the inviting aroma of coffee wafting in the fresh air. After a time, John gestured for July to come join us. And he did.

"You don't need to worry about that lot any longer," John said to him, gesturing at the wilderness. He extended his own plate to July, whose eyes got a little bigger, searching John's, as if he wasn't sure about what was happening. Was it another cruel white man's ruse? Slowly taking the food, he shuffled backwards, watching us carefully. Only then was I struck by how young and vulnerable he seemed, not more than fifteen years old, surely.

Finally, he sat and started in ravenously on his breakfast. John poured a cup of coffee and walked it over to July, who looked up, startled. John smiled at him, patiently nodding until July took the cup, his eyes never leaving John. I was transfixed, this simple, kind gesture of John, the Devil Preacher who with much shooting and noise had staged a jailbreak of seven strikers out of Alpika, toughest jail in Mississippi; who robbed a government payroll shipment from Florence, Alabama, only escaping U.S. agents and half the town after a merry chase by burning a bridge.

Now here he was, of all things, serving coffee to a former slave. What effect would it have on a man like July, who had already been through hell on earth?

July appeared to relax a bit, then and very hesitantly hunkered down nearer to the fire. I did catch him looking over his shoulder once or twice, peering into the woods, no doubt to ensure Semple really had gone, and harbored no more designs on him.

Other gang leaders might have simply dispatched a Billy Semple to be rid of them, but John's outlook on execution was miles away from any stories you might have heard about him. He never took to it at all. He saw that when you dealt with a man like Billy the way he did, and leave that in your wake, that had more effect on a man than simply killing him.

"Lasts longer and not as messy," he would say. "A man wandering around with tales to tell of how he had been punished goes a lot farther than a corpse moldering in the ground, wouldn't you say?"

I really couldn't argue with that. So, I didn't.

21

The outfit had become regionally vast. John figured it was time to put some real organization in place, for the express purpose of maintaining control. To that end, he had already burned a considerable amount of coal in that brain of his.

One morning, John sauntered into my quarters at our base near Ward's Stand, north of Jackson, Mississippi. He was wearing a very contented grin.

"Stephen, I have it!" He announced, the escaped slave, July, walking in behind him.

"That is happy news, John!" I nodded a greeting to July. These past two months or so, John had taken him under his personal wing after the incident at Billy Semple's camp – and he proved to be a very able and reliable young man. John had taken a great liking to him, as had many of the other men (though a few grumbled, not quite used to black folks entering our ranks as equals yet). Now with better, more consistent grub and more kindness and respect than he had ever known, July had a bit more certainty to his carriage, not as timid and distrustful, yet still wary at times, especially in large gatherings.

He stood straighter, taller, and working on the trail, managing wagons of our product, had made him somewhat broader in the shoulders.

"Indeed, old friend, happy news! How's the shoulder?"

I had gotten a fairly bad wound in one of our gang melees, falling directly on my shoulder while getting knocked off my pony. Hurt like hell, but my pride was more bruised. This wasn't helped by the fact that my brothers never let me forget I had been unhorsed.

"Still a bit stiff, but largely on the mend, thankfully." I hitched the shoulder up and massaged it. "Received the weekly report from the boys on the river this morning. Nothing new on the Mandley front."

"Might be good news," John pursed his lips thoughtfully. "Might not."

All we've heard since moving inland was that Mandley's recruiting efforts were fairly successful, and he had outfitted four boats designed just for the pursuit and destruction of river pirates. The boats had been named – rather loftily and overly ambitious to our minds after the Four Horsemen: *War, Famine, Conquest,* and *Death.*

Now, I would think, being maritime creatures – sailors, even fresh-water riverine types – would refrain from painting the word "Death" on the prow or stern of any vessel. Apparently, these men were not traditionalists and did not give a hoot in hell for any kind of superstition. It turned out that there was a fifth boat, too, but since it didn't fit into the mysterious and intimidating – for that is what the names really were all about, call a spade a spade – the fifth carried the simple inscription of *Maude* on its side, which struck me as comical next to her more menacing sisters.

Still, the fact that they had five vessels prowling a sizable stretch of the Mississippi told everyone up and down the river that Tedder and Company was dead serious about cleaning out the villainous driftwood and scalawags.

As their operations progressed, they pushed us further and further inland, too. We had adapted well, though, with John, Hercules Plumb, and I agreeing that it had actually assisted our organization in its burgeoning beyond our wildest imaginings.

"Now what is it you have, John?"

"Why the name, sir. The organization's!"

During this demonstration, July had meticulously packed John's pipe, which had become ever-present in recent days, alternating with his now beloved cigars, the brands of which had become a finer variety of late. Almost in the same movement, he scratched a match, holding it to the bowl. John puffed it to life.

"We are a *brotherhood* of survivors, Stephen. Many of our troops... we've sprung from the jaws of the law. Henry Duggs from Langford Prison, for instance. Charlie Peck now, no town or community would take him in thereabouts after they'd hung his boy for horse thieving. And we have July here, maybe the best example of all of our collective resiliency! Damned me, but I am proud of this boy, for taking command of his life, as most men should!" The affection John had for the kid was never plainer.

His eyes alight, fervor growing, he began pacing energetically about the room.

"Maybe brotherhood isn't a strong enough term. Brotherhood is a good word. A stout word, containing many meanings. Full of a kind of warmth. But we..." He thumped his chest with his fist this time. "We are something stouter even than that. We, all of us, came through a fire, a crucible, and came out sturdier. Went through hell, some of us, and survived tougher for it. Meaner, in some cases, and much more savvy."

John was really immersed in it now. July's eyes never left

John. They had a fierce, resolute shine to them. Even I was caught up in it at this point.

"Like some mystic beast, striving, forging through hell itself to live on, we are a *clan* of them." He was gesturing about with his pipe, stabbing the air at a particular point, spreading smoke around like some wizard heavy at his craft. "A mystic clan that may take its blows, but will never – never – be ground down to nothing."

I imagined how the rest of the gang – our clan – would be taking all of this in, how they might get caught up with a fever for it. I could see it happening, truly, these men and women doing almost anything for this man, and his clan. For a fleeting moment, I wondered if he could or would launch a political career. After all, the creatures populating that venerated swamp down east in Washington weren't all that far removed from the criminal caste.

"Alright, Stephen. That oratory was right from the gut and the heart, the spirit of what I am trying to accomplish with this clan speaking through me. Now, to lend some legitimacy to it. July, the register, if you please."

July produced a large ledger and laid it on my table. The cover had been lovingly decorated with ornate designs, framing large, filigreed words that read:

THE CLAN MYSTIC

"And what is this?" I lifted one brow. "Am I a bookkeeper now?"

"More like a keeper of names," John answered, puffing leisurely.

"Names," I said, blankly.

"I've been collecting them."

"I take it this is a list of purchasable government officials? Crooked judges? Enemies to be rid of?"

John chuckled. "All of the above, to be sure, son. So many to track these days. I thought it best to jot them down, else we forget our friends and enemies."

He patted the ledger.

"These are our confederates. Our friends. Our fellow Mystics, so to speak."

I cracked the ledger open.

John's handwriting was neat and orderly. The first heading I read was:

<u>The Heads</u>
(Council)

The first name I saw listed there was:

Hercules Plumb

I regarded that for a moment. The names descending from Mr. Plumb's fairly blurred into anonymity as I scrolled down the list.

I turned several pages.

<u>Strikers</u>

Then the next heading. These columns ran some pages, perhaps five or six hundred scalawags, ne'er-do-wells, horse thieves, and perjurers. With just about every entry was a location and sometimes a note regarding family, spouses, or friends in their respective areas.

I flipped back to where I started. "John?"

"Hmm," he murmured as he relit his pipe, genially waving away July's offer to help.

"I do not see our names. I assume the Heads are the captains?"

"Captains! I like it!"

"Then... Where are... Our names?"

The answer lay entirely in John's expression of incredulity. I spoke it aloud.

"Were the book to be captured, or elsewise compromised..."

He saluted me with the stem of his pipe like a professor recognizing a student that has experienced an epiphany of enlightenment.

He indicated the ledger with the stem.

"This, son, is a leash. One to which we will give a twitch, or a yank, if required."

I understood at once. This list contained intelligence on all of our agents, and it would facilitate control over the gang and protect us from immediate prosecution should the law get too close to the mark. A mystic beast we may be, and a mighty one, but possibly too mighty. Without this stratagem of John's, in time, it might devour itself and us with it.

I was impressed with the detail, but I couldn't help but remember that book from so many years ago. The one that John had purloined from Pastor Purdy. I looked at the ledger again. The hand-made cover illustrations and lettering brought to mind Ma Surgick's. The one with the bird, framed by similar designs.

Lists. Ma Surgick had been big on lists and had tried to impress on us their importance.

And now John had one of his own.

INTERLUDE

1877

Mr. Erastus Vinning
Secretary to Mr. A. Forepaugh
The Offices of The Forepaugh New and Colossal
All-Feature Show
Trust Company Building
Philadelphia, Pennsylvania

     August 24, 1877

Dear Mr. Vinning,

     Having received Mr. Forepaugh's communique
directly, I feel I must respond in a most
firm fashion. I am not, in fact, "dilly-
dallying" or "skylarking" in my duties here
in Georgia. I have never been given to
anything of the sort and strenuously object
to such a characterization. In fact, I view
it as a personal affront.

     It is difficult for me to believe that my
previous descriptions of Mr. Hue's insistence
on my hearing — and now dictating — his and
Mr. Murrell's tale have been completely
ignored.

     At last, we've arrived at the place where
Murrell has applied a moniker to his cartel,
thus I believe the saga will really begin
rolling and biting into the meat of the
legend.

     I do realize that I risk the prospect of
further employment with Mr. Forepaugh by
pointing this out, but I either stay, hear

Mr. Hue out to the fullest and obtain the object, or simply depart this place and seek employment elsewhere. I hear there is quite a market for attorneys in New York, and more particularly, Washington, D.C.

Additionally, I am mystified by Mr. Forepaugh's obvious agitation at my mere mentioning of one P.T. Barnum as "Mr. X" or any of the other ridiculous "code names" he has proposed. And I certainly have no intention of using the code name "Agent Mulberry" for myself in these communications or referring to the object we are seeking as "Judge and Executioner."

It is just all too silly. After all, I am not in the employ of Mr. Pinkerton and his Secret Service, nor seeking to secure this object as a critical matter of national security for President Hayes.

To the point that Mr. Forepaugh's eagerness to get hold of this thing of Mr. Murrell's is borne from the fact that he knows that Mr. Barnum is also desperate to attain it, I suggest that Mr. Forepaugh simply announce that he has it, and display something in its stead, and be done with this absurd game.

I must insist that you advise me, upon receipt of this letter, whether or not I continue to remain employed by Mr. Adam Forepaugh and his show.

I shall continue my mission while I await

your response, lest I be accused of further "skylarking," whatever that is.

Respectfully Awaiting Further Instructions,
     R.E. McElhany, Esq.

22

WE HAD BEEN on the trail – a slow one – for three days or so. West-bound, we were and had even crossed the Red River some miles north of Alexandria, Louisiana.

John was apparently following some directions and information that had been delivered about a week before, and all he said to me after looking at it was to gather up some packs and provisions and prepare to travel. He emphasized bringing along extra grub, a good amount of cash, and more gunpowder and tarantula juice than we might've brought on such an excursion.

So, July and I set to that task. He was quiet but very pleasant company altogether, and a hard worker, too.

John would not divulge to me or any other member of our small party where we were headed, staying very cryptic about these notes and messages he had received.

Fortunately, we had good weather for the jaunt, so I just took it for a recreational outing or hunting trip or some such, and just resigned to enjoy myself and leave it at that. It'd been about two years since the christening of the clan and the opening of the ledger. Since then, the clan was steaming right along, expanding its territory, licking a few rival crews, and absorbing others. The ledger's pages were filling with more names to the point where another one had to be cracked open. Thankfully, amidst these skirmishes and consequent paperwork, that shoulder of mine no longer troubled me as much. Still, we sure could use a vacation.

Finally, we came along to a region known as Kisatchie, what had once been known as the Neutral Ground or Neutral Strip. It was a vast section of land that was argued over by Spain and the New World for some years. All parties more or less agreed to disagree over its ownership and just let it hang. At last, it had been settled, around '20 or '21, I believe, but people still referred to it as neutral.

John pulled up the party on the trail underneath a huge cottonwood tree, almost as if he expected it to be there. He turned to us all and said, most grandly, "But a quarter of a mile from here lies a Heavenly place. A place where we may all take refuge in the coming days and years." He wore a big smile.

The rest of us merely looked at each other with varying degrees of blankness, unsure what John knew about those very coming days and years he just mentioned. Yes, the land was lovely and peaceful and looked to be a very good hunting ground, but Heaven?

None of us had heard John talk so before, outside of his occasional sermons, that is.

Anyway, we followed the trail down to a kind of shallow valley, and my instincts were buzzing and telling me this was a right dandy place for a bushwhack.

John led us down a little further, and I began to see what looked to be a large chunk of rock between the trees. As we finally came around to see it was a large chunk of rock indeed, with a big hole in it, too. Right before it was a fairly wide-open area, with a gigantic oak tree standing sentry there.

We pulled up again, falling silent as we looked into the mouth of a large cave.

"Why, John," I said, finally, "we could ride these ponies right into that place."

"Indeed, we could, dear fellow," he said jovially, and proceeded to do so.

I looked at July, and his eyes told me his senses were a bit jangled too. We followed him in but kept our necks twisting all the same.

John slowed his mount down. I could see him leaning to study another mark etched onto the cave wall nearby. I drew my horse up beside his.

"John–" I started, but he stifled this with an upheld hand, then urged his horse on again.

As we rode further, I noticed the cave tunneling off into various directions, all still large enough to steer a horse through. The light somehow stayed with us for a time, until we at last had to light some torches.

All the while, John followed more signs and symbols, some with arrows, and squares, and a time or two, there were even skulls, which I took to be warnings.

Even so, proceed we did, deeper into the gloom.

I finally started to see other signs, betraying further human habitation. Spent torches, the occasional bit of clothing. A scrap of leather that looked like it had been used for a harness, which I couldn't figure how it had ended up down in that place.

It was quiet as could be, though, save for our ponies' hooves clopping on the rock, and the soft rush of the torches.

We came to what appeared to be the opening of an enormous chamber, and sure enough, it expanded quite a bit as we pushed into it. We rode slowly in, examining the arching ceiling as far as our torches' light would allow.

As I moved in next to John, I could see something against a

far wall, near the cavern floor, and I went to it. It was a table. Perched there was an unlit lantern.

I turned to John. "Why, this place is spoken for, it appears."

"It is." The voice came from the darkness.

Startled, the men went for their rifles. John quickly held up a halting hand.

"Hold," he said firmly.

A man walked into our torchlight from the inky gloom.

This was a man of some dark complexion and a fierce countenance. He wore a frock coat of black wool and a dark red and black cravat. A broad-brimmed felt hat, also black, slouched just slightly over a strikingly handsome visage.

He lifted his head just a bit, staring menacingly.

John held up both hands as a sign of non-violent intent, then slowly dismounted. We all followed suit. As we did so, many others of what appeared to be this man's confederates came also into the light from the gloom of the network of natural tunnels that seemed to lead from all directions, thus surrounding us.

"I am Jack Bembry," their leader said, his voice all business. He looked at each of us in turn then, with a challenging eye.

"I know who you are, Bembry," said John in a business tone equal to Bembry's.

They stared at each other for a long moment until I was sure one or both of them would free up their respective barking irons and proceed with the parley in lead. An interesting proposition within those confines. I imagined the noise and smoke and blood suddenly filling up that tight space.

"You Redbones," John said at last, "know what you are about, I'd say."

"We do," growled Bembry, "and we would be about more, what without your Devil Preacher and Clan Mystic foolishness fouling our spokes."

I knew it, then, and I devised a maneuver in which I would dive for that table, turn it on its side, and barricade myself against this gang's volleys. I could see others of our group stiffen, as did theirs.

Suddenly, John and Bembry erupted into a gust of gruff laughter. They approached each other and clasped hands in sudden and unexpected friendship.

Bembry's men relaxed almost as suddenly, some of them offering what would pass as a smile, as they were clearly a rough bunch, and not to be trifled with.

Turned out this Bembry was captain of our western-most gang, inhabiting the Rapide perish out in this part of Louisiana. John had been in some communication with them and had settled their partnership separately from our river-bound endeavors. These two, we learned later, were thoroughly familiar with each other through earlier criminal enterprises.

They were a largely mixed-race band known as Redbones, and sometimes Melungeons, and were known to be a sturdy, reliable people.

"Clan Mystic, is it?" Bembry motioned John over to the table. One of his men produced a jug and some food.

"That is the name you picked for your lot, that right?" laughed Bembry.

John looked at him with some astonishment. Our crew had not been shy about spreading the name of the clan everywhere, boasting its fearsome reputation wherever they could, flaunting the law at every quarter, but hearing it had reached this far already was something of a happy surprise.

"Oh yes, your villainous reputation precedes you in a big way, old friend. I've even heard that your name is being used by parents to bring their unruly brats into line."

John guffawed. "I like that! Oh, I think there are ways I can use that to my advantage!"

"There is no doubt about that," Bembry said, with a leer. So, what do you think of our little hidey hole, Rev?"

"It will do right nicely," John looked around contentedly.

"You know," said Bembry, "Charlie Spiers and his crew hit a team of folks heading Texas way, about eight, nine wagons. Had all their goods on 'em. Well, Charlie hit 'em hard. Almost two thousand in gold, too. Anyway, the colonizers got out after 'em, and they were out to do some hanging too, after. Two of their members had been killed in the fracas, sad to say.

"Well, Charlie, after winding a bit here and doubling back there, made it to this here place and weren't never found."

"Yep, that'll do just fine. Charlie's a good man."

"He's got some bark on him, that one."

"Where is old Charlie, anyway?" asked John, peering about into the dark crevices as he struck a match.

"Set for Tennessee. His ma's poorly."

"Sorry to hear it," John said. Then he cleared his throat. "Ah, well. I have brought more than gab for you." He gestured to one of the men.

Bembry smirked. "For a change."

They placed a crate before Bembry. He slowly reached over and picked out a brown bottle. "I've heard tell of this here sauce. Most generous of you, John." He popped the cork, sniffed at the mouth. "God save us all!" He laughed and downed a swig.

"Jack, I believe your eyes are watering."

"That'll curl your dead relative's toes, I tell you." More laughter as Bembry gestured to his people. Another crate was brought out.

John whistled as this was prized open. He picked up a brand-new, gleaming rifle.

"The U.S. Cavalry will be looking for these," Bembry laughed. "Hall carbines. Latest model."

"Fine, Jack, just fine." John gazed lovingly at the weapon, taking aim down its sights. "These will do nicely." I looked at the rifles greedily and couldn't wait to try one myself.

Their palaver went on for a spell, and eventually I made myself scarce to explore the cave on my own.

Some of the places I could see were lit, but dimly, as the darkness was thick, and I took it for Bembry's men that were occupying them, so I steered clear when I could.

One chamber actually had a wooden door affixed to it, with a heavily armed Redbone standing sentry there, and I went by acting like I was just for a stroll. The guard cast me a warning eye anyway, but then nodded curtly at me like he just realized we were allies or I wouldn't even have been strolling by like I was.

We were all getting used to each other, and it fairly reminded me of two sets of hounds sniffing and sizing up the other.

After a time, all that wore off considerably, and those Redbones melded well into the fold of our growing clan, for Bembry's people were a rough-hewn lot who put up with no nonsense from any quarter. They were much respected and even feared in Kisatchie and beyond, reaching to Texas. Our flank in that direction was stoutly protected.

Some of the men jokingly referred to this new place as John's Heavenly Hole, but goodness, if that didn't open the possibilities of even more ribald jokes. John heard about all of it and laughed in his good-natured way, but that is how it came to be called Heavenly Hollow.

That stuck, and that is how we knew it from then on.

23

IT WAS ALONG ABOUT THEN, as we made our way back east across the Red River, that a man came upon our camp looking tattered and bloody.

He damned near got shot, too, as one of our Mystics unlimbered his rifle and brought it to bear on him like the flick of an eye – quickest I'd ever seen. This stranger would have right deserved it, too, barging foolishly into a camp like he did.

However, our man pulled up, thankfully, seeing also that the intruder had been accosted in some way, damaged by something along the lines of a Kiowa, or Lord forbid a Karankawa, since they are known to be your savage's savage and sometimes even cannibals, according to the Spanish, anyway. They wouldn't be this far north though; more likely to be found nearer the Texas coast. Yet in these crazy wilds, we'd all heard all sorts of fantastic tales, as you might imagine.

Anyway, it was clear he had been attacked, and it took us several minutes to calm him, and we even got some whiskey in him, which helped some.

Through the night, we kept a man on sentry, as always, but

he was to pay particular mind to this man, as to ensure that his state of mind wouldn't send him into a fit of hysteria and try to slaughter the whole camp, thinking we were some of those renegade Karankawas or Kiowas.

He just slept like a babe the whole night, and taking note of his position once we had him settled down, it looked like he hadn't even moved a hair at all during his sleep. In fact, once we roused up the fire again and got some coffee on, he still hadn't moved, and we started getting the uneasy idea that the poor soul had given up the ghost.

He finally did stir, though, sitting up so straight and sudden all at once, it was almost comical. He looked about the camp and blinked his eyes once or twice. Then a light of fear came into them and almost as quickly went away as he recollected his surroundings.

July slowly handed him a tin cup of coffee, which he carefully took, nodding his head slightly in thanks. John sat across from him, chewing on a biscuit.

"Name's Blackmon," said the man finally. "And I thankee." He looked around at all the men. "Thankee kindly."

John shrugged. "Haven't done anything yet, Mr. Blackmon. Murrell's the name. This here is Mr. Hue..." He introduced the men around the camp. Some looked at him with some alarm, but John nodded to them slightly as if to say it was all right. This man was no threat.

"You didn't shoot me, wonder of wonders," said Blackmon. He reached up and gingerly felt his scalp. His fingers traced the dried blood that had trailed down one side of his face.

John laughed mildly. "Well, I guess that is truly something we did for you right there."

Blackmon sipped at his coffee. Someone tossed him a biscuit.

He started chawing on it, then stopped. He gulped and looked at us with lost eyes.

"My people," he almost whispered. He looked down at the half-eaten biscuit and then suddenly threw it aside like it was a scorpion that had stung him. He dropped the coffee too, and that hot liquid had to burn his leg severe, but he looked at us without the slightest care about it.

"My people," he croaked again, trying to stand, but his legs wobbled under him and he started toppling. July half-caught him and eased him to the ground.

"Here I am eating biscuits and sleeping and my people..." He looked down at the ground between his splayed legs and sobbed, and I tell you that is something I don't care to hear again from a human being, much less a grown man. It was just too much.

John looked over at me, and I could tell from his eyes what he meant to do. Without a word, we stood and commenced to break camp.

We got Mr. Blackmon calmed again, his sobbing subsiding into morose silence. He stared right ahead with eyes seeing something awful and way off into the distance.

One Mystic who was a sight better tracker than most started out on Blackmon's trail back to his people, since the man was in no shape to guide us. Any of us might have been able to track his path, really, as Mr. Blackmon had torn through the brush and the bramble, leaving a trail that even a tenderfoot kid could follow.

As we alternately rode and walked Blackmon's trail, I pondered what might be going through his mind – if there was anything left to it, that is.

Maybe the reason he was all shut up was because he was reflecting on the revelation that he might be a coward. And going back on the trail that he had left over the landscape was bringing more light to that possibility the closer we got to the beginning of it. To be truthful, I did not think that the man would be able to see again the evidence of his people's fate without completely unraveling and screaming off into the wilderness. Maybe we would be serving him a kinder turn by letting him do just that.

Now you might think, for our part, that it would seem a bit contrary that there was a band of criminals heading out to aid travelers in distress, particularly when their leader just a few days before had casually discussed a raid on wagons bound west to Texas.

Those days were contrary in any number of ways anyhow, and when it came to a party of colonizers falling victim to a band of savages as opposed to the more standard bandits or road agents. Why, the calculation of what was then required tended to change on the spot. Don't ask me to explain any further than that, because I can't. I wouldn't even try.

It fairly astonished us to see that Mr. Blackmon had covered about four or five miles on foot, over rough ground. We came up on the first of his party. It was the body of a man who, in fact, had been scalped, but first he had been trampled to death, from appearances. His back was certainly broken, his corpse was contorted in a grotesque, unnatural way, which made the gorge rise up in me, I admit.

I kept it down, but another man did lose his breakfast. Don't mistake it – these Mystics had some bark on them, and many had seen truly brutal things in their time – but even a tough man has his limits, and when something comes sudden on them like that, there's no shame in it.

John looked about the area, his face clouding with growing fury.

We drew closer to what was the main gathering of these slaughtered colonists, and as I looked about the place, I was not convinced that it was Kiowas or Comanches or any other red savage who had done it.

Save for the one man who had lost his top knot, there was no sign at all in the direction Indians had been at all involved in this carnage. In most any kind of attack of that sort you would likely find at least one or two dropped weapons, maybe an arrow here and there. Arrows were one of the best ways to distinguish who made the slaughter, for each tribe made them different and usually displayed favored markings for whatever purpose. The kinds of wounds on corpses, and what had been left behind, were a sign too. By that, you could tell if it was just some vengeance raid – killing for killing's sake – or an assault borne from a thirst for violence coupled with lust for gold and booty.

Now, I'll allow that I wasn't as well-versed in all these particulars as some others in our party. Most of what I knew I'd gotten second hand, from talk around the camps and taverns and from news accounts and pulp magazines that I sometimes got a hold of, even when I was a kid, despite my mother's best efforts to keep me from their foul and grisly influence.

The expressions and mutterings of the more seasoned men about me started noting that this was not Kiowa work or the like.

There were eight corpses. Most had been just shot in the head by somebody who possessed some fearful accuracy with what looked like a pistol. One man remarked that the murderer served them a favor with this quick, merciful end.

This lot did put up a fight, though, that was clear. A couple still grasped their weapons, in fact. One of them was a fine Lancaster rifle that one of ours claimed, gently pulling it from the poor soul's hands. Understand, this was not a thing to be reviled in those days. It was not considered pillage or disrespectful in any way. It was understood that one simply did not leave behind a fine weapon in the hands of the dead, given only to rust and rot.

The three wagons had all been burned, along with their goods inside. In fact, the little bit of smoke still trailing up from their remains had helped us reach there in the last mile or so. Perhaps this was done to resemble a Comanche raid. They loved to burn it all down when they were done with their rage and fun.

As nightmarish as the scene was – and it's not something one would ever forget – the worst of it was discovering the carcass of a woman. It looked like they had tried to stuff her under a bit of debris but gave up. Her upper torso had been burned along with the debris, and there was a charred, grinning horror where her face should be. What remained of her clothing was in such disarray that there was no question she had been viciously violated.

It was here that my gorge did come up again, and I did not even try to stop it. Nor was I alone.

John came up beside me. His eyes never left the poor woman. He laid a hand on my shoulder and gently but firmly moved me aside.

And he stared and stared. To me, it appeared as though he forced himself to look at it hard because he did not want its image to fade from his memory.

Mr. Blackmon sat on the edge of this hellscape, his back to us, and we buried his people.

* * *

We interred the poor wretches as best we could in rough, shallow graves, owing to the hard ground and conditions. We piled as many stones as we could locate and devised crosses and markers from whatever lumber was left of the wagons. This seemed somehow fitting in an awkward, sorrowful way, given how and where they had met their ends. The markers seemed all the more desolate, being absent any names or dates. Over time, there would be nothing left of their resting places, and their bones would be lost in the ground forever. The thought left me despairing, even though I never knew them.

At last, Mr. Blackmon roused himself to come over to us and the graves, which surprised us some, for previously he looked like a man lost in the depths of his grief and not wanting to visit his friends' final resting place for fear of falling back into it, maybe forever.

He shambled over anyway, a sort of fierce bleakness in his eyes as he forced his gaze on the markers, a steady, long time for each. Much like John had before, looking at the sad corpse of the woman, like he wanted it seared eternally into his mind's eye.

Finally, he lifted his chin, his torso sort of twitching as he looked over the markers again and said, in a cold, flat voice, "We are short one."

The phrasing struck us right odd, for he sounded for all the world like a shopkeeper accounting for the proper number of hogsheads of salt he had expected to be delivered to him.

We all looked at him, expecting further illumination, and then it came.

"Was there a girl?" his eyes finally met ours, weirdly all business now, which was a sort of relief, watching the fellow find a certain measure of respite from that ponderous weight of grief on him.

"There was not," John answered. "Seven men, one woman."

"Nina," Blackmon said, in more of a gust of breath than a word. I, for one, wasn't sure I had heard it right. "They got Nina, they did."

Well, that might have been a clap of thunder over us. We looked at each other with a purpose anew. And this accounted for Blackmon's physical start after reviewing the set of grave markers, for it seemed he knew the answer to his query before he had even asked it.

Despite us being ragged and dog tired, all of it was forgotten in an instant, and our energies renewed with the thought that these murderous renegades had made off with an innocent. Something had to be done. No civilized being would put it off for even a moment more. The Clan Mystic was no stranger to committing violence ourselves whilst riling up towns and villages, stealing folk's horses, peddling contraband, or killing law enforcers and rivals that got in our way. But plundering women and children, or maiming them, was forbidden.

Perhaps it just came from the natural fact that we all came from mothers, and many of us had sisters, so the thought of them falling prey to villains of any stripe was more than most could take. John was not alone in his code throughout Clan Mystic.

We refreshed our animals what we could and started out.

These villains had not given a care to cover their tracks at all, no doubt anxious to spend their booty and ravage the poor girl. One didn't want to think on that aspect, yet there it loomed.

Mr. Blackmon was fiercely silent the whole time, and I remember thinking as dark and bleak as that time was, it appeared beneficial – even if temporarily – to bust him out of grieving blankness and the specter of his own cowardice.

Our quarry had a good day and a half on us, but we made good time, with sturdy ponies, most of them those Southern-bred Oupelousas that might even outlast the toughest of riders. These ponies had more hardiness than sense, thankfully.

For all we knew, these devils might stop anyhow – maybe a hideout or a farm that they had ranged from to begin with.

We finally came on their camp, by God, thanks to our tracker who had scouted forward and rode hard back with the news.

"Bastards've split, looks like," he said. "I tracked one group but got the idea it wasn't the one with the girl. So, I doubled back and found where they went asunder, and sure enough, these the ones got her."

Blackmon started, his face taking on anxiety and fury.

"Mr. Blackmon," John cautioned, holding out a restraining hand, "This calls for a steady hand. I know it doesn't seem it."

Blackmon seemed to catch himself, nodding. "Nina's a good girl," he whispered.

John caught my eye but said to Mr. Blackmon, "I do not doubt it, sir."

"How far?" I asked the tracker.

"Maybe a mile on."

"Good," And John laid out his plan.

* * *

We approached their camp as quietly as we were able, having left the horses behind as we neared them. We left Mr. Blackmon, too, with one man watching over him. Of course, Blackmon had made a fuss, which John put an end to right quick, politely yet firmly explaining that he believed his passions might put into question the outcome of any rescue attempt. It simply could not be risked. Mr. Blackmon finally had to agree, and we set out.

Some fellows were not far off from where Mr. Blackmon's mind was set, either, because there were those in our party that wanted to just go to the camp and raise hell right off, as many

Mystics were wont to do anyway, blasting and killing as many as they could in a surprise effort, and thus overwhelm them with general chaos. This tactic had worked to great effect before, after all, some argued. And this occasion, maybe more than some others, rightly called for it.

John argued that the girl's presence considerably altered that calculation, as these men who held her likely would just as soon carve her throat open amidst such ruin, rather than her be rescued or stolen – as they might perceive it – by a rival gang of ruffians. Not to mention the possibility of her being injured or killed in a confused tangle of violence.

So, we crept toward their camp later that night, on foot. We held our distance once they were within sight and sound, save for me and John, walking closer to them with great care and caution. The plan was to enter their camp, secure the bandits' confidence however possible, discover the whereabouts of the girl Nina, and hopefully spirit her away in the night.

We could not see her from where we were, though. Had she already been dispatched of? My stomach curled into a tight ball at the very thought.

"Hello, the camp!" John called from the dark perimeter. Some of their party started abruptly, one of them kicking something over in surprise. Another stood quickly, cursing and grasping a musket. There looked to be five of them. Our present numbers had that beat by three.

Two of them wore ratty, dirty military-style tunics, one even sporting the remnant of a cross-belt across his chest. From this, I figured these men were, in fact, renegade Mexican army types. That far east, though? Most intriguing. Again, anything was possible in these wilds.

Some words were exchanged, of course, a challenge from the camp. I couldn't make out the exact words from our position. We continued carefully forward, hands held aloft for all to see. John was smiling that fetching smile, but a man held a pistol on us all the same.

Many miles from anywhere, and here came two strangers right out of the gloom like ghosts; who could blame them? I was praying that we didn't get shot down right there, knowing that these same ones had murdered those colonists with likely no thought to it. I was sweating too; I don't mind telling it. A deep ache bloomed in my long-healed shoulder of a sudden, a distraction I didn't need.

"Damned us for a pair of tenderfoots!" John called. "We was making for Monroe, and our hosses gave out."

Well, they favored us with a skeptical eye, and it looked like they would send out someone to confirm our story, maybe scout the perimeter, but at last looked to think better of it. John gave them more theater as bedraggled travelers in peril, what with having torn our coats here and there, purposeful to bolster the image, which I hated, for I valued that coat.

Even rascals and murderers have a soft spot occasionally, it seems, for one of them motioned us closer to their fire, a man who wore a right dandy and handsome buckskin coat. For an instant, I thought about how good it might look on my own person, after all of this was said and done. That man poured a dram of liquor into a couple of tins and held them out to us. Of course, men cut of this cloth would likewise just as easily work it into their design to murder and rob us just as soon as feed us.

Oh, I still sweated, trust it, throughout the act. The annoying shoulder pain refused to die down. But I was fortified in the knowledge that our own men were lying in the brush, ready to commence violence when called for.

"You do look like men what's come down a hard trail," he remarked, and right then I could see just a tiny hint of a signal to someone somewhere. By some providential act, we had already met the leader.

I don't mind telling that my spine did tingle, but years of facing down many hard cases and roustabouts of every villainous stripe helped rein fear somewhat at arm's length. I ignored the temptation to look over my shoulder.

"Monroe, huh?" he asked, bringing it around to where John had told them of our destination. "Must have some pressing business." He took a long pull on the jug he had poured from. "But both your nags gave out, huh?" he squinted at us. The ghostly call of a far-off coyote drifted to the camp.

John groaned dramatically as he settled on his haunches nearer the fire. "Why, we killed the one, then rode double on the other. Poor hoss couldn't take it." I looked down, shaking my head sorrowfully, adding more flavor to the drama.

"Most pressing, sure." John continued. "Got word our dear Pa was near to the gates of Heaven and wanted to see us one last time."

I tried to spy out the whereabouts of young Nina through all of this, without drawing too much attention. My heart began sinking as I did, though, for I could detect no tell of hers. That is, until my eyes finally lit on a real low, hunkered-down tent that you would surely miss unless you were looking for it, just on the outskirts of the fire's light. There was a man sitting down that way, not far from it, hunkered down too, looking like he didn't want to be seen. At least, that was my impression.

It had to be her in that tent, just as sure as the sun was about to come up.

Something must have slipped in my performance, because when I turned back to the conversation, the light in Buckskin's eyes told me he had caught on. I cussed myself sore.

What did that Buckskin do, though? Well, he just smiled, showing rows of ruined teeth that roiled my stomach, and his eyes were black as a coiled rattler's. But he didn't move one bit, staying hunkered down opposite me. I could feel his boys getting all tensed and poised around us, and my skin started crawling like it does when trouble's afoot.

"You are back for her, are ye?" he said.

One of his men stepped around, just into my side vision, and the buckle on the crossed belts over his chest blinked brightly in the firelight. He said something in Spanish, and Buckskin answered like he was almost native to it, but not quite. One of his men lurked behind him now, another of the Mexican soldiers, and he drew out two short-barreled pistols.

The sound of his cocking each of them matched the snapping from the fire. His expression told me he was eager to use those irons.

"I saw you run, you damned poltroon," Buckskin said. The man to the side of me grunted a low laugh and muttered, "Maricon."

Now, the plan was simplicity itself, but it made no allowance for them to think of me to be Mr. Blackmon. We'd been in some tight spots before, but I confess I struggled to tamp down my curling panic.

That all became a moot development anyhow, for that was when a bright red bloom appeared on the forehead of the man what wielded those two flintlock irons, and then I heard the rifle shot.

Chaos erupted immediately. Buckskin jolted from the shot, and John jumped at him, having settled on his haunches just right for getting to a leap. His hands grabbed tight around his throat. They kicked and squirmed in the dust and got some into the fire even; Buckskin grasped for a knife that had been stuck in a hunk of wood nearby.

Thankfully, the Mexican renegade who was standing there had already run off, likely to address developing events elsewhere. So, I got to that knife first, thankfully, yanking it up just as Buckskin managed to roll away from John, but fast as a cat, he evened things out by getting to that other renegade's pistols, one of them still resting in his dead hand.

Now the renegade had already cocked that pistol before he was shot in the head, so I sort of instantly calculated my fate, and Buckskin aimed that thing at John with that rotten grin, and even in all that noise, I could swear I heard him squeeze the trigger.

And it amounted to nothing.

Right then, it got awful quiet, just around Buckskin, John, and me. Like we were in some big, woolly cocoon, because then I heard only a muffled silence, even though there was plenty of killing going on all about us. The pistol had misfired!

Then that cocoon just dissolved all at once, and Buckskin ran. Yes, he did. That poltroon or maricon or whatever that renegade muttered about me could be squarely applied to the villain in the buckskin coat.

He was making for where their mounts were picketed, but the Mystics knew their business and had cut that tether, pure Comanche style.

I threw the knife at him, and it sailed off into the dark somewhere. I always wished to be better with a blade, either carving or throwing, which would have come in handy about now.

I looked about for the head-shot renegade's pistol, but damned if I could see where it had gotten to in the dark and smoke, even though the sun was by then making an appearance. I snatched up a ragged-edged hatchet at random. There wasn't time to find a better weapon.

Who knew where John had scrambled off to; there was so much to attend to. Experience told me to trust him on his lonesome. Me? I trailed Buckskin as best as I could, but he did make it to a horse, jumped on it like an Indian brave, and started grabbing at something as it whipped around in a frenzied panic. I could see the silver roundels shining off the saddle in the newborn sunlight. Seems it was one of those beautiful, ornate Spanish saddles. It almost looked like one of those parade saddles of the military variety, and one could only wonder how these bastards had come by it.

Buckskin was trying to bring that mount under control while unlimbering a rifle from a scabbard there. I charged him, hatchet raised, hoping to close the thirty-something feet between us.

He finally wrenched it out, aiming clumsily with me about ten feet away. The flash from the weapon's muzzle blinded me, a storm of smoke and noise bellowing out, but the shot plowed past me. All sound around me turned instantly murky.

My blood was high, though, and I pressed the attack, bringing down the hatchet in an ugly slash, but just grazed Buckskin's leg as the horse skittered. Instead, I struck more of the saddle, a silver roundel flying off into the dusty air.

The horse wheeled around. I must've been deafened because Buckskin's mouth was gaping open, eyes wild, but there was no sound. He held the rifle high, useless now except as a club.

His arms chopped down at my head.

Blinding pain turned my legs to liquid, sprawling me into the dirt. The world turned into nothing but a dark, spinning blur.

I had the faintest idea of Buckskin finally loading the rifle, bringing it to bear on me.

Everything slowed of a sudden. Weirdly, I became very calm, looking into the barrel of the rifle, now smearing in and out of focus.

24

Suddenly, Buckskin jerked like some puppet whose strings twitched, then fell aside from his seat. I looked around, and there was John lowering his Collier revolver that had cut him down, direct to his black heart.

Even as my chest rose and fell, my loopy head did feel disappointment in some measure, as it ruined that fine buckskin coat. It wouldn't have mattered much anyway, as that horse just took off with Buckskin slumping in that parade saddle. He finally dropped from it after some distance, but he did get dragged quite a way after that, from what I could see. Hopefully, someone down the trail would get a rope on that hoss and recover that lovely saddle, at least. For some reason, I felt warm all over, like I was floating without a care in the world, as one does after a snort or two of tarantula juice.

The new sun bathed everything crimson. I looked over to that hunkered-down tent and spotted John there on one knee, head down, looking into it, and my heart sank low at the sight. I suddenly felt very sick to my stomach, before the world went black.

John told it exact when I came to only a few minutes later. My melon felt like a dray horse had trampled on it, before the fuzzy memory of Buckskin whopping me with the butt of the rifle rose up. As the carnage depicted, we did give them all a quick Hell. Only one of us at the time had been a military man, and he told us later that it looked like we were born to it, said he never saw men skedaddle like those renegades did, two of them that we knew to be Mexican soldiers, even. Apparently, there was no telling how much soldiering they had really done anyway, likely conscripts pulled from a prison, as was common in those days.

Those on the perimeter of the bandit's camp later calculated that they had spotted the girl's tent about the time I had, as there was a Mystic who was adept at stealth nearest to her. He was positioned to cut off one of the villain's avenues of escape when he found her.

It really was a happy accident, as this man stole up on her guard just before that first shot rang out, and when it did, the guard lurched toward the tent, tore the flap open, and pulled her out roughly, yelling in Spanish. Our man said this one plainly meant to dispatch of her at any sign of trouble. He had pulled a nasty, narrow blade from his tunic and was about to gut her right then when our Mystic beat him to it, driving his own Bowie home.

All but one of the renegades had been sent to Satan in right short order, and he mounted a beast and rode hell for leather to the west.

My head still ached something fierce. John approached, extending a tin of black brew. I winced, propping myself on one elbow, taking the coffee gratefully.

"How's the girl?" I nodded my thanks and sipped.

"She'll be fine, Stephen. When you're ready to move some, I'll take you to her."

I nodded again and stood gingerly. "I'd like that."

That poor child had been reunited with Blackmon after all the mess. She looked up at us with big, round eyes I liked to never forget. All of about twelve years old and as pretty as could be, one could see it despite the conditions we had found her in, all shot through with the starkest fear someone could have inside of them. My heart got clutched in a tight grasp of something right then, only imagining going through what she did, being so young and all.

Mr. Blackmon had wrapped a blanket about her. Still, we could see her body tremble. A little at first, and then she buried her head into his shoulder, and the shaking really started in.

"Come," John said quietly as she shook and shook. "Best give her some room."

"We're taking you away from here, Nina," I heard Mr. Blackmon say as we turned away. "We're taking you home."

* * *

It turned out that the colonists had not been traveling to Texas, but from it.

"That damned Austin," said Mr. Blackmon one evening over supper. "He about ruined me. Why, he ladled on a whole crop of lay taxes and finder's fees what ate up anything we might make for whatever harvest we could bring in, or goods we might peddle. It got ridic'lous. So, we pulled up stakes and made back for Alabama, damned his soul. And we felt fortunate to be able to do it, too, for there are plenty of folks that couldn't do even that much. They just had to stay put and hope for the best and had no wherewithal a'tall to get to home back east." According to Blackmon, that was why the bandits had taken to slaughter, more than anything. It was rage at the fact that the colonists were dirt poor and had nothing worth spitting on to surrender, but that young girl.

Poor Nina had settled down some and seemed right comfortable amidst us, even enough to ride on my own mount a few days (I walked beside her, holding the reins and occasionally giving her a gentle word). She didn't speak, though, not ever. At first, we found it peculiar but then quickly realized that was just how she was, maybe combined with the shock of everything what was done to her, and all the violence and killing she'd witnessed in her young life. Blackmon didn't act so much like it was anything unusual. He did stress the importance of getting her back to her uncle, and that's what we did.

All the way to West Alabama we took her, and there was her uncle, mighty glad to receive her. We were surely surprised, for it was none other than Colbert himself. "Thank you," he said, all gratified and humble, with fierce earnest eyes, and with a hint of fury to them, for advance word had gotten to him as to her ordeal.

Colbert's sister had struck out for Texas with the family, packing along high hopes and dreams, as most colonists do, of ranching out there and selling strong western ponies, lured by Stephen Austin's promises of rich land and full coffers.

Of course, we had to relay the full story of their sad end and assure him they had been buried proper with words said solemnly over their graves. We likewise made assurance that justice had been dealt to those who had wronged them. Nina was all Colbert had left of what would have been his western clan, and even he showed how much he treasured her being brought back to him, in his way.

As we started off, Nina just looked on with a stony, stoic expression, as her people do, but she held herself as someone commanding themselves to stay put and not allow themselves to betray that they were distraught in any way. It didn't occur to me until then that she really had bonded herself to me, of all people, and never strayed far at all as we had travelled. I found it comforting, in a strange, forlorn way.

Something about how the girl wouldn't speak gave it all a more sorrowful aspect.

* * *

Some days later, I awoke in camp to the sun just peaking over the horizon, coming out of a dream. The same one kept returning since we left Nina with Colbert. I was back at The Roost, reading father's letter for about the thousandth time. His voice even sounded solemnly in my ear.

Stephen, I hope to God I shall be spared until I see you arrive at an age to give protection to your dear mother and little sister. Remember that to you they will look for protection should it happen that my life should be shortened.

I lay there awhile, thinking. My heart ached worse than head or shoulder. I had flown right into the face of Father's wishes those years ago and abandoned Mother and Tiffany after all. The encounter with Nina and the bandits had brought these guilty feelings about, I knew deep down.

Perhaps it was time to settle down forever, leave outlawing behind at last. This wasn't the first time the thought of departing the Mystics rose up, though only once in a blue moon. But for once, these many years, I inspected the idea instead of shooing it away. The Clan could carry on well enough without me, myself having trained many Mystics along my journey with the outfit. I had amassed enough wealth to purchase my own plot of land. Also, I wasn't getting any younger, and the mileage I had put on myself was – I hated to admit, even to myself – beginning to take a toll. There's my shoulder, for one thing, and Buckskin had damned near split my skull open. A man couldn't live this kind of life forever; that was plain.

These thoughts tumbled about my brain for days and weeks as I went about my business, wrestling which way my life should turn. True, Clan Mystic had asserted itself as a stout, fearsome organization, and despite its criminality, stood for real liberty and independence. I was proud to be a part of it, something bigger than myself. I was proud of John, too, emerging as a strong leader who really cared about his people. But what would he think of these notions? Would he see me as a turncoat? A quitter? Someone not worthy of being a Mystic all this time?

But my heart would be neither still nor silent.

INTERLUDE

1877

Mr. Erastus Vinning
Secretary to Mr. A. Forepaugh
The Offices of The Forepaugh New and Colossal
All-Feature Show
Trust Company Building
Philadelphia, Pennsylvania

August 28th, 1877

My Dear Friend Erastus,

Your faithful servant, R.E., is in receipt of
your latest communique.

I feel that I have been "roundly sorted
out," as my loving Father was fond of saying.

I do humbly apologize for the overall tone
of my last missive, and beg you to understand
that I have been affected to a near-debili-
tating degree by the staggeringly oppressive
and punishing heat of this region. The
natives appear to be strangely immune to its
influence, but when I am out and about with
Mr. Hue (on his various and constant local
excursions), I could swear that my brain is
being thoroughly cooked inside my skull, with
or without a hat resting atop it. Mr. Hue is
an aged man, yet he does not appear to even
notice this, or any other meteorological
event, for that matter.

My only relief is the occasional, somewhat
refreshing servings of lemonade or cool tea
from Mr. Hue's lovely wife, Abby. She is as

dear and as close to a saint as I have ever witnessed, to put up with this Philadelphia lawyer appearing on her doorstep to pester her husband regarding the furtherance of his tale. She looks eternally vexed by the whole affair.

I admit I have privately entertained the notion of simply asking Abby Hue for the object, but owing to her demeanor and expressions when Mr. Hue happens to mention it in her presence (always in an elliptical way, I might add), she appears mystified as to what he is on about. She does not even know what it is, much less where it is.

To tie up this entire report, I do believe we are nearing the end of this whole process,

however, as it appears Mr. Hue is near to parting ways with the Clan Mystic. I am powerfully vexed as to how he obtained the object from Mr. Murrell though, mostly owing to the fact that at this point in the tale, Murrell was not only hale and hearty but will even use his finest weapon to great effect in his most daring campaign to date. I've always wondered just how illustriously history had covered it, this *Annie Franklin* job, so I'm eager to hear Mr. Hue's firsthand account. In the meantime, thank you, Mr. Vinning, for interceding on my behalf with Mr. Forepaugh. I do appreciate your having endured his outburst. I understand they can be rather volcanic in nature. You certainly are correct that you are most fortunate that he is a poor shot when he elects to launch objects from his desk to emphasize his displeasure.

You are also correct in your observation that I, in fact, would not wish to actually obtain employment in Washington, D.C. It is a fetid, miserable swamp, stuffed with creatures armed only with long, sharp daggers eager to be plunged into one's back.

Your Eternally Grateful and Loyal,
    R.E. McElhany, Esq.

25

Thankfully, distraction came in the unexpected form of news from the river. The thorny Mandley Problem had come to a head.

It got back to us that on top of his five river patrol boats, Mandley had fooled around with a steam engine, which would likely have been the death of us. Outside of the suspected reliability of the steam engine in those days, they'd have made Mandley's bunch far speedier and handier than our hand-and-wind-powered fleet.

Only it blew up, killing five men and taking an arm off a sixth.

John regretted he was not the author of this incident. "It would have been a gaudy feather in my cap if I had!" he declared.

Nevertheless, as the days passed, John obsessed over bringing ruination to their doorstep.

"I mean to stop Mandley's wind, here and now," he told us one night, lighting a smoke after going over our books. "Everything is in place."

I cocked an eye at him. Mr. Plumb sat back, looking satisfied.

"Is it, then?" I asked, as if I knew what they were about. I had been so busy monitoring and overseeing our various dealings on the Trace, not to mention dwelling on my latest turmoil, that the Mandley Problem had come to reside only in the back of my mind lately.

"We have inserted no less than four Mystics into the Mandley fleet," proclaimed Mr. Plumb.

"One for each horseman," John said, emitting a thick blue gust of smoke from his mouth.

"*Maude* shall be right offended," I joked. Even now, the fifth vessel's name amused me. John waved an impatient hand. "I've heard tell that *Maude* is the smallest of the brood. And the skipper is a rather timid sort. We can deal with *Maude* at a later time."

The plan was, at first blush, all too simple. Our Mystics would just resort to any sort of sabotage at hand, as opportunity presented. Even as early as a year hence, these men had spent a considerable amount of time wheedling their way into the good graces of Mandley's crews. It had been necessary to find men who were not well known to be part of our gang, which took some careful planning as well. Mr. Plumb had overseen this while John and I were expanding into the Trace.

"As I had previously stated, you will recall, direct confrontation is not in the cards," John said.

Our first Mystic, Cochran, reported back to us within about three weeks.

"It took me a time to win over the crew," he said.

"And which horseman was it?" asked Mr. Plumb, for our benefit.

"I got aboard *Famine*. The crew was fairly stout about their business, I'll say. We'd intercepted two flatboats runnin' about Island 99."

"Forsyte's bunch, I'll wager," John said. "Last I heard, anyway."

Cochran continued. "They's ruthless in their work, Mr. Murrell. Terrible ruthless. They put a shot right into the middle of these two we intercepted and made no bother a'tall about pulling them from the river neither."

John, Mr. Plumb, and I exchanged looks.

"So, we patrolled more into the night without seeing nothing more and shored in. Most times they'd sleep up on the deck, because of the heat and all, but I'd make for the hold to, I says to them, escape from the skeeters. It was those times what I begast to worry up a board on the keel, little fits and starts at a time. The knife-edge of m' Bowie done the job nicely, over a spell of time."

"You weren't worried about discovery at any time?" I asked.

"I covered any work with what cargo may have been stowed in there."

Cochran took a pull on his tankard.

"So, we was pullin' for another scalawag boat a few days on, in broad daylight, it was. Which was unusual, but the *Famine*, she could not make much speed like before, and this pirate got clean away as we bogged down more and more. The skipper, Bogdan or Bogdin or some such, got furiouser as we went and even directed us to get the sail rigged. But it were no good at all by then. We shored in closer near a sizable plantation jetty, and the *Famine* bogged to a rip and she was fair-on swamped by then. Bogdan or Din, or whatever, was squared away, fit to be tied, and hollered at us to clear out, and we fetched a ride back to the Mandley base on some borried horses. And they did not happen on them worried boards even then.

"I was looking to light out around about then, based on that very worry alone, but Bogdan or Din, or whatever, fetched up to us and said that yonder hole musta occurred at some point a tricky sawyer did the deed undetected, and we were caught up in the chase and weren't payin' no mind to it. And this in broad daylight!"

John clapped him on the shoulder.

"You are to be commended for your efforts, Mr. Cochran. Unfortunately, it is only a temporary setback for them. At least for their one vessel."

Cochran looked at us in surprise.

"Then you haven't heard tell of Lem Hackett?" he asked.

We patiently waited to hear what Hackett had been up to.

"Well, Lem got on with *War,* and I have to say he made me look like a piker. He made no bones about it and just made a trail of their powder cache for that six-pounder of theirs, and it sparked off with nobody looking, all of skylarking or whatnot, and the *War* just blowed up and torn asunder every man aboard!"

We looked at him, shocked. "Lem didn't make it, neither," he said. "I already told his wife." This last bit was delivered in an abrupt, matter-of-fact way that took even John by surprise.

"We will make it right with her," he said.

"Oh, I'd not bother about it," Cochran said. "She didn't so much as blink when I gave her the news. They was on the outs, as it were. I think that's why he gave it up and went hell bent for it, out in a blaze of glory and all that. He seemed right cavalier at his prospects to success when I seed him last, and he told me just how he was set to go about it. I guess it's what you'd call fatalistic."

We absorbed this news in silence. None of us Heads really knew this Lem Hackett well, but his reputation did surface up the ranks, as a reliable, loyal sort. From time to time reports would come in regarding the gang's various activities, and Hackett's name would be noted as a key figure in some of them.

John remarked, with some solemnity, that our organization had lost a respectably productive member.

"Indeed," intoned Hercules Plumb, his eyes fixed on the fireplace.

These events, particularly Hackett's end, smacked me more sober than I already was regarding the dangers this life posed. I might still seem on the younger side, but back then, it was not at all unusual for a body to expire at the age of thirty-nine or forty. Why accelerate my situation?

John's knuckles rapped the table suddenly, breaking all from our solemn reveries.

"That leaves, what, *Pestilence* and *Death*?"

It took a moment for the names of the remaining boats to register with me. "*Conquest*," I answered.

"Ah, yes," said John. "I would assume that the river titan Mandley is the master of *Conquest*."

Cochran merely nodded enthusiastically.

John stood and began pacing, relighting his pipe, which had gone quiet as we pondered Hackett's fate. "To continue this line of assumptions, I would surmise that the river is just a bit more freed up for us."

"Oh, we have some that are taking advantage, just so, Mr. Murrell," said Cochran.

John nodded curt approval.

Our boats had been scattered all up and down the Mississippi. Hidden, for the most part, in little-known dark and shady estuaries. We had individual keelboats and flatboats venture out from time to time. They were, in every case, skippered by captains and strikers who enjoyed some discretionary independence. Some made it pay and were able to turn a profit, pay their crews, and provide their Head's cut of the take. Some, though, paid the price. They were apprehended and turned over to authorities, most likely to hang eventually. Some had their boats overtaken by locals, plantation owners, or even rival independent criminals and were even killed in some form of vessel-to-vessel struggle. This was rare, but it did happen. I envisioned this Mandley to be reliving his glory days in the Royal Navy, imagining himself back at Trafalgar in his *Victory* (*Conquest*), going muzzle to muzzle with the Frenchie *Tonnant* and always coming out on top.

I could see John's mind working again.

"I ask you, Cochran," he said, "Have we seen this Mandley's fleet working in concert with each other?"

Cochran looked puzzled, very much like a vexed hound dog.

"Together, as one team," I clarified.

Cochran scratched at his head while he pondered, still working it out hound-like.

"As a team of horses, like?" Cochran's eyes finally lit up, excited that he had made out the meaning of the term. "None that we seed. They's trying to cover a lot of river."

"Although Mandley, likely as not, will combine his forces after this blow," said John. "We must move quickly, before *Famine* can again enter the fray."

"She's swamped square, Mr. Murrell. Likely be a week afore she can take to the river again, I'd wager," said Cochran.

"Anchor," John mused to himself. We waited politely, as we had learned to some time ago during his ruminations. Cochran resumed his vexed hound-dog expression.

"Yes. Anchor Line. And Old River. That will do nicely."

This was the area that *Conquest* had been last reported to have frequented while on patrol. The river was always shifting, sometimes miles at a time over months and years. Smaller, off-shooting rivers could be closed off or re-opened along the Mississippi. Entire towns, villages, and camps would come and go according to the whims of nature.

Over the next few days, John elaborated on his plan: Old River's path bent westward into Louisiana. It was not a large body of water, but John figured a keelboat could navigate its course fairly easily. Down Anchor Line's way it narrowed a tad before it eventually re-joined the Mississippi. Mandley's remaining fleet, if forced to navigate it, would bunch together near the shore, making easier targets. Even ruining two vessels would be a hearty blow. "A dandy place for a trap," John exclaimed. "We just need the right lure."

It took time, a few weeks at least, to gather supplies, weapons, and ammunition for this sizable an endeavor. Also, instructing and drilling the Mystics on the particulars. Day in, day out, with some captains beneath us, John, Plumb, and myself rotated amongst the troops to ensure everyone knew the business end of a musket from the butt. Once we got to Anchor Line, we might have even needed two more weeks to get folks used to operating on the boats.

I was almost grateful for the reprieve. In what private moments I had amongst all this busyness, I twisted up inside, trying to find an opening to lay out reservations I had for staying afterwards. I don't mind saying Lem Hackett's fate had a large part in it.

I was at my desk the evening before we set out for Anchor Line, staring unseeing at the ledger, pondering these very thoughts, when John came bounding in, eyes lit like a child on Christmas morning.

"The day is near at hand, Stephen," he sang. "Mandley and his damnable fleet go under."

"Yes," I absently slapped the ledger closed. "Yes... Mandley goes down tomorrow, to be sure... Yes." I looked out the nearby window at the distant river, silver in the moonlight like a mythical serpent.

"Mm hmm," John whistled a jingle. There came the rustle of hands going through pockets. "Something on your mind, Mr. Hue?"

His voice sounded somehow distant. I remained staring out the window. "Have you ever thought beyond all this, John? I mean, when our best years are behind us."

"Beyond..." I glanced at him. Having located his pipe, he helped himself to the matches on my desk. "Oh, some, I suppose," he struck one to life. "Brother, for now, I am content to live in the moment. There is time enough for all that."

"Is there?" The river, the moon low over it, seemed to beckon like the sirens of old. It brought back a simpler time, being a grubby cabin boy under Mose Bunton's legendary shadow.

"Come, Stephen, we must break you from these doldrums. I won't allow you to be so melancholy on the eve of our triumph."

"I have not slept, John." I turned to him. He gazed at me, puffed a cloud from his pipe and looked at me thoughtfully. "Can't. It's Hackett." I faced the window again. "Eating my guts out, it is."

A chair scraped the floor behind me. "I can't say it doesn't trouble me," he sighed.

I turned back to John. He sat back, taking the pipe from his mouth, watching me. I placed my hands flat on the desk, one to either side of the ledger, shuffling it about. *Just get it out, Hue.*

"I've a notion to take some time away. Away from this. After Mandley."

He put another light to his pipe, his eyes sparking with some amusement.

"I'm not fooling, John. I've been thinking on it for a time. Just– It has been awful busy lately."

"I see," he looked at me, more serious, then glanced out the window behind me. "Yes, I do see. Well, we can arrange for that, of course. A month, or two then... However much you need. Ask me for anything." He looked away a moment, then shot me a quick smile as he drew on his pipe.

"I mean to settle." My chair creaked slightly as I leaned forward, making myself look him square in the face. "Settle, John. Permanently."

John took in a deep breath and let it out slowly. His pipe dangled in his hands between his knees as he studied the tiny glow in the bowl. Were my fears of him thinking me disloyal being realized in this moment? What would I say if that were the case? What could I say?

"John?" I said finally after several minutes of silence. The ember in his bowl flickered a last time, then faded.

He looked up, more serious than I had seen him for a time. "Why, Stephen? Where is all of this coming from, of a sudden?"

Father's letter came to mind right then, Nina's rescue from the renegades, but it was all a jumble, and I shut that aside rather than try to explain it. "I don't know," I said quietly.

"I mean, what other life can come close to measuring that of a mighty Mystic's?" He chuckled mirthlessly.

My chair squeaked as I stood, walked around the desk to John. "The Clan... John, the Clan has been... well, it's been extraordinary. I've never even heard of anything like it. Hell, nobody has. You've brought all these people together. And for one purpose. But in doing so, it has served many purposes. You've united people, given them a brotherhood they didn't know they could ever have, a family to people who otherwise would have known only despair. And I'm damned proud of it. And of you, John."

I looked at him earnestly. "I'm proud of you."

His brow furrowed, his eyes flicking down and away. A tiny flare of regret needled at me. But it's too late to go back. "But... I feel as though I've run *my* course. Maybe it's time for another family, a wife, kids. A home to call my own..." I gestured off to the doorway. "Have another Mystic take my place. I've trained a few stout men. Trustworthy men."

There was a rap on the door before July popped in, holding a large jug.

"What is it, July?" John snapped. "Can't you see we are busy?"

"Oh," July stepped back, startled. "S-sorry, Mr. Murrell. I just brought that new tarantula juice you asked me to fetch. Th-that new blend, direct from Mr. Pilver's still." He darted his eyes at me. "So's you could celebrate proper with Mr. Hue." His eyes went from me, arms folded and leaning against the desk, then back to John, elbows on his knees, still studying his pipe.

"That's fine, lad." John's voice was suddenly tired. "Thank you. Please... ah... take it back to my quarters." July backed hesitantly out of the room.

John stared blankly at the ledger.

"I'm sorry, John." The words sounded flat in the little room. "Trust that you will always have my loyalty. As will the Clan–"

John waved a quick hand as he stood. I fell silent. He dipped his head, his mouth working. "Well I–" he choked out. He would not look my way. "I mean–"

After a moment, he blurted, "We will chew on this more. After Mandley. Meantime, prepare your Mystics to execute the plan. We ride for Anchor Line at first light, as agreed."

He stalked out of the room.

I stared at the ledger, then picked it up, my eyes looking over the cover's ornate illustration for about the thousandth time. But this time, *The Clan Mystic*, emblazoned in bold, defiant lettering, seemed to blare at me, shouting, mocking, *shaming*.

26

ALONG THE JOURNEY to Anchor Line – about two days' ride – John seemed to be generally his old, amicable self from what I could tell. That wasn't much, really, for he kept things mostly to the business at hand, maybe to avoid prolonged conversation with me, talking to the Mystics repeatedly about what was about to occur, to ensure everyone knew their role.

For all my talk of leaving the Clan, it did feel good to again be at the helm of *Minerva Underwood*. I pulled the canvas from my beloved swivel gun and inspected it, patted it, and spoke lovingly to it. We would depend on it mightily in the coming days.

It did not take but a day and a half to get her ready for the river, re-rigging a few areas here and there, and restocking stores in the event that this excursion extended beyond our expected duration. We had selected a team of good rivermen and strikers. If Mandley and his men lived up to even half their reputation, we would need them.

Cochran came along. With his recent experience with the

Four Horsemen patrols, we felt his knowledge may come in handy.

We convened a few miles north of Gravel Bay with *Vixen Mistress*, which John himself skippered. Not for the name, mind, but for her superior river-going abilities. When put to the test, even I had to admit the *Vixen* was swifter and handled lightly – much more so than *Minerva*. She responded like lightning to any command or maneuver, under pole or sail.

In any case, we lurked about a few days with no sighting of our nemesis, although we did see a steamer venture by and only hoped that she would pass on word that they had spied us. I wondered how they could tell we were not but legitimate traders, and John instructed us to behave "pirate-like" when spotted.

I took that to mean to act furtive and begin scurrying away as quickly as possible when spotted by a vessel that may be allied in any way with Tedder Company or Mandley.

Sure enough, that moment came.

On another boat further upriver from ours, Cochran, using a pre-arranged sign, signaled to John that *Conquest* had come into his view and was bearing down on him.

Within a mile of this chase, *Conquest* had pulled within view of *Minerva* and *Vixen*. Someone fired a warning shot from her, and some shouting could be faintly heard coming from Cochran's boat. As these vessels came nearer, I spotted a burly man on top of the cabin of *Conquest*. This had to be Mandley himself.

It was then that we heard a peculiar sound: rather sustained, high-pitched, piercing noise reaching from across the water.

I peered across to *Conquest*, and it appeared the burly man standing atop the cabin was blowing... a horn. I had never actually heard one before, but I did read about them. I imagined that this was what a bugle for a fox hunt sounded like.

A smile spread instantly across my face, for I was in the middle of some promising great sport. Mystic blood obviously still ran in my veins, settling down forgotten for the moment.

A few men on the *Vixen* took up muskets and fired them in the general direction of *Conquest*. They were still at enough range where they had no real hope of hitting *Conquest*, or anything at all, for that matter. *Minerva*, though, was heaving close now, just shy of a hundred yards. I ordered her crew to open up with our muskets. They banged madly away with great relish.

Mandley continued with the horn. Their four-pounder thundered again, this time with more authority, since the distance had closed some since their warning shot. A great geyser of water flew up in the river near *Vixen*, announcing they had about found their range.

I heard another scattered clattering on *Minerva's* hull. Had I encountered some unknown sawyer lurking in the river? Was *Minerva* about to be clawed to its clutches?

My mind then righted itself, matching the sound with its origin: *Conquest's* muskets had joined their rifles, and the balls were clattering along the hull and the deck. God, how many guns had they brought against us?

But there was some relief, for by now we had reached the mouth of Old River. Our men knew the waters there fairly well, as we had navigated them some days earlier to familiarize ourselves with its traits and any feature we might use to our advantage.

Speed and agility were our allies here, and we used them to full advantage. Old River wended about to the extent that we were even able to use the shore terrain to shield us from rifle and cannon fire from time to time.

We knew where the eddies and shoals lay. Hopefully, Mandley's crew didn't.

There were enough river bends to make aiming and accurately firing a cannon – four- pounder or otherwise - a bit more of a challenge than it otherwise might be. That is, unless Mandley had taken it upon himself to enlist former Royal Navy gunners and gun captains, in which case their accuracy and speed could not be called into question. I felt an urgent, close gust, before a plume of air plucked at my hair, towers of white water appearing in the river near *Minerva* – too near for anyone's taste. One of my men looked at another, laughing as water cascaded down on them. His neighbor looked back at him as if he had gone mad.

I stood in the stern of *Minerva,* manning the helm as my crew poled away as if their lives depended on it. Mandley's horn blew. That ugly buzz-whir of rifle shot sounded all around, making my skin crawl as before. They had the advantage on us there; we being only armed with muskets. My boys kept up with their own arms though, loading and firing as quickly and steadily as Tennessee militiamen, I'm proud to say, laying down fire on *Conquest.* There were about nine men on her, two manning their gun, three sailing her, and the rest trying to return fire under the withering volleys. Much shouting and gross insults to each other's wives, mothers, and ancestors filled the gaps between the gunfire.

Anchor Line finally appeared on the distant shore.

I felt myself inwardly bracing, scanning the shore for our expected allies, but not seeing any thus far. My stomach tightened into a fearsome clutch of muscles.

The chase went on. I ducked reflexively as a ball from *Conquest's* cannon tore off a chunk of Minerva's gunwale. Jagged splinters ripped into a crewman's throat. He fell to the deck, his musket clattering overboard. He screamed and thrashed on the deck, his blood splashing brightly everywhere.

There was shouting now from *Vixen*. John was gesturing wildly to the farther shore. With newfound alertness, I steered *Minerva* in his indicated direction.

The men drove the poles deeper, pushing madly for more speed. A rifle shot, very close this time – no, a pole had shattered, and the man carried over the side with the momentum. We could not stop. The crewman's face was as white as river froth, his eyes wide with terror. I knew him, knew he could not swim. I tried to shake it off, not think about it.

As I steered onto the shore, the man disappeared beyond our stern, the river claiming him. My throat tightened, my stomach churned. My eyes stung from the smoke of the muskets; the air was dirtied with the acrid smell of burned gunpowder.

The shore grew nearer, agonizingly slow.

That damnable horn had stopped. This was no longer sport. *Conquest* was overtaking its prey. A loud, piercing voice now replaced the horn. "Heave to now, rascals, and you may yet live on to torment your children!"

A volley of musket fire from *Vixen* and a few from *Minerva* answered Mandley's order.

A man on *Conquest* flew back as if kicked hard in the belly, a ball from a *Vixen* musket carrying him over the side.

The man on *Minerva's* deck was no longer thrashing. He was not moving at all.

The chase had finally reached the shore, just north of Anchor Line.

My eyes searched frantically for Hercules Plumb. By now, the shore should have been teeming with men and even a six-pounder gun and limber team he had told us he had acquired.

Nothing was there to be seen but one man on a bedraggled

and sorry-looking horse, a small boy, a girl, and a three-legged dog.

Conquest loomed closer, its bow and stern guns now bearing onto our vessels. Mandley stood, still on the cabin. He was a right lovely target.

Heads down, two of my crew were manhandling the swivel gun, mounting it on a yoke on the *Minerva's* foredeck. I watched as one man hurriedly opened the breech and installed a bag of powder while the other added a handful of musket balls. Their hands moved in something of a blur, weeks of training paying off.

Yes, that will do nicely, my fevered brain managed as I brought the *Minerva* about just enough to hopefully aid their aim. The *Conquest* was near enough.

A gigantic, bellowing explosion tore the air as *Conquest's* gun roared. Losing my hearing during the fight with old Buckskin paled to nothing against this blast. Futilely, I flung my arms over my face. A ghastly splash of bright red erupted on *Minerva's* bow.

The swivel gun was gone in an instant, and one crewman was cut in two, the other nowhere to be seen. As sounds started to creep back in my ear, the world slowing down its quakes, I surveyed my deck. A sizable part of the bow, in fact, had been obliterated in a storm of wood and iron, blood and flame.

In that moment, all I could think was that I never had a chance to fire that weapon in anger. It is sometimes amusing, when thinking on things later, what absurd thoughts will tumble through a man's brain in such times.

A second shot from *Conquest* likewise crippled *Vixen.* Much of the stern, including the rudder, was simply gone.

I could not see John anywhere. *We will chew on this more, after Mandley.*

Cochran lay dead on his boat, head and shoulders lolling across a hogshead on the deck, still grasping a musket.

Minerva and *Vixen* were sinking, the muddy water of Old River and the Mississippi busily claiming their hulls. Their crews were scrambling for safety, tossing muskets and poles away, shouting and crying to their companions, trying to throw lines to them, cursing the *Conquest*.

As I searched about for a means of salvation, some debris to grasp onto, I saw several figures now, coming through the trees and approaching the river. I could not grasp who they might be. Everything was happening so fast; my thinking was a muddle.

The current of the river was converging the wreckage of boats a little, moving ever closer to the shoreline. Blood slicked its surface. I then spotted John about twenty yards away, also clutching a piece of the shattered *Minerva.*

The fabric of his coat had been savagely ripped away at his right shoulder, exposing a red ruin of shredded flesh. A musket ball must've gone through it. He clung desperately to his support with his one good arm; his face twisted in agony and anguish. I made it to him and supported his body as best as I could. *I'm sorry, John. Trust that you will always have my loyalty.* The river water chilled me to the marrow.

We watched the gathering on the shore as it grew in numbers. Mandley steered *Conquest* nearer to shore, got out, and waded in with a satisfied smile on his face. His ridiculous fox hunt horn was now tucked into his belt.

The men coming through the trees were ours, looking sullen and defeated. They were being marched at gunpoint, with Hercules Plumb in the forefront.

Mr. Plumb's face wore an abject expression of absolute dejection and failure. His hands were tied behind his back. His mouth had been gagged with a grimy bit of cloth.

Mandley turned back to the water, his eyes searching for John.

"One thing I have always hated, even since a lad," he cast his voice over the crowd. His Irish brogue seemed more pronounced when speaking in a more conversational tone, "is not being invited to the best parties."

He stalked over to Mr. Plumb. "Plumb, you did wrong me. In more ways than one, didn't you?"

Mandley found John now, who was staring back at him through the pain, with unflinching hatred.

"Oh, you'll never know if Plumb here sold you out, Mister Devil Preacher. Could be any one of these river demons in your service." His mouth curled into a grimace. I realized after a moment that this was him smiling.

Mandley gestured to one of his men, who tossed him a coil of rope.

"Sadly, there are but a few ways to see to it this little game of yours ends forever. That's as I see it, anyway."

He threw the rope over a nearby overhanging tree branch. A noose dangled on the other end. Mr. Plumb flinched as Mandley looped this over his head. Someone brought up a horse, and Mandley awkwardly mounted it.

The river's current had already pulled us some distance away from most of the wreckage. God Almighty, it was *cold*. Our men who had been stationed on a few Mackinaws a bit south of Anchor Line came into view.

Mandley fastened the other end of the rope on the saddle's horn and began moving away on the horse.

Mr. Plumb was already twitching and twisting about as he instinctively endeavored to fend off the inevitable. Someone laughed. Mandley's mount clopped slowly down the shore, leisurely as the Queen's own pony in her garden.

Hercules Plumb's thrashing body rose, the tree's branch

bending and bobbing with the weight. I will never forget his bulging eyes, now almost fully red with blood. His men on shore tried to look away, but Mandley's crew clubbed them to the ground.

One of Plumb's men tried to run for it, running madly and clumsily over the shoreline pebbles. Mandley quickly grabbed a rifle from one of his men and took calm, careful aim at him. When the poor bastard was almost out of sight, a shot rang out. Plumb's man collapsed.

Mandley shrugged, gazing placidly back at Plumb's struggle, the rifle's smoke billowing around him and his horse. "It's shot in the back, belly, or hanged."

My body ached from supporting John and fighting the current. The river had pulled us a good distance away by now, so Mandley had to shout at us again. "Makes no never mind to me! You see?"

John's eyes never left the twisted form of his friend, Hercules Plumb.

The Mackinaw crews carefully pulled us from the water once we had reached them downstream. Mandley was content to stand on the shore and watch his troops bind the remaining of our men and march them back through the trees, to whatever fate - jail or gallows - awaited them.

I was puzzled as to why *Conquest* had not pursued us, but for only a moment, as I had my friend John Murrell to tend to.

27

SLOWLY AND CAREFULLY, we transported John to the nearest haven, about twenty miles from the river, a large cabin home to a worthy Clan captain by the name of Percy Garris.

"We'll look after him, Mr. Hue," Garris looked over John gravely. "He'll be mended proper."

"That he will, make no mistake." His wife Susanna, a small, no-nonsense woman, moved with urgent purpose and motioned to one of the bedrooms, already made up for John.

We laid up there for several months, the Garris's and I tending to John to heal his wounds. I sent for July right away. John had taken to the lad so much, having him about to help out would bolster John's spirits. He got to us in just a few days' time, with some other Mystics.

"By jings, son, I didn't know you could ride like that," I fanned away some dust his horse had kicked up with my hat. Susanna had come to the porch to see who the new arrivals were.

"Mr. Murrell is a fine teacher," July smiled breathlessly

back at me. The smile faltered as he looked distractedly toward the cabin.

"July, this is Mrs. Garris." I took his reins. "She'll take you to John." He made for the cabin, but I placed a hand on his shoulder. "Thank you, July." He stopped, looking at me. "Thanks for coming so quick."

He nodded, and Susanna led him inside.

There was no question that the Anchor Line fight had bruised our operation and repute, but we still had active captains and Mystics keeping things moving, just more and more of it away from river country.

Mandley had accomplished his chief object, it seemed. At least for the time being.

John was mending, better every day, aided by July's arrival as I had hoped, but Mandley's triumph, and of course the lynching of our friend Mr. Plumb, burned like an unquenchable ember in him. He would go long periods of never speaking, just staring, engulfed in a depression so profound it had me worried about him more than ever. I couldn't fault him for any of it, but I urged him to rest and concern himself with recovering.

Here he could hardly object, being severely limited in movement, but I often found him in his bed, face darkened in deep thoughts, sometimes scribbling like mad in his ledger and muttering to himself. His voice was frequently more subdued and thoughtful than before, certainly less boisterous and jovial. Clan members would look in occasionally, sometimes reporting to him the clan's adventures, or getting a weak smile or soft chuckle out of him with some ribald story or joke. I hoped that was doing him some long-term good.

I had to wonder if our exchange the night before departing for Anchor Line played a part in his present state. When I wasn't tending to John, or handling Clan business where I could so it wouldn't burden him, I found myself pacing, my mind running with a hard press of shame. My friend in such a state, and other comrades, fellow Mystics gone to God knew where or to what fate. And here I was, not long before all of this, thinking only of myself, leaving a brother - and brotherhood - behind.

"Clan Mystic suffers a mortal blow, Stephen, a mortal blow," John told me at one point, as I was trying to get him to eat a proper meal. "I feel it teetering now, by God." His eyes stared, vacant, nearly lifeless. "This can't be the end."

"John, no," I stopped myself from reaching for him. "It's merely a setback. It's bad, yes," I forced something of a smile. "But this is the Clan Mystic. It's not the end. Not by half." I wasn't sure I believed it myself.

"I should have seen it," John said, staring fixedly into the fire. He looked so profoundly lost. Not sure what words could help, I left the room quietly.

Another time, John looked at me very intently for several moments.

"You know," he said suddenly, "I do understand it. You might not think it, Stephen." I looked at him, somewhat vexed. "This impulse for a family, children, to carry on the line and all of that. After all, what happens to our names when we are all dust, hmm?" He waved a hand quickly. "Puff! It all just... ends? We must carry on the blood – no, more than that, my own bloodline isn't worth a drop of horse piss – the heart is more important, Stephen."

He tapped his chest twice, weakly. "The heart bears what we've gathered up in this life, you see? That's worth carrying on to the next line. And if we benefit from a woman's devotion and a child's affection while at it, why, so much the better, yes?"

I opened my mouth to reply.

"Now, July, my God, what a story, Stephen! It's one I

would have heard far and wide if I would have my way. I couldn't be prouder of the kid, grasping onto his humanity and not letting it go. I am damned honored to have known him. I understand you, you hear?"

I confess I had no response by that point. My heart warmed with John's wide-open display of affection for July and the comfort of his finally understanding my urge to move on. Yet how could I now, the Clan in such precarious state?

But John seemed to have retreated into his own reflections and lay without remembering my presence for a bit, murmuring here and there about the "impulse for a family" and that he "did understand." Soon, he fell blessedly asleep, and I took my leave.

Meanwhile, our investigation into the gang's betrayal had not yielded any real leads, which added to John's torment. Most of the men who had been intercepted by Mandley's men on shore that day had been already strung up or otherwise executed. Only a few yet were in prison, but to our knowledge, none of them had given Mandley or what authorities that were about any useful information in the direction of John's capture. It seemed that the power of the ledger and our various captains' influence held their integrity even within prison walls. The prospect of my being the traitor had not seemed to cross John's mind. I was, of course, relieved, but I anguished over just how I might have to respond if it had, given our discussion just prior to the Mandley fight. It was a bridge I prayed our friendship would not have to cross.

My own well-being was diminished as well, too often lacking sleep, tormented night and day by visions of John's body bobbing in the river's churning current, his gaping wound swirling the water from brown to white, to red.

As John's health continued slowly improving, he conducted more business than usual – even more than he previously had –

and almost all of it done verbally. He used runners and only occasionally on paper. He seemed almost unnaturally fearful of some form of written communication, even mundane or routine lists. Such might provide some kind of intelligence to Mandley, the law, or some other enemy. He had also become something of a voracious reader, reading everything he could get his hands on regarding military campaigns, logistics, and the like. Myself, I thought he was getting all a bit high-minded, devouring the likes of Napoleon, Frederick the Great, and even Julius Caesar.

He looked up at me one night from one of these books, his face with a healthier glow by his ever-present fire. It wasn't much, his face was wan, thinner, and he still winced some when he had to move that shoulder, but for one moment, some of the old, energetic John Murrell glinted briefly in his eyes.

"This ship will be righted, Mr. Hue." He nodded, more to himself than anything. His voice became an almost prayerful whisper, "It will endure. Yes. Yes, it must."

I looked into the dancing glow of the flames. Ghostly, gnarled hands of fear slowly clutched at my belly. This path John seemed to be on would only cut him down in the end. And I didn't know if I could stop it.

The mesmerizing fire brought to mind a time long ago, when we were lads on the run. "Always have a plan," My voice was soft, dreamlike.

"That's right, brother. Always have a plan."

28

"ANCHOR LINE. You've all heard about it by now, the details of it. I won't belabor it or cast any blame about. That would serve no purpose now, other than perhaps to drive division into our ranks. I'll have no part of it, and I expect none of you to."

It was roughly three months on, and John Murrell was addressing an assembly of his head captains and senior Mystics, gathered in a large clearing above the entrance to Heavenly Hollow, under the canopy of that enormous oak tree. It had taken them all about a week to arrive from all of the various far-flung reaches of the organization. There had been a pile of decent grub, a large fire, camaraderie, and a few brawls – after the typical consumption of a fair bit of alcohol, of course.

Things had settled down to business. There was, after all, a purpose for John calling this assembly, other than old friends meeting after years apart and sundry scores being settled between old rivals. This was a rare occasion.

"I will say that this beast, Mandley, was right about one thing. Now, every man here has a different reason for joining this crew. I harbor no illusion about that. Some of you have been running from John Law for the better part of your lives, like me!"

Appreciative laughter and knowing looks rolled through the assembly.

"And many of you ran into the loving arms of a like-minded band of men. Men with a talent for crime. And has it not benefited us all? Rather than each man out in the wind, on his own, we are better and stronger united, working together.

"It's true, our renown has been bruised. As has our purse. I'll not deny it. The loss of those vessels hurt, and soundly. Sadly, some of the clan's more lucrative earners were lost as well. You have all done yeoman's jobs in filling that gap what you could. For that, I thank you.

"But we are survivors, my captains. That," he thumped the table before him, "is what we do." Judging by the men's various expressions, they were caught up in John's passion.

"It'll take more than two sunk vessels, beloved as they may be," he gave me an apologetic look. "And cash blown into the wind to topple our hard-built, longstanding empire, I should think." John raised his voice. "What say you, lords and gentlemen?"

Enthusiastic huzzahs and cheers sounded from the ranks.

"And do you know why?"

A chorus of voices erupted, variously. "Why, John?"

"Tell us, sir!"

"Why?"

"Because of every single one of us here tonight, and every Mystic son and brother we command under us."

"You there, Josiah! Why, you and your Mystics sure did put the fear of the Clan in that Biloxi banker and got half his fortune while at it!" Some chuckles passed around. The Biloxi banker had raised a motte-and-bailey settlement in his lands some ways east, like one of those Anglo-Saxon ramparts, denying the Clan its rightful tithe in his dealings. For all the good it did him.

"And Elwood over there, that grift in Mooresville, well, I haven't seen that one pulled off in a time."

A man I recognized as Judge Joe Fox proudly clapped Elwood on the back.

"You freed men in our ranks. By God, you can hold your heads proud. Joseph, there, and Emanuel, why that Rutledge job? At the farm? Hell, that was one for the books, sirs, yessir."

The white men in the ranks applauded loudly, some shrilly whistling their approval. The Rutledge family was famous in the region for the prime horse flesh they raised. Exceptionally fine stock, fast, sturdy stallions that brought a pretty penny. A mite too pretty for the likes of us, at least, while slave hunters always found some optimal haggling choices. Until Emanuel's job nearly put the Rutledges in the poor house a good while.

"You see?" John paced up and down, pausing intermittently. "You see, Clan Mystic? What is one soggy defeat for a kingdom like ours?"

The captains began to cheer, many of them hoisting their steins in salute to the rousing speech and the clan of mystic beasts. My neighbor, whom I knew as a constable of Lynchburg, glanced at me and, with a grin, said, "It's not Henry V, but it'll do."

I smiled slightly. My heart was gladdened to see the old John emerge. Rallying the clan from its rough times seemed to be doing him as much good as the men.

"Gentlemen," John continued after the hubbub subsided, "I did not rally you here to a criminal camp meeting, a convention, if you will, of criminal brethren to merely boost your spirits. You are all confident men, else you would not be here. This is certain.

"I have gathered this *Mystic Clan* to a grand purpose. A purpose that will, in time, make us all kings!"

He paused, looking about. "At least dukes and maybe earls." His audience again emitted a collective laugh, and a charitable number of cheers and applause.

"We have a sizable clan. I'd wager a formidable force, by any calculation. Our reach goes deep into every southern region. What we have at hand, should we choose to properly exploit it, is a veritable army at our disposal. An army, really, that has been right under our noses and primed for action all this while."

Some of the captains looked questioningly about. Sure, we had our share of skirmishes and battle experience, but calling us an army was a mite rich. Others just puffed on their pipes and cigars patiently, awaiting further details.

"I speak, gentlemen, of the slaves."

I took in a quick breath. I really had not expected this. The assembly fell to a further hush, with just a clattering of steins and pitchers being set down, as they settled in for more. John had really bolted down their attention now.

"We all know of the Haitian Rebellion, and its successes. I propose none but the same *here*, with the Mystic Clan at its head."

Naturally, at this pronouncement, the meeting erupted into exclamations ranging from shock to disbelief to excitement and enthusiastic huzzahs. Most of the freed black men smiled broadly. One laughed, while another stood with a fierce expression and fists to his sides as if ready to spring to action at a moment's notice.

John held up his hands to quell the hubbub and was successful to the degree that Judge Fox was able to stand and make his voice heard.

"But John," he said, "This seems too far-flung a design. An impossible endeavor. I cannot conceive of such a thing."

"And I am sure there were Haitians who believed the same, Judge," John replied.

Another man spoke up, cutting in before Judge Fox.

"Haiti is an island, sir, and such a contrivance is no doubt more easily attained there. Here, the scale is just too great."

"Easy to say, in hindsight, I declare," John responded. "The Haitian experience relied more on a growing mob of terror and greatly benefited from rapidly gained speed. A wildfire of violence and voracious thirst for revenge not seen since revolutionary France."

"But is that not what you propose here?" said Judge Fox. "I cannot see how else to accomplish this otherwise." Others around him nodded in agreement. "I mean to the aspect of sheer violence and terror."

"There is no other way, if we are to achieve our aims, early on," said John. "We have already set in place in all our cities within our reach, agents that will set things in motion. To be supremely successful, these things must be accomplished all at once, on the same date and time."

Many captains sat calm and passive throughout these pronouncements. Those were men, I assumed, that John had already been working with, which accounted for his flurry of correspondence and constant runners, day and night, during his period of convalescence. Some of these were freed men, former slaves. They watched the assembly quietly, expressions stony, arms folded.

"I have every confidence that our connections among the Negro community are already substantial and vast enough to afford this early success," said John.

"I can attest to this," said Loney Pilver, standing, then spitting into the fire. "I am the overseer at Rooks Hope, never mind what many of y'all might have heard. I have men ready for it. Just give the word."

Another man, known to be a merchant with dealings with several plantations, offered known support amongst at least three very large plantations in his region.

A general buzz of conversation among individuals and small groups started up, showing a general sense of enthusiasm and mechanisms already in place for the ambitious scheme.

John managed to settle everyone down again.

"The twenty-fifth of December, this year, gentlemen," he announced.

A hush again fell over the crowd. Loney Pilver spat into the fire again and barked a laugh.

"And it'll be a warm yuletide this year. Store up them chestnuts," he said.

Someone cackled.

"We design to have our companies so stationed over the country, in the vicinity of the banks and large cities, that when the Negroes commence their carnage and slaughter, we will have detachments to fire the towns and rob the banks while all is confusion and dismay."

The assembly sat in rapt attention. I pondered on this operation of calamity, and I confess it held me rapt as well. I suppose that could be chalked up to the sheer audacity of the thing. All the same, at that moment, I shivered inside a little, pondering the calamity that was Anchor Line, and how far-flung that operation had been, and depending so much on the actions and dependability of others. This thing that John was now proposing was even grander. Perhaps too grand. Involving the slaves, as he had, brought to my mind the Nat Turner revolt, which had occurred only nine years prior and failed after only a week's time.

I decided to keep my reservations to myself and bring them all to John after the council.

Knowing he had them, John seized on his audience further.

"The rebellion, taking place everywhere at the same time, every part of the country will be engaged in its own defense, and one part of the country can afford no relief to the other, until many places will be entirely overrun by the Negroes.

"Now, it's true that the slave population may be weaker in some areas, but if we back them with a few resolute leaders from our own clan, they will murder thousands and huddle the remainder into large bodies of stationary defense for their own preservation. And then, in many other places, the black population is much stronger, and under a fierce leader, would overrun the country before any steps could be taken to suppress them."

"John, I can't see how this is made known to the Negroes without the scheme being exposed wide and fast," said someone. "You know the gossip in their towns and quarters is just as buzzing as a Boston quilting bee."

"This is easily done, my good man," replied John with an easy flow. "We do not go to every Negro we see and tell them of the Christmas Rebellion. Oh, no. We find the most vicious and wickedly disposed of them on the large farms – the ones who have been most aggrieved in their punishments – and poison their minds ever more. Implore on them that they are entitled to their freedoms as much as any man, and that all of the wealth of the country, having so far gathered, is the product of *their* sweat, *their* labor."

John let that sink in for a moment. I confess here that I myself had not thought in that vein before. I could see from some expressions that this was a revelation for them as well. The freed men looked about at their white fellows, stern aspects to their faces, some exchanging nods, as if confirming an ancient truth long known.

"To reinforce this idea," John continued, "I propose also that we convey to them that all of Europe has abandoned slavery, and that the West Indies are all free, and that they achieved this freedom by rebelling a few times and slaughtering the whites. If they hence follow the example of the West Indies Negroes, they too will obtain their liberty!

"It is imperative that we assure ourselves that we have secured a bloodthirsty, rebellious leader in as many key regions as possible. Of course, secrecy is of utmost importance. Swear them to it, and convince them of the exact starting mark in each place, and that every other state and section of the country where there is a population of slaves is set to step off on that same mark. We must assure them that there are thousands of white men – and there are – engaged in endeavoring to free them, who will die by their sides in battle.

"Our emissaries – your strikers – will be furnished with money to procure spirits to ply them with, and then they will open their secrets to them as such: 'Fellow slaves, this is the night we are to obtain our liberty! All of the Negroes in the South rebel this night and slay the whites. We have long been subject to the whips of our tyrants, and many of our backs wear their scars. The time has arrived when we can be avenged. There are many good white men who are helping us to gain our freedom. All of you who refuse to fight will be put to death, so come on, brave fellows! We will be free or die!

"Our strikers will be at hand to encourage their handpicked Negro leaders. You see, there will be enough slaves that will follow these men, enough to force all of the others to engage, under the belief that the slaves have also rebelled everywhere else, just as it is happening around them."

"You are talking about a mob army," someone else said. "These things have a way of getting out of hand."

"Once this beast is unleashed," said another, "how do you intend to rein it in?"

"The strikers and their cohorts are very well armed," answered John. "And a select number of them and the slaves will have access to them. There are a number of former military men who have already been put in command positions and know to act accordingly. There are many of them that will fight like Turks!"

There was a murmur now running through the assembly. Those who knew in advance of the plan were busily convincing others that it was sound. Someone broke off from the debate and stood. "For my part, this is all madness, for the very reason just broached. John, we have a good thing going. It would be a tragedy for it to all come raining down on us should just one or two of these leaders in some far-flung area fail to ignite these flames. And for it to be done all at one mark! Too much would have to play out perfectly. The risk is too great."

John pointed at the man, as if he had anticipated his concern.

"This may seem overbold to you, brother, but that itself is the *glory* in it!" He paused and looked around at his captains. There was a loud crack from the fire.

"All of the crimes I have ever committed – the crimes that many of you have perpetrated – have led to this point. Have you not asked yourselves – despite any success and wealth gained in life – is this it? Is this all there is?"

Here, there was a long, quiet pause.

"I tell you, gentlemen, there is. There most assuredly is, and it is a place in history. An indelible imprint chiseled into granite. An imprint of *your* name. *Your* accomplishments. The annals of the Mystic Empire will be the annals of your life, and its legacy, for all time. This is your day, gentlemen. Your time. Seize it with all of your strength. All of your soul."

Things grew very quiet.

"Riders!" John called suddenly.

Men who had been in the back in the gloom of the surrounding trees came forward, leading Rutledge mounts. In a quick glance, I spotted at least seven.

"We have our word," John said solemnly. "And you have your orders and contacts. Ride forth and deliver."

The riders silently turned as one, mounted their horses.

Christmas Night, 1834, was five months away.

29

It was well after the Grand Council had disbursed, leaving John and I sitting under the enormous oak tree and contemplating the dying fire, that John spoke to me directly of the plot that he had announced and expanded upon to the captains.

"I didn't think you would approve," he said.

I looked at him.

"As Mr. Cotton said, it is a large chunk to bite off," he said.

I shrugged. "Maybe so. But if it works, you're a mad genius."

John barked a laugh. "I am!"

"They do say that of Napoleon."

He stared into the fire. "Napoleon."

It was quiet for a time. A nightingale sang in the distance.

"Nat Turner," I said. John arched an eyebrow at me.

"It would be fresh in people's memories," I said. "Could be too soon for adventure such as this, I'll say that."

Turner was a slave who began a rebellion by first slaughtering his owner and then the man's family, following what he claimed was a message from God. He saw visions, spoke to spirits. Said he had foreseen everything he was then perpetrating himself. It started with an eclipse, as one of his signs, which started all the murders. About sixty people had succumbed to Turner's violence. They tried to capture an armory near the county seat, but that had failed. Turner escaped for a while, but they caught up and strung him up. Nevertheless, in white folks' revenge, they slaughtered twice the number of Turner's victims in a bloody rampage.

Word of it, of course, got everywhere in very quick fashion, and the South had been on high trigger since those events. It had caused a fearsome amount of anxiety and fright in the white population in the region, and even deeper hatred of the abolition movement that even then existed. If the law-abiding whites, plantation owners, and farmers even got one whiff of anything like it being afoot, why, it would be all over for Clan Mystic.

"In any case," John said, standing and stretching, "The die is cast. The riders have been dispatched." He looked at me, clamped his teeth on his pipe, and smiled, supremely satisfied.

"John," I said, "what about the bloodshed? You've never been for it. Something on this scale, Lord... Those things in Haiti. It was just... slaughter. Murder."

He stared at me. There was a coldness there. Even though I knew it wasn't for me, it was like I was looking at another person altogether. Someone I no longer really understood.

"This is a war, Stephen. It's that simple."

"War, John?" I asked. "War on your own people?"

There was a long pause. John's eyes trailed down to the still-glowing embers of the fire. His right hand drifted to his left wrist, seemingly without him realizing. It grasped there and rubbed through his coat and the long sleeve of his shirt.

"My people," he said, with a bitter starkness. "I don't see them as my people, Stephen. I don't see that at all. I don't know as I ever did." He shook his head. "Stephen, I fear that you have lost sight of who I am, if you don't know who my people truly are. It's the downtrodden, the castaways, the slaves, the whores, the mongrels. Not ever civilized society."

After a moment, I stood, then slowly walked away.

I left him there, staring into embers, no doubt seeing in them his people.

30

THE WORD WAS SPREAD INITIALLY by the riders, all trusted men, John assured me, and then to further loyal strikers. As to the thoroughness of his communication and its security, I could not attest, but we were trusting to the word of our various captains and clan members holding official stations across the land.

In the meantime, one of our agents had come upon reliable intelligence regarding the steamboat *Annie Franklin,* carrying a significant cargo of whiskey and other spirits.

Another of our more enterprising strikers had finagled getting a man aboard her into a position to influence the roustabouts and take over the vessel.

John instructed me and July to meet him with a suitable number of men and carts to haul off the supply of whiskey. I also armed myself and many of the men with our new Hall carbines stored in Heavenly Hollow, gifted to us by Mr. Bembry. I had spent a great deal of time honing my skills with the Hall, loading and firing as quickly and efficiently as a British army rifleman.

We arrived at Lake Chicot at the appointed hour.

"Your timing is perfect," John said with a grin once he had reached us. "*Annie Franklin's* is not, however. They are hung up at the Sweet Plantation, apparently."

The place had taken its name from its chief product, sugar cane. Hence, sugar.

"The captain will be much disturbed, but that may well work to our advantage. He is liked to be distracted by his impatience."

"Do you know this captain, in particular?" I asked.

"No, but if he is true to the model, he will be agitated at being behind schedule. These steamboat captains are all cut from the same canvas."

It wasn't until the hours just before dawn that we were aroused by a distant banging: the distinct, obnoxious engine of a steamboat.

John hurried some Mystics to ignite a sizable fire on the shore – a signal to our men on the *Franklin*.

Shortly after, we heard a commotion on the nearing vessel. There was an unmistakable crack of a pistol. A pause, then another, more muffled report. I thought I saw the briefest flash from within the pilot house.

In came the *Annie Franklin*, directly at us. From the sound of it, the engine was not reducing speed by any detectable measure. Some started stepping back from the shore, unsure of the intent of whoever was at the helm.

"Cuss me for a Kiowa!" John exclaimed with a laugh, "I believe he means to beach her right here!"

Annie Franklin did veer then, as if directing herself away from John's voice, but it was too late by then. A tremendous crash violated the morning air as the boat lumbered first into the low tree branches hanging over the river from the shore. The hull of the vessel met the shore with a heavy grating sound coupled with the creaks and groanings of the hull grinding itself apart. Pushed by the *Annie Franklin*, the river spilled onto the shore, sluicing heavily past tree trunks and washing away leaves and dirt, a small flood.

At the same moment, most of ours took advantage of the chaos and boarded the *Annie Franklin*, brandishing rifles and some with knives and a variety of blades. It really had all the color and sound of a real piratical moment right then.

The crew of the *Annie Franklin*, in most cases, just gave up without much fight. Some had already jumped ship. Those who could swim were making their way to various gaps on the shore. Others, I can only assume, had already drowned. There were a few scuffles here and there, and two or three shots fired, but these appeared only been loosed in the air for effect. The only casualty we could see, at least right off, was the poor captain.

"Did it have to be done?" asked John with some anguish.

Our man, I remember him only as Beales, simply shrugged with a sheepish look. He tucked his pistol away and heaved off.

John's reaction to the captain's death was quite mystifying. Was this the man who, only days before, expounded as to his plot to revolt the slaves and kill white people wholesale? Perhaps he had some kind of soft spot from his childhood, or reading books or some such, for steamboat captains and other uniformed men. Law officers being the exception, of course.

The men set to relieve the *Annie Franklin* of her precious golden liquid cargo, working with a will not witnessed in any previous enterprise. I would go so far as to say that some records were broken and made again in the time it took for the unloading of cargo from a steamboat. Maybe even a Spanish galleon.

A team of men took the steamboat's own fire axes and began destroying the hull in various places, at John's direction.

"See to it the *Annie* never floats again," he said, with a certain malice in his eyes.

"This beast is the property of Tedder and Company," he continued, turning to me. "And I mean to bruise them."

And now I saw it, what this event truly came down to.

"They will come down on us like fire, John."

"Let them."

After this considerable daring and enterprise, John allowed the men a celebratory pause. Amidst this, they proceeded to become well-fumed, of course. After all, John had not revealed any sense of urgency as to departing the area, even projecting a sense of perfect security. Apparently, his scouts had reported no activity whatsoever in the region, nor information as to when *Annie Franklin* was expected at her next stop.

I couldn't quiet the alarm rattling inside me. John seemed to be throwing away all caution by luring on all-out war with Tedder, and in particular Mandley, blinded by the desire for revenge. What instincts I had as a man and as a Mystic screamed that only disaster and misery lay on this path. A bolt of fear jarred through me. What might this mean for my own future?

For the moment, I resolved to set those thoughts aside and simply let folks relish the revelry.

As the day wore on, most of them quieted to a happily drunken stupor, or slept on whatever free bit of soil they might have found. Some had succumbed to the effects of the drink directly under the hot, unshaded portions of the ground. Particularly uncomfortable, that.

I surveyed the now relatively quiet landscape of drunken men, stoved-in crates, and half-empty hogsheads of whiskey, thinking on how to rouse this lot and collect any remaining booty into the wagons and carts.

The sudden crack of a rifle rattled me from my thoughts. Heart instantly pounding, I sprang to my feet, looking about.

No one stirred. I made out the pounding of hooves right behind the rifle shot, distant at first, but approaching rapidly. Our horses and mules stamped their own hooves, ears twitching.

More rifle shots. I saw a man sprawl backward. A collection of fifteen mounted men tore through the trees toward us.

When I turned to find John, he was already up and moving. His coat was on, and he had his two hands full of pistols, firing and loading with cool deliberation. A howl split through all the noise as a horseman fell to one of his shots. Another man's head twisted grotesquely, the ball from John's pistol taking off his jaw. I reached for my carbine, set against a tree stump nearby, but one of the men charged by, knocking it out of reach into the river reeds. Cursing, I scrambled after it, my feet sinking into the mire of the riverbank.

This troop stormed into the camp, shooting down two more Mystics as they did, and trampling another.

One man brought his horse quickly up to John, knocking him to the ground. One of his pistols flew off into the reeds.

Surely winded, John got to his feet while trying to bring his remaining pistol to bear on this rider, who appeared to be leading our antagonists.

Most of the Mystics had scattered through the forest near the riverbank. I heard scattered shots, no doubt some seeking to engage these raiders. My heart sank. Most would not mount much defense, still drunk or staggeringly hungover. Not to mention being caught with their knickers down.

I waded a bit deeper into the reeds. The damned carbine had been knocked further than I had thought. The posse was mostly dismounted now, taking off in individual chases after fleeing Mystics. Some of them boarded the wrecked *Annie Franklin*, looking for fugitives hiding inside her.

The posse leader, still mounted, had now brought his rifle around, aiming directly at John about twenty yards away. His horse's hooves dug furiously at the turf, the air filling with dust.

John, fully recovered and steady as the rock of Gibraltar, stood stock-still, legs spread wide, pistol cocked and aimed at the leader.

"John Murrell," exclaimed the leader, steadying his mount's churning. It was a statement and question all at once. "I am Constable Joab Asher, of Barge Port."

John looked up at him defiantly. "Pleased to make your acquaintance, I'm sure."

Asher smirked nastily. "I'll have you on your knees, now, Murrell. Come, drop your weapon." He shifted the rifle just the slightest bit closer to John.

John did not move. His extended arms did not waver, the pistol barrel staring at Asher.

My hand had hit something ridged and unforgiving in the reeds. My rifle! I scooped it up as stealthily as possible.

My throat pulsed with each blow from my hammering heart. Unable to move quickly, standing almost up to my knees in the river mire, I took a bead on the posse leader from there. The Hall, for all its range, was a single-shot breech loader. If I missed, this man would surely gun John down before I could even reload. The notion turned my mouth dry as desert.

Asher did not turn even as another mounted man rode up. "This is your man, Colonel."

The man whom he addressed was a very dignified-looking sort, adorned in fine riding clothes that you might see on some English lord out on a fox hunt. His magnificent riding boots fairly gleamed in the morning sun. He looked John up and down disdainfully, as he might survey a dead cow blocking a road, then looked away toward a commotion just behind him. A man came through the reeds, tugging viciously on a rope.

"Come on now, you black bastard! Heel now! Heel, damned your cussed hide!"

That voice. High, reedy, that unmistakable deep Southern drawl...

He burst through the tall reeds and looked up at the men on their horses with a broad, scraggly-toothed smile through a filthy, unshaven face.

Billy Semple.

"Damned near got away, this one, Colonel," he said, breathing heavily, looking at the dignified-looking man. "But I got this old blackbird for you, I did." He reached over and thumped the head of the man on the other end of the rope. This one's hands were trussed with another bit of rope, and his scalp was bleeding freely, blood glistening over his dark face. His arms were lashed with ugly cuts.

It was July.

John's eyes darted to July, his mouth working in anguish. I could see him gritting his teeth, his fierce scowl deepening.

"I'll thank you not to further bruise my property, Mr. Semple," said the dignified-looking man, his horse pawing impatiently at the ground.

"That's right, Colonel, sir. I'll leave all of that up to you," Billy grinned slyly. "Yes sir, I will." The rattle of gunfire cut in for a moment, increasingly scattered and distant around us.

"Should have stayed with horse thieving, Murrell," Asher said with a humorless slit of a grin. "This will surely get you hung, you damned villain."

My breath quickened, and my skin crawled watching all this, my mind scrabbling for something of a plan. Sweat kept slicking my hands as I watched Asher's rifle becoming steadier. I had one try.

Billy's mouth twisted into a sneer. He tugged down hard on the rope. July collapsed to his knees with a pained grunt.

"Mr. Murrell," the dignified man said, his horse pawing at the ground, "I am Colonel James Antrum of Madison County, Tennessee. This man is my property, and you shall be deprived of your liberty for a very long time."

John shifted his footing, baring his teeth. One arm twitched slightly, then swiveled the pistol to aim at Semple.

"My, my. How the mighty have fallen, huh, Mr. *Devil Preacher?*" he said, belching out a high-pitched, sarcastic guffaw. "And I brung you to this, Murrell, and don't forget it. You think I'd just slink off like some kicked hound-dog? You had some answering to do, by God, you did. Nobody treats Billy Semple like that with no price to be paid."

The Colonel simply looked on with granite stillness.

"Traced that there blackbird back to his owner, the Colonel, that is. That's right. And it serves you right, too, rotting in that old hole up there in Tennessee where you're going. Serves you right for treating that old nigger over there better than this here white man."

He hawked and splattered a large gob of snot and spit in front of John.

"Jesus," Asher chortled, almost under his breath. His rifle barrel angled a tad unsteadily, slightly away from John. I took a breath, let it out slowly, and squeezed the trigger.

My shot flung Asher from his saddle like a locomotive pounded him. Even as I worked to pull my legs from the muck, fumbling in a new ball, I almost felt the thud as he slammed onto the ground and heard the air blast out of him. His horse tossed its head, neighing loudly.

John fired. Billy Semple jerked, contorting sideways, hands at his throat, wet sounds gurgling through gushing blood. The Colonel's mount had bolted, carrying him off a fair distance for the moment. Cursing, he tried to control it with one hand while his other scrabbled for his sidearm. River mud sucked and water slushed at my legs as I finally reached the shore. Shouts in the distance blended with the sound of baying hounds.

I rushed to John, now sawing at July's ropes with Billy's knife. I swallowed hard, looking at the poor kid, his brown head matted with dark blood. He looked up at me with pleading eyes.

"We've got you, July," John eased his shoulder under July's and stood, moving carefully but as swiftly as he could.

"There!" I gestured to the *Annie Franklin*, the hubbub around it having cleared away some and hopefully forgotten in all the confusion. John and July made for the wreck. I turned to the nearing posse, took aim, and fired. A man went down, clutching his leg, but got off a shot with his pistol, the ball whizzing past with hot fury. Another ball dug up a clump of sod in front of me while I reloaded, spraying my eyes with dirt. Cussing, I tried to calm my breathing as I scrambled backwards. Keeping these men in view would be near impossible soon, as they were spreading out. I licked my lips, but I had no saliva left. This was some damned thirsty business.

Finally, we found some cover behind the crates from the *Franklin*. I gusted out a relieved breath.

July leaned against part of the steamboat's beached hull, John sheltering him with his body as he drew his Collier revolver. Wood shattered from a corner of the crate before me. Their aim was getting sharper. The baying of the dogs became an incessant moaning, as from a damaged church organ.

I blinked away the stinging sweat dripping into my eyes, obscuring my aim down the sights of the Hall. The hammer came down, the ball sent away, only to knock off a man's hat. I snarled, my hands becoming numb as they reloaded the carbine, machine-like.

"Mr. Murrell," July gasped.

"It will be alright, July," John soothed. He came next to me, aimed and fired, brought back the cylinder of the Collier and turned it. "One left," he hissed just so I could hear.

I reached into my ammo pouch to find barely a few balls and caps left. There were more... back at the damned wagons. Smoke and noise wrapped around me like some insane, other-worldly cloak. Was this it? Enemies at the gate, back to the wall, powder and ball dwindling to nothing?

"Mr. Murrell, listen," came July again.

John went back to him. "This is just a minor scrape. They're nothing."

"No."

I laid down another fellow before I dared to look back. John was frozen, looking earnestly into July's eyes.

"No," July said firmly, his face wet. "I ain't going back, Mr. Murrell. Not ever."

"You won't."

"No, sir, I won't," July said, and he grasped John's hand, the one holding the Collier, resting the barrel just under his chin.

John stared at July with horror. "There's always a way, son." He said slowly. "Why, I've been in tighter squeezes. Right, Stephen?" He offered me a weak smile.

A rifle roared outside. Almost gratefully, I peered carefully past the crate, sighted a target, let a shot go, loaded swiftly, and banged away another. A man fell to his knees. He slumped into a pool of his own blood, twitched, then lay still.

"There isn't, Mr. Murrell. Not this time." July squeezed his eyes shut. "Nine, ten of them now to us... to you two. All them hounds. Heard that kinda ruckus before. They don't give up. No, they don't. And you with the one round to your name in that there pistol." He smiled weakly. "I heard you tell Mr. Hue."

To my satisfaction, one of the posse howled and cussed wildly after I fired another shot – but this was my last.

Please," July whispered in the wake of the blasts, one hand moving up to the trigger guard, placing his thumb over John's finger there. "It's hell. In a black man's life, it's only hell."

"July," John sobbed. He tried to jerk the pistol away, but July grasped it harder, gripping John's hand fiercely over the trigger.

"You know, it was lovely," He smiled softly. "It was all so lovely, this taste of freedom. And I thank you. I thank you for it, John. You see that there's just no going back from it."

He let go of John's hand. "You got to see that."

A tear streamed down John's face. He nodded then, almost imperceptibly.

The report was deafening. I gasped suddenly, falling hard against the crate, the smoke enveloping everything in a sorrowful shroud.

John did not move, only stared for what seemed forever into nothingness.

"He was just a kid." He finally looked at me, tears smearing his dirty face. "Damn it, he was just a kid."

"Yes," I replied softly.

"–rush 'em!" A shout from the posse as it stirred, working up their courage. Antrum's voice gave commands, rallying, encouraging them. The dogs were howling in anticipation, mad with bloodlust.

"John. John, come on..." I tried to keep my eyes from straying to July's sad remains. "There's no time."

"You must go, Stephen. Now." His voice was forced, faltering. He wiped his face, smudging the dirt even more. He pulled the cylinder back on the Collier with some effort, hands trembling.

"No, John. Here..." I went to him, grabbing his sleeve,

looking to my left up the riverbank. "There might indeed be a way…"

"Best this way, brother." His voice was stoic, certain. "It's over. You have a life to get to." The cacophony of the dogs reached a crescendo.

"You get now, son," John grimaced slightly. "Get on with it…" His eyes smiled at me as he grasped my arm. "Make it a long life, Stephen. Make it better than this one."

I gulped in a breath, trying to control myself, tears threatening.

He reached the Collier firmly to me, wrapping my hand around it. "Take it, I can't look at it." I looked down at the weapon. The memory of John and I firing it together for the first time at Natchez-Under-the-Hill came to mind. The night of our reunion. A good memory.

John Murrell looked at me squarely. "Go, Stephen."

I tore myself from him, eyes stinging, my throat tight.

Keeping low, I scrambled away as quickly as I could, the *Franklin*'s wreckage and beached cargo screening my movement on the riverbank.

"Never mind anyone else," Colonel Antrum's voice rose behind me. "This is our prize, gentlemen. The Devil Preacher himself. For ruining my property, I'll see him suffer for a long time."

I prayed for my friend John Murrell as I looked about for a horse.

* * *

Extract from Tennessee State Penitentiary record

    August 17, 1834

    John A. Murrell was received in the Penitentiary this date. He is five feet ten inches and a half in height and weighs from one hundred and fifty-eight to one hundred and seventy pounds. Dark hair, blue eyes, long nose and much pitted with smallpox; tolerably fair complexion, thirty-one years of age. He has a scar on the middle joint of the finger next to the little finger of his left hand and one on the middle finger of the same hand; two scars on the upper portion of the left hand and near the wrist, appearing to be the letter H and the letter T; a scar on the inside of the end of the finger next the little finger of the right hand; Was found guilty of Negro stealing at the Circuit Court of Madison County and sentenced to ten years of confinement in the jail and Penitentiary House of the State of Tennessee.

<h1 style="text-align:center">31</h1>

I WENT to ground in the aftermath of the *Annie Franklin* job.

As the clan endeavored to ward off the authorities everywhere it could, I was, being the de facto head of the Council now, the recipient of numerous reports about events meant to lead up to the planned Christmas Night Insurrection.

"They have riders everywhere about the roads," reported Hobbs, who had gotten to me as quickly as he was able. He was a squat, large-jawed man who looked nothing like the courier riders that we routinely employed.

"The town folk are calling it 'The Excitement,'" he told me breathlessly. "Word is spreading fast, Mr. Hue."

"Back to the original occurrence, if you please," I implored him.

"Yes. Yes, one of their patrols came upon two Negroes near Bucks, off the river, a'course. They lashed them severe, they did. And the Negroes 'bout sang it out. Admitted they were of the plan. Leaders of the plot, they told them. For their towns, that would be. Lynched them right then and there."

"Did they divulge any other leaders thereabouts?"

Hobbs shrugged helplessly, his over-large jaw working back and forth as if he were chewing something raw and tough. His eyes spoke of nothing but fear.

"The plan is asunder, Mr. Hue. All of us will hang, sure."

"Please get hold of yourself, Mr. Hobbs," I assured him, trying myself not to get caught up in his hysterics. "This is likely just the one incident."

"The word is spreading, like lightning, it is."

"So you have said," I replied. I searched my mind for any semblance of a plan. Day after day, I racked my brains, but nothing. I had to wonder what John would do in such a fix.

Unfortunately, Hobbs was indeed correct. Reports then came in from even further south, not far from Natchez, even.

Two of our captains this time had been seized by vigilantes. These two men had been described as "steam doctors," practitioners in various aromatic medical treatments, fashionable in that day. They were fairly influential figures in the county: Joshua Cotton and William Saunders.

The vigilantes who had arrested them immediately charged them as conspirators.

Saunders pled his innocence, staunchly at first, it was said, and then more frantically as his captors searched about for a suitable place to hang them.

"The vigilantes were having no discussion about it, neither," said one witness I had interviewed. "The courts don't exist for matters such as slave rebellion, said one of them possemen," he said. He visibly shivered at the recollection of it. "Nor none on the road, neither. They were fierce set on hanging a man, that's a plain fact. Saunders went up quick as you please, crying like a child, whimpering he did, 'til it was strangled off.

"Mr. Cotton was more resolute – firm, if you like. He looked about at the vigilantes with a right vengeful eye, as if to spit in them. 'I declare,' he told the riders, 'Death is coming to you all if you do not flee the country. Our Negro army will soon be upon you. You will pay for your transgressions!' Then he smiled at them, a ghastly, morbid thing it was, too. Even a few of the posse-men later admitted it made them quake, even for a moment.

"In others, though, it filled them with a fury, they said, thinking about their families, their wives and their children, fearful in their homes. Indeed, jumping at every sound and rustle outside their places, any flicker of light may be a coming vengeful and bloodthirsty horde.

"And Cotton, being caught up in the passion of events, bolstered his claim by naming other leaders in several other counties, two or three more counties out from there – the fool – and such is the case everywhere, Mr. Hue, it's told.

"Our men that's left have scurried to ground right quickly, and this insurrection is dead before born, really, I am fearful to report."

There was even word of some collection of gamblers in Vicksburg who were rounded up and hang, accused of conspiring with the Mystic Clan, though I never managed to verify their names against our ledger.

As the "Murrell Excitement," as it came to be known popularly, subsided, I was able to make contact with John through a network of men who worked in and around the Tennessee State Penitentiary.

And even though I was loath to put anything into writing, this generated a kind of correspondence with John through a James Whitaker, Lieutenant of the prison's guard troop, once the appropriate skids had been greased. He offered the following clandestine communique:

J.M. is in receipt of your messages and
wishes to express his apology for not
having answered sooner. Is in fair
health and relative spirits considering
current situation. Will be corre-
sponding with more frequency as opportunity allows. At this time subject to
severe restrictions imposed by solitary
confinement and daily work details.
Learning new trade as blacksmith. Will
write again soonest.

Somehow, I continued an effort to meet with John, naturally with a careful view of security in the forefront. In the meantime, I had to be content with sporadic and at times unexpected communication from my friend. Eventually, Whitaker allowed John to send letters and notes directly – with a commensurate increase to the lining of his own pocket, of course.

The smithing moves along. Believe it or
not, I have even been enlisted in
crafting objects that strengthen my own
confinement. The absurdity of it.
First, to construct chains and bars to
replace such here at T.S.P. Have
learned to repair broken hinges for
heavy doors, too.
    Best, J.M.
    April 1835

Have not heard from anyone in a while.
Kept to my cell all night with nothing
but my dwindling thoughts. Very quiet
here and no good. Some yelling sometimes, though. And screams from a long
way off. Thoughts of July's fate keep
me from sleep.
  J.M.
  December 1835

It is damned cold in the barrel. As
freezing and unforgiving as hell
itself. I almost don't care about it,
though. Not wanting to feel anything
anymore. What thoughts I still have are
all darkness. Don't know if I even wish
to see the next day.
  Hoping for some visits soon, might
save me my mind. Put guards outside my
door. Don't know why. Come and see me,
if you can. Not now, however.
  J.M.
  June 1836

The mention of this barrel was both puzzling and unnerving, enough to give me chills. The idea of John spiraling into a deep depression sent my own thoughts to a dark, sobering place.

```
Still smithing. Don't know what it is I
am   making.   Told   shapes   and   sizes,
nothing  more.  Pins,  iron  slabs,  some
with  holes.  Marched  back  to  cell  in
silence.  No  talking.  See  July  all  the
time,  like  he  is  here  with  me,  then
gone,  and  it  all  comes  back.  He  won't
let me be. I cannot fault him.
    J.M.
    October 1836
```

As sparse and bleak as they were, with months in between them, I treasured these notes, desperate to maintain any connection with my friend after all the calamity. While I struggled under the leadership of a slowly collapsing empire, they helped me grapple with the tremendous guilt that weighed on me like a great, rusty anchor, for the lives lost during the "Excitement" and our men imprisoned for God knows how long; for the heartrending end to July's all-too-brief life in freedom.

My mind's eye wanted to sift out the vision of his death. I resisted, though, as I did not want his life to be simply lost to the ages. Though July himself wanted that end, that fact hardly diminished my sorrow.

I could not bring myself to look at John's Collier pistol, but

I kept it in a crate just the same, bearing the memory of his dream of empire, crushed under Fate's unremitting iron boot.

A boot that had missed me by inches. All this while, I wrestled with the bald fact that I was indeed free to pursue the life I had dreamt of, free from the troubles of a criminal pursued, an existence which very well might come to rotting in prison or wearing the hangman's noose. Any sense of relief was sullied in no small way by knowing this only came about by John's being captured. I wasn't sure I would be able to truly enjoy that new life, after all. The irony of having John's blessing to pursue it was not lost on me.

In return, it was my duty, at the very least, to try to keep the Clan intact and operating. Without a plan to speak of in the bargain.

Only time would tell, and time was not on my side.

32

As the years went on, the Mystic Clan dwindled ever further into obscurity. John's southern empire and his dream of rebellion had died a pauper's death with his incarceration.

Over that time, his letters or notes ceased altogether. This I expected. Our enlisted contacts at the Tennessee State Penitentiary had withdrawn their Clan activity to protect themselves, died, retired, or otherwise simply moved on.

Myself, I eventually took up the quiet life of a tradesman in the small town of Blythesburg, Georgia. I found that I wanted to be as far away from the Mississippi River as circumstances would allow. I hoped – like most other Mystic Beasts – that the passage of time would forever fade our connection with the Clan Mystic, freeing us of the same fate that had been John Murrell's.

The routine of everyday life distanced my connection with John. He was never forgotten, don't mistake me, but his memory became almost like the sad remnants of someone who had long since passed away. The faded dreams of another life.

I married a fine woman, my Abby, who had what I regarded

as the overwhelming and near-superhuman politeness not to ask too much about my past. Together with two children, we led a peaceful, common mercantile life among the Blythesburg township.

It was in the summer of 1845, a particularly heavy and punishing Georgia one, when Abby came to me in the back of our shop, where I was sorting through newly delivered crates. I was pondering as to why my order of three-inch nails was not among them. Such was my new professional life.

"A man is here for you, Stephen." Her pretty face wore a vexed expression. The addition of worry and caution in it did not elude me.

"A man?" I asked stupidly. After all, men did occasionally arrive at our shop, where we did, in fact, sell things. "If it's Mr. Downs, please tell him the damned nails still have not arrived."

"It's not Mr. Downs, Stephen," she said, in a rush, then looked behind her as if this visitor had perhaps crept behind her to some illicit purpose.

I chuckled at her strange demeanor, having never witnessed the likes from her before.

"Fine," I said, dusting off one knee of my trousers as I straightened up from the crates. An old ache in my shoulder reminded me it was there. Every year, it turned less forgiving. Wincing, I wound my arm around a bit to work it out.

Abby took a step closer.

"He looks like–" she said in a hushed voice, pausing abruptly.

"Looks like what, darling?" I smiled. My smile faltered, though, and then my stomach clutched up, like it was suddenly enclosed by an invisible fist. Was it John? The memory of when we were last together tumbled through my mind. My throat tightened again with the memory of John's anguished features,

July's destroyed body beside him, his voice choking with emotion as he implored me to flee.

"He looks like a man pursued," Abby finished.

"Thank you, my dear," I said, but I do not know if she heard me, it having to get through the lump now gathering in my throat. I nodded firmly, hoping to assure her that all would be well, then whisked the remaining dust from my hands onto my apron and stepped awkwardly around her.

I walked through our modest shop, past the linen stacks, bean cans, and broomsticks on somewhat weak legs. I found breathing hard to come by before I realized I was holding it. In those brief moments, my mind ran through reasons why I was reacting in such a way at the prospect of once again, possibly, seeing my old friend. My mind provided no immediate answers.

My eyes sought out this man, but I did not see anyone right away, until I approached the front of the store.

He was on the porch, one hand on a small anvil newly arrived at our shop from Pittsburgh. Abby had inexplicably placed a ribbon about it, apparently to make its ugly shape more attractive to a potential buyer. His back was to me, and I at once thought that John had been reduced to nothing compared to how I remembered him.

Hearing me, the man now turned.

"Hudgins," he introduced himself, head bobbing like a man addressing his superior. No one had greeted me this way upon our first meeting, not in a while. I felt a pang of foolishness, then immediate embarrassment for this stranger. His eyes darted from mine, as if fearing to make direct contact for too long.

"Please," I said, extending a hand, not only in salutations, but to ease his discomfort what I could. His demeanor had already made *me* uncomfortable. "Stephen Hue. How can I help you, Mr. Hudgins?"

"Selmer Hudgins," the man made a small, grateful smile.

"Do come in, sir." I gestured to the door, looking quickly about. I saw that Tom Smedley gazed at me from across the street, cigar in hand, watching curiously from under the awning of his photography studio. He nodded politely.

We entered the shop. "Please, sit down," I motioned for Mr. Hudgins to a chair near the counter. I looked over at Abby, who ducked away to retrieve something from the back office.

Hudgins sat, looking this way and that.

"Frightful heat, isn't it?" he said, smiling nervously.

"Indeed, sir, and we are only just now getting it under way," I pulled up my own chair.

"I've not been to this part of Georgia afore," he said.

Abby appeared and placed a pitcher of badly needed lemonade on the counter.

"I hope this is still cool enough," she said, gracing our guest with a soft smile.

Selmer kept his eyes down. "Thank you, ma'am. Very kind." His agitation seemed to ratchet up some at her presence. Graciously, Abby returned to the back of the shop.

I poured each of us a glass.

"Cherokee County is the jewel of northern Georgia, to be sure," I said with a joviality I didn't exactly feel. My mind was still squaring with finding this man in place of where it had figured John was supposed to be. Why was he here...?

"I know, sir, that you were a confederate of John Murrell's," said Selmer Hudgins.

"Yes," In my mind I had simply croaked out the syllable. I was sure my eyes were staring fixedly ahead, not at Selmer but at some other distant place and time.

This Hudgins does not look like a law-man. Nor did he

comport himself as someone bent on avenging a capture or death or other crime. Nevertheless, my mind went through various evolutions of a hunted man's impulse, fight or flight. Then it rapidly began calculations of the years past, sifting through the exploits of John Murrell and the Clan Mystic, trying to pluck out Hudgins' face.

"I, too, regard myself as a friend of Mr. Murrell's," continued Hudgins. "Were it not for his kind attentions in the confines of our imprisonment. I would like as not be here before you otherwise."

My brain was still processing, at long last, some word of John, indeed, the mere mention of his name. I barely registered then that Mr. Hudgins' words had tumbled in a stilted and awkward way, as if he had rehearsed them many times over.

In the corner of my eye, I observed only a fraction of my wife's form in the back office. One of her tiny, delicate hands tightly clutched the back of the office chair.

Selmer Hudgins' eyes looked into mine; for the first time, holding it more than the fraction of a second. There was an interminable sorrow there.

"It is a pitiable place, Mr. Hue," he said. "This Tennessee State Penitentiary. Men are ground to nothing there." He finally looked away. "It is made to reduce us," he continued, almost in a whisper. He slowly clenched a fist, which trembled ever so slightly. A bird flapped past lazily.

He blinked out the window several times, then returned his attention to the interior of the store, to me. I held my breath.

"It was the silence, all the time quiet. Funny to think a thing like silence can wear a man down. You wouldn't think that would be so, would you? Some men crave silence and solitude. Intolerance can build against anything most desired. I know that now." He paused. "You'd get flogged even if you looked at another inmate, much less a guard."

He let out a shivering puff of air. "Don't look at the guards, sir. No, you don't. Your eyes meet theirs, and it's the barrel for you, sir."

"The barrel..." That word... John had mentioned this barrel long ago in one of his notes.

Selmer nodded slowly, put a hand to the back of his neck. "Collared you with a wooden yoke, they did. Like common livestock. Try moving your head a'tall, you couldn't. Couldn't move anything, really. Then water from the pipe right above. Icy water, over and again. Never dreamed I could shiver so much, liked to shiver me right apart. Wished it would shiver me right out of those bonds. Out of that barrel, least-wise. Shiver me all to nothing just to get out of there. That place."

Engrossed as I was, two thoughts raced through my brain – John's face, tortured and white beyond description, enduring this unspeakable punishment, and not wanting my Abby to hear this. I chanced to shoot a look her way, where she still stood in the back office. That hand quickly withdrew from the back of the chair.

"Sometimes you could hear the floggings, the screams. They would only do it at night, you see," said Selmer, gaze fixed blankly on a hogshead of sugar. "Sound carries. All sound does. That's why they did it at night, see."

He tapped the side of his head. "It does it. It gets in there and slams around and dents the insides of your skull, like... Like a big ugly bird looking for a window out."

Selmer slumped a little in his seat, rested his elbows on his legs and smiled up weakly, tiredly. "I am sorry," he said.

"Mr. Hudgins," I said after a moment, realizing I was holding my breath again. I exhaled with my next words. "No need." I grasped his shoulder lightly to assure him.

He composed himself with a deep breath. "Thank you, sir," When he sat up. I let my hand drop.

"They march you everywhere, and you best keep step. They marched us to our chores. We all had chores. Lots of us learned new ones, too. Useful ones, I admit. So, there is that. I myself learned to make harnesses." He offered me what felt like his first real smile thus far. A smile of genuine pleasure rather than just basic politeness, I mean.

"And that's a useful thing," he said, then seemed to catch himself. His eyes took again a distant, angry aspect, before snapping back to the present. "That's what Ambrose used to say. Chief guard on our block. Marching us to our labors, he would say, 'We'll make you into useful things. Like it or not.'"

Just then, a customer, Mr. LaRay from the Blakely farm, came in for some salt and a frying pan his wife had asked for some time before. This time we had it, in from Hinesville.

Mr. LaRay politely addressed Selmer Hudgins, saying hello, exchanged the usual words regarding the day's heat, and then made to leave. Not before shooting me a questioning look with one arched brow, unseen, of course, by Selmer.

I at once resented the expression and simply nodded courteously. "Good day to you, Mr. LaRay."

Selmer watched Mr. LaRay exiting. The store was quiet even while the sounds of footsteps on the boardwalk dimmed away.

I waited patiently.

"That was where John befriended me," said Selmer. "At the shops. It was the only place, really, where we could talk. Oh, not like we're talking here, like. Oh, no. It had to do with our labors, a'course, mostly, and what I need him to forge for me. We snuck in, here and there, some idle and friendly talk where we could. Where Ambrose and his men couldn't pick up on it. If it weren't for that..."

I didn't reply. Even though I had a thousand questions, I

figured by now the best thing to do was simply let the man speak.

"And John helped me with those parts, yessir. Everything that makes a harness a harness, he'd say. You had your hame clips and chains, rein hooks, tugs and tug stops, and breast plates – depending on the type and style, a'course. And terrets – have to have those, I learned it all."

He took in another deep breath, released it, and shifted his shoes on the floor, looking down. "So there's that."

"And John made them all for me and, mister, he got so *good* at it. I did, too. I mean good at taking his hooks and stops and tugs and making something of them along with what the leatherworks provided, naturally.

"But the years," he looked up again. "The years, sir, of it. Became a prison in itself, it did. There were no change in anything. Just over and over and over... That'll chew a man down, just like anything will, I s'pose.

"And John, well, every man in that place took it different. I mean, some got just mean. Dumb and mean, I thought of 'em, 'cause they just went past caring how many beatings they got, or barrels. Prolly, they just wanted the guards to end their misery and be done with it. I don't know if that was the purpose of it all. But it appeared that way, sure, after long enough. Some just sort of walled themselves off and proceeded with the daily marches and labors with eyes with nothing behind 'em and doing things like a dray animal or machine. They weren't men no more, really."

He stared for a time, well past that hogshead.

"That is what become of John. Started out really mostly a normal man. I say mostly, because his eyes, well, you could see he already was suffering. Sort of inside of him, you know? Sometimes you could see the smartness in his eyes, too, though. A light of brains in there, but it seemed like that only came when we were able to talk. Can't truthfully explain it. Even that light, I saw dimming over time. He could still make things, though.

"He made parts for me – and others – that were like from one of those machine factories. Better! My harnesses – Our harnesses, why, people from two states over was asking for them. That's true. In the end, well..."

My heart crawled into my throat.

"And he talked of his gang, the clan. The Mystic Clan, and how they's all waiting for him when he gets out of there. There was no talk of escape, not from that place, believe it. He did talk with some regret as to the things he did, that the clan did. How it ended. He looked real sad, too, said it was him that brought it all down, in the end."

Selmer sighed out another breath and fixed me with a sad smile. I felt a whole new despondency right then, knowing that John somehow blamed only himself for the end of the Clan Mystic for I felt a part in it as well, that I had somehow let him down in its execution.

He stared again at the floor. The world grew very quiet. Down the street, a dog barked. somebody hollered something to a neighbor.

"He did get out," said Selmer finally. "There was really nothing left of him. He took up a blacksmithing job in Pikeville, the only thing he knew by then. The whispers among the townsfolk was that he really was nothing more than a harmless idiot. I hated that was said about him. He deserved better. The idea of the Tennessee State Penitentiary, I read, was to reform a man after his wrongdoing. Well, if that's reforming a man, I think most would prefer death to it.

"Before it was all over," Selmer said, and an icy hot ball developed instantly in the center of my belly. "John fessed up to all the things he done."

His eyes took on a spark of defiance. "'Cept murder. He said he done none of that."

"And the skipper of the *Annie Franklin*? He said he would have punished the Mystic that done it, too, if things'd gone different after that job."

"Did he..." I hesitated, suddenly finding it urgent to clear my throat. I self-consciously looked away, to the office, then down to the floor. There was a soft scraping sound as Selmer shifted his feet.

After a moment, I forced my gaze back to Selmer. "Speak of a young man? July?"

"He said..." Selmer swallowed. "Ah, John said none of that needed to happen. Shouldn't have happened. But he said he got careless. Let the men laze about after the *Annie Franklin* job. Let them get drunk, no guards set or nothing. It was this foolishness got July killed. Even said it was his devil pride done it. Never saw him so down 'cept when he spoke of this. And in there, that's saying a shit lot."

I stared at him without seeing him, imagining John grappling with the past and how it must have weighed on him.

"Funny enough, John said that was when he felt Master July was most free. Selmer's voice was very soft, but he stared at me earnestly. "That was when John was very clear, Mr. Hue. Very clear. The freest he ever was or ever would be."

"Yes," I managed, tears coming. My heart ached more with each beat.

After a minute, Selmer reached for his drink and gulped thirstily. He wiped his mouth with his sleeve. There was an overly loud clatter as he set the glass back down. "That's right good lemonade, that is."

He paused for a long time. "I am sorry, sir," he finally said. "To have to tell this part to you. It was consumption that did him in."

He opened his mouth but abruptly stopped. His features took on a worrisome aspect, which surely meant his next bit of news was somehow as troubling as what he had just delivered.

"Among all the things he done," he finally continued, "John helped me secure a job as sexton. At the Smyrna Church. Steady work, too. I have to say it was a good one. I liked it." Just then, his eyes took on an angry light, and he looked away again.

"Something fierce wicked happened. After they buried him in the churchyard, I mean." He shook his head emphatically.

"Fierce wicked!"

* * *

Excerpt of report made to the office of Sheriff Thomas Waymer, Bledsoe County, in the town of Pikeville, Tennessee, by Pastor Lucas Martins, Smyrna Methodist Church
November 24th, 1844

It is with utmost horror and revulsion I report to your office the desecration of a grave on the premises of Smyrna Church.

A fellow member, Brother John Murrell, whom you may have known, had been interred on these grounds in recent days. It was not more than three days hence that the grave had been greatly disturbed. It is my opinion that the disturbance is the work of grave robbers, though I do not know if anything of value or indeed even any personal effects of Mr. Murrell that had been buried with him. He was not a man of any particular means. I do not know why his grave in particular would have been so violated. This most detestable act, however, was made more egregious, if you may imagine, by a report made by our sexton, Mr. Selmer Hudgins, that the head of Brother Murrell was removed from his body to some inexplicable and dastardly purpose. It has also been reported to me that the thumb of his left hand had been likewise removed.

Do let me know in the instant if there is anything I might do to facilitate and indeed expedite the arrest of these criminals. Any men capable of committing such a thing can only be considered to be villains of the deepest dye and must suffer the most dire consequences for this barbaric act.

Your Humble Servant
Pastor Lucas Martins, Smyrna Church

<h1 style="text-align:center">33</h1>

To say I was shocked at the revelation of this depraved act does not do my reaction – both exterior and interior – any kind of justice.

I sat there in a stupefied revulsion, which soon developed into quiet rage. Mr. Hudgins seemed to be reading my thoughts and emotions through my face's various contortions.

"But, who–" I stammered. "Why...?"

"I know. I know, Mr. Hue," Selmer blurted, who seemed to become further agitated as I stood and started pacing, trying to find some outlet for my growing anger.

"You... know?" I shot him a look.

"I think I know who done it, sir." He proceeded to tell me. I stopped still and grabbed the back of my chair, my knuckles quickly turning white.

I still found myself unable to form words. I don't believe that anything would sound proper.

Shortly after he was all talked out, he said his goodbyes, and that he regretted being the one giving me the sad news, and extended his condolences.

This Selmer Hudgins had been a good friend to John, at least as good as a place like that would have allowed. I could see it in his eyes as he shook my hand.

My friend John Murrell, head of the Clan Mystic, was dead. After all the suffering and joy and mistakes and adventures, he was dead. I went back into the shop, locked the door behind me. Then I sat down in my chair and wept.

* * *

My dear wife confronted me after Selmer's visit. She was considerably distraught after learning of my association with the Devil Preacher. John's fame and reputation were regionally known, and I daresay the Clan Mystic's exploits had risen to the heights of legendary criminal acts, well past the point of fact and even reason. She told me she was hard pressed to believe I had ever been a part of it at all, much less a lieutenant or close confederate of John's. After some interior debate as to whether to encourage this belief or minimize my past role, I decided that I owed her the truth. I loved her too much to let this villainous past cloud lurk forever in the background of our lives, awaiting another chance to make itself known and possibly become further magnified.

Imagine my shock when I saw her eyes light with relief at the truth. She grasped my hands and looked at me earnestly. "Thank you," she said.

Why, I physically staggered a bit, I was so pole-axed.

She at once grasped my hands ever tighter, smiling a little as she gently pulled me to her.

"You see, Stephen, I have always known," she said to my astonishment. "Well, mostly." She giggled. "Mr. Hudgins' visit and the tale he provided only firmed it in my mind."

"I- I don't understand," I stammered, like an idiot.

384

"Those years ago, after we first met, well, Mr. Haney, of the town committee of Overton?" I nodded, vaguely recalling Mr. Haney and the geography of a place called Overton. My head was still swimming then, so I couldn't think what it had got to do with Selmer Hudgins or John Murrell or my villainous past.

"He told Father that he believed you were in some way a criminal type and our family should be quite wary, and skirt you a wide berth. There were moments where those fears did arise in our minds, like that incident over to the Sedgewick place?"

"Two slaves had gone missing," I replied stiffly.

"Yes. And there was some chatter about them having been stolen, and Midge Potter even joked about those dastardly Murrell men back at it!"

I chuckled, just knowing the smile pasted on my face really resembled a grisly rictus.

"Father even had some fun with it and told me that I should ascertain your whereabouts, only to be sure." She smiled slyly.

"Huh," I grunted, stunned with the thought of all this fun going on while I was blissfully ignorant, thinking all was well.

"Now, father being the fair and just man that he is just simply would not believe it. Nor would I. I confess, at times, I would lie in bed at night and think about it until I believed it might drive me mad. And in time, those thoughts honestly came to blows with other thoughts that I–"

"Yes?" I prompted, hopeful and desperate.

"Well, that I knew I was in love with you, you silly man!" Her eyes glistened with the beginnings of tears. She reached for my arm, then drew it down to hold my hand again, ever so gently. "And that it didn't really matter what you did those years ago. I knew what kind of man you were – had become – and you weren't that any longer."

Her soft hand squeezed mine comfortingly. I put my other hand over hers.

"Another life," I croaked, and indeed, seeds of tears were growing in my own eyes as my mind whirled with images of the life we had built and the boys we had made and all of that evaporating in a heartbeat. A crushing weight on my heart had been mercifully lifted.

I confess that this episode, alarming and shocking as it was, made me love Abby all the more. From that moment on, I swore to forever strive to be a better man than she could ever have hoped for.

* * *

All that said, Abby was not convinced that I should, at a moment's notice, go with our new acquaintance Selmer Hudgins.

"It's just so outrageous," I declared that evening, when William and Theo had gone to bed. "Poe himself could not have contrived this!"

"But do you believe him?" she asked.

"I believe that something evil and wrong has happened, yes."

"And only you are able to right this wrong," she said, sitting back in her seat, exasperated. We had been skirting around the issue of my association with the Great Western Land Pirate John Murrell. Here, the skirting stopped, however.

"Yes." My voice was low, audible mostly to myself. I was looking just past Abby's shoulder, at nothing.

"Stephen?"

"Yes," I said, firmer. I fixed my eyes on hers. "It must be, Abby. Only myself." My voice cracked involuntarily.

"But why, Stephen? Good God, how many years has it been?" Abby stood and started to pace, then pivoted to me. "This Mr. Hudgins, he can–"

"No, Abby!" I blurted, more forcefully than I wanted. Abby flinched.

"Stephen, I've never seen this in you." Her voice was small, slightly wounded. I went to her and clasped her hands.

"I'm sorry. But you must understand, all the things I haven't revealed to you... Well, there is a reason for it. For all of it."

Abby backed away slightly but still held my hands. She sat down slowly, her eyes not leaving mine.

"John Murrell... He was more than a friend to me, or just some bandit I ran with. We were only kids when we met, all those years ago. And the times we had... Started out a little rough, but oh, the times we had." I paused, chuckling slightly. "But then we fought side by side, all up and down the Mississippi and along the Trace. Had some close scrapes too! Had one hell of a fight on the river, with the Mandley bunch. Wasn't sure we'd get out of that one."

I took a deep breath. "I watched John become a leader, Abby. A leader of men. He took outcasts and wretches, the detritus of society, and molded them into... Well, it was something none of them thought they could ever be a part of. It wasn't just about the gold, and the booty, and... the *business* of it. And even though we were criminals, it still meant... something."

I fell to one knee, stifling a sob burbling in my throat. Abby squeezed my hands ever so softly. Finally, I looked at her, and that's when the tears came. "This life we have, our family, the boys, all of this. I... We owe it to him."

Abby sat back, looking at me with confused wonderment. "Owe to... him? I don't understand, darling."

I stood and turned away. One hand wiped my tears. "It was at Lake Chicot, a whiskey boat raid. The *Annie Franklin* job — yes, that one. We lost... July, a dear friend. Just a kid really. He..." I swallowed hard. "Then... John was captured"

Abby came to me, tentatively reaching for me. "And you were not, love. You were not and came to me. That should be enough–"

"He traded his freedom for mine! His empire, his future!" It came out in a loud rush. "Don't you see?" I could not look directly at her. "I failed him," I whispered. The room was quiet. "I failed him."

She watched me for a moment, taking it in, working through everything. Finally, she put her hands delicately on my cheeks, then kissed me very softly, and stood back, hands falling to my arms as she stared at me. I knew that look well by now. "Will this be the end of this, then?" she asked, the frown that had grown deeper not leaving her pretty face. I stared stupidly back at her.

"This Clan Mystic life of yours. If you right this wrong, this will be the end of it forever?"

"Yes."

"Then you will come back to me anew, and that name will never be uttered again," Abby said, with an unmistakable finality.

34

BLEEKER AND SONS TRAVELING MARVELS

THE BANNER READ; Selmer Hudgins and I knew we had found them.

And this is where I saw it.

I laid my nickel down and walked into the dark tent. My eyes cast about for one specific marvel among the other grotesqueries and oddities, gradually growing used to the dim light. All else was blocked out for me, the barker's strident voice, the catcalls of the other patrons, the smell of canvas and sawdust and cigars.

A cone of light from a harsh, amber-hued lantern rested on a large jar, sitting on an oddly dainty cloth atop a somewhat rickety pedestal. As I approached the display, my stomach clenched, my mouth drying to cotton. I don't even recall blinking as I approached it, the features becoming more defined with each slow step onward. Through the liquid, murky confines of the glass container, it stared back at me.

The words "pickle jar" flashed through my brain right

instant, and I just as quickly shunted it away, not wanting that every-day object attached to what I was observing. At the same time, a hysterical giggle scrabbled to be unleashed from my mouth, but then I stopped in my tracks. The sounds around me bled away into a formless void of noise like a very loud, rushing waterfall.

For there he was. There *it* was.

The head of my friend John Murrell.

* * *

"It's him," I gasped, as I exited the tent and hurried to Selmer, who had waited respectfully outside.

"You are sure?" he asked, his eyes wide.

"Of course I am!" I snapped.

Startled, Selmer looked around, as if to ensure that nobody nearby heard the exchange. He reached into his coat pocket. This appeared an absent-minded motion at first, but then I recalled a pistol which he had used to ward off would-be bandits during our travels.

"There will be none of that now, Selmer," I cautioned.

He looked at me with reproach. "How else, then?"

I took him aside. "Firstly, violence here will only reduce our mission to nothing in an instant," I said. "Do you want to go back to the penitentiary for a fleeting moment given to passion and no thought?"

"No," he said petulantly, but withdrew his hand. "Course not."

"With men like these, it is best to employ the language of coin," I said.

Selmer nodded grudgingly.

"Are you known to these men?" I asked. He shook his head.

"These aren't the men who took it, to my mind. Who

knows how they came by it or what they'll ask for it. I figure they can point us in the direction of those that... That dug him up."

I silenced him with an upheld hand, and with the other patted my belly, where a money band rested. "I believe I'll have enough." Selmer raised surprised eyebrows, a small smile on his lips. "Just don't tell Abby."

Later that evening, long after the crowds had melted away, I approached the show's camp, gathered around a fire under the boughs of an impressive oak tree. It brought me back to our Grand Council Tree, where John had held forth to the clan heads about his Christmas Rebellion.

"I'm Bleeker," said the man, approaching after I asked for the show proprietor. Those around the fire found other things to do at a distance after he gave a silent signal.

"James Dunleavy," I said, using the name I picked beforehand. I reached out my hand first, and he shook, albeit with a hint of a suspicious eye.

"I take it you enjoyed our wares," he said, his expression now evolving into one of business-like appraisal, much in the same fashion as a fox appraising a hen. "Come this way to enjoy more of them, did you?" He nodded behind him.

A ways off, I saw a man exiting the cabin of one of the wagons, reaffixing his clothing. A woman came partly out of the wagon, looked my way, and stared blankly at me a moment. Then she receded back into the wagon.

"Some other time, maybe," I said, wondering why a stranger had paid me such prolonged attention.

"Ah!" said Bleeker suddenly. "You're the one, yes? My boys told me of the man with eyes only for Mr. Murrell!" He laughed. "Most folks stare at it only a moment."

He leaned in for emphasis. "It's all they can take."

I managed to stifle down anger and revulsion. "About him,

yes," I barely kept from stammering, I don't know how. I found myself glad that Selmer Hudgins had stayed behind.

"I have come to purchase him– It," I said.

Bleeker had taken the enormous cigar from his mouth, which now snapped shut. "Have you now." It was not a question. He leaned back on a nearby large wagon wheel, crossing his arms. "I don't know that it's rightly for sale."

He returned his cigar to his mouth and proceeded to produce an impressive cloud of smoke.

"Come now, sir," I replied. "Everything has a price. And probably, most especially, a human head in a jar." I could not believe I was saying these words.

Hopefully, I sounded matter-of-fact, all professional. But was I succeeding? Of all unique situations in my lifetime, this particular one beat all of them to hell and back.

"I'm curious, Mr.–" Bleeker squinted, as if trying to recall.

"Dunleavy," I replied, glad to remember my lie.

"Dunleavy," he pointed at me with his cigar. "Curious what your interest is in this artifact."

"Purely scientific, sir," I said. "No other purpose. I am with the Rappaport Scientific Society and Conservatory, you see. In St. Louis."

Fictional, of course, as far as I knew.

"They have embarked on a new line of inquiry into the criminal mind."

Bleeker's eyebrows arched up. I seem to have marginally impressed him, at least.

"A man of science," he said, his face like stone.

I shook my head earnestly. "No, no. Not me, exactly. I am merely an acquirer of specimens for the society, nothing more."

"That sounds like a fascinating line of work, I must say."

"It is true," I nodded. "Keeps me busy, traveling far and wide."

"I'll bet." He paused, puffed on the cigar again. The cloud of smoke had by now encompassed his head like a blue weather system about a planet.

His eyes still bored into me, gleaming with wariness.

"Well," he said, "Far be it from me to stand as an impediment to science. I'd like to think on it some, if I might."

"Of course. Might I ask when your show will be embarking toward its next venue? I would like to plan accordingly."

"Not until tomorrow, latest, more than likely."

"Very good. Then tomorrow, say mid-day, I should return?"

He nodded formally, bending at the waist. "Your obedient servant."

"I will await your decision."

I tipped my hat and left.

* * *

I returned to our own camp, set up in the woods only a few miles from the show's camp rather than in town. All the quicker access to the show so that we may begin our journey home all the sooner – whether our mission had been successful or not.

I found Selmer anxiously awaiting.

"So...?" he asked, coming up before I had even halted my hoss.

"We wait," I dismounted and walked the horse over to where his had been picketed.

"Whatever for?"

"For them to decide."

Severe disappointment clouded Selmer's face. He turned to the fire he had prepared, grabbed a cloth, and used it to raise the coffee pot he had brewing.

"Smells good," I said as he poured me a tin. "Thank you, Mr. Hudgins."

"They ain't a-gonna sell it," he said flatly.

"I believe they will."

"How much did you offer?"

"We didn't reach that point in the palaver, I'm afraid."

Selmer rolled his shoulders and bobbed his head in a gesture of frustration.

"They ain't a-gonna sell," he repeated. "I know it."

I sipped my coffee, trying to project a sense of calm. I did truly feel it. I thought about Bleeker's eyes piercing through his cigar's smoke at me.

"If there is anything I have learned, Mr. Hudgins, as I have walked this earth, it is that patience is, indeed, a virtue, just like the wise men say."

"Hmmph," he grunted. "Virtue." He stalked off into the surrounding darkness.

"Hang virtue all to hell," I heard him mutter.

* * *

My body shook suddenly, jarred rudely from dreams of Abby's warm embrace.

"We gotta git!" Selmer Hudgins kicked dirt on the embers of our campfire in a frenzy.

"What–?" was all I was able to muster as my mind tried to muddle itself awake.

"Come *on*, Hue," he barked at me, tossing me my hat.

I sat up and looked around. He was dashing about the camp, gathering this and that in an almighty rush, shoving items roughly into saddle-bags.

My brain was still all a blur, but I managed to dump the contents of the coffee pot into what was left of the fire. I sat back again, taking in the frantic Selmer. Then I saw the horses. Both were fully saddled and ready, but it was clear that his had been recently ridden and ridden hard.

"Selmer," I said as calmly as I could. "Selmer, what did you do?"

He glanced over, then away.

"We gotta git," he repeated.

I stood, put my coat and hat on, and got to my horse. My shoulder was complaining again. I looked about the camp, and it looked like we had everything. Selmer was swinging up into his saddle. I followed suit and we headed out.

It was still dark, so our progress through the woods was slow. We were riding close, but I really could only see Selmer in bits and pieces in the sparse and scattered moonlight that managed to filter through the trees. I started addressing him, but he hushed me impatiently.

Then he stopped suddenly, a hand still up for silence.

I heard voices then, in the distance. After a moment, I could discern that they were slowly approaching. My blood started to run cold.

"Selmer," I whispered. "What is happening? What did you do?"

By then, I had already put together what had happened, but my mind refused to accept that conclusion and was hoping for a different one altogether.

Selmer only nudged his pony on.

It was slow going for a long time, but after several stops and careful listening, we appeared to have widened the gap between us and our presumed pursuers.

Sunlight at last began to beam through the branches, and I started to feel pretty licked. Selmer did not look the least bit weary. He still looked somewhat nervous, though he had shed a great deal of this agitation during the ride.

As we had moved, from time to time, my eyes fell on one of Selmer's saddlebags, noting a slight bulge I did not recall noticing before. I had regained a clearer mind after our frenzied departure, since then putting together what Mr. Hudgins had been up to while I slept.

Still, I did not let on my ruminations. Our trying to keep down the noise of our passage added to my silence.

When we stopped at a stream for a moment of relative respite, I moved upstream from the horses and closer to Selmer. I dipped in one cupped hand and drank cold, delicious water. Finally, I looked over at Selmer, also slaking his thirst.

"You have it," was all I said.

He met my gaze, smiling grimly. "Yes."

I sat down and breathed aloud, looking into the woods.

"What have you done?" I said with an exasperated sigh.

"What had to be done, Mr. Hue," he stood suddenly and looked mutinous. "You know it." He shook water from his hand, his eyes not leaving mine.

Now I stood. "I do *not*, sir." I walked to his horse, raised the flap of the bulging saddlebag. I saw the object and shook my head.

"Mr. Hue– Stephen," said Selmer, who seemed to be trying a lighter, more reasoning tone, "This is a trifle, in the grand scheme. Think of it. Our aim is to right this wrong. We can't let these people profit from our friend's misery. Not in this ghastly light!"

This did hold some truth. His words, his conviction, took me back to the first impulses I felt when I first learned of John Murrell's fate and the indignity done to his remains.

Any method or device that I could imagine would have served to correct that crime.

So here we were, in possession of the object of our mission.

Now to evade pursuit and get it back to the Smyrna Church yard, where it belonged.

"What has been done has been done," I said as much to myself as to Selmer. I looked up, offering a resigned smile. "Do you think they will long give us chase?"

He shrugged, "I don't know, Mr. Hue. I suggest we keep at it in case they do. I doubt there is a proper tracker with that bunch. We keep riding."

And ride we did, several days' worth of exhaustion. We kept off the main roads, best as we could, which naturally made the traveling more painstaking and arduous.

35

I started awake, squinting against the very bright sun in my face. As I attempted to look about, I realized I couldn't move.

Almost immediately, my head and eyes throbbed with pain, which only seemed to intensify as I awakened further. Again, I found myself in a tremendously confused state.

I lay on my side on hard, rough ground. I tried to move my hands, but in vain too. They were tied very tightly behind my back.

"Ah, welcome back, Mr. Dunleavy," a rough voice said. I attempted to look around for the owner of the voice and was rewarded with a spike of fire through my brain and eyes. What I could see was my hat, lying on its crown very near a low campfire.

Someone stepped over my extended leg, knocking it indelicately as they did so. A face then appeared to me: Mr. Bleeker's.

"I'm so disheartened that you simply could not wait for the appointed time," he said, rising back out of view.

A shadow passed over my face.

"I have to say I would not rightly have you pegged as a common thief," said Bleeker, sounding genuinely disappointed. "I suppose you should take that as something of a compliment."

Suddenly, someone seized my shoulder – thankfully not the aching one – bringing me upright. I blinked against the sunlight again. One of Bleeker's men stepped back from me after turning me upright. He sneered disdainfully.

"Thieves," he muttered, and spat into the fire.

"I believe I know how they dispose of thieves in this county," Bleeker said. He struck a match and began lighting one of his apparently ever-present cigars.

I looked about at the several men now surrounding me. Some I recognized from the carnival's show, and then later, the camp.

One I did not recognize. He looked at me with the deadest eyes I have ever seen. "We hang 'em," he said. "Usually from trees." He turned his head just so. I looked around for Selmer, then, taking the meaning of what Dead Eyes had said, into the trees, as best that I could.

Then I saw him, lying beyond Dead Eyes and his horse. A few other men stood back in the shadows of the woods. There on the ground was a heap, a man's body, covered in dirt and leaves and blood. His clothing had been ripped asunder, and part of his scalp had been torn away.

There was no mistaking that it was the body of Selmer Hudgins.

"I love it when they run," Dead Eyes told me, his voice hollow as a crypt.

"That was a lucky shot, what took you down when we finally got you two in range," said Bleeker.

Dead Eyes huffed at that. "Luck," he grumbled. "Lucky for this lot. Just creased that miserable scalp."

Bleeker shrugged. "Unhorsed him, and that's what counts.

Better this way, anyhow. But your friend, why, he just had to up and run again."

It was then that, through a haze of pain, I recalled having received a sudden sharp blow to the head as Selmer and I rode. And that was all.

Bleeker blew out one of his eternal clouds of blue smoke.

"Of course, it didn't have to come to this. Did it, Mr. Dunleavy? After all, we had an appointment. You simply could not wait."

He reached behind him and produced a canvas bag. I knew, naturally, what was in it.

He placed it on the ground, then lifted part of the canvas to reveal the large jar, John Murrell's head floating serenely within.

Through the glass, the sunlight lit the murky liquid around the head with a phosphorescent, other-worldly glow. The details of the right side of John's face stood out clearly through that glow. My gut wrenched more forcefully than when I first saw it the night before.

"It loses some of its drama out here in the daylight, doesn't it?" Bleeker said thoughtfully, considering the jar like a man viewing a specimen of nature that he found wanting.

"One thing that I have surely learned in this business," he said, "is that some things call for a greater degree of showmanship."

He lifted the jar again and carefully put it back in the canvas bag. This he handed to one of his men, who dutifully took it away.

"Which brings us to you," Bleeker said. "What to do with you?" Through another cloud from the cigar, he glanced over at Dead Eyes, who shrugged, his lifeless eyes staying on me.

Bleeker gestured with his cigar hand, and the men around us went into motion, mounting their horses. I was pulled up to a standing position, my arms wrenched painfully behind me. A man threw a rope around my neck, and I thought that was it – I was done for. I looked over at poor Selmer's broken body, then up at the sun through the tree branches.

Dozens of thoughts barged through my brain. First among them were images of my beloved Abby and my boys William and Theo, and the lovely Georgia town where we had established a life, and for me, a new existence. Then at once it raged back at me that I had thrown all this away in a rash pursuit of the head of a dead man. Something that was not in any way rational affected this new self I had managed to build, replacing my former criminal existence. True, John was my friend, and I mourned his loss. For all of his faults and weaknesses, his remains did not deserve such desecration. Such an outrage must, of course, be addressed, but was I rightfully the man to do it? Was my striking out with Selmer Hudgins on such short notice, not knowing the situation entirely, so sinfully foolish? After all, Selmer might still be alive had we not begun this insensible and foolhardy endeavor.

As these questions slammed through my head like unforgiving lightning strikes, I hardly noticed that another rope had been looped about my waist. I staggered, almost being pulled to the ground again as Dead Eyes nudged his horse forward. I was being tugged behind him like cattle. Was I about to be dragged to death like poor Mr. Hudgins?

There is no doubt that Dead Eyes pulled me with a purpose past the remains of Selmer. Flies were swarming the bloody pulp of what was left of him. The gorge of my belly quickly rose to my mouth. It was an automatic response that most of us would not be able to contain.

"He ran like a rabbit," Dead Eyes murmured coldly, without looking back.

Another man giggled– a high-pitched, demonic sound if there ever was one.

And I trudged through the woods.

* * *

I was forced to trail these mounted men for what seemed like weeks. Though in reality it was only days. Most likely, they had found the roughest, crudest variety of rope that they could employ, so that my neck was rubbed raw. The constant jerking and twisting of the rope about my waist also put painful bruises there. Normally, my bad shoulder would be screaming; I barely noticed because of the punishment the rest of my body endured.

During the day, as we travelled, my captors only gave me water but once throughout the ordeal, and even then, it was brackish and unrefreshing from one of the men's underused canteens. Meanwhile, when stopping at a creek or stream, the men would make a grand show of refreshing themselves and their horses in the cool waters, while keeping me from it.

We travelled in some places on the main roads, and as I looked around, I realized we were in a somewhat familiar area. At one point, riders stopped our group, and although they spoke to Dead Eyes some distance away, I made out that this conversation erupted into an argument. These riders seemed to be challenging my captors on some basis. Their leader's voice rose briefly into an undiscernible shout.

Finally, Dead Eyes returned to where his men guarded me beside the road.

He walked his pony up, his face somewhat animated – more than I had witnessed up to this point, anyway – in anger.

"Tell me how to comport my prisoner, by God," he muttered tightly. "Never seen the likes."

He leaned over and said something to one of his men, and for the first time, I saw a badge on Dead Eye's vest when his coat opened a bit.

He straightened up then, and looked at me, his eyes turning dead again.

"I'm no vigilante, by God."

One of the men removed the rope from around my neck.

So, I had, in fact, been apprehended by the law. My blood fairly froze right there. If these men learned my true identity and my affiliation with John and the Mystic Clan, I could indeed meet the same fate as my friend. The dark aspect of the Tennessee State Penitentiary and the enforced isolation within its grim walls penetrated my soul. I never considered myself a coward, but this notion alone sent waves of sheer terror through my very bones.

Eventually, by that very sundown, we reached the encampment of Bleeker and Sons Traveling Marvels. They had indeed been traveling ahead, which accounted for Bleeker's absence from our group and the days it took to catch up with them. A man on foot – even being dragged behind – will be much slower.

I could not tell what town or city the encampment was near, but there appeared to be local men making their way into the camp, as Bleeker greeted them most enthusiastically, as he had greeted me all those nights ago. That seemed from another life entirely now.

They had set me well apart from the main camp, still trussed up with my back affixed to a tree stump. I observed the local men making their way to the wagons of the "sporting women," as Bleeker called them. And once again, that woman who had exchanged looks with me before caught my eye. I could not figure why she would look at me so. It did not seem like any ordinary curiosity about a man new to the group, prisoner or no. There seemed to be a more meaningful, investigative quality to her gaze. Curious indeed.

Entire days and nights went on like that, seemingly without end. I endeavored to number them as best I could, but they became a blur by around the second week of my captivity, by my reckoning.

I really could not ponder what Bleeker intended to do with me, as I was more of a burden than a benefit of any kind to his band. They kept me by turns in a wagon or in a tent, always trussed up, and all I could do to pass the time was listen to the sounds of the show as it displayed its wares from town to town. They gagged me, sometimes even putting a bag over my head to further reduce any utterances I might make. This, along with plenty of threats to my gullet or knives to my innards and whatnot.

From time-to-time, Bleeker would look in and examine me with a glare. Sometimes he would talk to me. Talk *at* me would really be more appropriate, me being almost always gagged.

One night, he revisited me, canvas sack in hand. The last time I saw it was that day: The day they dragged poor Selmer Hudgins to death.

He placed it down and tugged my gag free, then sat on a stool that he had pulled up. He looked down at the sack for a long time.

Of course, I knew what was in it.

"Funny how you never asked me how I came about it," he said.

I said nothing.

"Yep, it was up Tennessee way. Some of my boys had wandered into some little old cornpone town up there and were raising hell. Sometimes I don't mind that. They have to get the starch out now and again, don't you know. This particular time, though, it rubbed at me, and I had to go in there and rouse them out. Some of these idjits just don't understand that you *don't* go into these places and agitate them. Our customers, that is. Leaves a foul taste in their mouth. Not to mention it might give some of them the impulse to run us out. And I hate that. Then I have to go avoiding places for a spell whilst they cool down, or move on, or die. Some folks have a long memory, though.

"Anyway," he cleared his throat, then spat. It splattered thickly on the wagon's side. "I got their hash settled, and turned out they'd gotten into a tangle with townies that felt wronged by somebody, and already were looking to punch someone for it.

"Well, once everything got a mite friendlier and the boys were reliving the fight and who threw the best punches and all of that nonsense, they started to spell out the particulars of their sourness. You could say without a doubt it was an *odd* job, a queer and distasteful one, I might throw in, too. One they were not the best equipped for, either."

Bleeker laughed, low and without humor.

"I mean, they was young, too young by half to be asked to do it. You ask me, the fools who hired them should have known better, or just do it themselves. Too many tongues to wag away, if you take my meaning. Knowing their type, they just didn't want to get their hands dirty."

With this, he held up his own hands and wiggled his fingers about, grimacing his face up.

"Can't have that now, can we?"

He let his hands drop, stared back down at the sack for a moment, then leaned back.

"They were doctor types, you see. Probably a lot like your bosses, back in St. Louie? That, uh, institute of theirs?"

I blanked out on what I had told him. He waved a dismissive hand.

"No matter. You know the type."

He leaned forward, a mocking grin on his lips. His eyes grew wide.

"Mighty men of science!"

He smacked his lips grotesquely, staring at the sack.

"All of it for this. They wanted this. Something about studying the skull. Fen... Fre..."

"Phrenology," I croaked. I don't know where it came from, perhaps surfacing from untapped depths of memory from a Harper's Weekly article or some such.

"That's it!" he made this funny little smile that people get when something lost to their mind comes back to them, and they find it to be some kind of miracle. He brought his hands up to his own skull, his fingers dancing merrily around the top of his head. "Said they could figure a man's mind and how it was set just by the shape of it, and the bumps and ridges and such. They thought they might learn even more by studying Murrell's bean, too, and his criminal habits and designs. Doesn't make a bit of sense to me, but there it is.

"Well, these two giants of the medical field aimed to swindle these young lads after scooping Johnny's head right out of his grave for them. Never had even a notion to pay them. Despicable act, if you ask me. They tried to stiff them for it, see, but the lads had the sand and smarts to stay hold of the goods – if you will – and fair to pummel those ghouls for their trouble. Left them to be treated by another doc, I s'pose.

"Anyways, I negotiated a good piece with them and got it for a fair price, I'd say. Came out well to the good on it, in fact, after the long haul and Johnny's turned me a tidy profit. They had another piece too, some kind of finger or thumb or something. I wasn't really interested in that. One of them boys said he wanted to keep it anyway, so I let him have it. He seemed an odd sort, so it kind of seemed right for him.

"Anyway, word gets out, see, and in these parts Johnny

Murrell – or at least part of him, anyway – still intrigues and terrifies the masses."

He reached down and rapped his knuckles against the glass. It made a dull, distinct *thonk* through the canvas.

"Hear that, Johnny? You done me good."

Bleeker's eyes crept up to mine. They held a flat, menacing quality.

"And you'll do me good for some time more, old sock. Yes, you will."

36

After a time of this, I started praying that they would simply end the misery. Hang me, shoot me, do *something*. I pondered that, if given the opportunity to actually speak, I might be able to make the case that it was Selmer Hudgins and not I who had taken the precious artifact. Not *stolen*, as that would be accepting that it was Bleeker's to begin with.

Not that Bleeker would ever believe me, let alone care. No, he just took a simple pleasure in having this power over me, and my life or death.

My meals were mere scraps when they thought to feed me at all. Perhaps their intent was to starve me half to death and use me as one of their gruesome exhibits. I had lost so much weight that I very much doubt that my dear Abby would recognize me at all. Not to mention my growth of beard and bedraggled, unwashed hair. I had heard tell of some of these road shows having wild men as part of their bizarre, ugly acts, so much so that only the men-folk were allowed to view them. Women and children had far too delicate sensibilities to be exposed to something like that. The thought of me inside a pit voraciously dismembering a squirrel or raccoon that had been thrown to me, and devouring it before a rapt, horrified crowd, did once send me into a fit of giggling.

I knew then that I was, in truth, at least halfway to madness.

One dismal night, I was trying very hard to stay dry within my prison wagon. It was not easy. It was very cold, raining quite hard, and the wind was blowing like it was the end of the world. This tore to shreds what was already a tattered, dilapidated canvas cover, so the rain poured quite liberally into my pathetic "quarters."

Through the darkness, a figure approached, bearing a chunk of meat and a tin of water that, for a change, appeared drinkable. There was no sign of any spit in it that I could see.

In the wet, murky light, I could make out the features of a young woman from underneath the cloak. It was the woman who had, from time to time, cast curious looks my way just before and during my imprisonment.

I nodded my head gratefully at her offering. She nodded in response as she removed my gag so that I could eat. Of course, far from being very fresh, the meat very well could have been rancid or on its way to it. However, a starving man will eat almost anything. By that point, even the canvas and wood that surrounded me looked tasty.

It was probably just as well that I could not see very well what I was chawing on. I let out a mad little giggle at the thought. The woman looked at me most oddly, and from her expression, I did indeed look the very picture of a lunatic.

She looked around cautiously before gesturing furiously with her hands, holding them out as if they were bound together by an invisible rope. It was when she looked up at me and grunted softly that I knew that she was a mute.

She pulled her hands apart as if suddenly freeing them,

then whisked one away, gesturing into the distance. She pointed at me with a serious, emphatic expression, then repeated the gesture.

She was planning on helping me escape, that was clear.

She quickly looked around again for anyone who might have observed this. But she had picked the right night to come, as apparently nobody wanted to be moving about in that nasty, soaking darkness. All was quiet save for the downpour of the storm.

She held out a hand to me, palm forward, as if signaling me to wait. Although exactly where was I going to go in this state? She looked me very earnestly dead in the eyes, held up two fingers, and uttered a low grunt that sounded like "Ays..." Two fingers up again, then "Ays..." once more.

Two days, then. My heart went out to this woman, and tears sprang to my eyes all at once. She returned my disgusting gag and left.

Two more days in hell.

* * *

The next day passed with much the same routine, save for its interminable length, brought on by my fresh knowledge and hopes of possible escape.

The show was rolling again. Here and there, I glimpsed through the gaps in the tattered canvas what again appeared to be a familiar landscape.

Through the trees, I swore I even saw distant, glistening bits of what appeared to be a huge river. It was the Mississippi, no? Surely? But in reality, it could have been anywhere, for all I knew. My mind was just working to create a comfortable, familiar place in which to couch my thoughts in this comfortless world.

Bleeker visited me again that night to continue my torment with that ghoulish artifact. But even he was intelligent enough to understand that even this horrid jar containing my friend's head really no longer horrified me.

I stared at the grisly thing and back at Bleeker with dulled eyes. I had been numbed by the constant repetition and cruelty of my captivity and the ever-present companions of hunger and the unknown. Fear was no longer part of the picture, really.

Bleeker seemed to derive some satisfaction that he was now gazing upon a man who had become a mere broken, lunatic thing, and that he alone had authored this.

At one very fleeting point, the eyes that had penetrated what was left of my soul betrayed a certain pity.

It did not give me any false hope, as I believed in my heart of hearts that Bleeker was nothing more than a cheap monster, one suitable for display in his own show. A surly beast beyond all hope of any redemption.

Indeed, any thoughts that I may have previously harbored on revenge had very much evaporated along with my wits. The atmosphere about me consisted only of a resignation to some forlorn fate, and cold death's peaceful embrace.

At last, the day came that I could look forward to the possibility of escape. The anticipation of it by turns excited all senses that had previously been deadened.

I had not seen the mute girl all day. I prayed that it was only because she was avoiding being around me to reduce any suspicion about our new connection. Otherwise, she had been discovered and dealt with, and that was that.

As the sun sank, the camp fell to its usual rhythms of life. One of Bleeker's men came to give me a grudging drink of brackish water, then checked my bonds and secured the gag on my mouth. Soon, that evening's customers would arrive for the show's offerings.

From my distant wagon, I could perceive that the show seemed to be proceeding accordingly, as they always had before. Some music drifted here, as always. And though it always carried a very cheap quality – it was a small show after all – it gave me some little spark of light to an otherwise dismal existence. There was fiddling, accordions, and on this night, even some drumming. The show appeared to be really putting on the dog tonight.

I sat there, trying to ease the discomfort of my bonds and my now bony bottom on the wagon's unforgiving boards. In the distance, the lights of the main square of the show winked. I always looked for some sign of what I thought of as other, normal life out there. Whenever I could see boys running about or an unmistakable female form, it gladdened my heart just a bit – and helped me hold some useful dram of sanity. I occasionally indulged myself with a daydream about how one of these nights, one of the boys or ladies or men of the town would discover me in one of their curious wanderings into the show's camp. I could only surmise that Bleeker had posted some of his more intimidating roustabouts to guard the camp, thus warding off any would-be intruders.

So, this night began like any other. I heard the showman's barks imploring visitors to investigate – if they dared – the interiors of the tents holding various wonders and horrors that Bleeker and Sons Traveling Marvels had collected in their wanderings of the world.

My senses came to life at once at a violent eruption of shouting, yelling, and screams from the concentration of what lights I could see. These shouts took on an immediate and intensely angry quality.

As it reached its peak, I heard reports of gunfire in quick succession. Then there was a muffled, explosive sound followed by the distinct shrieks of women and a low, growing roar. Fire?

Indeed, the area that I had before seen under the soft glow of lanterns was brighter with a ferocious orange glare. Smoke billowing above the conflagration seemed to glow from within itself, giving the thick cloud an ever more menacing aspect.

Though the fire was still a fair bit away, I began feeling the unrelenting grip of panic. I wrenched as mightily as possible against the ropes binding me to the wagon, to no avail. Such efforts were even less effective than they might have otherwise been, owing to my weakened state.

Silhouetted figures ran about in the fiery-gold glow, some with purpose, others in a chaotic bid to escape the violence and flames. More shots rang out, and a man screamed in agony.

Suddenly, a figure had jumped up on the sideboard of my prison wagon, looking in hurriedly. I couldn't make out features, only a great shadowy mass that seemed to have a savage intent. Something flashed in the fire-light: an enormous Bowie knife.

I recoiled, not knowing if it was Bleeker or one of his men sent to dispatch me.

Instead of going to work on me, the knife cut through the rope around my hands, then my feet.

I am free? My panicked, fevered mind was trying to make sense of the situation. The figure said nothing, but quickly removed my filthy gag and grabbed me, hustling me out of the accursed prison wagon and into the inky darkness of the nearby woods.

He stopped, once we were safely in the shadows of trees, and then darted back to the wagon for something. My head was still swimming with this rush of activity; I did not fathom what he could be doing, and I didn't care. I just wanted to make good the escape.

All was still chaos in the camp as the figure returned, and we continued deeper in the welcoming blackness of the forest night.

Further and further into the woods we ran, and the sounds of the now burning show camp finally faded behind us.

My mysterious rescuer had yet to utter one word to me this entire time. Were all of my allies mute? I stumbled, tripped, and fell numerous times during this hectic departure, and the figure barely made a sound at all, as if he were a creature born to the night.

We finally reached a creek where men appeared to have been waiting for us, as they had horses saddled and ready. A bit of moonlight on the shore allowed me to see the man who had retrieved me from the clutches of Bleeker and his damnable Show of Madness.

I started a bit to see that it was none other than Colbert, a near-forgotten ally of a long, dusty criminal kingdom.

He was little changed over these many years. The suddenness of the appearance of a familiar face amidst this insanity and violence added to the unreal quality of it all.

He looked at me and offered what, for Colbert, passed for a smile.

"We're even, hoss," the specter said.

I stared at him, unbelieving.

"You look like hell," Colbert said, and though his lips still bore a smile, I saw by turns pity and then anger light his eyes.

"Yes," I croaked. "I know."

"We even brought you your own mount," he said after a long breath. He looked in the direction from which we had come. Smoke could still be seen billowing up over the tree line, and distant shouting could still be heard.

"We had best git," Colbert said.

We mounted the horses, and I carefully followed him. I did

not know in what direction we were heading, and really didn't care, as long as I was away from that misery.

* * *

Near dawn, Colbert slowed our escape owing more to my exhaustion than anything. He looked none the worse for wear, of course, but doubtless I looked the very portrait of death itself. Likely taking pity, he commanded his men to pitch camp.

Something occurred to me suddenly as we sat down at a fire they had kindled, and I looked about, into the surrounding woods.

"Will they follow? Attempt to find us?"

Colbert gave me an offended look. "Truly," he said, "You think that little of my trail craft? Daniel Boone himself couldn't track us."

I scratched out a relieved laugh. There was a long pause as the fire crackled.

"What of Bleeker?" I asked.

Colbert shrugged, his eyes not leaving the depths of the fire.

"The fracas that broke out at their show, the shooting, the fire, really all to distract them. To find you. We had pictures, so we knew where to find you. The lowliest wagon, furthest from the show, and the show camp. That was easy."

He paused, threw something into the fire.

"Bleeker was easy too, from them pictures. I almost would have known him without them anyway. The way he carried himself or looked at people. He was giving orders, too. Until I closed on him. It all happened so fast. And that I regret. It should have lasted longer, goddamnit."

He must have felt my stare, because he looked over. His eyes held a very intense, wrathful glint that I never forgot. At the same time, he looked very satisfied, like a man would after a job well done.

"Rest assured, my good friend," he said, "he has met the end his like deserves."

I sighed, hanging my head a bit. I had never before felt such complete exhaustion.

"You still look like hell," Colbert observed suddenly.

I blinked up at him. Colbert smiled and let out a grunt, or a laugh – the first I believe I had ever heard from him. It was like hearing a friendly, long-forgotten melody, and I joined in. It felt so very good to laugh again.

The laughter died away a little at a time, as we stared into the fire. His men quietly conversed as they tended to the horses.

I wondered about these pictures he spoke of. It seemed an out-of-place component to all of this strange, terrifying journey. I also found myself profoundly touched that Colbert had been so intent on my rescue, if a bit shocked at the vindictiveness that came with it on my behalf.

"These pictures... How did you come about them? Who–"

He eyed me thoughtfully, his mouth working. "The mute girl what let you know of this," his voice was low, hesitant, uncomfortable even. "She drew them."

I sat back, as if someone had pushed me, my mind scrambling to piece it together. "Her– Yes! Yes... w-what happened to her? Who... who is she...?"

"Nina," he grunted, after a pause. "That girl is Nina, my niece."

"Your... niece?" I was stunned at the thought that this was again Nina, little Nina that we had rescued all those years ago from the renegades.

He nodded.

"She was missing for many months. Sabine Redbone

traders we know and deal with saw her when that show came through their parish. They kept it to themselves and got a runner to us about two weeks ago. That pig Bleeker took her and raped her, they said, until he couldn't use her anymore."

He snapped another thick branch easily with his bare hands. It was not difficult to imagine that the branch was, in Colbert's mind, Bleeker's very bones. It all made sense then, Colbert's drive to attack the show. That bitterness in his eyes, the way he wished Bleeker's end came slower. That wasn't all for me.

"She got out of there, though, somehow."

After a moment, listening to the crackle of the fire, I asked, "Where is she now?"

"She is safely home." He looked at me. "She risked a lot going back to that hell."

"But why, when she had already made good her escape?"

"She remembered you from those years ago, when she was a little one, and what you had done for her then. She got word to me that that pig had you as well."

I looked at him, utterly dumbfounded. No sane man would have blamed her if she had escaped and never looked back. But she did, for me. The notion that she went through that hell again, even later in life, gave me the despairing thought that the poor girl suffered under some ugly, vile curse. She had already endured far too much in her short, heartbreaking life.

"But how could she have fallen prey to a beast like Bleeker? I mean, after... after...?" I had to ask.

Colbert shook his head. "That's a stubborn one, my Nina. Got more that way as she got older. And after her cousin Louisa nagged at her forever about it, she moved on, with her aunt and uncle, out west, Fort Smith way. Said she needed more room." He snorted, spitting into the fire. "Guess she chafed at my trying to keep her from the Bleekers of the world." His eyes glittered coldly, maybe even sadly, in the firelight. "If she'd only listened."

I knew then that Colbert must harbor a deep hatred for anyone who would again make her a victim. There couldn't be a decent living soul that would blame him, either.

Colbert must have read my expression.

"We never forget."

* * *

We traveled to Colbert's town. Weeks passed and I slowly recovered my weight and strength, thanks to his people's kindness. Soon after arriving there, I asked for writing materials so that I could get word to Abby and the boys that I was alive and would be making my way home soon.

My savior, Nina, was there too. Through tears, I took it upon myself to thank her profusely for the tremendous risk she took on herself to secure my survival of what I had come to think of as the "Hell Show." My thanks seemed to embarrass her, and she quickly withdrew. I do not believe she meant to be at all rude. I certainly did not take it so. Nevertheless, I reflected sadly that what I had been through paled in comparison to what Nina had endured. It was most frustrating that my gratitude was feeble and weak compared to her service.

Of course, I understood Nina's desire for independence, even though that desire led her to suffer at the hands of the likes of Bleeker. She could not have known what would be on that path. None of us do. After all, look at me, my own choices.

As I finally prepared to depart, everyone said their brief goodbyes, as Colbert's people are wont to do. Some said no goodbye at all, but just looked at me for a pause and turned away. For them, that is enough. For these stoic people, a friend never really departs, as they are always together in heart, mind, and spirit.

"Stephen. One last thing," Colbert said as our horses stopped on the edge of his village.

I looked at him curiously, and he produced a leather bag of some size and held it out.

I knew instantly what it was.

Wordlessly, I took it from him. A bit hesitantly, I admit. Take it I did, though. It was heavier than I thought, but maybe I was still weak.

After all, it was for this, ultimately, that others and I had come so far and gone through so much. Lost a friend, endured torture of body, mind, and soul. I would carry the scars for the rest of my days. But it was my duty to remember the past and restore where I could.

Speaking of remembering...

As I rode, I couldn't help hearing John Murrell, that old Devil Preacher, in my head.

Make it a long life, Stephen. Make it better than this one.

I struck out for northern Georgia, for home.

Epilogue

Mr. Erastus Vinning
Secretary to Mr. A. Forepaugh
The Offices of The Forepaugh New and Colossal
All-Feature Show
Trust Company Building
Philadelphia, Pennsylvania

SEPTEMBER 1, 1877

Sir,

This letter is to inform you that my negotiation with Mr. Hue is at last concluded. It is with great pleasure that I further inform you that said negotiation has reached a beneficial conclusion for all parties.

I have secured the object of my mission here, as gruesome as it is: The head of John Murrell, the Devil Preacher's finest weapon.

Sometimes code-named by Mr. Forepaugh — perhaps with good cause — "Judge and Executioner".

Though let that be the last time I acknowledge it. In general, I still find Mr. Forepaugh's penchant for code names irksome.

If I have taken anything from this task, it would be a respectable measure of appreciation for the life and exploits of John Murrell. Most are woefully unaware of the humanity of the man as described to me. History never recounted his liberation of a young black man, let alone the close relationship they shared. Almost familial. Remarkable, truly.

I dare say that I continue my habit of editorializing despite your imprecations to proceed otherwise on recent events, to say that I am heartily relieved to be at last making my way homeward and thus putting a great distance between myself and the state of Georgia.

While the people that inhabit this place have been exceptionally friendly and welcoming as reputation has heretofore allowed, the heat of the region I find what I imagine to be as oppressive as, say, the deepest parts of equatorial Africa.

That is to say that I am glad to escape it. I will strike for home soonest. I would skip my way to the train depot if they had one, and if my constitution had not been drained of all its energies.

Your Exhausted and Perspiring Servant,
R.E. McElhany, Esq.

* * *

The house was quieter than it had been for a while. Abby Hue had come to enjoy having Mr. McElhany around, despite his unpalatable business. He had been a daily visitor for over two weeks, much longer than even their sons stayed when they visited. They seldom had guests those days.

She stood at the open window in the foyer, hoping for an evening breeze to cool the house. People were emerging from their own homes and onto their porches up and down the street, seeking the same respite from the heat.

The rhythmic ticking of the grandfather clock was the only sound in the hall. It always reminded her of the marching of tiny mechanical soldiers.

Might be time to have Stephen wind it, she thought vaguely. She had inherited the clock from her folks, but Stephen had long insisted on being the clock's chief custodian.

Stephen.

She turned from the window to the house's darkening interior, listening for her husband's stirring. Hearing none, she went to the drawing room.

He was still where she left him directly after Mr. McElhany's departure, gazing out the window, a book forgotten in his lap. One thumb marked his place amidst the pages. Trim and fit as he still was in their seasoned age, no doubt he was tired after narrating and storytelling so animatedly for days.

She went to his side, settling into the comfortable chair opposite his, Mr. McElhany's half-full water glass still on the end table. She glanced at the book's cover.

AROUND THE WORLD IN EIGHTY DAYS

"Mr. Verne not holding your interest these days?"

Stephen looked up, startled. After a moment, he chuckled softly, holding up his spectacles.

"Even with these, not enough light."

"I'll get the lamps then." She started to get up, but he held out a hand.

"No, thank you, my dear." He nodded to the open window where a gentle breeze chanced to stir the curtains. "It's nice."

They sat in the quiet, the mechanical soldiers clicking off to battle.

"I liked him." Abby's voice was light, cheerful. She smiled to herself. How much the young man had enjoyed her cornbread.

"Hmm," Stephen grunted. A whisp of white hair fluttered a little with the small gusts of air. The rascal had managed to keep most of it, even as the rest of him withered gracefully. "Oh yes. Nice enough fella. I mean, for a lawyer."

They laughed.

"Stephen…"

"Yes, love?" He was gazing out the window again. Three boys ran past in the street, chattering excitedly. Stephen smiled.

"Why did you give it to him? To Mr. McElhany?" Sometimes she had pictured him refusing to part with the… artifact, after all, though it still gave her the shudders to imagine it under her roof.

Stephen sighed, then placed the book on the end table. One wizened hand went to a vest pocket, searching.

"I mean," Abby ventured gently, "after… Everything… It seemed safest with you."

He turned to her, ceasing the quest for whatever was in his

pocket, smile faltering a little. He blinked, then looked at her firmly.

"It's not him, Abby."

She sat back, reading his face. "Not... him." After all their years together, she knew her husband's tells. Out of the stoniest expression a face could devise, he would tug at his chin when he thought he might cave into a smile or laugh. Any cigar, lit or unlit, would be stowed in the corner of his mouth as he looked away, clucking his tongue for punctuation. This was not one of those times.

"I wouldn't have handed it over if it were." He produced a cigar from his pocket and lit it.

Abby's expression transformed from mild shock to vexation, then to a hurt frown.

"I didn't want to trouble you with any of that." He waved a hand at her. "Those sordid outlaw tales. I wanted all that left behind anyway, after I came home." He gestured with his smoldering cigar, warmly yet bluntly. "You did too, darling."

"Fair enough, Stephen." She remembered the firm line she drew all those years ago. Abby glanced out the window. "Fair enough."

The curtains stirred with another welcome breeze. A cigar-smoke galaxy spun above the old couple.

"What happened to it, then? What *did* you give to him?"

Stephen looked askance at her, then cheekily shifted his attention back to the window.

"Come now." She batted playfully at his arm. "One last sordid yarn."

He turned back to her, eyebrows arched.

"Out with it, you old villain."

Stephen drew on the cigar, blew out a large plume of smoke, looking satisfied.

"Well, Abigail, before I come back to you and the boys, I paid a visit to Pikeville."

"Pikeville?"

"Yep, up Tennessee way. At that old Smyrna church. John's buried there, you see."

After a moment, Abby sat back thoughtfully. "I see. Yes, I do see."

It was quiet again. The faint pop of a buggy whip cracked through the air from the streets.

"But whose... I can't believe I am asking this... But whose head was it you gave to Mr. McElhany? I mean, if it was a head at all?"

He reached out to tap the ash of his cigar into a tray. "Oh, it was a head, alright. You see, the bag Colbert gave me had two heads. One was John's, of course. And yes, my dear, people will plunk down their two bits to gaze in horror at a human head. But I'll be damned if it'll be the head of my friend.

"It will be the head of Abraham Bleeker."

THE END

HISTORICAL NOTE

Contemporary records regarding the life of John Murrell and the exploits of his Clan Mystic are few and far between. Other than the record of his physical description and state when being received at The Tennessee State Penitentiary, as noted in the novel, the only other record is a mere name, date of incarceration, and a short description of his crime as "slave stealing."

Murrell's life seems to have become pronounced as more of a legend than fact, appearing in books and movies, but usually as a side character or presence, such as in Mark Twain's *The Adventures of Tom Sawyer*. The $12,000 that Tom and Huck come by is speculated to have been part of a Murrell treasure by Injun Joe and his accomplice. Twain again mentions the Murrell gang briefly in *Life on the Mississippi*, describing the slave stealing operation.

Humphrey Bogart played Murrell in the 1940 western *Virginia City*, sporting an appropriately villainous moustache opposite dashing hero Errol Flynn. It is a fictional anachronism since the film takes place in 1864 during the American Civil

War. The gang was called Murrell's Guerrillas in the movie. Whether that had anything to do with his inexplicable Mexican accent in the film is anybody's guess.

Murrell was, in fact, branded with the letters "HT" in his youth, as a horse thief, and part of his modus operandi did involve him captivating audiences with his oratory skills while his men made off with their horses, as described by Twain in *Life on the Mississippi*.

Depending on which source one consults, the number of clan members varies from hundreds to thousands (Twain had it at one thousand).

Whiskey Chute, Arkansas, is named for an actual incident wherein a steamboat transporting a large amount of whiskey was captured and sunk. Local citizens organized and attacked the bandits as they enjoyed the purloined cargo. It is not clear if this was a Clan Mystic operation, but it does fit the bill, which is why I borrowed this event to depict the final capture of John Murrell.

Murrell reportedly confessed to almost all his crimes on his deathbed but declared himself "guiltless" of any charges of murder. He died of pulmonary consumption in Pikeville, Bledsoe County, in November 1844.

Murrell's grave at the Smyrna church was desecrated shortly after his burial, and the head was removed. Tales told in the day involved medical students looking for inventive ways to supplement their tuition by supplying bones and skeletons to their schools. Sadly, his head did make the rounds of carnivals and county fairs, some sources note, for "ten cents a peep." Its whereabouts today are unknown. The Tennessee State Museum does proport to possess his thumb, and for years it would be put on display annually – usually on Halloween. It appears, however, that 2011 was the last time this had occurred.

Other than his thumb – left or right is unknown – the rest of John Murrell's remains lie peacefully beneath a stone marker bearing only his name.

Acknowledgments
For Devil Preacher

When I embarked on this journey, I confess I was somewhat ignorant of not only how much time is devoted to such an endeavor, but also the number of people ultimately involved by the time one gets to publication. Being an avid reader all my life, I have read hundreds of acknowledgements in books (yes, I do read them), so you would think I would have a better appreciation for it. As in most things in life, one does not really know the realities of something until they do it themselves.

My family's support was, of course, vital to the very survival of this project. A very special thank you to my wonderful wife, Christine, for her unwavering encouragement. Our son Alex has my gratitude as well, primarily for his unique sense of humor. Thanks, son, for the laughs. I needed them. They both helped keep me (relatively) sane, not just through the writing and editing process, but through the general stress of life. I don't know where I would be, or if this novel would even exist, without both of you.

A tremendous thank you to my amazing friend and editor, Ian Tan. I'll always feel that our having met was truly serendipitous. His instincts for story and character are impeccable (and honestly, I'm a little bit jealous of them). He mentored and guided me to see things within my own novel that I likely would never have seen without his insight, thus giving it much more emotional agency and thematic weight. Ian possesses a genuinely rare gift, and I can't thank him enough for sharing it. Everything you did, Ian, made this better.

I cannot express enough gratitude to Abigail Wild and all of the fine folks at Wild Ink Publishing for giving me this opportunity. Like virtually all authors, I have suffered the outrageous fortune of rejection after rejection from agents and publishers. This is a breakthrough the likes of which I had only previously dreamed. Their faith in me and my creation will be forever treasured.

Finally, I want to thank you, dear reader. I find my own time to read a precious thing. It is no small thing for me that you've spent your own valuable time reading my tale. I hope that you found it to be time well spent.

About the Author

Christopher DeWitt lives in Phoenix, Arizona with his wife Christine, son Alex, three dopey but lovable dogs, and a weird, vegan cat. When he isn't writing and reading, he is exploring the beautiful and sometimes eerie Superstition Mountains and the haunts of Tombstone. He also occupies his free time trying to figure out if his house, built practically on top of old western mines, is as haunted as The Copper Queen Hotel in Bisbee, Arizona. (It is.) A United States Air Force veteran and licensed pilot, he loves anything that flies and earth-bound racing machines that go very, very fast. He is an incorrigible and unapologetic Godzilla and Star Wars geek and loves to read history, historical fiction, westerns, sci-fi, and horror.